THUG LOVIN'

THUG LOVIN'

WAHIDA CLARK

GC

GRAND CENTRAL
PUBLISHING

NEW YORK   BOSTON

Grand Central Publishing
Hachette Book Group
237 Park Avenue
New York, NY 10017

Visit our website at www.HachetteBookGroup.com.

Printed in the United States of America

First Edition: August 2009
10 9 8 7 6 5 4 3 2 1

Grand Central Publishing is a division of Hachette Book Group, Inc. The Grand Central Publishing name and logo is a trademark of Hachette Book Group, Inc.

Library of Congress Cataloging-in-Publication Data
Clark, Wahida
   Thug lovin' / Wahida Clark. — 1st ed.
       p. cm.
   Summary: "Tasha and Trae, the hood's favorite couple, are still together and have moved far away from the drama in New York for the sunny skies in Los Angeles...or so they think"—Provided by publisher.
   ISBN 978-0-446-17809-9
   1. African American criminals—Fiction. I. Title.
PS3603.L3695T47 2009
813'.6—dc22   2008051427

*To all my readers, I would not
be here without you.*

*Karen Thomas, once again you showed me
how awesome you are. Special thanks to you for
having and using your editor's eye.
I really do appreciate you.*

ACKNOWLEDGMENTS

Keisha Caldwell, Tobias Fox, Antoinette B. Barnes, Treena Wright, Nydia Benders, Tracy Bebe Johnson, and my Lil' Wahida. You all are the best critics. To my typists, Roz, Kisha, Sherry Porter, Hadiyah and Zakiyyah Muhammad, and Hasana. Thank you again and again.

Linda Duggins, thanks for getting me in wherever I could fit in. I'm ready to do it all over again.

To all the booksellers and book clubs... *THANKS*!

TASHA'S NOTE

Listen up, everybody! My name is Rosalyn Tasha Macklin. But everyone calls me Tasha, my middle name. That's right, I'm married to the one and only Trae Macklin. His ass is supposed to be officially retired from the game and enjoying life as a family man. But I've learned that you can take the thug out of the streets but you can't take the thug out of the man.

The ladies love Trae, thanks to his arrogant, cocky, by-any-means-necessary, I'ma-make-it-happen attitude. And you can't discount the fact that the nigga is the real deal and I hear how all of y'all chicks be sweatin' him telling Wahida that he is y'all's man. But don't even think about it. I know he's fine as hell. It's a fact that he's a cross between Tyson Bedford and DMX, thugged out with a pinch of Tyrese. That bald head and Hershey chocolate skin, a little over six feet, 210 pounds, with the body of a god. He's all the thug lovin' I could handle.

Shit, I'm known to turn a nigga's head as well. After three kids, yes three! I still got it going on. As big as I got with both pregnancies, I didn't even think I would get back down to 155 pounds. Trust and believe my body is bangin' and them babies did something good in all the right places. I told Wahida when she gets my story on the big screen, she better represent and don't do me dirty and have some B-list actress play me. She better have somebody like Megan

Good, Gabrielle, Sanaa Lathan or somebody on that level play my character. Somebody cute.

But anyways, there is no doubt in my mind that Trae is my soul mate. He is ecstatic that I gave him three sons. A set of twin boys, Kareem and Shaheem, and then I had my baby, Caliph. He undoubtedly loves the ground I walk on and vice versa.

Everybody is all in our business and wants to know what happened after Trae got out the game and him and Kaylin beat that drug case by the skin of their teeth. Well, me and Trae hightailed it to the Islands and laid low for a minute. But now we livin' Hollyhood large up in Cali. We live in O. J.'s old neighborhood. But now I'm not so sure that movin' to Cali was the best move for us. Shit has gotten downright crazy. The transition from illegal to legal hasn't been all peaches and cream. I thought I was going to catch a case at one point. And the club? I wanted to burn that bitch down to the ground. Let me stop before I tell it all. I'll let Wahida, "The Official Queen of Thug Love Fiction," put it down for y'all.

Peace!
Tasha

PART I

CHAPTER ONE

Ocho Ríos, Jamaica
Three years ago and before the twins were born . . .

*B*oom! *Boom! Boom!* The sound of the first-floor door being kicked down woke Tasha, Trae's wifey, out of her deep sleep. Trae jumped out of bed, going for his gun.

"Baby," Tasha said as she jumped up and peeked out from behind the curtain of her third-floor bedroom window and saw jackets with huge lettering—FBI, ATF, DEA—and unmarked squad cars stationed in front of the three-family house and in the middle of the street.

She placed her hands on her pregnant belly as her knees hit the floor.

"Baby, throw something on." Trae Macklin was rushing to put on his boxers and some sweats. "You see they're coming in. C'mon, baby, please get up. They're coming, baby." He hopped over to her, one leg in the sweats, one leg out.

"I love you, Trae." She looked up at him in disbelief. She was a hustler's wife, undoubtedly. But she had been sure that this hustler would be out of the game before it was too late and before it came to this.

"I know you do, Ma, but I need you to put something on."

"Then why are you doing this?" she screamed. "Why do

you keep leaving me? The babies, Trae, our babies, they need you." Tasha was expecting twins any day now.

Trae's adrenaline rushed through his veins and he fought to remain calm as the sounds of steel-toed boot-wearing police rushing up the stairs grew closer. "C'mon, baby, you gotta put something on." Concern over Tasha's frame of mind was evident in his voice.

I know she is not going to fold on me, he thought.

Tasha had been through raids, search warrants and this same drill numerous times with her ex, Nikayah. It all came with the territory of being a hustler's wife. But she had sworn she would never get involved with another hustler again. Not in this lifetime. Trae had managed to convince her and swore to her that he was getting out and it would be different with him. He was going legit. Now here they were. However, she would rather her door get kicked in by law enforcement than by some niggas trying to take their heads off.

Seeing that she wasn't going to move, Trae snatched up his T-shirt, put it on her, then hurried to the dresser and grabbed a pair of panties for her. "C'mon, baby, they're at the door. Get dressed." He managed to get her to stand up. Just as Tasha pulled up her panties the front door damn near flew off its hinges and the law enforcement agents pushed their way into the bedroom, screaming.

"On the floor! On the floor, now! Let me see your hands! Get down!" Trae knew the routine all too well. Most of his life he had heard these orders.

"She's pregnant, man!" he yelled as they threw a distraught Tasha to the floor and handcuffed her. "Why the fuck are y'all handcuffing her? Y'all came here for me!" he yelled as they put the ghetto bracelets on him.

"That's right," the agent in charge said. "We don't need her. Not yet." He smirked. "And read Mr. Macklin his rights."

"It'll be okay, baby," Trae assured Tasha as they led him away with nothing on but sweatpants.

"Okay? Okay? They are taking you away and I'm eight and a half months pregnant with twins." She screamed, "Trae, you promised me. You promised me you wouldn't leave us." Tasha was trying to run toward Trae, but the white female DEA agent was holding on to her.

The agents began searching—more like destroying—their one-bedroom apartment. They went from room to room ransacking the apartment and flipped over furniture, emptied out drawers, snatched clothes out of the closets, tossed papers around and dishes out of the cabinets. In a few short minutes it looked as if a tornado had struck. The agent in charge yelled, "Oh, he's leaving you all right. He's leaving you for a very long, long time, unless you tell us where he keeps his drug money. If not, by the time he has a chance of getting out of prison, that baby you're carrying will be raising a family of its own!" Tasha spit on the agent and he lunged at her throat. The entire room burst out laughing.

"Aaagh!" Tasha sat up, gasping for air as she awakened from this horrible nightmare. Her fingers clenched the bedsheets so tightly her knuckles were turning white. Her breathing was rapid; her body was pulsing from the thundering of her heart as it tried to beat through her chest. She tried hard to shake her head clear. As she wiped the sweat from her brow, Trae sat up and turned the lamp on.

Since the day their drug case was overturned, and Tasha picked up Trae and his partner in crime, Kaylin Santos, from the courthouse, they had been at the bungalow in

Ocho Ríos. They had the same bungalow where he had promised her that after he got out of the game they would come back and chill until they got tired of it. It was a gift from the dons. Their first couple of nights there, Tasha had begun having that awful nightmare, but after about a week it had stopped. Now, exactly three months later, it was starting again.

"What's up?" he asked as Tasha kept shaking her head from side to side and rubbing her eyes to make sure she was dreaming. As he reached over to comfort her he realized how badly her body was shaking and saw the tears rolling down her cheeks. He pulled the sheet off her to make sure she wasn't bleeding. He wanted to be certain that the babies Tasha was carrying weren't in any danger. She was expecting twin boys. He sighed in relief as he looked between her legs. "Baby, what's the matter?"

"That dream. It's starting again. That same dream."

"It's okay, baby. It's over. I told you, I'm not going anywhere." He used his thumbs to wipe her tears away. "Are you listening to me?" He grabbed her face.

"It was so real, though. Oh, God, it was real," she gasped. "It's a sign, I know it."

"It's not real, Tasha. Don't say shit like that. You're jinxing a nigga. It was only a dream. Trust me, Daddy ain't going nowhere." *Shit, I'll hold court in the streets first.* "I'm free. Me, you and the babies are far away from Jersey and New York. Aren't we?"

She hugged him. "Sorry, baby."

"Don't apologize. Everything's fine. It was only a dream." He could still feel her trembling. "I need to be the one apologizing. It was my lifestyle that got you so shook. I'ma make it right, baby. I promise."

"Just tell me you'll never leave us." Tasha felt as if she could never get enough of his reassurance as she held him tighter.

He reached down and rubbed her stomach. "Baby, you should know by now that if I have my way, I'm never leaving my family. But you know I did so much shit in the past. I don't know what's going to happen." She pushed his hand off her stomach, jumped up and stormed into the bathroom, slamming the door behind her.

Trae followed her to the bathroom. They had decided to move to California and start fresh as soon as Trae stopped hustling. "Maybe it's time for us to raise up outta here," he suggested from the other side of the door.

"What you think?" he yelled as he turned the doorknob. Of course it was locked.

CHAPTER TWO

A jet-lagged and exhausted Trae hopped out of the limo before it had fully stopped, as it pulled up to the entrance of the Wilshire Grand Hotel. It used to be one of the best-kept secrets in LA, sitting on the corner of Wilshire and Figueroa. Trae watched as the bellman retrieved their luggage and the driver helped a sleepy Tasha out of the limo. He decided right then and there that this spot would suit their needs perfectly as relocation central. It was the beginning of September and the weather was sunny. A picture-perfect day.

They were so exhausted that after they settled in they slept until almost noon the next day. They were chillin' while waiting for Tasha's cousin Stephon to come over. They had about six houses to look at and he had volunteered to be their official tour guide. They were sitting on the couch in front of the big screen, which was on mute, watching ESPN2. Tasha was devouring a bowl of fruit salad and had her legs thrown across Trae's lap as she listened to him dish out demands to the Realtor.

"Listen, I need somewhere to stay, like, yesterday. I'm expecting my first child." Tasha popped him on the forehead. "I'm sorry, we're expecting twins any day now so we need to get settled in as soon as possible." Trae reached over and began rubbing Tasha's belly. He was silent as he listened to the excuses the Realtor came up with. Tasha placed her hand over his as she guided it to where the movement was.

"What's up, twins?" Tasha whispered to her belly.

"Call me within the next hour. If I don't hear from you, I'm moving on to the next man." He pushed the end button, then leaned over and began kissing Tasha on the belly. "Man, these LA clowns are crazy. They got so much money they don't wanna make no more! They acting like my money ain't green. I have no understanding of this bullshit. Couldn't be me. I don't give a fuck how much bread I got, I ain't stopping until I see Bill Gates type of bread!"

"Give the poor man a chance, baby." Tasha laughed. "I mean, what you want the man to do? Throw the people out of their houses today?"

"Hell yeah! Daddy needs a house."

"And Ma Ma needs for Daddy to chill out."

"I need to chill?" He tongued Tasha down.

"Mmmmmmmmm, mmmmmm," she moaned as she came up for air. "Yes you do. That's my job, to clock out on niggas."

"Aiight then. You got that," Trae told her.

There was a knock at the front door.

"Thank you. Now go answer the door," she ordered.

"I love you more than anything. You know that, right?" Trae leaned over for another kiss.

"Of course I know that. You show me that every day." She kissed him back.

"Aiight then. Just don't forget that shit."

"Don't you forget it. Don't get out here and get caught up in this Hollyhood lifestyle and lose your mind," Tasha warned him. "I'm not going to put up with no bullshit."

"What?" Trae laughed.

"You heard me loud and clear. Now go open the door, nigga!"

"We gotta talk," Trae teased and winked at her as he walked across the room to open the front door.

A feeling of nervousness came over Tasha as she overheard Stephon's voice when he entered the suite. Even though they talked and kept in touch she hadn't seen him since twelve years ago, when they were teenagers. He was the one to bring her the bad news about her brother getting shot to death. He was around when both of her parents were hauled off to prison. He was there when Social Services came and took her sister Trina and brother Kevin into state custody. She felt that seeing him was like reopening a door to her past, something she wasn't ready to do. She didn't like that feeling.

He had spoken with Tasha and Trae over the phone on plenty of occasions, especially when they had confirmed that they were coming to LA, which Stephon called his playground. He promised them that he would do everything to make their transition from Jersey to Cali as smooth as possible.

"What up, man?" Stephon greeted Trae. They gave each other dap followed by a brotherly embrace.

"Good to finally meet you in person," Trae told him.

"Meet you? I feel like I already know you. My cousin talks about you all the time and she sounds like you're keeping her very happy."

"Well, actually we do that for each other," Trae said with sincerity. Then he turned to his wife and said, "Yo, Tasha, your cuz is here!"

"Damn, look at this room. Y'all rollin' like this?" Stephon was admiring the plush suite. He looked around at the marble floors with gold molding, eighteen-foot floor-to-ceiling windows, leather sectional couch and fully stocked bar, and that was only the living room.

From talking to Trina and Kevin, Tasha's siblings who were living in New York, he knew that Trae had stashed a shitload of drug money, but damn!

"Ewwwww, ugly boy," Tasha said playfully when she got up on her cousin, immediately forgetting those bad feelings she had just been having. "You look just like Uncle Bill." Stephon could grace the cover of *GQ* any day and stood six foot tall, with broad shoulders, a clean bald head, coal-black goatee, light brown skin and a perfect set of pearly white teeth. He was fine. Absolutely a lady's dream. Wet dream, that is. She gave him a big hug while Trae stood back and watched his wife interact with family. Stephon twirled her around before staring at her face.

"And you look just like Aunt Seleta. So I don't know why you turning up your nose. My dad and your moms is sister and brother, remember? So if I'm ugly, so are you." He held her back to get a good look at her. "Damn your belly looks like it's about to burst. Even though I look better, I must admit you do look good. But for the most part, you look very satisfied and pregnant," he teased. "I'm happy for you." He hugged her again.

"Thank you. I'll be happy when these boys come out. I feel like a whale, but I'm still a dime, big belly and all. But you're wrong about looking better than me. I see you're going to be a problem already!" She pushed him away, joking. "So where are you taking us? I'm ready to get out and smell some of this Cali air. You know, see some sights. That Realtor you referred us to is moving too slow for Mr. Make-It-Happen-Right-Now over there," she said, referring to Trae.

"You damn right. I ain't got time to be playing with the

type of money I'm trying to spend," Trae snapped. "Later for the bullshit."

"Later for that bum. That's what I wanted to tell Trae. What I got to show y'all you're gonna love. It's in stupid-ass O. J.'s old neighborhood. It's nice, quiet, and most important I should be able to get the keys in less than a week if you want it. And if you got the paper, which I know you do, my man who owns the house got other moves he tryna make. Plus he got the connections to make the deal close very fast. Y'all couldn't have arrived at a better time." Stephon was elated. "I can make it all happen," Stephon said as he pulled his cell out of his pocket.

"Now see? That's the shit I'm talking about," Trae said, ready to go.

Stephon proved to be a man of his word. It was just a matter of days before Trae and Tasha were able to move into their new home. The owner had no problem once Trae gave him a hundred grand down payment. Since O. J. was no longer in the area, Stephon promised that the Brentwood Estates was a quiet, upscale neighborhood. Other than Trae and Tasha, the family of the detective who lived a few houses down the street seemed to be the only visible black family on the block.

The house was a monstrous 6,200 square feet. To both of them the challenge of getting it furnished and decorated was almost overwhelming. However, Tasha was so excited about their new home on West Eric, but Trae was even more worried about Tasha overdoing it with her pregnancy. Nevertheless, Tasha was in heaven. And as far as Trae was concerned, if Tasha was in heaven, everything else would fall into place.

Trae heard the phone ringing but refused to answer it.

"Baby, pick up the phone!" Trae yelled from the family room. He was posted in front of his sixty-inch flat-screen TV.

"Hello," Tasha said into the phone. She knew Trae wasn't moving from his favorite spot.

"What's up, girl? How the hell are ya?" It was Kyra. Tasha could recognize her childhood friend's distinctive voice anywhere. Kyra and Marvin Blackshear had moved—to some suburbs in Long Beach, Cali—right before Trae and Tasha did. Marvin and Trae had become tight in Jersey on the strength of the girls and their respect for one another being in the game. Just like Trae, Marvin had retired from the game. They were all like family.

"When are you coming over?" asked Tasha. "Can I see my peoples for a change?"

Kyra laughed. "Awwww, your fat ass miss me? You need to be resting because it's a wrap once you hit that delivery table. Plus, I told you we'll get over there. It's not like I live right around the corner. I'm taking two online classes that are kicking my ass, Marvin has been doing some things, and I know you and Trae are trying to get settled in. And I know your hyperactive ass is overdoing it."

"No, I'm not. I'm just excited and anxious at the same time. Trae just put up the cribs for the twins, so my main concern is their room and our bedroom. I'm dying for you to see it. It was empty the last time I spoke to you, but now I got a few thangs going on," Tasha bragged.

"Trae told Marvin that your belly is about to burst. How are you feeling?"

"Tired. But like I said I am soooooo excited!" Tasha crooned.

"Look, Tasha, you don't need to be overdoing it."

"I'm not. When I feel myself getting too worked up I chill out."

"Umm-hmm." Kyra doubted her. Plus she knew how Tasha was. "Ho, I think I need to come visit your ass for real now!"

"You gotta see the twins' bedroom and I need to see my niece Aisha. You know every time I talk to her she tells me how she is going to help me with the twins, right?"

Kyra laughed. "Let her help, 'cause she is only five, and I ain't having no more no time soon that she can play house with."

"Yeah, right." Just then Tasha's phone beeped. "Hold on, Kyra, let me take this call."

"Girl, just call me back."

"No, Kyra, hold on," Tasha told her.

Kyra sucked her teeth and said, "Girl, go 'head. Call me back." Tasha didn't want her to hang up, but reluctantly did and clicked over.

"Hi, baby." The voice on the other end cracked.

"Hello, Nana." It was Trae's mother.

"How are you feeling?" Nana asked before her voice began to break up. She was not sounding like her usual vibrant self.

"I'm fine, thank you. How are you and Pop Pop? Is every-thing all right?" Trae appeared in the doorway.

"How long are you going to be on the phone?" Trae asked in an agitated tone.

"It's your mom," she mouthed.

"Give me the phone," he demanded.

Tasha rolled her eyes at him. "Nana, here's your rude son. I love you." Tasha covered the mouthpiece. "I think something's wrong," she whispered before passing him the phone.

"Hey, Ma. Everything aiight?" Trae was silent as Tasha watched his facial expressions. When he ran his hand over his head and those nostrils flared she knew something wasn't right. "Ma, calm down. Put Daddy on the phone."

"What's the matter?" Tasha was now standing in front of Trae.

"Pop, what happened?" Tasha watched as the tears rolled slow and steady down Trae's cheeks. He then took the receiver and began banging it repeatedly against the wall. Tasha jumped back, not knowing what to do.

"Baby, what's the matter? What happened?" Trae threw the cordless phone across the room, knocking the lamp over.

"We gotta go back to New York."

CHAPTER THREE

B aby, are you going to tell me what's going on?" Tasha pleaded as she followed Trae, who was pacing from room to room in an attempt to calm himself down. His last words to her had been, "We gotta go back to New York." But those words had been spoken over a half hour ago. "Trae, be fair. You can't keep me in the dark like this."

"Shaheem. It's my cousin Shaheem." His voice cracked.

"Shaheem? What about him? Isn't he still in New York?"

"He's gone."

"He's gone. What do you mean he's gone?" Tasha asked, even though in her heart she already knew the answer.

"They found him bound and gagged. They stuffed him in a New York Housing Authority bag, Ma. They treated my cousin real dirty. Muthafuckas!" he spat before he punched the wall.

"Baby." Tasha embraced Trae warmly. She squeezed him tight and whispered in his ear, "I am so sorry." She held him close as he cried, releasing a lot of his frustrations and hurt. She had a flashback and thought about the day that she met Shaheem for the very first time. She had been with Angel, her other childhood homegirl. She and Trae both considered Angel like family.

Angel was dragging Tasha to a party that Kaylin, Angel's newfound man and Trae's partner, was going to be at. Tasha didn't want to go because she hadn't heard from Trae in almost a week and wanted to be home in case he came by. And of course she was very worried, especially since Kaylin hadn't seen or heard from Trae in a couple of days either. Then on top of that Angel hadn't told Tasha that the party was damn near three hours away from where they lived in Trenton, somewhere in Wildwood, New Jersey.

Angel kept saying, "You know I would do it for you."

"Angel, three fuckin' hours? You can't just wait for the nigga to come by your house? This shit is crazy." Tasha rolled her eyes and slammed the passenger-side door, damn near tearing it off its hinges.

"It's not three hours. Two, two and a half tops. Tasha, you don't understand. This nigga just does something to me. He's like a drug. I'm telling you, he is the one. Watch what I tell you. This nigga is going to have my babies," she joked. "Plus, you know he didn't want me to come by myself. He told me to snatch you up."

"Bitch, just drive before I jump out this car and take my ass back in the house," Tasha snapped as she whipped out her cell phone and dialed Trae again, only to get his voice mail. She had started to hang up but decided to leave a message, only to be surprised by Trae's message recorded on his voice mail. "Yo, if this is my baby, Daddy is on his way over. So take ya ass home. To everybody else . . . fuck y'all! Please leave a message after the beep." Tasha decided she would do just that.

"Trae, you went through all of this trouble to change your voice mail message when you could have easily exerted that same energy to call me. So if Mommy is not home when you decide to stroll in . . . fuck you!" Click. Tasha sighed.

"Bitch, you dick-whipped and the nigga got you open like

7-Eleven, so just chill out and take this ride with me. He got the key; he'll be in the bed asleep when you get there."

"Angel, I swear you done lost your fuckin' mind. I don't even know who you are anymore." Tasha and her girlfriend Jaz had met the cousins Kyra and Angel in the seventh grade. They all had bonded like sisters and been a clique ever since. They had all hooked up with drug dealers, because at the time it was the thing to do. Angel's boyfriend was a pimp and a dope boy who had disappeared and who they all assumed was dead. So Angel had moved on. She and Tasha were at a club in Philly one night when Angel spotted Kaylin. Even though she had vowed to leave all hustlers and thugs alone, Kaylin had her at hello.

When they arrived in Wildwood it was still early. There was no need to wonder which house was the party house because cars lined the street all leading in one direction, plus the music, people and decorations made it obvious. Lanterns of various colors lit up the property and even though there was a chill in the air, partygoers were hanging outside drinking and partying.

Angel flipped open her cell phone as they got out of her car and dialed Kaylin.

"Yo, beautiful, where you at?" Kaylin always called her beautiful.

"We're walking towards the house now. Where are you?"

"I'll be there in a few."

"What?"

"Wait there for me in the front."

Angel flipped her cell closed and slipped it in her bag. She had a huge grin on her face as she looked over at Tasha.

"Bitch, don't be cheesin' at me." Tasha rolled her eyes at her.

"Tasha, lighten up. I know I owe you one. You know I got you."

"You don't owe me shit but a ride back home and to name your firstborn after me."

"Okay, you got that," Angel told her.

"Yeah, right." Tasha flipped her off.

Angel led the way up the front steps of the mini-mansion. A big dude wearing dark shades stopped them.

"I'm here to see Kaylin," Angel informed him.

He looked the both of them over from head to toe. "Wait right here." He turned to a guy standing behind him. "Marlo, these two ladies are here to see Kay."

Marlo, who also looked like a linebacker for the New England Patriots, looked them over as well and nodded. "This way ladies."

Tasha made a mental note of the fancy shade of burgundy of the thick carpet and furniture as they headed down a set of winding stairs. The color was bangin'. Marlo knocked on the door and growled, "It's me. Open up."

The double doors to the basement opened and he stepped aside. "Have a good evening, lovely ladies," he said, and then blew both of them a kiss.

They both grimaced and looked at each other and then back at him. There was a ruckus in the front of the room. This was obviously the game and gambling room. There were card tables, craps tables, pool tables, chessboards, you name it, spread around the room. In front of the huge fireplace were about seven dudes standing in a semicircle, but then they quickly broke up as blood was squirting everywhere. Kaylin held the iron poker and was beating the scream-ing dude down to the floor. His right-hand man, who was *mocha-colored, six feet two, bald-headed, a tatted Tupac-looking cat who looked as if he killed for a living, repeatedly stomped the dude wherever he could. Losing patience and wanting to inflict more pain, he grabbed a pool stick off a nearby table, unscrewed it and with a smile on his face joined Kaylin in the beat-down.*

Tasha gasped and Angel stood frozen in place. Kaylin was in a zone, beating the guy to a bloody pulp.

The next thing you knew, Angel was on the floor. She had fainted.

"Kay!" Tasha screamed. "Kaylin, get over here now! Angel! Oh my God, Kaylin. Help me."

The words "help me" snapped Kaylin out of his zone. He looked over toward Angel and Tasha, mumbled something under his breath, threw down the poker and yanked off the now bloody work gloves.

"Who the fuck let these broads in here?" Shaheem spat. None of the other cats in the room said a word. Instead they all looked away.

Kaylin hurried over to Angel's side and swooped her up. "What simple muthafucka let my lady up in here?" he screamed. "Don't let that pile of shit move, Shaheem."

"Move? This fool ain't going anywhere. Man, handle your business. I got this shit over here. You should have let me handle this in the first place. White muthafucka wanna cheat somebody outta thirty grand! In they own house! I'ma clean this shit up. Better yet, I'ma take out the trash." Shaheem then yelled for someone to bring him a trash bag. They handed it to him, he popped it open and wrapped it tightly around the guy's head. Dude began kicking his legs and flailing one of his arms. The other one appeared to be broken. Shaheem squeezed the bag tighter, not turning it loose

until the dude released a pile of shit and piss. There were a couple of snickers among the onlookers.

"What the fuck is so funny?" Shaheem was breathing hard. "Ain't nothing funny about a muthafucka tryna beat you out of money in yo own damn house. Muthafucka tryna hustle me?" He beat at his chest. "What? Y'all pussies was in on this shit?" he challenged as he looked around the room. The room grew dead quiet but they were all shaking their heads. "Any one of y'all niggas try to do that shit"—he pointed at the limp body on the floor—"this is your future. Now, who wanna play another hand?"

They all mumbled, "Nah, no thanks, I'm out," and "Nigga, you crazy," as they filed out of the room.

"Aw, y'all punk-ass muhfuckas. All y'all niggas wanna be killers but don't wanna kill shit," Shaheem barked. "Get the fuck outta here!" he screamed at them. "But wait! Who the fuck let those broads in here?" He stormed past Kaylin, Angel and Tasha in search of Marlo and his boy Black, the two bouncers. When he found them they were standing tall on duty, not having a clue that they had fucked up.

"Didn't I tell y'all stupid, dumb muthafuckas not to let nobody downstairs? Didn't I give y'all specific instructions to not let anybody down there?"

Marlo was the first to speak up, "But Kaylin said he was expecting the girls, so I thought—"

"I don't give five fucks about what you thought. I don't pay yo goofy ass to have thoughts. I pay you to take orders. And if you can't do that then what the fuck I got you working here for?"

Neither one of the bouncers said a word.

"You two simple Simon muthafuckas go down there and clean that shit up." They both stood there staring at him,

scared to move. "What the fuck y'all staring at me for? Go clean that shit up!"

"Red, baby." Kaylin called his nickname for Angel. She was still out cold. "Somebody get me a cold cloth," he yelled. "Angel!" He whispered in her ear. "Angel." He was relieved to see her eyes open but they immediately closed. "Shit," he gritted.

Someone handed him a clean wet cloth. He dabbed at her forehead. "Tasha, you need to toughen your girl up."

"Don't blame me. If you were handling business you shouldn't have sent for us."

"I sent for her. Trae sent for you. And this wasn't supposed to be business. This is a party. But hey, shit happens. Your girl here is going to be fine but she does need to toughen up a little." He shook her mildly. "Red, can you hear me? Red, baby, I'ma sit you up, all right?" He dabbed at her face some more.

As if it had just hit her, Tasha snapped, "What do you mean Trae sent for me?" Tasha's heart was now racing. "He told me to be at the house because he was on his way over."

Angel's eyes fluttered open and focused on Kaylin. "Kaylin, what are you doing?" Angel groaned as if she were in pain. "Kaylin?"

"I'm right here, beautiful." He planted a soft peck on her lips.

"Where is Trae?" Tasha asked, but no one was listening.

"Kaylin, I just witnessed you attempt to commit a murder," Angel whispered. "Why, Kaylin? Why are you still testing me? Do you ever stop?"

"Baby, that wasn't a test. C'mon, let's get you out of here. I told you to wait out front for me."

He helped her up and they started walking toward the

door. Angel kept trying to look back at the bloodied body with a trash bag over its head, lying crumpled up in front of the fireplace, but Kaylin was blocking her view.

"Where is Trae?" Tasha asked again.

"I'm ready to go, Kaylin. Let Tasha take me home. I've already had enough of you for one night. Let me leave you to do what you do. Look at you! You got blood all over you." Angel pulled away from him.

"Red, you know I didn't plan shit to go like this. Them stupid niggas wasn't supposed to let y'all down here. I'll take you home." She was shaking her head and trying to pull away from him.

"I need to use the bathroom first," Tasha said. "And when I come out, you better be ready to tell me where Trae is," Tasha threatened.

"So do I," Angel snapped.

Kaylin kept his hold on Angel's arm as he led them to one of the bathrooms. He waited until Tasha closed the door before he embraced Angel and kissed her on the forehead.

"Kaylin, I'm at a loss for words. Am I supposed to—"

He kissed her softly on the lips, cutting her off. "Red, I'm sorry, baby. And believe me when I say it. You weren't supposed to see that. But damn, baby, it is what it is."

Tasha burst out of the bathroom as Angel pushed Kaylin off of her. "It is what it is," Angel mocked him, before storming into the bathroom and slamming the door. She covered her mouth and began to cry.

"You need to toughen your girl up," Kaylin teased.

"That ain't funny, Kay. Shit, I'm tough but if I walked in on my man beating a nigga with an iron pipe to a bloody pulp, my knees would get weak too. Plus, you gotta remember, your living on the other side of the tracks fucks with her.

She's a square for real and you're, um, you're a gangsta thug, as she would put it.

"Your little lawyer girlfriend Angel is living in two worlds fuckin' with you. There's her little all-American legal world and then there's your big all-American illegal world. I think that shit is tough on her mentally, especially since she's determined not to let either one go."

"Your girl is cool, that's my lady. Every Thug Needs a Lady. She'll keep riding that double-sided train until she decides to get off on my side of the track or pull me onto hers."

"Whatever, nigga. Now, where is Trae? I am so losing patience with your boy, Kaylin. I haven't heard from him in almost a week. He hasn't even called me. Is this shit a game to y'all?"

"Chill out, girl. He's right outside. I don't see how y'all missed him."

"Outside!" Tasha shrieked. "Outside where? So he knew I was coming and his ass is outside? He had the audacity to tell me to stay home? What is the matter with him?"

"He's drunk, Tasha."

"Drunk?"

"Yeah. As in liquor. As in he drank too much."

"Kaylin, I—"

"I'm ready to go, Tasha. Now!" Angel came storming out of the bathroom, cutting her girl Tasha off and almost knocking her over. "C'mon, let's go."

"Go? I told you I got you," Kaylin told Angel.

"Tasha, bring your ass on." Angel ignored Kaylin.

Tasha ignored Angel.

"Why is Trae drunk, Kaylin? You know he can't hold liquor! Why do you have him drinking?" Tasha was screaming at Kaylin.

"Kaylin, I'm leaving with Tasha. Go handle your business. Don't let me stop you from doing what you do," Angel told him.

"Hold up. Hold up!" Kaylin needed to get a hold of the situation. "I got this." He took ahold of both of the ladies' hands. He turned to Angel and said, "You're staying here with me." Then he turned to Tasha and said, "You're going to have to drive your drunken-ass nigga home."

"Kaylin, you know Trae can't hold liquor. I can't believe you let him drink," Angel scolded him.

"That's a grown-ass nigga!"

"You're supposed to have his back," Tasha snapped.

"I do have his back. But if a nigga wants to get his drink on who am I to stop him? I ain't the nigga's daddy. All I can do is make sure he don't get into anything or do something stupid. That's why his ass is in the car. Now both of y'all need to chill the fuck out."

Shaheem turned on his charm as the lovely ladies came his way. His bloodshot gaze roamed over Angel and then fell on Tasha. He then broke into a wide platinum-filled grin.

"My bad...uhm, ladies." He flashed them his million-dollar smile and they both frowned. He still had blood on his hands. Kaylin, embarrassed, tossed him a handkerchief he had in his back pocket.

"Oh, my bad. My bad. How y'all ladies doing? Y'all want something to drink? Damn, y'all fine. I thought these country-ass bums was just talkin' shit. Y'all must be Angel and Tasha. I'm Shaheem. Introduce us formally, nigga," he snapped at Kaylin.

"Oh my God. This is so crazy," Tasha exclaimed. She stood there staring at Shaheem, then finally said, "He looks so much like my baby."

*"You don't need no fuckin' formal introduction," Kaylin
snapped back. "You ain't the fuckin' President."*

"Man, stop playin' and introduce us."

*"Tasha, this is Shaheem Macklin, Aunt Marva's son. He
just came home from a four-and-a-half vacation upstate.
That's as formal as it gets," Kaylin said.*

*"Shaheem, take me to Trae, please," Tasha requested.
"Since this nigga Kaylin refuses to do so."*

"Uhm, okay. Follow me." Shaheem beamed.

*Tasha's heart rate sped up as they navigated around the
cars parked on the lawn and people standing around getting their drink and party on. But the closer she got to the car
the angrier she was getting.*

*Trae's truck was kitted out and its windows tinted, but
the front passenger window was rolled halfway down. "Trae
needs to wake his drunken ass up," Tasha snapped.*

*"Yeah, unable to hold liquor runs in the Macklin family,"
Kaylin cracked. "Both these niggas have been partying for
four days straight." Kaylin was talking about Trae and Shaheem. And that was the first time Tasha made the acquain-
tance of Shaheem Macklin.*

CHAPTER FOUR

The next morning Trae and Tasha caught a flight to New York. Trae was in his old bedroom at his mother's house in Hollis, Queens. He sat in the old wooden chair in the corner, looking around the room. Posters of LL Cool J, KRS-One, Vanity 6, Lisa Lisa, Salt-N-Pepa and Run-DMC were still on the wall. The set of full-size beds was neatly made.

Damn. Here I go back on the hunt again. Just when I thought I could put this shit behind me, I'm pulled back in, he thought.

His mother tapped on the half-closed bedroom door. "Come in, Ma," Trae told her.

"Trae, your wife is eight months pregnant. Why did you bring her way across the country? And I know you don't expect her to sleep on these little beds while you're out running the streets, now do you?"

"Ma, our stuff is in the guest bedroom with the king-size bed. And as far as her traveling, she insisted. I couldn't make her stay if I wanted to."

"She probably was trying to talk some sense into that big head of yours. Before you leave out of this house, make sure you talk to your father."

"Ma, how is Aunt Marva holding up?" Trae asked, knowing that his mother would tell him the truth.

"She's not, baby. Just like you are my only child, Shaheem was hers. I can't even begin to imagine what she's
going through. I can, but I honestly don't want to."

Tap. Tap. The bedroom door eased open. It was Omar,
Trae's other cousin. "Hi, Nana." He gave his aunt a warm
hug, hovering over her and kissing her on the forehead.

"Omar, what are you and Trae getting ready to do?" she
asked, already knowing the answer.

Mrs. Macklin wasn't new to the game, she had married
a hustler. Trae's father had snatched her up pretty much the
same way their son had snatched up Tasha. Her husband, Walter, had done time, survived a gun battle and its injuries and
managed to retire from the game with his life. The rumor on
Walter's side of the family was traced as far back as the days
of Bumpy Johnson. One of the sisters had supposedly put a
blessing on the family. That's why Mrs. Macklin knew that
Trae would be all right. How long that blessing would last, she
didn't know. *Did it stop with Shaheem? "Is that why he got murdered?"* Even those close to the sons were blessed, like Omar
and Kaylin. Even though Kaylin's younger brother Kyron was
still locked up they all seemed to be protected. Her husband
Walter had had a long run, hustled and balled with the best of
them. The rest of the hustlers were dead or still in prison.

"I'ma take him out to clear his mind. I'ma watch over
him, I promise."

"Omar, you look so much like your mother. I miss my
sister so much," she sighed.

"So do I, Nana. But you and Pop Pop have always been
there for me." Omar planted another kiss on her forehead.
This was the only family he had known since the age of
fourteen when his mother was gunned down. That was
fifteen years ago.

"You discussed this with Walter already?" Nana asked him.

"Nah. He was in the den when I came in. I slipped right past him and came up here."

Tasha tapped on the door, pushed it open, walked in and sat on Trae's lap. Nana nudged Omar, indicating that Trae and Tasha should be left alone.

Nana stood and turned to Trae. "Make sure you speak with your father."

"Aiight, Trae." Omar followed Nana's lead. "I'll be downstairs."

Nana and Omar left, closing the door behind them.

"You understand why I gotta do this, right?" Trae held on to both of Tasha's hands as he kissed them. She was giving him a blank stare. "C'mon baby, don't be like this. Answer me. You know I'm going to do this anyway. I just need you to tell me you understand."

Tasha sighed. "Look baby, I know what you do. I don't like it, but I deal with it because I love you regardless. I've been with you long enough to understand how you are feeling right now." She let out a sigh and her voice cracked. "But damn, what if something happened to you? We are getting ready to go to Shaheem's funeral, I don't want to have to start preparing for yours. Don't do that to me, Trae." She kissed him softly on his bald head and stood up. "Do what you gotta do, Trae, as long as you come back home when the work is done."

When Trae's father stepped into Trae's bedroom he found his son sitting on the edge of the bed staring into space.

"So what's the next move?" his father asked him.

"Pops, you know what it is. You been there and done that more than enough times that I can remember."

"Yeah, but you know damn well I didn't want this for you. Plus the game ain't the same no more. Shit, I ain't got to tell you that. But this shit here is spookin' me and your mother."

Trae released a huge sigh. His father sat down on the bed next to him.

"Pops, I'm out. I don't know why you don't believe me. Just like Sha. He didn't believe me either." Trae chuckled. "I told him to get out with me. Come to Cali. We good. Good for life."

"What did he say?"

Trae smiled. "As usual he said what he was feeling. He said he was gonna die in the streets and fuck Cali. He a East Coast nigga for life and ain't nothing like some New York pussy." Both men started grinning. "I told him I wanted him to be the godfather to the babies. That fool said he's already the uncle and that's better than godfather. Then the crazy nigga said he would as long as I named one of them after him." Trae choked up and couldn't hold back the tears.

CHAPTER FIVE

For a black funeral, a rare calm blanketed the service. Quiet sobs and sniffles were barely heard above the organ music that played softly in the background. Nobody knew where Trae was when the limos arrived to take the family to the church. There was a sea of flowers. All the young boys from the 'hood who idolized Shaheem wore T-shirts with his picture on it. Trae spared no cost, down to a horse and carriage. He laid his cousin out in style. They all thought: Puff did it for Biggie, Trae did it for his cousin.

Aunt Marva was very snippy. "Let's go! Fuckin' niggas ain't wait to kill my son, so I damn sure ain't waitin' to bury him," she snapped before pulling the veil over her face, shocking the shit out of Tasha.

Despite old folks' tales that a pregnant woman shouldn't go to a funeral, Tasha was right there. The twins were kicking as Tasha's hand glided across her belly. She was doing her best to hold back the tears. She diverted her attention to Trae's father, who was standing in front of the room having a few words with the pastor before he delivered the eulogy. Trae wasn't even there yet. Tasha glanced over at Aunt Marva. She sat tall and proud. Her face was blank. Tasha had not seen her shed one tear and that sent chills up her spine. She was being too calm for her, which spooked her.

For the one life that had been taken, the lives of two would soon be entering the world.

Aunt Marva must have felt Tasha looking at her because she turned toward her.

Tasha tried to give a reassuring smile, but it wasn't until Aunt Marva looked down at her round belly that the cold blank stare turned into a warm smile. Then a tall white lady with a wide-brim hat and a white young man came up to Marva. They looked alike so Tasha assumed that she was the young man's mother. The lady handed Marva a card. The young man leaned down and mumbled something and Marva started screaming at him, "How dare you! How dare you!"

Before Tasha could blink, Omar had the dude in a choke hold, and Kaylin, Kendrick, Bo and Mr. Macklin had surrounded the two white guests.

"Get them the fuck out of here," Kaylin kept yelling as they tried to stop Omar from breaking the dude's neck. The white lady's face was beet red and she stood there petrified.

Everything happened so quickly, Tasha didn't realize she was holding her breath. Nana had grabbed Marva and they had disappeared. Tasha had no clue what was going on. Everyone was mumbling, turning in their seats and trying to figure out what all the commotion was about. Tasha was now wondering what other drama could unfold. About fifteen minutes later the pastor had gained control of the funeral. Everyone was back in their seats except for Marva. Nana now had that same blank stare that Marva had. They both were spooking her. The pastor began his eulogy and he began speaking highly of Shaheem. It was obvious he knew very little of him.

*   *   *

Trae lay in the cut as he watched everyone leave the burial site. He couldn't bring himself to go to the funeral. Instead, he had spent the day getting high and reminiscing about the good times. He, Kaylin, Kyron and Shaheem had plans on taking over the city when they were young and getting in the game. Shaheem's favorite words were "I got you, Cuz."

He stepped out of the car, zipped up his jacket and pulled his fitted cap down low. The climate on the East Coast was much cooler than in California. New York always seemed to remind him of how cold the world could be. He had a bottle of Corona, Shaheem's favorite. He smiled at the thought of Tasha looking around. He knew that she felt his presence.

"Daddy will be home in a few days," he mumbled as he trudged up the walkway, stopping in front of the burial plot. He stood there.

Just a day after Trae had arrived in Queens, word of Shaheem's murder had already spread throughout Hollis. During Shaheem's four-and-a-half year bid he had bumped heads with Magnificent, a ruthless drug dealer from Newark, New Jersey, who had gotten caught up in a buy-and-bust investigation in Spanish Harlem.

Magnificent had already served a year of his five-year sentence before Shaheem arrived. Magnificent had managed to take control of his tier. He paid off the guards, along with a few jailhouse enforcers, and made examples out of anyone who didn't see things his way. That was until he got a taste of Shaheem Macklin.

Shaheem quickly turned the tables on Magnificent by giving him a serious beat-down in the prison yard in front of many spectators, which allowed him to take control of the tier, not to mention that he doubled the guards' salaries. Magnificent was at the mercy of Shaheem until he was paroled. It was obvious that Magnificent refused to let prison beef stay behind prison walls.

As Trae stood over Shaheem's burial site, a weird feeling came across him.

Why did God spare me? And my pops? We were both in the game and retired from it. That shit rarely happens. My Aunt Marva and all of her roots and shit said she and our ancestors would save us. But why couldn't she save her own son? "Damn," he mumbled. Trae pulled out the blunt as he sat on the ground next to Shaheem's plot. "Dawg, I got your favorite." He pulled the brown paper bag off the Corona and poured some out.

Then he took a huge swig of the brew. "It's ice cold, just like you like it." He got choked up. *I can't do this.*

"I'm sorry, man. I'm sorry I wasn't there to have your back. I'm sorry. You got my word that I'm going to fix this shit. I'ma make it right. I won't stop until I do." He emptied the rest of the bottle of Corona and tossed it out as far as he could.

CHAPTER SIX

Tasha's due date was less than three weeks away, but the triggerman who had taken Shaheem out was still breathing and to Trae that was unacceptable, so he was anxious to go out on the hunt. The hunt for blood.

His parents' family room was where Trae, just like his father, went to clear his head. Trae slid the glass doors shut and turned on the dimmer. Tasha had gotten him hooked on scented candles so he lit a vanilla-scented one, grabbed a blunt and stood in front of the window staring up at the New York moonlight. He still couldn't believe that he was out of the game, married; living in Cali, and any day now would be a father. He couldn't help wonder what the Creator had in store for him.

He inhaled on the blunt filled with purple haze and smirked. "Lord, I hope you ain't got jokes. You didn't bring me through all of that dirt I was doing for nothing. Whatever you do, just spare my wife and kids. As for myself, come what may." Trae spoke in a whisper as he continued to gaze up at the stars. He was a firm believer in karma. He had sold and poured tons of poison into his own community. He had numerous bodies under his belt, had fucked more women than King Solomon himself and now here he was on top. The drug game had allowed him to stash millions. Shit couldn't be better for him. But he couldn't help

but wonder, *What did the universe have in store for him?*
The thought continued to nag at him. *What's next? What's
around the corner?*

His heart went out to his cousin Shaheem. Shaheem
hadn't been out of the bing six months and he was already
gone. Trae knew that he wouldn't be able to rest until he
served street justice. Tasha and the twins she was carrying
would just have to wait. He knew Shaheem would have
done the same for him.

Shaheem was a Macklin and they had been raised as
brothers. Each was his parents' only child. They had played
together, gone to school together, lost their virginity together,
and both accepted Kaylin and his family as their extended
family. The only time they had been separated was when
Shaheem went to juvie hall and that was when he took the
weight for Trae, Kaylin and Kyron. The same with this last
bid. It was for having Trae's and Kaylin's backs. Shaheem
and Kyron were always the muscle in their crew. They loved
getting down and dirty, just for the rush.

Tasha, as always, was in tune with her man. She lay in her
bed back in Cali wondering what Trae was doing and if he
was safe. She had not heard from him since that day in his
old bedroom.

Aunt Marva peeked in and interrupted her thoughts. "You
still up? What? You're worrying about him, aren't you?"

"I can't help it," Tasha replied.

"You want something warm to drink?" Aunt Marva offered.

"No thank you."

"Okay then. I'll see you in the morning."

"Marva, thanks for coming home with me. I really do
appreciate you making the sacrifice."

It was the day before Trae disappeared when Trae had asked Aunt Marva to come live with him and Tasha in Cali. Aunt Marva protested at first, but Trae convinced her that she would be a great help around the house, especially after Tasha gave birth and since he didn't want Tasha to be by herself.

After some serious thought and constant nagging on Trae's part, Aunt Marva finally gave in. She could now have a new start at life along with helping to raise other children. It would be a way of correcting the mistakes she had made with Shaheem.

"I told you, there is nothing in that city for me anymore. Everything's gonna be just fine. Good night, baby."

"Good night, Auntie."

Tasha hugged her pillow tighter, closed her eyes and went back to thinking about Trae. Knowing him so well sometimes spooked her. The love she had had for her last boyfriend, Nikayah, was nothing compared to the oneness she felt with Trae. The two men were so much alike, yet they were so different. They both were laid back, but Nikayah was more trusting and chilled; Trae would be watching you like a hawk and ready to pounce. Trae wouldn't sleep. They were hustlers, but Nikayah again was laid back with his and would be content. Trae on the other hand wanted it all and wouldn't stop until he got it all. Trae saw Tasha and he didn't stop until she was his. And then when it seemed that Nikayah had a problem with it, Trae got Nikayah out of the way permanently. His body was found in a Dumpster just like Shaheems. Talk about karma. She would always say that if something happened to Nikayah, she would be able to go on. And she had. But if something happened to Trae, she didn't see how she could do it. She closed her eyes and for what seemed like the thousandth time prayed for Trae to come home safe.

CHAPTER SEVEN

Newark, New Jersey

Sabeerah lived in a second-floor, two-bedroom apartment on Hawthorne Avenue. This week had been pure heaven for her. She was preparing for college and as a graduation present she had gotten a new digital camera. Now all of her family was gathered around for her older sister JuJu's baby shower. Sabeerah watched out her second-floor balcony window as her family exited the cab. They had traveled all the way from Haiti. And they had all moved over here to the States in search of the American Dream, but instead found the Ghetto Dream. JuJu nabbed a baller. Her baby daddy Deontay sold crack for a living. And his drug proceeds upgraded their lives. Sabeerah's belly had never been empty again like in those old days in Haiti.

Deontay was holding Deontay Jr. with pride written all across his face as he beamed down at his new son of three weeks. Then JuJu opened the framed picture of Deontay Jr. that Sabeerah had painted. It got oohs and aahs from everyone in the room. It was lifelike.

Toying with her new digital camera, Sabeerah used her graduation present to zoom in on her sister's gifts. She focused the camera on her sister's new diamond earrings. She zoomed down to the Prada gym shoes on her feet, and then to her expensive outfit. Sabeerah fantasized about going to the beauty salon, getting her hair fly, nails done, a whole new outfit with those same Prada shoes on and going to school. Sabeerah wanted to be just like her big sister. Now if she could just snag her a baller. She hadn't figured out how to do that yet, especially since her mother kept her under lock and key and couldn't wait to send her off to college. But Sabeerah had made up her mind. Once she was out of here and off to college, she was going to get loose. Her mom was already disappointed in JuJu for having a child out of wedlock. But Sabeerah was determined to get her a baller or somebody who would afford her the glamorous life. "As soon as I'm out of here," she mumbled.

After another twenty minutes of recording everyone fawning over her new nephew, Sabeerah grew bored and decided to go on the balcony and get some shots of the block. If she had been back in Haiti, she would have been guaranteed to get some award-winning footage. But the block would have to do for now.

It wasn't quite winter yet, but it was definitely a brisk afternoon. She focused in on the regular runners on the block. The Hawthorne Avenue Posse worked the corner from sunup to sundown. Then they moved shop down the street. There were Ja, Cassie, Dre and Lil' Spruce. She then panned over to a long stretch Mercedes limo as it pulled up. The scrawny Caucasian driver jumped out, looked both ways and jogged over to Cassie. They slapped hands and the driver turned around and jogged back to the limo, not giving a damn that he almost caused an accident. She had seen this same limo driver buy crack off this block on several occasions. Didn't he realize this stretch limo, smack dab in the hood, stuck out like a sore thumb?

"Oooh. There he is." Sabeerah froze in place as soon as the words slipped from her mouth. Magnificent the God. Sabeerah had a serious crush on him. Ja, Cassie, Dre and Lil' Spruce all came running over to him. "Damn, y'all, just bow down and kiss the God's feet, why don't you!" she hissed under her breath. Magnificent was as close to Ne-Yo as she was going to get and he ran Hawthorne Avenue.

Beep. Beep. The limo driver was lying on his horn. Sabeerah focused on the limo, and figured that he had probably just finished smoking his rock and was now hyped and ready to go. Two cars with New York license plates had blocked him in. Magnificent the God was flexin' for his workers when two of the dudes from the New York vehicles came over to him. Magnificent looked over the two dudes standing before him and then he arrogantly waved his runners away. But as soon as he did that the dude with the long leather Pelle Pelle jacket pulled a hammer out of his waistband and shot him right between the eyes.

Sabeerah dropped her camera and stood there frozen in place as everyone down below scattered. The two gunmen both looked up at her, and the cute triggerman aimed the gun at her. She quickly hurried back into the house and stood peering out behind the curtains. The triggerman turned around and smiled at the dead body, and then both men jumped into the car and sped off. *Oh shit! Forget Mr. Magnificent. Mr. Triggerman was gangsta. I'ma have wet dreams about you tonight, Mr. Triggerman.*

"Sabeerah, get your behind out of that window, gal. It sounds like dem fools are out there shooting dem guns." Sabeerah was still peeking from behind the curtain.

Slowly Sabeerah eased out on the balcony, picked up her

video camera and came back into the house. She went into her bedroom and locked the door.

"JuJu, I don't know if I should send Sabeerah away to college. What if she gets sick and does something bad?"

"Mom," JuJu sighed, "Sabeerah only talks to herself. That is not a sickness. She'll be okay. Let her get away from here."

"JuJu, have you listened to her? She sounds different when she talks to herself," her mother pleaded.

"Mom, then take her to the doctor's, if you are so concerned. I think you don't want her to go and you are using not going away to college as an excuse," Juju snapped.

Sabeerah's mother, Winsome, was getting ready to argue with her daughter but changed her mind. She could hear her grandson crying. "Go on and get your baby," she sighed.

"Mom, she'll be fine." JuJu waved her off as she went to get Deontay Jr.

"Trae, why the fuck did you shoot him, man? That wasn't the plan," Omar barked.

Trae was emptying out the Philly as he calmly said, "I didn't like his attitude and plus you know I gotta get back home to Tasha. I don't have time to fuck around with the nigga. He did Shaheem so I had to do him while I had the chance. Who knows when we would have caught him again? Hell, it took us damn near a week to find him."

"Man, there were witnesses and one of them had a video camera!" Spit was flying out of the corner of Omar's mouth.

"Chill nigga, with ya scary ass," Trae's cousin Bo snapped from the backseat. "Dee's people live in that apartment. I'll take care of it." He turned to Trae. "And Trae—"

"Bo, at this point I really don't give a fuck," Trae said, cutting him off. He looked at Omar and said, "My cousin...our cousin is gone. Plus, that's our man's people who had the camera. Ain't that what Bo just said?" Trae leaned back in the seat, lit the blunt, took a drag and closed his eyes as if he didn't have a worry in the world.

"I hope you don't think you're going back to the West Coast before we get that videotape," was the only response Omar could come up with.

"Nigga, can you let me enjoy this moment, please?" Trae snapped as he shrugged Omar off.

CHAPTER EIGHT

Tasha and Aunt Marva were standing in the twins' bedroom, going over it for the twentieth time. Tasha had to admit it to herself, it felt good having someone around the house to help out and keep her company, especially since Trae was out of town. Slowly but surely everything was beginning to come together. Tasha was surprised at how much she was able to get done with the help of Aunt Marva.

"Girl, this room is ready. You can't put nothing else in here," Marva scolded. "You've changed the curtains a hundred times. The babies aren't going to be paying those curtains any attention. Hell, they can't even see. They will only be interested in eating, shitting and sleeping. I'm going over to my friend Ms. Millie's house." She left Tasha standing in the middle of the room. Tasha had started to protest but changed her mind. Aunt Marva had already made new friends. She was doing all she could to deal with the pain of losing her only child and keeping Tasha from worrying about Trae and for that she was grateful.

Tasha looked around the room, fluffed up the crib pillows once again and then headed downstairs to the family room. She settled on the couch, grabbed the remote and turned on the TV. She then felt it, warm fluids wetting her thighs.

"Oh, my God!" she whispered as she felt her thighs and crotch to be sure. "Oh, my God. My water broke!" She jumped up and ran over to the phone and called Trae. "Baby, it's time," she sang into his voice mail before hanging up and racing upstairs to change her pants and underwear. She was both excited and nervous. But before she could get inside her bedroom her first labor pain practically folded her. She grabbed ahold of the doorknob, squeezed it and began doing her breathing exercises.

The pain was so sharp it brought tears to her eyes. "Oh, God," she sighed a sigh of relief after it subsided. She grabbed the phone to call Trae again. When the voice mail came on she said, "Baby, where are you? I just had my first contraction and it was a big one. Hurry home." She hung up and put some dry shorts and panties on. She then called her doctor and told her that she had had her first contraction and that her water had already broken. The doctor told her to get on over to the hospital. With twins and with Tasha being past her due date Dr. Cannon didn't want to take any chances.

Tasha hung up with her doctor and called Trae, again leaving a message, and then she called Marva.

Taking care of Magnificent had eased a load off Trae's shoulders. Trae was slowly coming down off of that high. The high he had gotten from taking Magnificent out. He was in Omar's basement along with Bo, and of course Omar. They were sitting around drinking, passing blunts around and reminiscing about Shaheem's crazy ass.

Omar said, "Kaylin said since you don't know how to answer your phone come over to the crib. He needs to holla at you before you leave. I told him you ain't going nowhere until we get that tape back."

"Leave? Leave for where?" Then it dawned on Trae that he had a wife and soon-to-be family at home. "Shit!" Trae spat. He jumped up and began pacing back and forth. "I've been so caught up in finding that damn Magnificent cat, I haven't even checked on my wife. I can't believe this," he mumbled. He searched all of his pockets for his phone and turned it on. He dialed his voice mail. "Shit!" he spat as he realized that Tasha had been blowing his phone up.

Bo and Omar watched as his whole demeanor changed. He went from killer Trae to worried daddy.

He could hear the panic in her voice but at the same time she was trying to be strong. He could also hear it in her voice that she was scared and disappointed. He snatched up his jacket.

"Tasha is in labor. Y'all gotta get me to the airport on somebody's plane and I mean right now. I can't miss the delivery of my first babies." He was already headed for the door, with Bo and Omar on his heels.

Trae arrived in California and walked in the delivery room just as his first son was coming into the world.

PART II

CHAPTER NINE

Fast-forward, Manhattan, New York City...Game Over Records

G ood morning, Game Over Records. Please hold. Good morning, Game Over Records, how may I direct your call?"

Bobbi the receptionist was going crazy for the third morning in a row since the headlines read REGGAETON SUPERSTAR AND MOTHER FOUND SLAIN. The news was on every radio station, every news channel and just about every newspaper.

When she looked up she saw Angel coming into the office. She had on a pair of dark shades that Bobbi knew matched her mood. She stood up and said, "Mrs. Santos, I'm glad you are back safely from your business trip and I am sorry about Papi Chulo. I still can't believe it, but y'all don't pay me to do public relations." Bobbi rambled on all in one breath.

"Bobbi, just take a message like any other normal secretary would do. We have a publicist. Several. Give them Courtney's number. Is Kaylin in yet?" Angel snapped as she held *The New York Times* tightly under her arms.

"He was here when I got here, Mrs. Santos. He's been on the phone all morning."

Angel stormed off in search of Kaylin. His door was open,

his back was turned and the phone was glued to his ear. Angel slammed the door, causing him to turn around. She tossed the article in front of him. "Hang up the phone, Kaylin."

His smile turned into a frown.

"Now, Kaylin." While she was in Colorado on a business trip, she had been calling Kaylin repeatedly since she heard about Papi Chulo's and his mother's deaths. Kaylin had refused to talk to her over the phone. He continued his conversation as he watched her pace back and forth. He knew she was pissed because he wouldn't talk to her. He knew that all she wanted to do was grill him. He ended the call and stood up.

"I'm glad to see you too. How was your trip?"

"Kaylin, don't even try it. If you would have answered your phone you would have known." She picked up the newspaper and tossed the article on Papi and his mother at him. He caught it and placed the newspaper on his desk. Papi had taken his mother on a cruise and they had both been found murdered.

"Red, I found out about this the other night. You know I wasn't going to discuss this with you over the phone, so I don't know why you trippin'." Kaylin turned up the music in his office because he knew what was coming next. He walked over to her and Angel started crying.

"You know I liked him, Kaylin."

"So did I, Red. He was our number one moneymaker."

"Why did they do this? We should have never sent them on the cruise," Angel bawled.

"Baby, it's not our fault," Kaylin assured her.

She looked into his eyes to see if it was true or not. What she saw made her stomach clench. She pushed him away and went into her office.

*   *   *

California here and now...

Trae and Tasha were sitting in the family room. The twins were now almost three years old and Caliph was going on one. Caliph was in his playpen and the twins were playing with their toys. Trae was filling Tasha in on Stephon's pitch for the nightclub. He could sense that Tasha wasn't quite sold.

"The bottom line," he continued, "is that I can clean up a nice amount of this cash we sittin' on. The longer we have it sittin' around the more uncomfortable I'm getting. You understand what I'm saying?"

"Of course I understand. But do you understand what I'm saying? Matter of fact, are you even listening to what *I'm* saying?"

"What are you saying, Tasha?"

"Why does it have to be a club? Nightclubs are very risky. There are so many other business ventures that you could use to clean up some money."

"Yes, but a business venture with your peoples that I can control, baby. This opportunity just fell into my lap. And to make it even sweeter, he has a board of directors that are made up of the most powerful people in California. I won't have to explain to them where the money came from. It's like I'm doing business with the connect's connect. Plus, it's *our* club. When we go out we will be going to *our* club."

"I don't know." She was shaking her head.

"You don't know what?"

"By no means am I insecure, but a club? I don't know about these West Coast hoes having access to my husband," Tasha said, clearly not feeling this nightclub thing.

"Oh, so now we're getting to what this is really about."

"Trae, be for real. I'm looking at the future. You know you will be swimming in bitches. Bitches mean drama. We both know this."

"Tasha, this is business."

"Nigga, you must have forgot who you talkin' to. Y'all niggas say that same shit when y'all out there hustlin'. *This is business*. It's always business, but business and bitches don't mix. Look, I'm done talking about it because obviously your mind is already made up."

"So, you don't want me to invest in the club?"

"Baby, I've said all that I'm going to say. You've already made up your mind. I'm with you. Just don't let me have to act a fool out here in Hollywood."

"Uh-oh. This just in: Tasha threatens to get ghetto," Trae joked.

"Ha, ha, ha, nigga. I got your joke, Chris Tucker." Tasha rolled her eyes at him. "For real, keep playing if you want to. You can mark my words, it's gonna be some shit. Just be sure to remember what I'm telling you. A club guarantees drama. And Trae, I promise you, I am not the one to be putting up with the bullshit. Watch what I tell you."

Trae was out taking the Navigator for a ride on the LA streets. He had several cars: the Benz, the BMW, the ole skool and the Denali. But the Nav was by far his favorite. He had just gotten it detailed and wanted to show it off. Riding in the Nav brought back lots of memories. This was his hustle ride. Trae opened up the sunroof, allowing the noonday sun to warm his bald head. He turned the CD player on and lit a blunt. Jadakiss came on telling everybody to "fuck the frail shit." Trae smiled but the moment was instantly lost as the flashing lights were right behind him. *Shit.* Trae put the blunt out and pulled over.

The dark blue Chrysler with the tinted windows pulled up behind him. Trae called Tasha and told her he had just been pulled over and the Nav smelled like weed. He then told her to call Benny, his attorney, if she didn't hear from him in thirty minutes. Trae watched as the driver-side door of the Chrysler came open. A brown-skinned brother with long dreads stepped out wearing plain clothes and talking animatedly on his cell phone. *What the fuck?* Trae thought as he rolled his window down.

As the officer continued to talk he was admiring the Navigator. He finally hung up and said, "I had a silver Nav just like this. Same year and everything. Muthafuckas stole it and chopped it up. You know your left brake light is out?"

"Naw, man. I didn't. It's been sitting in the garage for over a month. I had to take it out today," Trae told him, wondering if he was going to say anything about the weed.

"How she running?"

Trae smiled. "Like she been sittin' for months."

The detective started laughing. "Aiight, man. Get your light fixed." He turned and headed back for his car leaving Trae wondering, *What the fuck was that really about?*

CHAPTER TEN

It was a little after three in the morning. Trae and Tasha were just getting into the house. They had been out with Stephon, Marvin and Kyra scouting out the hottest clubs, those they would be competing against.

As Trae fumbled with the lock, Tasha was standing behind him, kissing him on his neck and squeezing his dick. As soon as he opened the door she began to unbuckle his belt and unzip his pants.

"You know you were the finest thing out there tonight, right?" he said as he looked at her over his shoulder.

"You told me that already. You gonna give me some dick or continue to tell me what I already know?"

"I'ma do both, smartass," he told her as he yanked her dress up over her ass and lifted her up. He slammed her back up against the wall as she wrapped her legs around his waist.

"Ohhhhh, I like it rough, big daddy," she teased him as she slid down onto his dick. They both released subtle and seductive moans.

Her pussy was hot and juicy. "Oh, you ready for Daddy, huh?"

"Mmmmmm," she moaned as she wrapped her legs around his waist tighter. "All night long I was ready to fuck," she whispered into his ear. "You were the finest nigga out there tonight. And this big fat dick is all mine."

"Is it?" He pounded deeper into her pussy.

"Yes, oh sssss, right there, baby. Oh...my...right there, baby. Fuck this pussy," she moaned.

"Whose pussy is this, Tasha?"

"You know it's yours." She clenched her teeth together and threw her head back as he pounded away.

"Is it?"

"Baby, yes...oh God, my spot. My spot, nigga," she gritted.

Trae felt her legs trembling. "Whose pussy is this?" He began pounding harder into her G-spot. Every time he hit it, he wanted to smash it. "Whose pussy is this?" He smacked her ass.

"Yours, babeee. Ohhhh, I love you so much," she squealed as her orgasm erupted. Her body was still trembling and her legs were weak as he slowly eased her down. "Turn around." Trae guided her around and bent her over. She was still spent and was moving in slow motion. He spread her legs and began hitting it from the back. He wanted to watch his dick slide in and out of her pussy but it was feeling too good. All he could do was close his eyes, grab on to her hips and get in as deep as he could. After four more strokes of being in that gushy gushy, his knees buckled and Tasha was makin' the pussy do what it do, clamping the muscles down and around his dick and he was no longer in control as he shot a heavy load up into her. Now it was his turn to be spent as he rested all his weight on her.

"Nigga, you better get your heavy ass off of me," she giggled. He leaned harder onto her back. "Trae, stop playing. What? You trying to tell me that you want me to give you a piggyback ride? That's too freaky for me." He pulled her up slowly, smashing her into the wall, and began sloppily kissing her cheek. "I love you too. Now let's go and check on our babies and quit slobbing on my cheek."

Trae slid her dress down over her ass and she bent down and pulled his pants up. They shared several more passionate kisses before they headed upstairs to the twins' bedroom.

Aunt Marva startled them both as she met them at the top of the stairwell.

"Yo, Auntie, I was about to pull out my piece and start blasting," Trae teased.

She ignored his comment. "Those little boogers have been up all night. They just went to sleep and Concita left, right before y'all came in. Don't go in there messing with them babies and wake them up," she warned. "I don't know why y'all had to hire a nanny. That's what I'm here for. I'm going to bed, so don't call me, I'll call you and good night." Then she stopped and turned around. "Why won't y'all use your bedroom? The last time I checked, that's what it's for. Y'all making all that damn noise in the hallway. Voices do carry around here," she snapped. "And I hope you wrapped that thang up because at the rate you going, her body will never get a rest. Baby after baby. It don't make no damn sense."

"Yeah, that's how I like her, pregnant and barefoot. I told y'all I need my own team." Trae laughed.

Tasha yanked on Trae's arm. "C'mon on, Coach." She was ready to fuck some more.

"Good night, Auntie." It was Trae's turn to ignore her. He grabbed Tasha and pulled her along with him.

"Are you sure there is only one of her?" said Tasha. "She is all over this house. Remember I told you she was spooky? What's up with the praying over the boys? And blessing the house every damn fifteen minutes?"

"Tasha, stop trippin'. Everybody is spooky to you. Auntie is spooky, the last nanny was spooky. Concita, the new one, is spooky."

"Now you're exaggerating. I didn't say that."

"Yes you did."

"I did not. I like Concita. We can't have any ole body up in our house, watching our children."

Trae turned on the hall light and went into the boys' huge bedroom. Caliph had a crib that turned into a bed and a playpen. There were three toy chests, three dressers for each of them and two closets. Tasha had outdone herself creating a serene suite for her babies, who were growing faster than she liked. Every detail she had overseen with the help of one of LA's most famous interior decorators, A. J. Deville. The sea-blue color scheme drew you in to the stars and open sky that were painted on their walls with the boys' names detailed throughout the sky. With every baby gadget and toy spread throughout the room you would have thought it was a small day care.

All three of them were sound asleep. Trae watched proudly as Tasha felt Caliph's diaper, kissed them all and adjusted their blankets.

Breaking the silence, Trae said, "C'mon, let's take a shower together."

CHAPTER ELEVEN

Trae and Tasha had established a routine. The week was for the children. Saturday was Tasha's day, when Trae catered to her and she decided what she wanted to do and where she wanted to go. As the head of the household, Trae made sure everybody got attention and everyone stayed happy.

But Sunday? That was the king's day. It was all about Trae. He would hang out with his boys and do him. Most of the time it would be about business. If he felt like it, he would just kick back with the remote in his hand and just chill out and of course enjoy his favorite pastime of getting his knob slobbed. He loved Sundays. Tasha loved them too. She would cater to him and be at his beck and call. She would feed him breakfast in bed, lunch and dinner if he wanted it.

This particular Sunday the twins were having fun in their play area. Trae was puffing on a blunt while channel surfing and Tasha had just finished up his pedicure and was giving him a foot massage.

"Baby, I'm thinking about getting ready," Tasha told him.

"Ready for what?" He looked down at his queen, the love of his life. She definitely completed him and was everything he wanted in a wife and soul mate. She confirmed all the time that merking Nikayah had been necessary and well worth the risk it had posed at the time.

"To open my physical therapy office."

Okay, Trae thought. He definitely hadn't seen this coming. He was sure the twins had taken her mind completely off opening her own practice. *Why the fuck is she trying to work?* He knew plenty of professionals who had private practices who wished they could stay home and do whatever they wanted.

"Trae, I know you heard me."

"What brought this on? Aren't you busy enough?"

"What do you mean what brought this on? You talking like this is something new. Did you forget I graduated with that as my major? Did you forget how you told me, 'We got enough money, we can hire someone for the kids. Kids don't stop anything. You can still do your thang. Just have my babies,'" she mocked. "Do you remember that, Trae? Do you remember that you made me that promise when I got pregnant the first time?"

"Yeah, I remember. But damn, why you gotta spaz out? All I'm saying is that the baby is only one year old, Tasha. You don't think it's too soon?"

"No, I don't. By the time I put my business plan together, find a suitable office, staff, equipment and furniture, the boys—"

"Baby, hold up. Hold that thought," he interrupted.

She leaned back and watched as Trae took another toke off his blunt. This was her baby. The love of her life. Shit, he was her life. Both of her parents were in federal prison serving lengthy sentences. You name it, they done it. Her sister and brother were on the East Coast doing their own thing. And she was more in love with Trae now than she had ever been. And she believed in everything he told her. So far, every promise he had made to her he had kept.

He put the blunt out and came up to the edge of the chair. "Come here, baby." He grabbed her by her hair, leaned down, and began to kiss her. "You know I love you more than anything, right?" She nodded. "You know I only want to keep you happy, right?" She nodded again. "I can't lie, and call me selfish if you want to, but I want you to stay home. I don't think I'm going to like you being gone all the time running a business. That's my job, to provide for this family. I want you here with me and our babies. At least until I see what's going to happen with the club."

"Trae, you know as well as I do, it's never going to be the right time. Let me at least get started on it. Hell, I don't even have my business plan done. This is a dream of mine, Trae. Don't make me put it on hold. I got the itch now and I want to do it now. I need you to support me *now*."

"Baby, give me six months. All right? Let me see what's up with this club and I got you. All right?" He could tell that she wasn't happy about waiting. "C'mon, Tasha. Trust me. I just need you to hold up for a few months. Okay, work on your business plan."

"That's all I was saying. I just don't want you to forget about what I want to do."

"I'm not going to forget. I gotta go and meet Stephon and Marvin." He leaned forward, gave her a kiss and went to get ready.

"Yo, dawg, I'm telling you. This is the move. Look at the market research. A nightclub in this spot?" He tapped the blueprints for emphasis. "We gonna laugh all the way to the bank. Marvin, Cali is your old stomping ground. You was raised out here, so tell him," Stephon prodded.

"You already told us about five times," Marvin said. "And

I'm sure I speak for the both of us. We have to run the numbers and go over everything one more time."

Trae nodded in agreement as he was focused on the market research report.

"But I'll tell you now," Marvin continued. "If everything looks like money, then I'm in like Flynn."

"Aiight then. But make up your mind. I got some other investors lined up and the construction crew is ready," Stephon said.

"Bullshit," Marvin teased. "You know we the only niggas you came to."

"Shit, we the only niggas who got a couple mil to put up," Trae added.

"Fuck the both of y'all." Stephon couldn't help but laugh. Trae, Marvin and Stephon were seated at a table inside the famous Beverly Hills restaurant Mr. Chow.

"Man, I always wanted to come to this joint." Trae was looking around and acting like a tourist. There were a few celebrities, like Lil Mama, Charlize Theron, Xzibit, Tobey Maguire and Mike Epps, getting their grub on, but he wasn't sweatin' them. Shit, as far as he was concerned he was the supastar.

Stephon on the other hand was ecstatic. He didn't have enough capital to pull it off by himself, but he did have the blueprints to a nightclub. He just needed to find the right people, and he had been searching high and low for the past two and a half years. Since his cousin Tasha had moved to Cali it looked as if he was getting ready to fulfill his dream of opening one up. "Look, here is a copy of the business plan. Y'all got copies of the blueprints and market research report. I did all the legwork for y'all. So again, make a decision soon. Now, for our next order of business." Stephon was anxious to get down to the business at hand. He waved the waitress off. "The cable channel, Trae, all you gotta do is be ready to flip it. This is designed especially for you. Don't you agree? You looked over their offer and you're in, right?"

"I'm in, man. I told you that. Plus Tasha didn't even give me no beef over flippin' the cable channel. It's the club that she bitchin' about."

"Man, handle that, because the club is going to be crazy. Now, the attorney who is handling the financing of the club and who wants to take the cable channel off your hands has an office about twenty minutes from here. Her name is Charli Li. She wants to meet you. It's actually one of her father's businesses."

"So is there a problem?" Marvin decided to jump into the conversation.

"There are other bidders. I went into this thinking it was going to be a slam dunk since I've dealt with her a few times. But the last word I got was her pops was ready to play, so that's why we gotta go to her office. They seem to be leaning toward our offer. The focus has been all on you."

"On me?" Trae wanted to know.

"Man, I tried to tell y'all. You are playin' with the big dawgs now. Where the name of the game is the almighty dollar and you have to be in it to win it," Stephon said. "These people get what they want." Stephon lowered his voice. "They checked you out and know your background. I think they like what they found."

"Fuck his background. What do you mean, get what they want? That shit sounds suspect to me," Marvin said.

"Marv, chill. That's why I got my own lawyer, nigga," Trae told him. "The shit sounded suspect to me at first too," Trae admitted.

"Look y'all, I got this," Stephon the dealmaker explained. "But after I checked with a few contacts, if you need to clean up large amounts of loot this here is the move, these are the people to see. They got reps to protect and Charli is always bringing me something. Between the club and the hotel, I'm straight. I'd figure Trae could use the club and the cable channels. I'm trying to find something for Kaylin, but as of yet, nothing has piqued my interest."

"Well, he'll be up here next week to talk. From what he told me, he's expecting you to present him with something. He also is looking for something for his brother Kyron," Trae said.

"I'm working on a few things," Stephon assured him. "Trust me. I'll have something for him."

Marvin waved the waitress over. "I don't know about y'all niggas, but I'm ready to order."

As they enjoyed their meal their discussion was all about the club and its renovations, which were scheduled to start the next day. It had once been a rubber warehouse. They had named it Club New York. They were looking forward to bringing their New York flavor to the people of Cali.

Marvin let out a long whistle as they pulled up to the offices of Li, Hammerstein and Burke. The complex held eight office buildings six stories high, two each to the north, south, east and west according to the type of service. The outside was ultramodern, complete with landscaped layouts, glass and marble exteriors, beautiful atrium gardens, fountains, waterfalls and marble and granite statues. The men marveled at the building's layout and were shocked that all the buildings belonged to one law firm, the Li, Hammerstein and Burke legal team. Trae had never seen anything like this before.

"Damn. They doin' it big. The whole complex is nothing but lawyers? And all of them are on Li's payroll?" asked Trae.

"Sheeit. 'Big' ain't the word. It's enough lawyers up in this bitch to get a nigga a not-guilty verdict on trial with the feds," Marvin added.

"Yeah, I told y'all these people were major. What? Y'all thought I was bullshittin', didn't y'all? Every one of these buildings house lawyers that specialize in something for Li, Hammerstein and Burke. This whole layout is them. This is money on another level. You thought you was gettin' it in the streets, fuckin' with these cats they gonna have you Donald Trump rich," Stephon swore.

They walked in silence as they stepped into the softly lit foyer. The walls of the plush leather waiting area displayed very expensive artwork. They stepped onto the round glass elevator. "Awww, we gotta put one of these here in the club," Trae marveled at the elevator as the glass doors smoothly slid shut and it took them up to the top floor.

They stepped off the elevator just as Charli Li was walking by.

"Ms. Li," Stephon greeted her with a gentle handshake.

"Stephon, how many times have I told you to call me Charli?" Her four-foot four-inch frame was swallowed up inside Stephon's embrace.

"Charli, this is Trae Macklin and Marvin Blackshear."

"Pleased to meet you both." She lightly squeezed both of their hands. "Let me drop off these files right here. It will only take two minutes. Stephon, you know where the conference room is. Feel free to help yourselves to the refreshments."

"Not a problem." They all watched her sashay away.

"She got some black in her?" Trae was actually surprised.

"She's Jamaican and Chinese," Stephon clarified for him.

"That sounds like a dangerous combination and damn the bitch reeks of money. But yo, she is too fine to be named Charles," Marvin commented.

"It's Charli, not Charles," Stephon corrected him.

"Y'all on a first-name basis?" Trae noticed.

Stephon blushed. "Naw, man. She on a first-name basis. I like to keep it professional. I think she be wanting some black dick though. Shit, my life is more important to me. Do you know who her pops is?" Stephon's voice went down to a whisper. "Charles Li. The Chinese mobster in the flesh."

"Man, go 'head with that Hollywood bullshit, son," Trae cracked and they all shared a laugh. On a serious note, Trae may have been laughing but he already had the office of Li, Hammerstein and Burke checked out. He wasn't going to be shelling out millions of dollars without no real facts on these people and what he had found out was big. Hammerstein and Burke were both squares. But the infamous Mr. Charles Li, his nickname should have been Mr. Heroin. He too had gotten out of the game but was still a boss. Even though Mr. Li and they were cut from the same cloth, after Trae discussed his findings with Kaylin they had come to the conclusion that this was the next step up from the drug game. And it made them wonder if they would ever become one hundred percent legit.

"She got enough money to buy all the black dick she wants too. Why would she want yours?" Marvin asked, still on the "black dick" comment.

"You know how those spoiled rich bitches are. They know they got it like that and they'll want it just because."

"Fuck it. If I was you, I'd trick with the bitch," Trae said.

"Naw, man. It ain't worth it. You don't want to fuck with her like that. Trust me. I'm telling you who her father is. Plus, I know bitches. She the type that gets a taste of the black dick and it's over. You won't be able to get rid of her. Listen to me, my brothers. If you want to keep your dick attached to your body and not stuffed in your mouth then don't fuck with her."

They stepped into the conference room and it mirrored the rest of the building.

"Check this out." Stephon pushed a button and a wet bar came out of the wall.

"Stephon loves to play with that," Charli said as she stepped into the room. "Please have a seat, gentlemen. Unfortunately, I have a car on the way to get me for another meeting, so I need to get right down to business with the owner of that cable company. That would be with you, Mr. Macklin?" She took him in from head to toe.

"Yes, that would be me."

"Great. And then I need to talk to everyone about the financing of the club. From what I understand everyone is ready to proceed?" All of the men said yes.

"I am so excited for Stephon, that his dream is getting ready to be fulfilled. You guys don't know how much he has been talking about this. Stephon and Mr. Blackshear, help yourselves to whatever is over there at the wet bar and the refrigerator. That guy there even knows where the secret button is for the big screen."

She was of course talking about Stephon. "Come. Follow me,

Mr. Macklin. My office is right across the hall." They headed out of the conference room. As they got seated in her office, Trae was surprised. From the reputation of Charli's father, he still couldn't get over the fact that she was mixed. Men of his caliber usually didn't do the race mixing, unless it was on the down low. His eyes wandered over to the left of the wall to where the pictures were hanging. Her father was a Chinese man who resembled the Chinese actor Sammo Hung but was much taller. Her mother, Trae discovered, was Jamaican. Trae studied her picture and said to himself, *Damn. She is fine. She puts the J in Jamaican.* From the side he could see that her ass was bangin'. *I wonder how Mr. Li got his little dick up in all that ass?* Trae laughed to himself as he studied the picture. *Charli resembles them both. Dark eyes like her father's. Round nose like her mother's. Smile like her father's, but mouth like her mother's. Head shaped like her father's, hair her mother's, long, curly and jet black. Thick hips and phat ass definitely her mother's. Attitude probably from her as well.*

"Yes, those are my parents." Charli's voice was dripping with sarcasm.

"You don't sound too pleased," Trae commented.

"I'm a mutt as my grandmother would say. Can I get you anything before we get started?" She quickly changed the subject.

"No, I'm good."

She took a seat behind her huge mahogony and glass Donald Trump–style desk. It was accented with diamond corners. "The cable company that you want to sell is already done. We have four investors that are clamoring all over it. But what did Stephon tell you about the land deal that we are inviting you to invest in? That makes the cable company chump change."

Trae got comfortable in his seat. "I didn't want to hear third-party information. I told him I needed to hear everything from you. And for starters, why should I get involved with this venture? Y'all talking sixteen million? That's a lot of dough."

"Look at it like this. You're getting thirteen from the sale of the cable company. You only need three million more." The "three million" rolled off her toungue as if she had said "three hundred." "You've got funds that you need to clean up and this is the fastest and best way to do it all at one time."

"Who told you that?" Trae got defensive. "And if I don't like what you tell me, I'm outta here."

She liked his style and had to hold back a smile. "Mr. Macklin, just as you had us checked out, we did the same on our end. And it just so happens that this project requires this type of funding and that's one of our specialties, matching buyers and sellers."

She felt that she had said what he needed to hear and that he would not get up without sealing the deal. She had to admit that she was impressed. To date she had never met a black man like Trae. One who had some brains and some balls. It was always one or the other. She kept him talking and ended up rescheduling her next appointment. She could see that he was bullheaded, driven and focused just as much as her father. When he finished talking she came from behind her desk and began pacing the floor.

"Glad to see you thought this out, Mr. Macklin."

"Why wouldn't I? Come on now. I'm not your average joe from off the streets. I'm sure Stephon told you that. So choose your words carefully."

"I apologize if I offended you. I'm not used to dealing with black men with balls and money." She smirked.

She grabbed a file off the table and handed it to him. She watched him as he flipped through its contents.

Finally he said, "I have a meeting with my attorney next week. His name is Benny Brown. I have no idea what his schedule is. So is it okay if he sets up an appointment with you?"

"Sure. Have him call my assistant, Jill. Here's my card. Let me grab Club New York's files and I'll meet you back in the conference room."

Trae stood up and she watched this hell of a black man swagger out of her office.

CHAPTER TWELVE

Even though it was a weeknight, Stephon and Marvin came by Trae's house. They called him and told him to be ready. They wanted to go by Club New York to check on the construction crew.

"Ready to get to work?" Marvin asked, and winked at Trae.

"I'm always ready to work," Trae said.

Tasha shot him a look that said, "Nigga, I know you don't think you going out tonight!" And she caught Marvin's wink.

Stephon read her expression. "Y'all married niggas got too many restrictions for me. Can't go there, can't say this, and can't say that! Y'all can't do shit."

"Nigga, I'm the king of my castle. Tasha knows what it is. You see, she only *looked* all crazy but ain't say shit. Give me a minute," Trae told him.

Tasha rolled her eyes at Trae and left them in the living room. In the blink of an eye Trae went upstairs, changed clothes and was out the door with Marvin and Stephon. They jumped into Stephon's burgundy Escalade and were headed out of the driveway.

"Ain't that some shit," Tasha snapped. "Nigga ain't been home for an hour and already he's gone," she said to Marva.

"Chile, please. You know what kind of man you got. And

if you don't get it out of your mind that Trae is going to settle down as if he has a nine to five and is no longer in the streets, you are going to be in for a rude awakening," Marva told her. "All the business in the world won't satisfy his craving for the streets. It's in his blood. He is his father's son. A born street nigga." Marva didn't give Tasha time to respond. She got up and left out of the family room.

"Yo, where we going? This ain't the way to our club," Trae yelled over the Styles P lyrics Stephon was blasting.

"I know. We got something special planned for you." Stephon flashed him a devilish grin.

Trae looked over at Marvin, who simply shrugged his shoulders.

"Nigga, don't act like you ignorant," Trae told him.

"Trae, for once, I want you to just chill out and go with the flow. Can you do that for me, man? You ain't kicked it with the fellas in a minute. What's up with that?" Marvin tried to ask with a straight face.

Trae smiled. "Chill out? What the fuck you think I've been doing? You know. I've been doing the family thing."

"We know. That's why we hookin' you up, dawg," Marvin said. "Shit, you got the keys to the club; you can see that anytime."

Trae sat back, cracked his window and marveled at the Los Angeles sky. Marvin passed him a blunt as Stephon navigated through traffic while talking on his cell. About forty minutes later they pulled up into a club called Spinners that was in the cut.

"Trae, tonight is your night. Anything you want is on the house. This is my treat." Stephon threw the Escalade in park and jumped out with Marvin right on his heels.

"This is what y'all niggas be doing when I'm not around? Hanging at seedy-ass strip clubs?" Trae shook his head in mock disappointment.

"Man, don't hate. But at the same time don't let the raggedy outside fool you. Now get yo' doing-the-family-thing ass out of the car," Stephon barked.

"Steph, don't let this nigga spin you. He's only puttin' on an act. Just in case you wanna run back and tell Tasha on him. This nigga is down for whatever." Marvin put Trae on blast. The three of them walked up the rickety stairs.

"Damn. Y'all couldn't take me to a better place than this?" Trae cracked.

"Nigga, I asked yo ass to chill out," Marvin said as he knocked on the door.

A small Cuban man opened the door, looked at the three of them and moved to the side. Stephon placed a few bills in his hand and kept walking to another set of winding stairs that were carpeted and led them to a steel door. Stephon pressed the buzzer three times and the steel popped open.

A half smile appeared on Trae's face as they stepped into the colorful club and he saw so many beautiful women. There were dark ones, light ones, Asian ones, Indian ones, Latina women, white women.

"Damn, y'all. I take back what I said about y'all niggas earlier," Trae apologized.

"We not tryna hear that shit," Marvin bellowed as he led Trae over to their VIP booth and took a seat.

Stephon waved the waitress over, placed their drink order and then sat down. "I told you, boy. I got you," he yelled over the music to Trae, who was checking out his surroundings. The club was crowded but not packed. Trae noticed that cats of all calibers were in attendance. There were thugs, ballers, business suits, nerds, geeks, even women who were trying their damnedest to look like men.

Sitting back in the booth Trae surveyed the club. One cat caught his eye. Actually it was the dancer who was doing tricks with her ass that caught him off guard and caused him to look in that direction. He looked the dread head right in his face. "That's the nigga that pulled me over the other day."

However, the dread head looked more like a baller than a cop this evening. He had about six honeys in his booth and one on his lap, a sexy bootylicious sister. He was poppin' bottles and was flossing as if he was on big willie status. It reminded Trae of how he used to do it. Dude with the locks must have felt Trae looking at him because he turned around and caught his gaze. Trae nodded in approval and turned his attention to the honey who had sat on his lap and was working on getting his dick on swole. Marvin had disappeared and Stephon had two, a sister and a snow bunny on his lap.

"Yo, why you get two and I only get one, Steph?" Trae wanted to know.

"I'm taking it easy on you," Stephon joked. "You gotta work your way up."

"I'm enough for you, big daddy," the honey in his lap purred.

"You think so?" Trae asked, twisting his face and thinking to himself, *Yeah right.*

A waitress came over with a bottle of Ace of Spades on ice. "Compliments from King Dread over there." Trae looked over at the detective and he was holding up a glass as if to give Trae a toast. Trae held up his empty glass and toasted him back.

"Who is that cat?" he asked the chick on his lap.

"Oh, that's King," she replied.

"King of what?" Trae asked.

"Let him tell it, he says LA."

King made his way to the bathroom. As soon as he walked in there, he noticed Marvin standing at the sink nodding. It surprised him. Recognizing the nod he had seen on so many junkies, King looked at him in total disgust. He didn't know Marvin was getting high. Rockin' this nigga's world was going to be easier than he thought. "Weak niggas use drugs," he said, hearing his father's words ring in his head. *And when you are weak you get used up.* And King was already trying to figure out how he could use this weak-ass nigga up. After all, he was the king and LA was his.

Marvin looked up at him as if he had heard his thoughts and shot him a look that said, "Yeah, try me if you want to, nigga." As he watched King walk out, he checked himself in the mirror and he said to himself, *Damn that could have easily been Trae or Steph who walked in here on me. This shit is fire, I'ma make a killin'.* He floated out and rejoined the fellas at the table.

The young lady on Trae's lap whispered in his ear. Trae grinned as he said, "My wife will do that. Shorty, you gotta come with something a little more creative than that."

Marvin and Stephon both started laughing.

"All right then." The stripper got up. "That sounds like a challenge to me." She smiled at him. "Don't go anywhere. I'll be right back."

"Awww shit," Stephon said, instigating, and started laughing. "She said she'll be coming back."

"Sheeit, I'll be ready for her. But yo, why ain't nobody smokin' up in here? Fire it up," Trae said.

"That's the only thing you can't do in here," Stephon said, almost apologizing. "You gotta go out front or out back. Drink up, nigga. Give your lungs a rest."

"That nigga ain't no drinker. He a smoker," Marvin said as he passed Trae a blunt.

Trae took it from him and said, "Come on."

"I'm good," Marvin said. The heroin he had just snorted had him on easy street.

Trae stood up and looked around for the honey who had been on his lap. "I'll be right back." He took his time making his way to the front door as he admired all the luscious eye candy all around him. When he got out front, a group of smokers were just finishing up and coming back inside. Trae looked around, lit up and started walking.

"Yo, money."

Trae turned around and saw King, so he stopped and waited.

"Let's keep walking," King told him as he lit up his own blunt. "This is my first time seeing you up in here." He took a slow pull and admired the blunt. "So, we meet again." King Dread smirked. "I'm Detective Rick Bryant by day and King Dread by night."

"King, huh? King of what?" Trae was anxious to know. "And good lookin' on the bottle."

King smiled. "King of whatever I choose. You remind me of someone. And just like him, always curious and he was never a hater."

"That nigga *must* be a boss. And you couldn't put the word hate in the same sentence with me. I'm Trae and I don't have to hate. I gets mine."

"See, now that's what I'm talking about. It looked like you used to roll like that."

"Used to?"

"Yeah, what happened? You got married?"

"Damn, it's that obvious?" Trae grinned.

"Only to a nigga of my caliber. But check it. It ain't no thing. I got hitched too. I married a rich bitch. She already had a house, money, everything. But that ain't stop nothin'." They both started laughing. "You from the East Coast?"

Trae nodded as a pickup truck turned the corner on two wheels, jumping the curb, damn near running them over. Two crazy-looking cats jumped out with guns, aiming and yelling at King and Trae.

"What the fuck?" Trae mumbled, surprised that he was getting jacked. "Whoa, niggas. Y'all don't know me and I don't know y'all." He reached for his burner, and then held up, realizing that if the fools had intended to shoot they would have done so by now.

"Then get the fuck on," the albino cat said. "Go ahead and kick rocks, black nigga, while you got the chance!" he screamed at Trae.

Trae picked up his pace and began walking off. But the two dudes were stripping King of all his bling, emptying his pockets, even taking his car keys, and were beating his ass viciously.

Trae glanced back at them and stopped. Then he started back walking. *Mind your business, nigga*, was his first thought. *Naw, fuck that! You know you like to get down and dirty. Karma, muthafucka. What if that was you back there getting your ass whupped?* was his next train of thought. *Plus, you ain't had no action in a long time, chillin' all up in the house like some punk-ass bitch.*

Unable to resist, Trae turned around, Glock .40 in hand, and started walking real fast toward them. When the albino cat looked up, Trae blasted. POW! POW! Catching the albino cat in the chest, sending him flying backwards. Trae smirked.

Seizing the opportunity, King was then able to grab his piece and put several rounds in the head of the other cat. "Pussy muthafucka," he spat before lying back, groaning in pain and coughing.

Trae stood over King and cocked his burner. King raised his up at the same time.

"What? We gonna kill each other now?" King asked through a bloody grin.

"Give me a reason why I shouldn't take you out? You's a muthafuckin' witness and I ain't going to jail for nobody."

"Shit, me neither." King laughed and groaned in pain, dropping his gun.

Trae grinned.

"Look, money, you on my team now. Face it," said King. "You and me cut from the same cloth. So go on ahead and get the fuck outta here."

"Team? Come on now, don't insult me. Imagine *me* as a team player when I own the team and the whole damn franchise. All I know is, it's two bodies out here and one has my signature on it. And I don't know you or what type of shit you into so I have to handle my own shit." Trae spat as he paced back and forth, looking at the bodies and wondering where he was going to dump King's body.

"Yo, money, listen. Don't do nothing stupid. You can't do me and get away with it. I promise you that. Too many people watching me. Plus you would need to get in line. But know this, I'm a nigga that you need on your squad, and a nigga like me you need because you can call me night or day to do whatever you need done. Watch what I tell you. I'm an asset that a lot of niggas wish they had on their team. For starters, watch both your boys in there. We'll talk later.

"Get out of here. I don't want you here when my people show up. I'll take care of this. I owe you one."

"Nigga, owe me? You don't even know me."

"I'm the King, nigga. I know everybody. We neighbors, money. Now go ahead and get the fuck outta here so that I can clean this shit up." He pulled out his cell phone, dialed and then said, "Yo B, I'm over here at Spinners. I got two flat tires. I need you ASAP! Yeah. I'm okay." King spoke in code, letting B know that there were two bodies. He ended the call groaning and coughing up more blood.

Trae called Stephon on his cell phone. "Yo, I'm out front. Problem, man. Y'all get the fuck outta there now. I'll be walking. Hurry up and pick me up." He looked back at King. *Fuckin' neighbors? What the fuck is he talking about? So much for a quiet night out on the town.*

CHAPTER THIRTEEN

Two months after Trae's California murder and encounter with Detective King Rick, he was finally able to relax a little. Rick lived on the same block as he did and Trae hadn't even known it. But now Rick had become a pool partner and regular vistitor to his home.

Tonight they were attending Club New York's official grand opening and King had promised that he would come through.

"Oh my God. This is really real." Tasha was in awe as they pulled up to their own club, New York. "Baby, this is us?"

"This is me and you, Ma," he said as the stretch Aston Martin limo came to a complete stop. The paparazzi was all on them. Stephon and Marvin were waiting for their arrival. They had someone Trae didn't recognize holding a video camera. "Fuck," Trae spat. "All of these fuckin' cameras." He sat frozen into place.

"Baby, don't start. This is an important night for our family. We gotta record this one. C'mon, do this for me," Tasha pleaded.

Marvin snatched Tasha's door open. "C'mon, big mama. Y'all late. You said you were going to have this nigga here on time." He helped Tasha out of the car. "Damn, girl. You are heavy, what y'all been eatin' over there?" Marvin teased her.

"Marv, you better leave my wife alone," Trae warned.

"Tell him, baby," Tasha snapped.

"Congratulations, Sir Trae. You are now a co-owner to this fabulous nightclub of all clubs. I present to you, Club New York!" Stephon was showing all thirty-twos as he stood next to Marvin. He could hardly contain himself.

"This shit is real and legal, dawg!" Marvin beamed.

"No doubt." Stephon proudly held out a set of keys. Trae grabbed the keys and took Tasha by the hand.

Club New York boasted a huge New York–style illuminated marquee filled with bright white starlights that looked like diamonds. Without a doubt New York was definitely in Cali tonight.

Stephon had to be given his props. He had gone all out with the promoting of the grand opening. Leading to the entrance of Club New York was BET's Black Carpet.

"Baby, y'all were able to get BET here?" Tasha asked Trae.

"Not me. Kaylin and all of his industry connections did this. Let's keep walking." Trae leaned over and kissed Tasha on the cheek in an attempt to avoid the cameras.

"Don't even think about it, Trae." She smiled through gritted teeth as she grabbed onto his arm. "You look good enough to eat and I want to show you off and record this moment. I am so proud of you."

Stephon, Marvin and Trae were in black Armani tuxes. Stephon's date was a model chick and of course Marvin was sporting Kyra on his arm. "Steph, you went all out. Look at this shit," Marvin beamed. They all turned to the crowd. The line was wrapped around the corner. Stephon was really feeling himself.

"C'mon, y'all. Someone from BET has been waiting to interview us. It's showtime! Welcome to Hollyhood," Stephon told them as he led the way onto BET's Black Carpet.

The BET VJ saw them coming and signaled for his camera crew to start rolling.

"Good evening, everyone. I am Touré, your host of BET's *Black Carpet*, and I'm on location tonight in the heart of LA, taking part in history in the making. Tonight is the grand opening of Club New York, LA's premier black-owned nightclub. And here with me tonight on the black carpet are the men behind it all. We have Stephon Cole, Marvin Blackshear and Trae Macklin. Guys, first off I'd have to say congratulations. What you have done...I mean, this is huge. Everybody has been talking about this grand opening. Well, not just talking, they are here. This is *the* star-studded event of LA. I've seen Vivica A. Fox, Kim Kardashian, Reggie Bush, Allen Iverson, Dwyane Wade, Lindsay Lohan. How did you get her out?" He directed that question to Marvin.

Marvin pointed to Stephon. "This guy here, Mr. Cole, was behind the promoting. From day one, he had vision and he didn't stop believing. So here we all are."

"You guys are from New York. Why didn't you build this club there?" The mic was in Trae's face, who was frowning.

"We have been in the city all of our lives and relocated because of that. When Stephon presented the concept for the club it was a no-brainer."

"The people of Cali wanted New York, so we brought it to them," Stephon interrupted, loving the spotlight.

"I couldn't agree more. You got Biz Markie as the opening DJ. He passes the baton to the legendary DJ Red Alert and to close it out DJ AM to Travis Barker. People, it doesn't get more New York than that," Touré beamed. "I'm ready to get my party on, New York style. This is Touré live in Los Angeles at the grand opening of Club New York."

The three couples stood around for five minutes posing for the photographers and pushy paparazzi before finally making their way inside the club.

Tasha's eyes lit up as soon as they stepped inside. Her eyes scanned the renovations, which included a second and a third floor. Everything was encased in glass, so she could see all the way up. The second and third floors were identical. Of course there was the dance floor. There were two huge open bars, VIP booths, poles and stages for the dancers, and two DJ booths. The waitresses carrying trays of drinks were covered in body paint depicting New York's famous skyline.

Tasha did a double take as the crowd parted for Kaylin, Kyra, Jaz and her husband Faheem and Lil' E's entourage. Lil' E was the white female rapper on Kaylin's record label. After her brush with death she had slowly gotten it back together and the crowd was showing her much love. They were so busy partying they didn't even see their friends. "Check that shit out." Kyra nudged Tasha.

"I see them niggas."

"C'mon y'all. This way," Stephon yelled over the music. "I'm taking y'all to our party. Kaylin said he'll get with us a little later."

They rode a glass elevator up to the second floor, where there was another huge dance floor identical to the one on the first floor and a special presidential VIP area. To the left side of the elevators were a small kitchen, a security office, and three separate offices, one each for Marvin, Stephon and Trae. All of their offices had identical setups of security cameras, full baths and closets. Stephon's and Marvin's offices were already furnished. Trae had left instructions for them to leave his alone because he wanted Tasha to furnish it.

"What's that room over there?" Tasha pointed behind Trae.

"Oh, that's Trae's little project," Stephon told her.

"It's my surprise to you, baby." Trae turned to Steph. "The key to that room is on here, right?"

"It's the gold one. But yo, you approve of everything or what, dawg?" Stephon hollered at him. A little disappointed that Trae wasn't jumping up and down brewing with excitement. "I mean, damn, you ain't say two words. What's up? Did I handle business or what?"

"That's how he do. Don't take it personal. If he ain't say nothing that means it's all good," Marvin schooled Stephon.

"Yeah, you did your thing my nigga," Trae acknowledged.

Stephon now had a huge and satisfying grin on his face. He then yelled out, "Now come on. We got a party in the presidential VIP area."

"We'll catch up with y'all in a few," Trae said as he grabbed Tasha's hand, leading her to a shut door. He unlocked it. "Close your eyes, Tasha, and don't open them until I tell you to. You got that?"

"Just open the door," Tasha snapped.

"C'mon, Tasha. You're going to spoil it. Close your eyes."

Knowing how stubborn Trae was, she finally conceded and closed her eyes. He grabbed her by both wrists and backed up into the room. When he got into the middle of the room he stopped.

"Okay. Open up."

Tasha looked around and then slapped Trae on the head.

"What?" Trae started laughing.

"Don't play ignorant. What is this?" She was standing in front of a small stage with a stripper's pole.

"What do it look like? This is our private VIP room." He watched her smile.

"What? You done lost your mind. You want me to strip in front of all of these huge glass windows?"

"Naw baby, we can see out, but nobody can see in."

Trae was feeling like a king on top of his throne as they took in the view. Directly across from them was the dance floor and the view below was unobstructed. They could see everything.

"Will you look at all of these people? Each head is money," he bragged.

"Naw nigga, later for the people. Let's get back to discussing this pole. And where's the rest of the furniture?"

"I wanted you to see it first and let me know what to put in here. Why you trippin'? You know you would have been mad if I wouldn't let you do you."

"What about the pole, Trae?"

"What do you mean *what about it?* The pole is for you. Shit, the way I see it we gonna be fuckin' in here a lot. I want lap dances, blow jobs, the whole nine. I got my dollars already stacked."

"Dollars? Dollars? Nigga, before that will happen you betta get some hundreds and stack those. You should already know that."

"But we married now, baby, why it gotta be hundreds?" He tried to sound innocent. She swung at him and he ducked. "Okay, okay, you know I'm only playin'. I got you, Ma. Can we christen the room right now?"

"Nigga, please. Since you got all the answers, you set everything up. *We* gonna do it right. Get your stacks together

and then we can make it happen. But for now let's go celebrate our grand opening." She headed for the door.

"Get my stacks together? Shit, my stacks are always
together. Tasha, wait. Stop playin'." He adjusted his hard-on
and went chasing behind her.

CHAPTER FOURTEEN

Tasha was seated outside of Houston's at the Beverly Center. At the last minute Kyra had called her and asked her to go pick up Trae and to let Trae know that the business appointment Marvin had scheduled had been postponed. Marvin had dropped Trae off and was supposed to come pick him up from Houston's so that they could go to wherever it was that they needed to go.

Shortly afterwards Trae, an Asian woman and a guy, whom Tasha assumed to be Trae's attorney, Benny, stepped out of the restaurant. Besides Trae, they were dressed in business attire. Benny and Trae were talking excitedly. Then she began to pay attention to the little Asian chick. Trae and Benny ignored her and kept conversing. She was staring intensely at Trae. When she finally opened her mouth, both men looked over at her. Benny grinned but Trae didn't. She began talking to Trae. Trae's body language was displaying a standoffish stance. Benny gave Trae some dap and gave the Asian chick a quick hug, leaving them standing there. When Trae turned to walk away, she placed her hand on his arm, said something else and walked away.

Tasha beeped the car horn. When Trae saw her he hurried to the car and jumped in, greeting his wife with a nice long kiss. "Where the fuck is Marvin?" He looked at his watch. "We were supposed to go meet some people fifteen minutes ago."

"Don't start me to lying," Tasha said as she turned off LA's Power 106 FM. "All I know is Kyra called me and said that I needed to come pick you up because Marvin couldn't make it."

"What the fuck he mean he can't make it? He dropped me off and said he would be coming right back," Trae spat. "Let me call this nigga." He dialed Marvin and it bounced to his voice mail.

"If the meeting is that important, then why don't I take you?" Tasha suggested.

"Naw. Don't worry about it," he told her. "It was his contact, his people, and the both of us were supposed to be there."

Tasha shrugged it off but was also skeptical. "So, tell me. How did your meeting go?"

"Just the way I needed it to. I feel like I just sold about a hundred keys. Benny's on top of them wiring the funds from the cable company sale to my account first thing Monday morning and this land deal I'm looking at investing in is a go."

"Well, you look happy," Tasha commented. And happy he was. They had just wrapped up seventeen hours of back-and-forth negotiating; Benny had gone over every single detail with a fine-tooth comb. He was ecstatic because he prided himself on negotiating the best deal for his clients. Trae was on cloud nine. A huge weight had been lifted off of his shoulders. Just when he had given up and thought that he was going to be stuck with the cable company, it was sold. He had bought it for pennies from a client who had an astronomical drug habit and owed Trae too much money. But now Trae was statisfied that that was all in the past and he had damn near quadrupled his investment and now had an abundance of clean money to work with.

"Benny looked happy too."

"He should be. He is getting paid."

"Who is the Asian chick?"

"The attorney who put the deal together."

"I thought Charlie was the attorney on this."

"That is Charli. That's her name."

"Oh." Tasha was surprised. "I thought Charli was a man."

"Well, you thought wrong."

"So, what was her problem?"

"What do you mean what was her problem?"

"What was she saying to you?"

"That was business, Tasha, that's all."

Umm. Hmm. Business all right, Tasha thought and decided to let it go...for now, especially since he seemed to be getting agitated.

CHAPTER FIFTEEN

The doorbell rang while Tasha and Kyra were chilling in Tasha's family room. Tasha answered the door to let Detective Rick Bryant in. He had lately become a fixture in the Macklin household.

"Come in, Detective Bryant. Trae is down in the basement."

"Mrs. Macklin, why do you insist on calling me Detective Bryant?" he asked in an irritable tone.

"Because you keep calling me Mrs. Macklin."

"But that's different," the detective told her.

"How so?" Tasha challenged.

"It's out of respect for Mr. Macklin."

"Mr. Macklin? Don't even try it. You call him Trae."

When he didn't respond Tasha turned around to see what had captured his attention. It was Kyra.

Kyra and Detective Bryant stood there staring at one another. Tasha stood watching the both of them with a smirk on her face. She cleared her throat and said, "Detective Bryant, this is my girl Kyra, Marvin's wife. Kyra, this is Detective Bryant."

"You can call me Rick," Detective Bryant said. He extended his hand and grabbed Kyra's. He then leaned over and kissed it.

"Nice to meet you, Rick."

Tasha sucked her teeth and rolled her eyes. "Detec-

Bryant, Trae is in the basement." He stood there staring at Kyra as she walked past him.

"Rick, Trae is in the basement," Tasha reminded him. "And you better not lock my husband up for smoking weed."

"I'ma be down there smoking it with him." He smiled at Tasha and winked at Kyra as he headed down to the basement.

Tasha turned and went into the kitchen. As soon as she was sure that Rick was gone, she went up to Kyra and pushed her.

"What?" Kyra shrieked.

"I saw that, Kyra."

"Saw what?"

"You know what I'm talking about," Tasha snapped.

Kyra grabbed a chair and sat down. Her hand was over her heart. "Shit! I honestly couldn't help myself. That nigga got my heart about to jump out of my chest. What...I mean who was that?"

"Kyra, I suggest that you snap the fuck out of whatever realm you are traveling in and act like that little confrontation did not happen."

"Those locks. I never liked locks on a dude, but he is wearing the shit out of those. And that body! That chest and arms. The way those deep brown eyes were looking at me," she continued in awe.

"Bitch, I suggest you shut the fuck up before you get yo ass in big trouble," Tasha snapped. "We are supposed to be talking about Angel and planning Aisha's birthday party, remember?"

"Okay, okay," Kyra said unconvincingly, trying to pull herself together. "I'm only messin' with yo bitch ass," she lied. *Damn*. She was really having difficulty shaking off her encounter with Rick. Finally, she pulled herself together and her voice went down to a whisper. "Girl, can you believe that she killed that nigga Snake? I mean, damn. Who would have thought it? She's a murderer!" Kyra said with a twisted-up face. "She never said anything to you?" Kyra asked in disbelief, not wanting to believe that a little over a year ago her cousin Angel had killed her ex-pimp boyfriend Snake.

"Kyra, you sound like you've been watching too much *Law & Order*. You sound just like a juror ready to convict. 'She's a murderer,'" Tasha mocked. "Shit, if it was me, I would have killed that crazy-ass muthafucka. Nobody liked his ass, nohow."

"Girl, I would have never!" Kyra said.

"I would have never!" Tasha mocked her. "Fuck you been hangin' around? Must be all of those soap operas you've been watching or them white chicks up at the school."

"Tasha, stop playing. I'm serious," Kyra said.

"For real I didn't even know how to approach her. I was actually scared to talk to her after it all went down," Tasha confessed. "I didn't know if she had gone crazy or what."

"Sheeit, so was I. I had to talk to her moms first to get some advice."

"And Carmen?" Tasha sighed. "Angel will be going to therapy over that situation for years to come. I can't even imagine." Carmen was Angel's little sister who had started messing around with Angel's ex Snake, before ending up dead because of him.

"And Kaylin? Kaylin is a good nigga fo' real. He's not a stranger to this, but this time this shit is up close and per-sonal. I gotta give him his props. She picked a good one when she picked him. I see why she was so determined to marry his ass. Any other nigga would have cracked under all of this pressure," Kyra said.

"You right. Kaylin ain't new to this. It probably made his dick hard knowing his wife bodied a nigga," Tasha added. "But shit, we all got good niggas. Look at what you and Marvin been through. Jaz and Faheem. Me and Trae, we all counting blessings."

Just then, Kyra's daughter Aisha entered the room. "Auntie Tasha, the twins are asleep now. I straightened up their room. Can I spend the night?" Tasha didn't mind her spending the night because she loved to help out and play with the boys. She took the big-sister role very seriously.

"Aisha, you are such a big help around here. But I thought you had to get ready for Candice's birthday party? You're still going to wear that pretty dress, right?"

She shook her head. "My daddy brought me some Prada shoes," she beamed with pride.

"Did he? And what do you know about Prada?" Tasha teased.

"Everything," Aisha responded. "I know they got some pink ones coming out soon. The lady at Nordom's told me," Aisha said, trying to say Nordstrom.

"Nordstrom's! Kyra, she knows the name of the stores?" Tasha said, shaking her head.

"Don't 'Kyra' me. Shit, that's Marvin's ass. He buys her everything."

"And you expect me to believe that?" Tasha asked.

"Your lunch is on the kitchen table, Aisha. Please don't make a mess," Kyra told her.

"I won't, Mommy." She took off running for the kitchen.

"Prada shoes? Marvin is creating a monster," Tasha said. "Men never learn."

"I said the same thing. But his philosophy is, she's the next man's monster, not his."

"Oh my God," Tasha said in disbelief. "That is so sad."

"Bitch, you can't talk, you just brought the twins matching David Yurman bracelets," Kyra checked Tasha.

"What about you? You brought Aisha her own set of Louis Vuitton luggage, with the shoes and skirt. She was the talk of the last sleepover she went to," Tasha shot back.

"I'm just glad we are blessed to be in the position to afford these things. So what if we all take part in creating monsters in the process?" Kyra said, laughing.

CHAPTER SIXTEEN

Everyone in the Macklin household was in the kitchen. Trae was skimming through the paper while eating breakfast; Tasha was holding the refrigerator door open, guzzling down a Powerade. Her body was glistening with sweat and her clothes were soaking wet. She had just finished running three miles on the treadmill.

"Tasha, where are your stretch marks? For goodness sake you have three babies. I had one and was marked for life," Marva recalled.

"Aunt Marva, everybody is different. My mom never had stretch marks either. Nor did my granny. But I'm back in shape because I kill myself every day in that exercise room. I have a husband that I gotta stay fine for." She winked at her.

"Chile, please. Your husband loves you, no matter what." Marva said it as if Trae weren't sitting at the table.

"Mmm, hmmm. That's what they say and that's what they want you to think. But for real, they want you to stay fine as the first day they met you. But it's okay for them to grow old, fat, bald and out of shape."

Marva started laughing.

Tasha went over and kissed Trae on the cheek. "Ain't that right, baby?" He ignored her. "Aunt Marva, you see your nephew is pleading the Fifth because he knows it's true."

"What are you getting ready to do?" he asked without looking up from his paper.

"Take a shower and then take the boys out back. It looks beautiful outside."

Aunt Marva watched on as he whispered something in Tasha's ear. She burst into giggles like a little schoolgirl before she bounced off and disappeared out of the kitchen.

"Why is that little Chinese lady coming here? Ain't no beauty supplies around here," Aunt Marva questioned Trae.

Trae looked up from his paper. "What?"

"Don't play stupid with me. I know a snake when I see one. You playing a dangerous game. Business and pleasure never mix, Trae. Whatever it is, she shouldn't be coming to your house. You're playing with fire," she warned.

"Auntie, she has my number, so I don't know why she stopped by. Nobody called me and said anything. I'll ask Benny."

"Whatever, boy. You know damn well why she is popping up. You and Shaheem always did let the little head get y'all into trouble. You better fix it and I mean fix it now. Shoot, in my day if one of them little whores would have come to my home I would have had my trusty blade waiting for their ass." Aunt Marva made a slicing motion in the air. "Anyway, that one is a snake and a bold one at that. I've seen her kind before. She won't stop until she gets what she wants."

"It ain't even like that, Auntie," Trae said, getting up from the table, kissing her on the cheek.

Kaylin and Trae were down in the game room. Kaylin had jumped on a flight first thing that morning with a message for Trae from the dons. Trae was racking up the balls and Kaylin was chalking up his pool stick.

"So spill it, nigga. What's up? You looked stressed the fuck out," Trae said to his boy Kaylin. "How's your record label doing?"

Kaylin was now sitting on the sofa. "Nigga, you know I ain't here to talk about my damn record label. I'm here delivering a message. Don Carlos wanted to know why you didn't come to him? Why did you go to Charlie Li? He don't want you fucking with him. He said you could have come to him."

"What the fuck? Yo, we done, Kay. We out. What the fuck I got to go to him for? I can fuck with whoever I want to. This is my money. I worked and gambled with my life and freedom for this money," Trae spat. "Ain't this some shit. I made them muthafuckas millions upon millions. I'm all the way out here in fuckin' California and they know what the fuck I'm doing?" he continued to rant. "What kind of shit is that?"

"Nigga, it is what it is. I don't know if it's bad blood between Don Carlos and this Charli cat or not, but he said whatever you need he got you. Leave dude alone." Kaylin was used to Trae's stubbornness. He had actually used it to his advantage when they were out there hustling. But this was different. Trae was crossing the line.

"Kay, I already got money with dude and getting ready to get more. It's legal, man. C'mon now. Slavery is over." Trae was not going out without a fight.

"Well, dead that relationship, aiight? And don't say I ain't warn you."

"Man, fuck that. Yo, let's talk about you. Why you look

like you just lost your best friend? Yo, what the fuck happened with my nigga Papi Chulo and his moms? This shit looks like it never is going to end. They keep blasting it on the news as if the President was killed," Trae said.

"I got so much blood on my hands, I can't believe the shit myself. I couldn't leave those loose ends. I kept hearing him saying his moms was looking into this and looking into that. I had to be safe. Kaylin made an attempt at justifying his actions for bodying Papi Chulo and his mother. But now I'm regretting the decision I made to make that move."

"But damn, Papi too? That nigga was a cash cow. He went what, triple platinum?"

"Yo, what if I would have left him alone and he decided to take over where his moms left off? Then I'd be right back to square one. Shit, I can find another cash cow."

"Dawg, I know you. This shit is eating at you and I'm curious to know what's Angel saying?" Trae smirked. "I know she's not sitting this one out."

"Aww, man. She's getting on my fuckin' nerves. I don't know if the fact that we are finally married is driving her ass crazy or that she is a good-ass lawyer. Too smart for her own damn good. She keeps saying little shit trying to make me say I did it. She treated Papi like he was her son and shit."

"Why she wanna know if you did it or not?"

"I don't know, man. That lawyer shit went to her head. And the fact that she married a street nigga, it fucks with her sometimes. Especially when shit like this comes up. She'll be aiight," Kaylin said. "But yo, tell me about this five-o cat. What's his name? Sounds like we both into some shit."

"Nah, it ain't like that. Rick. Rick Bryant. Dude lives right down the street and I didn't even know it. But what I gathered, he is into all kinds of shit. If things get ugly with this Papi Chulo shit let me know."

"Yo, you trust him like that?"

"Hell naw! But I got a feeling that we may need to use him for something. What? I don't know. Plus, he owes me. I saved the nigga's ass. Now I can't get rid of him. He said I remind him of his little brother. I haven't been able to find out why he playin' me close, but I will."

It was Saturday night at Club New York. Trae and Tasha stepped into their club ready to get their party on. Security escorted them through the crowd as they headed for the VIP section as Raheem DeVaughn's praise for the "Woman" blazed through the speakers. All the ladies' hands began to wave high up in the air and they all headed for the dance floor, including Tasha.

Trae grabbed a seat, popped a bottle and fired up a blunt. He leaned back in his chair as he watched Tasha sway her hips to the beat. He got off on watching her dance. He never saw anyone command the beat with the movements of her body the way she did. After she danced straight through four songs, he waved her over. She sat down on his lap and felt his hard-on. She smiled and kissed him gently on the lips before taking a sip of what was in his glass.

"Let's go upstairs," Trae suggested.

"Baby, we just got here. I came to party."

"We can party upstairs."

"Nigga, that's what you said last week. Un-uh, nigga, come on." She stood up. "Come on." She grabbed his hand. "Come dance with me." She dragged him out of the VIP section onto the main dance floor. The DJ was obviously trying to prove himself because he was murdering a remix of 50 Cent's "I Get Money." It even had an actual live verse by the old-school rapper Milk himself.

Marvin and Stephon were looking down from the balcony at the dance crowd like proud partners and business owners.

"Man, look at Trae and Tasha. We might as well get them Friday-night passes," Stephon joked.

"Yeah. My man is already making the most of his investment." Marvin began nodding his head and did a full spin to Gerald Levert begging the DJ not to play a slow jam.

Tasha was all over Trae's dick. When she turned around he grabbed onto her hips and began walking her off the dance floor toward the elevator.

"Trae, hold up."

"Don't even try it. You feel what you've done."

"Excuse me. Mr. Macklin, can I have a moment with you?" Charli said, appearing out of nowhere.

Trae and Tasha both stood in place. Tasha looked the small woman up and down. This was the first time she had been up close on her. She reminded her of a petite Kimora Simmons.

"Charli, this is my wife, Tasha. Tasha, this is Charli." Neither one of the women said anything. Trae kissed Tasha on the cheek. "Charli, what's up?"

"I have a proposal that I think may interest you."

"Make sure you give it to Benny."

Tasha pressed the elevator button, letting Charli know that the conversation was over. She turned around and tongue-kissed him for emphasis.

Charli frowned and said, "I came here to talk to you

because I've been unable to reach him. Can you go get us a drink?" she asked Tasha.

"Ohhh shit," Trae mumbled and held Tasha tighter.

This bitch. Tasha snapped, "*Do* I look like the help to you?"

"Charli, I'll call your office tomorrow," Trae butted in.

"Don't call. Come by." She placed her hand on Trae's bicep and smiled at Tasha.

Before Tasha could snatch Charli up, Trae grabbed the back of Tasha's neck with force. "Ignore this shit so we can get on with our party."

"Nigga, I will fuck you and that bitch up," Tasha spat. Her eyes moved to Charli, who had walked away. She started going after her. Trae caught her just in time.

"Tasha, fuck her," Trae barked. "We are getting ready to enjoy our evening and don't make me tell you again." He pushed her toward the elevator. She knew he was not playing with her. "Chill out, aiight." He waited until she got herself together.

As soon as they stepped onto the private elevator and the doors closed, they were all over each other. When the doors opened up, Tasha's panties were off and stuffed into Trae's back pocket. He put in the code to their private room and the door popped open. The smell of vanilla potpourri assaulted their nostrils. Tasha had made sure of that. Their feet sank into the six-inch plush carpet as Trae kicked the door shut behind them and hit a switch. The lights automatically dimmed and their music came on.

Tasha headed for the bathroom to freshen up. When she came out she had on a sheer silver sarong, silver star pasties that covered her nipples, a matching silver thong and a pair of clear six-inch stilettos. Her diamond belly ring reflected the dim lights. Trae was leaned back in his chair at the foot of the stage. He motioned for her to come to where he was. She kept going toward the stage.

"I can't get a lap dance tonight?"

She ignored him and began winding around the pole. Slim 112's new joint bumped from the speakers. Trae stood there mesmerized throughout the entire song. He finally grabbed his chair and pulled it close to the stage. He pulled out a stack of bills and sat down. She seductively untied the sarong, allowing it to fall to the floor, then turned around giving him a nice ass shot. "Make that ass clap for Daddy. Shit, I'm a paying customer." He tossed a couple of hundreds onto the platform. She closed her eyes, feeling the music. It drove him crazy when she ignored him and danced as if she were the only one in the room. Her fingers ran over her pussy, thighs, abs and tits before tossing the sarong onto the floor, revealing the sexiest body Trae had ever seen, glistening with glitter.

Now Trae was standing up, ready to put the bills into her G-string.

She bent over slowly, giving him an ass and pussy shot. As Trae slipped a few bills into her G-string he grabbed an ass cheek and planted a big fat juicy kiss on it. Tasha stood straight up and made it clap and jiggle. She then turned around, putting her back to the pole, sliding down, squatting and opening her legs. Trae couldn't take any more. He crawled onto the platform and had his face in between her thighs. In a flash he had moved that G-string to the side and was tasting her pussy.

As she slid slowly back up the pole, his face stayed glued to the inside of her thighs, until she eased his head away.

He couldn't take his eyes off of her as he sat down in his chair. She seductively stepped down off her throne and stood in front of him. He ran his hand up and down her thigh. His eyes glistened as she began to sway to R. Kelly and Public Announcement begging for that "Honey Love."

She began grinding on his dick with the intention of giving him a lap dance that he wouldn't be able to forget. It was obvious that she was getting that result because he had gripped her thighs and was dry fucking her wet pussy.

Realizing that he was about to nut, he lifted her up and led her to the glass wall. The club was jumping. She placed both hands on the cool glass wall, bent over and spread her legs. When she looked back his dick was in his hand and he was ready to put in work.

"C'mon, Daddy. Make this pussy talk to you," Tasha purred as he slid it inside of her, not stopping until her warmth sucked him all the way in.

As he stroked they both felt exhilarated as they looked down onto the crowd that couldn't see them. The lights, the people, the height...got the both of them off.

"Shit," Trae grunted as he pulled back, not wanting to come this soon. But Tasha reached back and grabbed his ass, pulling him back in. She threw her pussy back at him.

"Make it talk," she screamed as he came a few seconds before her.

"Why'd you do that?" he panted. "I wasn't ready to bust yet!"

She giggled and was out of breath. "But I wanted you to."

"Well, you just blew a chance to get your back blown out."

"Nigga, you better bring my dick back to life," she threatened. "Remember, this is my night."

"Then let me run the show," he complained.

"Trae...Never mind. I'm not going to argue. Why don't you give *me* a lap dance now?"

"Naw, you give me another one."

"It's my night, Trae."

They argued and fucked for the rest of the night.

Tasha went home with a smile plastered on her face.

CHAPTER SEVENTEEN

Marvin promised Kyra he'd take her to UCLA to see what credits were transferred and which ones weren't, but she would have to ride with him and Trae to take care of some business in the area. He pulled up in front of the university entrance and let Kyra out. She had some loose ends to tie up before the next semester started.

"I'll be right back." She jumped out of the backseat and slammed the door.

Trae was in the front seat admiring the architecture and landscaping surrounding the university campus. "You ever think about going to college?" he asked Marvin.

"Hell to the naw. I'm retired. What I look like starting a new career? Why? Are you thinking about going back?"

Trae pondered the thought for a minute. "Nah, it's just that being here gives you that feeling."

"Nigga, if you want to go back then by all means go back. What's stopping you? Other than a houseful of kids. Man, is you trying to get Tasha pregnant again? What you wanna do, start your own country?"

"Nah man, she ain't trying to get pregnant. Lately she's been hinting about getting her physical therapy practice off the ground. I'm lucky to get the three in that I got." Then his eyes went over to a young lady who looked like Tasha.

She was standing at a table trying to sell what looked to be pictures. She then pushed a young man down into a chair, picked up a huge tablet and began drawing him. "I'll be right back, man."

When Trae made it to the young lady's table he was in for a surprise. Not only could she have passed for Tasha's younger sister, but her art skills were exceptional. Then, on closer inspection of her features, he was in for the shock of his life.

"Do I know you?" The artist stopped sketching the small guy who was seated in her chair. He looked Trae over and got up.

"I changed my mind," the customer snapped.

"Wait a minute! You can't do that. I'm almost done with your sketch."

"Then you should have finished!" The customer snatched up his backpack and stormed off.

"I hate broke-ass college niggas," the artist yelled at him.

"You were wrong for stopping. I know I look good, but you weren't supposed to allow my good looks to distract you. As you just witnessed it's not good for business," Trae told her.

"I know that, but it wasn't your good looks, you look familiar. Where are you from?" she asked.

"Where are you from?" he shot back.

She cocked her head to the side as she studied him some more. "I know that I know you."

"Yeah, they say we all got a twin. How long have you been drawing?"

"It feels like all my life and the life before this one," she laughed.

"You got nice skills and I'm impressed." Trae was checking out the sketches she had displayed across the table. "Do you do murals?" He turned to face her.

"I haven't, but I can. I can work on anything."

"Give me your card. I'ma throw some business your way."

"How soon?" She handed him a business card.

He looked it over. DESIGNS BY SABEERAH. "Real soon, shorty. Real soon." He headed back to Marvin's truck.

As soon as he got seated he dialed Bo.

"Who the fuck is this calling me so early?" Bo growled into the phone after finally answering it.

"Early? It's almost noon, doughboy."

"Trae, what's up, nigga? Fool, have you forgot, you three hours ahead of us?"

"Three hours behind you, nigga, and that means it's almost three o'clock in the fuckin' afternoon, East Coast time."

That caused Bo to burst out laughing. "What's up, my nigga?"

"Yo, your mans and that videotape. You took care of that, right?"

Bo was quiet for a couple of minutes as he figured out what Trae was talking about. "Nigga, I been told you that. What the fuck is wrong with you? Here you go, with yo scary ass! That shit happened damn near three years ago."

"Man, I just saw shorty."

"Who the fuck is shorty?" It took a minute before it dawned on Bo whom Trae was talking about. "Dawg, you seeing things, you know they say we all look alike."

"Bo, this is me you talkin' to. Trust me, I know who I saw. And I rarely forget a face. Just check with her peoples to see if she's going to UCLA, and named Sabeerah. Hit me back." Trae hung up and looked over at a baffled Marvin.

"What's up, man?" Marvin asked.

Just then Kyra jumped into the backseat. "Baby, I am so mad I could scream." Marvin turned around and looked back at her. "What's the matter?"

"These are some racist muthafuckas. That's what's the matter. They are trying to make me take four of my classes over! This is bullshit!" she snapped.

"Did you talk to who was in charge?"

"Yes," she pouted.

"Did you talk to his boss?" Marvin continued.

"Yes."

"Did you talk to his boss?"

"It was a her and no. She's not in."

"Well, do that before you give up. My baby is a fighter and we don't take no for an answer."

She ran her hands over her face. "I will die if I have to take these classes over."

"It ain't over yet. We are going to talk to her boss and then if that don't work, we'll just transfer to a college that will take all of your credits. This ain't the only college in town. Right?"

"Baby, you know this is where I had my heart set on going."

"You want me and my little friend to go and make them an offer they can't refuse?" Trae asked her, mimicking Al Pacino's character from the movie *Scarface*.

"No, Trae, but thanks. We have to do this right. We didn't relocate out here to catch a case. We are starting clean, remember?"

"Oh, I forgot," Trae teased. "Sorry about that."

"Sure you are. You know you meant it."

*   *   *

It was a Saturday morning and Tasha was running around the house trying to get out. The kids were driving her crazy and it seemed as if the phone had been ringing nonstop.

"Aisha, let the twins play with their toys, not your dolls. Okay?"

"Okay, Auntie Tasha," Aisha said with little enthusiasm.

Aisha made it her mission to make her way over to Tasha's every chance she got to help out with the twins. To her, they were life-size baby dolls. And today was no exception. She not only called herself looking out for the boys, but keeping their room straightened up as well.

The doorbell and the phone were ringing.

"Auntie Tasha, the doorbell," Aisha called out.

"I got it," Marva yelled.

"I got the door, Aunt Marva. You can get the phone." Tasha headed for the front door. "Your friends have been calling all morning wondering why you didn't come shopping with them. Why aren't you going out with your girls? It's Saturday," Tasha yelled out hoping she would catch the hint to get out of the house and do something.

Tasha pulled back the front door curtain to see a deliveryman. Baffled, she opened the front door and asked, "Can I help you?"

"Is this the Macklin residence?"

"Yes it is. I'm Mrs. Macklin."

"Is Trae Macklin home?"

"No, he's not. I told you I'm Mrs. Macklin. How can I help you?"

"Uh, okay," the surfer kid said. "Can you sign right here?" He pointed to a yellow arrow. "And right here." He pointed to another arrow.

"What did my husband order?"

The delivery kid tore off the copies of the transaction and handed them to Tasha. "A Harley-Davidson." He then handed her a big envelope with the keys and other documents.

Tasha and the delivery kid both stood there as the other deliverymen unloaded the truck and sat a brand-new top-of-the-line Harley in the driveway.

"What's all the commotion?" Aunt Marva came to the door carrying Caliph.

"Your nephew bought a new toy and didn't even tell me. A dangerous one at that."

"A motorcycle? Since when did he ride those things?" Marva shrieked.

Tasha was just shaking her head. "I don't have the slightest idea. I can't wait to hear what brought this on and if I don't like it, it's going back. The nigga even had the nerve to get it wrapped with a red bow tie."

"Have a good day." The delivery kid waved and jumped into the truck.

"Can I see?" Aisha was trying to squeeze in between Marva and Tasha, who were blocking the doorway.

Tasha left them standing there to go check on the twins, who were in the family room. Shaheem and Caliph were watching *Super Why!* and Kareem was still playing with his toys. Tasha sat down and thumbed through the paperwork. She frowned when she saw that the delivery address was the offices of Li, Hammerstein and Burke from Ms. Charli Li. "That bitch! That sneaky-ass ho! She is just determined to disrespect me."

"Concita," she yelled out. "Come in here with the boys, please. I have to go do something real quick."

"Can me and the twins go?" Aisha asked.

"No, baby. I'm not going anywhere. I just need to run upstairs."

When she got upstairs, she began ransacking Trae's things, looking for a number. She finally yelled, "Bingo!" She held up the business card and went over to the phone and dialed the number, only to be greeted by the voice mail. She then pressed zero to get transferred to the switchboard.

"Good afternoon, law offices of Li, Hammerstein and Burke."

"I need to speak to Charli Li."

"I'm sorry, but Ms. Li is usually out of the office on Saturdays. Would you like to leave a message or have one of our other associates call you back?"

"No, but tell Charli that Mr. Macklin's wife Tasha called to inform her that her little gift was unprofessional and disrespectful. And if she keeps on fuckin' with me she will see what an East Coast ass-whipping is firsthand. As a matter of fact, tell her if she doesn't get her little confused ass over here to pick it up personally, I will have it stripped and sell the pieces to a junkyard."

The operator paused. "Um, can I have your name and number again?"

"The name is Tasha Macklin and the bitch has the number and my address." Tasha hung up. She then went and put on her sneakers, put her hair into a ponytail and headed for the basement, almost knocking Marva over.

She grabbed a can of black spray paint, a pair of gloves and a baseball bat. She then ran back up the stairs. This time Marva stood blocking the basement doorway. "What are you doing, chile?"

"That Chinese bitch bought that motorcycle for Trae."

"Oh? Oooh." Marva slowly moved to the side as Tasha whizzed by.

"You and Concita, be sure to keep Aisha and the kids in the house for me."

When she got outside, she put the gloves on. She looked at the bat and the spray paint and tossed the bat on the ground. She stood back and began shaking the spray paint.

Marva's fingers couldn't dial Trae's number fast enough.

"Auntie, what's good?" Trae asked, sounding as if he was chilling.

"I suggest you get your ass home to your wife ASAP."

"Why, what's the matter?" Trae sat up straight. His seat was in the reclined position as he drove around the town with Marvin.

Aunt Marva looked out the window and Tasha was spraying black spray paint all over the brand spanking new Harley-Davidson.

"Your wife has gone mad. You need to get here as soon as possible."

"Auntie, you gotta tell me more than that. What the fuck is going on?"

"Watch your mouth, boy! All I know it's concerning a Chinese bitch and a package being delivered." She hung up.

Trae looked at the phone and frowned. Marvin saw the puzzled look on his face. "What's up?"

"I don't know, man." He called his house and this time Concita answered the phone.

"Concita, what kind of package came for me today?"

"Oh yes, Mr. Macklin. You got a big shiny motorcycle on the front grass. And your wife, Missus Macklin, she must not like it because she runs through the house looking for cans of paint. And me and Missus Marva have the kids and your wife is outside spraying and painting." Concita rambled away.

"What? Slow down, Concita. She's spraying and painting what?"

"The big shiny motorcycle on the front grass. We all standing here watching her. But no one doing anything. Oh, Jesus. Aye yiyi yi yi," Concita gasped.

"Concita, what is going on?"

She held her heart as she watched Tasha swing the baseball bat as if she were hitting home runs. She was trying her best to crush the Harley-Davidson to tiny pieces. "Missus Macklin has a baseball bat and she hitting and beating de bike. But Mr. Macklin, this is your house. Your business. I just here for de kids. None of my business," Concita said.

"Thank you, Concita." Trae ended the call with Concita and began dialing Charli's cell phone but got no answer.

"What's up?" Marvin tried to find out what was going on. They pulled up into the club parking lot and got out. "What's up, nigga?" Trae had his back to Marvin. Trae ignored Marvin as he continued to try and reach Charli. Marvin followed Trae into the club, all the way to his office.

"Yo, what's up with you? Are you sending shit to my house?" Trae finally reached her.

"Ooh, straight to the point," Charli purred as she spun around in her chair. "I heard that you were thinking about a Harley, so I had one brought over. No big deal."

"Don't send shit to my house."

"Was it the color?" Charli was very calm when she asked him that.

"Yo." Trae couldn't even finish his sentence. All he could

do was laugh since he had been caught off guard by her response. "No, it wasn't the color," he mocked her.

"What color would you like? Just say it and it's done."

"Charli, listen to me. You don't have to buy shit for me, and definitely don't be sending shit to my house. I'm telling you that for your own good."

"So, I see that it is not the color, it's the wife. Maybe I'll stop by with someone and have them pick it up. Maybe I won't. However, I'm not one to be denied so I suggest that you handle her." Charli hung up the phone.

Trae looked at the phone. "Ain't this a bitch."

"What?" Stephon barged into the office smacking on an apple.

Marvin was sitting there grinning since he had ear hustled enough to know what had just gone down.

Trae called his house and Marva picked up.

"Hello."

"Let me speak to my wife."

"Boy, she ain't thinking about no phone. She too busy out there banging up that damn motorbike. I told you to get your ass here ASAP."

"Take her the phone, Auntie. I need to speak to her."

As Marva went to open the front door, Tasha burst in huffing and puffing. Marva held out the phone. "This is your husband."

"Please. Not now."

"You heard her, didn't you?" Marva said to Trae.

"Tell her I said to get her ass on this fuckin' phone."

"Tasha, your husband said to get your ass on this fuckin' phone." She shoved the phone at her. "Chile, take this phone. Y'all got me in the middle of this mess. I need to check on Concita and the kids."

Tasha snatched the phone from out of her hands. She was so mad that she couldn't even speak. All Trae heard was her breathing.

"Tasha, I know you ain't trippin' over this bullshit."

"No, I'm not trippin'. Just bring your ass home right now, Trae. And you better hope your little Asian mistress is not dumb enough to bring her stupid ass over here. If she does, I'ma mop the cement with her ass."

Trae was left with the dial tone. "Damn," Trae snapped. "C'mon. Take me home."

"Do I need to break the speed limit?" Marvin wanted to know.

"What you think, man?"

Marvin pulled out his car keys and stood up.

"Tell us what's happening, nigga," Stephon said. "Y'all leaving already? Y'all just got here. What about our meeting?"

"It's Charli, man. Which one of y'all muthafuckas talking about me to her? You or Benny? Y'all the only niggas knew I was lookin' at the Harley."

"Yo, she hooked you up?" Stephon said excitedly, not answering his question.

"Yeah, but from what I hear Tasha fucked that shit up."

"Dayuuum," Marvin gritted. "She fucked up a hundred-thousand-dollar bike like that?" He visualized himself riding it down Highway 10 at eighty miles an hour.

"Awww, man. My cuz get down like that?" Stephon said as he followed them to the car. "Aiight, then handle your business. I'll hit y'all up later." He watched them pull off before going back inside the club.

As soon as they pulled up in front of the house, Trae jumped out of the truck, glad to see that Charli hadn't shown up. Tasha had used black spray paint and a can of red. It was all over the grass and driveway, and all over what was left of the bike. Trae picked the baseball bat up off the ground. The headlights and mirrors were busted and the pieces were scattered on the ground and dents were covering the bike. It was totaled.

Marvin came up and stood next to him. "Damn. This is fucked up. Where she get the strength from to destroy a machine? I wouldn't go in there if I was you, dawg. Wait until she cools off, playa."

"You don't know Tasha like I know her. She isn't going to cool off. I might as well go and get the shit over with." He left Marvin standing there and headed for the front porch.

"Hold up, man, let me get Aisha and take her home."

When they walked into the house it looked as if no one were home. "They must be in the backyard." Trae led the way out back, dropping the baseball bat next to the basement door.

"Daddy!" Aisha yelled, running and jumping down the steps into Marvin's arms.

"What's up?" He kissed his daughter on the forehead and threw her up into the air, causing her to yell with glee.

"Twins and Caliph! Your daddy is here," she yelled. Before you knew it the twins were running for the kitchen. When they saw Trae they both rushed over to where he was. He stooped down and started playing with them.

"Aunt Tasha said I can spend the night," Aisha told Marvin.

"That may be so, but I think your mother wants me to bring you home."

"Aww, Daddy. Can't I stay?" she pouted. "I don't want to go home. It ain't no fun at home."

"Daddy ain't no fun?"

"I like having fun with the twins."

"Well, we have to go home and talk to your mother about it."

"Mommy ain't home."

"Mommy *isn't* home," he corrected her. "And she is home."

"Mommy isn't home. You dropped her off at school, remember?"

"Yes, but after she finished talking to the teacher, I took her home. Now go get your things."

Tasha was upstairs on the phone with her girl Jaz. She was furious. Jaz was always the first person she consulted with whenever she had a beef with Trae. When she lived in Jersey she would run over to Jaz's house. Now that Jaz was living in Georgia, she could only call her up.

"This bitch had the nerve to have the shit delivered to my house, Jaz."

"Tasha, calm down. Have you heard Trae's side of the story?"

"No, his black ass ain't home yet."

"Here I go right here." Trae waltzed through their bedroom door. When he saw the blotches of red and black spray paint on her face he smiled.

"Oh you think the shit is funny?" Tasha snapped. She hung up on Jaz without saying bye and popped up off the bed and stood in Trae's face. "You think the shit is cute?" She poked him in the forehead.

"Tasha, I don't know why she bought me the bike. I damn sure didn't ask her to."

"Nigga, that's bullshit. Just say it. You fuckin' her. Say it, Trae."

"Why am I going to say something that ain't true? I'm not fuckin' her and don't be accusing me of no bullshit that I'm not guilty of."

"Nigga, ain't no bitch gonna put that kind of money out and ain't gettin' no dick. This is me you're talking to. Plus, I saw how she was looking at you when I picked you up from that restaurant. And I remember that stunt she pulled at the club."

"Tasha, how was she looking at me? Wasn't it dark outside? What the fuck is the matter with you? Where's the fuckin' calendar? You gettin' ready to come on your period?" He went over to the calendar. She was right on his heels and snatched it off the wall and threw it at him. He ducked and by reflex grabbed her neck. "What is wrong with you?" He let her neck go, realizing that he hadn't meant to grab her. When he let her go she smacked him across the face.

"How dare you put your fuckin' hands on me? How would you like it if a nigga delivered me a brand-new car? You would be acting the same way."

"Nah, I'd be acting much worse." He grabbed her by the neck again. "Then I'd put some bullets in the nigga. Remember that." He tossed her across the bed.

She jumped back up and went to swinging at him. He grabbed her.

Marva was standing in the bedroom doorway. "Tasha, take Caliph. He's sleepy. Me and the twins will be back. Here's his teddy bear." She laid him on the bed with his favorite bear and left, acting as if they weren't fighting.

Trae still held her tight. Her body was trembling.

"I don't want to fight with you in front of my son," he told her.

"Turn me loose." Her voice cracked. "You hit me over some bitch?"

"Tasha, you are blowing this shit all out of proportion. First off, I didn't even hit you. And like I said, I ain't fuckin' nobody but you. You know that shit. We shouldn't even be having this senseless conversation."

"Why is she sending you gifts, Trae?"

"She obviously thinks a nigga is for sale. And she is probably used to getting whatever she wants. But I told the bitch don't be sending me shit and stop calling my house. I told her to send messages through Benny. You know you ain't got shit to worry about." His cell phone began ringing so he turned her loose.

"It better not be that bitch."

She grabbed the phone out of his hand and looked at the caller ID, recognizing one of the family's numbers. She threw the phone at him and headed for the bathroom and turned on the shower. She needed to wash the spray paint off her face and hands. Plus, totaling the Harley-Davidson had caused her to work up a nice sweat.

Trae sighed as he checked the caller ID. It was Bo.

"What's up?"

"Damn, I'm happy to hear from you too. You sound like you just got caught creepin'." Trae just shook his head. *If he only knew.*

"What's up, man?"

"Listen, you were right. That is shorty who had the video camera. The name, the school. Everything matches."

"Damn," Trae hissed.

"But yo, her brother wanted to thank you for handling Magnificent. He wanted to know how much you wanted. I told him to just give us the tape and he did that. So tell me, how did you know it was her?"

"I didn't. Not until I walked up on her. Y'all already destroyed the tape, right?"

"Of course, nigga! I told you our peeps run that strip."

"How do we know she had only one?"

"It was only one," Bo assured him.

Trae ended the call. He knew that his crew was thorough, but damn, it had to be a reason he had run into her. What were the odds of that happening? His gut was telling him he needed to check shit out for himself.

CHAPTER EIGHTEEN

It was comedy night at Club New York, where Kat Williams, Jim Jones along with Juelz Santana, was in the house representing Dipset. Paul Mooney and Capone the Gangsta of Comedy were preparing to grace the stage. The club was packed to capacity as Trae, Marvin and Stephon were sitting in Trae's office, chillin' while watching the security cameras and monitoring the promoters who were in charge of the event.

"Why are you so quiet, man?" Stephon asked Trae.

"His little Asian fantasy got his ass in trouble," Marvin answered for Trae. "That little Chinese hood chick done got a taste of some thug lovin' and went crazy. And the sad part is your cousin Tasha don't even know if Trae fucked her or not. She only speculatin'."

"What?" Stephon asked. "Tell me Marvin is exaggerating. What have I been missing?"

"Nigga, you ain't gotta take my word for it. Tell him, Trae," Marvin prodded. "Tasha done sent for her sister, had a *girl's night out* and you know what they do at those. They bash a nigga's reputation to the ground. I bet you ain't had no pussy since that motorcycle shit went down two weeks ago, did you?"

Trae swiveled away from the monitor and faced Marvin. He held up his arms in surrender. "What? Marvin, are you my official spokesperson now?"

"Nigga, you ain't sayin' nothing. And it's not like I'm lying," Marvin teased.

"Don't worry about if I'm fuckin' her or not," Trae snapped.

"A Harley? Nigga she done felt your swag. Just come out and say it." Marvin snickered, refusing to let up.

Stephon started laughing. "But damn, Tasha done sent for her sister? My cousin Trina?" Stephon was still on that part of the conversation.

Trae swiveled back around to the monitor. "Here she go right here." He pointed at the screen. Stephon came over to take a closer look. Tasha, Kyra and Trina were seated at a table in the middle of the floor. There was a bouquet of roses in front of Tasha and a bucket of ice that held three bottles.

"Damn, look at my lil' cuz! She is fine! The last time I saw her was back in '97. She is all growed up. And I guess you sent the roses? Nice touch!" he said, not giving Trae a chance to answer. "I gotta go say hi to my lil' cuz." Stephon's phone chirped.

"Boss man," the voice bellowed.

"What's up?"

"Your attorney is here." The voice faded out. Trae and Marvin turned to look at Stephon, who had a huge grin on his face.

"Say that again?" Stephon beamed.

"Your attorney is here. Smitty is covering the back area tonight. He's bringing her up to your office. She got some papers for you to sign."

"Tell him to bring her to Trae's office." He put the phone on the clip. "I'm so glad y'all niggas moved out here. Y'all keep shit going."

"Speak of the little devil," Marvin smirked.

"You got an office, nigga," said Trae. "Take that bitch to

your office. All I need is for Tasha to come walking up in here."

A few minutes later there was a knock at the door and Stephon rushed to open it. Charli stood there with her hair up in a bun, perfect makeup, an all-white Chanel dress and white stilettos. Even her briefcase was white. "Stephon," Charli greeted him with a hug. "Marvin." She held out her hand and smiled as he gently shook it. "Mr. Macklin, I'm glad you're here. I have some documents for you to look over. I'm telling you, you are going to love this one. How does a resort sound added to your investment portfolio?"

Trae swiveled around to face her. "I told you to go through Benny."

"Benny has been impossible to reach. So here I am."

Trae stood. "Yo, Marvin and Steph. Let me holla at this girl in private."

"Not a problem." Marvin was the first to stand up and leave. Charli handed Stephon a folder. "This is for you." Stephon took it and left Trae's office, closing the door behind him.

"Check this out, shorty. You official on the business tip. And I'm feelin' your swag. But it ain't nothing personal between us. So what's up? What you want?"

"What do you think I want?"

Trae felt her small hand grab his dick and she wasted no time getting on her knees. "Whoa." He grabbed her wrist. "I don't think you want to do that."

"Aren't you the least bit curious?" She massaged his dick right out of his sweatpants, making it stand at attention. Her finger circled the head with immaculate skill. She then licked the tip, causing the precome to ooze out.

"Yo, you know this is going to cost you, right?"

"Name it," she said, even though her tongue was already

lapping his pole. Trae tried to look back at the monitor to see where Tasha was. He knew that if she were to walk in at that very moment, the both of them would be taking their last breath, but he couldn't see it from where he was standing.

Sensations shot through his body like electricity. He didn't know what she was doing to his dick but he knew that he didn't want her to stop. Watching the door and trying to look back at the monitor wouldn't allow him to enjoy it.

"Yo." He grabbed her head. "Get up."

She looked up at him, slid his dick out of her mouth and smiled.

"Get up."

She stood and began to unzip her dress.

"You now got me fucked up. My wife is downstairs, so I hope you got your shit off because you gots to go," he said as he stuffed his massive hard-on back into his sweats.

"What? Is she coming?"

"That ain't the point. I said you gots to go."

"It's a point if you want to make it one." She gazed into his eyes as she fixed her dress and then checked her watch. "Well, I do need to be going, I'm running late. Make sure you and Benny go over that file. You'll see that the offer is very generous." She spoke as if she hadn't just been on the floor sucking his dick. She then grabbed her briefcase and left.

He grabbed the folder, put it on his desk and headed for the elevators.

Tasha, her sister Trina and Kyra were sitting at a table on the floor enjoying themselves. Tasha had needed to see her sister so she had sent for her.

"You got some roses, dawg," Kyra teased Tasha, trying to sound like Tommy from the hit sitcom *Martin*.

Tasha waved her off. Kat Williams was mad funny, but he still wasn't cheering Tasha up. She wished she had followed her gut and stayed home.

"Don't look now but somebody is on his way over here," Trina sang as she watched Trae steal somebody's chair.

Tasha sighed. She knew she had been hard on Trae the last couple of days since Trina had been in town. Trina was in the guest bedroom and Tasha was sleeping in there with her. She was actually depressed and was thinking that this California trip had been the wrong move, marrying Trae had been the wrong move, having three children had been the wrong move. Shit, nothing seemed to be going her way as far as she was concerned.

Trae set the chair down next to Tasha, who had her legs crossed and her elbow resting on the back of Trina's chair. Charli appeared out of nowhere, whispered something in Trae's ear and sashayed off.

"What's up, brother-in-law?" Trina smirked. "So that's the Chinese bitch?" Trina yelled loud enough for her to hear.

"Tasha, let me go beat that ho's ass," Kyra pleaded. Tasha waved her off.

Trae ignored them as he pulled Tasha and her chair closer to him. He took his time and lovingly admired his wife. Her hair was hanging loose in spiral curls. She had on a halter top and a pair of True Religion low-cut jeans with Gucci sandals. She had on one of his favorite perfumes, Escada. She was stunning to him. And on impulse he planted a soft kiss on her shoulder.

"How long are you going to be mad at me, Tasha?"

She kept her eyes straight ahead, glued on Kat Williams.

"How long, Tasha?"

"Until you tell me what went on between you and that Asian bitch!" she said, still looking straight ahead.

Trae let out a sigh. "What? You want me to make up some-thing so that we can put this shit behind us and move on with our lives? Is that what you want, Tasha? I mean, come on now. You letting this bitch disrupt our happy home? Ain't shit to tell you, Tasha."

"The bitch just came by and whispered in your ear. And you know what? I'm tired. Too tired to put my foot all up in her ass. Any other day I would have snatched the bitch up and broke her neck. But for some reason, today I just don't give a fuck. So do you, nigga."

"What's that supposed to mean?"

Tasha stood up. "C'mon y'all. I'm ready to go." Kyra and Trina weren't paying her any attention because Kat Williams had them slapping each other five and laughing. Kyra had tears running down her cheeks she was laughing so hard.

"Tasha, c'mon, Ma. Don't be like this." Trae grabbed her wrist.

"I said c'mon, ladies. It is time to go."

They both looked at each other and then at Trae and stopped laughing.

Tasha gritted, "Let's go."

They both stood up in a hurry. Tasha looked down at Trae's hand on her wrist and stood up. He looked up at her and snatched her back down. Kyra and Trina jumped, looked at each other with wide eyes and eased back into their chairs.

"Let this shit go, Tasha," Trae spat.

"You are hurting my arm, Trae."

"I'ma hurt more than that if you keep up this fuckin' unnecessary drama."

"What you want me to do, act like I'm fine with every-thing when I'm not?"

"I'm not telling you again, let this shit go. It ain't nothing."

"Nothing? I know what I see. And you are going to sit here and insult my intelligence? If you want to be with that bitch, go right ahead. Just leave me the fuck alone. I'll be damned if you think you are going to have your cake and eat it too. Now let go of my arm, Trae. I'm ready to go."

One of the security guards came over and tapped Trae on the shoulder. He needed to tell him that Charli was waiting for him. Tasha used the opportunity to snatch away from him, and the three of them marched out of the club with Tasha leading the way.

They made it to Kyra's car without saying a word. Kyra started it up, and then she and Trina both turned to Tasha, who was sitting in the backseat with her arms folded across her chest, pouting.

"Ain't this some shit!" Trina beefed. "I was into some Kat Williams and this trick spoils it."

"Where to, bitch?" Kyra snapped at Tasha.

"Why are you yelling at me, Kyra?"

"Bitch, hurry up. Don't you see one of Marvin's goons behind us? He followed us out here and now he's on his phone. You better be glad I got your back," Kyra told her.

"Just drive and hurry up before Trae decides to come out here and snatch my ass out of this car."

"Let me call Marvin before he calls me," Kyra said.

"Just hurry up," Tasha ordered.

Kyra pressed the speed-dial button. "Hey, baby, it's me. We left out of the club."

"You *left*? Where are you?" His office line rang. "Hold up." It was Grip, one of the bouncers.

"Yo, you know Kyra got the Lex?"

"She what?"

"She driving the Lex."

"Don't let her leave, man." Marvin hung up on him. Sweat beads began to pop up on his forehead. He had to think fast. That monkey was on his back. "Kyra, hold up. I'm coming out there. Where are you parked?"

"I'm in the car. Who you told not to let me leave? I'm leaving."

"Why?"

"Trae came over and said something to Tasha, she got mad, stormed out and dragged us with her. You need to talk to your boy," Kyra told him.

"You need to mind your business. And where the fuck do you think you're going?"

Tasha could hear Marvin yelling through the phone.

"She wants me to take her for a drive. Damn, Marvin, what's the big deal?"

"Kyra, you didn't ask me shit. So you might as well get your ass back here. I have some people here I want you to meet."

"Baby, I already told her I would take her for a drive. She needs me right now. After all, I did drive her here and she is my girl. I'll call you a little later." Kyra ended her call.

"Can we go now?" Tasha yelled from the backseat. "Here comes the goon."

"Do you hear this bitch?" Kyra looked over at Trina. "I just got done pissing off my husband thanks to her and she got the nerve to be impatient." Kyra didn't say anything as she started the car.

The goon was standing next to them. "Marvin wants you to give me the keys." He tried to sound threatening.

Kyra ignored him and pulled off.

"So, where are we going?" Tasha wanted to know.

"We're going to a strip club," Trina yelled.

"A strip club?" Tasha shrieked.

"Ooooh," Trina squealed. "C'mon y'all, let's go to a strip club. Please! Please!" she begged. "Dicks flying everywhere. C'mon, Kyra."

Kyra started grinning and looked in the rearview mirror at Tasha. "Fuck them niggas, you down?"

"I'm with y'all," Tasha said as if she was bored.

"Whoop whoop," Trina yelled. "Let's go then!"

They ended up at the Raw Dogg, a bougie joint up in LA. This was Tasha's and Kyra's first time inside a strip joint. Trina took fifty dollars from each of them and when she came back to the table she handed each a stack of ones. And then the lights dimmed and "Jack the Ripper" by LL Cool J came on and the first stripper came onto the stage.

"Dayaam!" all three ladies said in unison.

"I bet that big-ass dick will rip a bitch's pussy," Kyra said in shock.

"Come over here!" Trina yelled out, waving some dollars.

It was now on.

After sitting there listening to Paul Mooney, Trae waved Big Black, the bouncer, over. "Yo, what's up?" Trae asked him, already knowing the answer.

"Ole girl upstairs in your office. You want me to tell her something? I got Jack in there with her." Big Black wanted to know.

"Nah, she can wait." Trae got comfortable in his chair. Paul Mooney was a genius to him. His jokes were mixed with very obvious and relevant truths.

Trae pondered how he would handle Charli. He knew that she was more than likely watching him on the monitor and he knew that he was driving her crazy. He hated to admit it, but this game she was playing was thrilling to him.

After twenty minutes of Paul, Trae got up and headed for his office. When he walked in, Jack walked out. He closed the door behind him. Charli was sitting on top of his desk with her legs crossed. She appeared to be very relaxed. Trae closed the door and went to where she was perched. She seductively uncrossed her legs and eased off the desk. Trae leaned over and she went for his lips, but his lips slid to her neck and his hand slid down her back to her ass. Trae felt her body quiver and heard her gasp. He yanked up her dress off her ass, lifted her up and sat her back on the desk. She spread her legs, leaned back and rested her heels on the edge of the desk. She watched as he admiringly glided his hands up and down the inside of her thighs. The anxiety was heightening her desire to feel him. She had wanted this from the first time she laid eyes on him. She didn't do black but this she had to have. Her pussy was dripping wet, and if he didn't hurry up she told herself that she would scream.

She felt his fingers plunge inside her and just as quickly he pulled them out. Her heart dropped to her pussy. She closed her eyes and lay back. He spread her legs wide and entered her.

She groaned. She looked at him. He was watching the monitor. She felt as if her body were floating. *How could a dick be this good?* As soon as she asked herself that he put both of her legs over his shoulders.

Trae kept his eyes on the monitor as he felt her pussy muscles tighten and clench around his dick.

She mumbled something that Trae couldn't understand and then she started coming. Trae grabbed her hips and stood still. He watched the monitor as Marvin knocked on his door and his cell phone rang.

He pulled out of her, stuck his dick in his sweats. Her legs were left dangling off the desk. "You gotta go. I gotta handle something." He saw that it was Kaylin so he answered his phone. He listened as Kaylin told him about an upcoming project and at the same time watched Charli as she got up off the desk.

"Mr. Macklin," she purred. "I need to handle something as well," he heard her say as she got down on her knees. In one swift motion his massive hard-on was in her mouth. How she was talking in another language and sucking his dick at the same time was beyond him. He ended the call with Kaylin just as he was ready to burst in her mouth.

She gazed up at him, smiling as his come dripped down both sides of her mouth. She seductively licked her lips, stood up, fixed her dress, grabbed her belongings and left as quietly as she came in, leaving Trae standing there.

CHAPTER NINETEEN

The infamous Charles Li was in his bedroom getting dressed. He had a business engagement that he needed to attend with his wife Lucinda, Charli's mother, who was sitting on the chaise studying his every movement.

Lucinda was a beautiful Jamaican woman. When he first laid eyes on her, he said that she was Jamaican royalty. Charles Li had been in Jamaica vacationing. He had a beach house that her cleaning service kept up year-round. But everywhere he went he found her signature. She was running the local restaurant, pub, massage parlor and tourist shop. She was too young to be running anything in his opinion. When Charles Li told her if she came to work for him she wouldn't have to work as hard but he would triple her income, Lucinda didn't think twice, she packed up and beat him to the airport.

But instead of an employee, she became his mistress and gave him his beautiful daughter, Charli Toi Li.

Almost two hours later, Tasha, Trina and Kyra were pissy drunk and horny. Tasha was sipping on her third Long Island iced tea. Trina's speech slurred as she tried to get her mack on with one of the strippers. Kyra was standing on wobbly legs in a corner, trying to avoid the loud music as she called Marvin.

"Kyra, why in the fuck did you turn your phone off!" Marvin barked.

Kyra giggled. "Because."

"Because? What the fuck kind of answer is that? Because what?"

"Because...I don't know, because." Marvin listened as she slurred.

"Kyra, you're drunk, aren't you?"

She nodded her head in agreement.

"Kyra!"

She nodded again.

"Ain't this some shit," Marvin snapped.

"Where are they?" Trae asked.

"Kyra, where y'all at?"

"I...I don't know," she whispered.

"Kyra, give somebody else the damn phone!"

"This is my phone, Marvin. I bought this phone."

"Kyra, let me speak to somebody. Anybody!" he yelled.

"Okay, okay. Here," she said to the first person who walked by.

The lady looked at her and kept going.

"She said no, baby."

"Give the phone to the security guard, Kyra."

"Why?"

"Baby, give the phone to somebody," he pleaded. He was glad that he wasn't in her presence because he would have smacked the shit out of her.

Just then, one of the waitresses walked by. "Here." Kyra held out the phone.

The waitress, realizing that Kyra was wasted, took the phone. "Hello."

"Hey, that was my wife who just handed you the phone. What's the name of this place?"

"The Raw Dogg."

"The Raw Dogg? What the fuck is a Raw Dogg? Where the fuck is that?"

The waitress gave Marvin all of the info, including her name, Dottie. She promised to look after Kyra and the other two ladies until he got there. In return, she was promised a nice big fat tip.

"Ain't this some shit!" Marvin swerved in and out of the late-night traffic as he headed for the Raw Dogg. He was driving while Grip was riding shotgun. Trae was trailing close behind him in his truck.

Grip didn't say anything. He only snickered every now and then when Marvin was going off. He knew that Marvin had left his stash in the trunk and needed a fix. Like a few hours ago and had customers waiting at the club to cop.

They pulled up in front of the strip club and Marvin jumped out.

"Yo, let me come in with you," Grip yelled.

"Naw, wait right here, and watch Trae's ride. We'll be right back. I got it from here."

Marvin watched as Trae double-parked next to Grip. They hurried to the entrance only to be greeted by two oddball Mexican bouncers.

"Can I help you?" the shortest one asked.

"What the fuck you mean can you help me? I'm going into the club."

The bouncer looked at Marvin, then at Trae, and back at Marvin again. "Y'all look like trouble."

"I'm here to pick up my wife. I spoke to Dottie the waitress." When the short bouncer didn't respond he turned to the tall one and held out a fifty.

The bouncer took the fifty. "You only want to take her home, right? We don't want any trouble."

"No trouble, nigga. Let me get in, get my wife and get the fuck out," Marvin barked.

He let Marvin in, but not Trae. "What's your business?" He stood in front of Trae, blocking the door.

"Nigga, I'm here for my wife too."

"He's with me, man. I told you we'll be in and out."

The short one moved to the side and let Trae in. "Keep an eye on them," he said to his partner, while not taking his eyes off of Trae.

When they got inside the club and scanned the room they shook their heads in disgust. The women were going buck wild, feeling on nigga's dicks and asses. One chick was getting fingered by one of the strippers.

When their eyes fell on Kyra's table, they both wanted to go off. Trina was rubbing on some nigga's dick, Kyra and Tasha were stuffing dollars in the same nigga's G-string, and he had a hand on one of each woman's ass cheeks, squeezing and rubbing.

"Give me seventy dollars, Tasha, so I can get me some of this dick," Trina said, before looking up into Trae's mean mug, and then at Marvin's screw face. "Oh, shit. Never mind. The party's over," she giggled. "Y'all hoes are busted."

Neither Tasha or Kyra was paying Trina any attention, as they were now dancing with the stripper.

"Oh shit, I'm getting dizzy." Tasha stumbled and turned, falling into Trae. She burst into giggles. "Sorry." Not even recognizing him.

"Where's your purse, Tasha? Time to go."

She gasped as she looked up. Her legs gave out and she reached for her chair and fell into it.

Trina had this stupid grin on her face as she watched the event unfolding in front of her.

Marvin was holding on to Kyra's wrist, and she was looking as if she were about to shit on herself. He gave Dottie, the waitress, the fifty dollars he had promised her and dragged Kyra out. He didn't say two words to her.

"Get up, Tasha."

"I can't. My legs are drunk." He grabbed her purse, yanked her up and pushed her toward the exit. Trina jumped up and followed them, realizing that was her ride.

"Hey, I thought you wanted to get with me." Jack the Ripper sounded disappointed.

"My ride is here, playboy. Next time," she hollered as she kept it moving.

Trae helped a drunk and giggling Tasha into the front seat and a drunk Trina into the back and slammed the door.

"I'm in trouble," Tasha whispered and they both started snickering but stopped real quick when Trae jumped into the front.

Marvin pulled up on the side of him and said, "I'll holla at you tomorrow."

Trae nodded and drove off. Trina stretched out in the backseat. Five minutes later she was snoring.

Marvin parked and got out. Of all days Kyra had picked this one to drive the Lexus. Since she hardly drove it he kept his stash in the trunk. He opened the trunk and breathed a sigh of relief that his stash was intact. He opened one of the little baggies, stuck it up close to his nose and took a long and satisfying sniff. He closed it again, put it back in its spot, wiped his nose and closed the trunk. His body began to tingle as soon as he sat in the car. He looked over at Kyra, who was fast asleep.

*   *   *

"Tasha, I don't give a fuck how drunk you are, but you need to listen up. Do you hear me?"

"I hear you."

"Don't let me ever catch you up in another strip club!"

She sucked her teeth and said, "You go to them." He pulled over onto the shoulder lane, stopped the car and snatched a handful of her hair and pulled her toward him. "Did you hear what I just fuckin' told you?"

"Yeah." She was startled and sobering up fast.

"What did I say, Tasha?"

"Don't go to no more strip clubs."

He grabbed her hair tighter and glared at her for another minute before turning her curls loose. She breathed a sigh of relief as she felt the back of her head to make sure her hair was still attached to her scalp. He put the car in drive and eased back onto the highway.

Trina's head popped up. "Pull over. I feel sick, Trae. Oh, shit," she groaned. Trae pulled over and before he could stop the back door flew open and Trina hurled.

"Ewww," Tasha said with disdain as she rubbed the back of her head once again.

"You got some tissue?" Trina groaned.

Tasha opened the glove compartment and passed her some napkins. Trina wiped her mouth and lay back down. In no time flat she was back to snoring.

"Trae," Tasha said.

"What, Tasha?"

"Do you love her?"

"Love her?" Trae was agitated. "Love who?"

"The bitch that you creepin' with."

"Tasha, ain't nobody creepin'. You drunk and talkin' crazy."

"I'm not drunk."

"Yes you are."

"You don't fuck me anymore."

He looked at her as if she had just sprouted another head. "Fuck you! Fuck you, Tasha? You don't speak to me, and you've been sleeping in the guest room! So what the fuck you talkin' about? Fuck this, Tasha, you're drunk. We'll talk when you're sober."

"You don't find me sexy anymore?" She leaned over and began squeezing his dick.

"Of course I find you sexy," he snapped.

"I still find you sexy and I don't want to."

"You're drunk, Tasha." He moved her hand off his dick.

"Why you not getting hard? You fucked her tonight, didn't you?"

"Tasha, you want to know why I'm not hard? Because I want to punch you in your fuckin' mouth for saying dumb shit, accusing me of shit I ain't doing. And then I want to slap the shit out of you for feeling all over another nigga's dick in a strip club. So don't push me, Tasha. Just do me a favor and shut your drunk ass up."

She grabbed his dick again, this time pulling it out of his sweatpants. He pushed her hand away and covered himself back up.

"So now you're saying I can't get no dick?"

"Tasha, your sister is in the backseat."

She sucked her teeth. "I want some dick, Trae."

"What? Them stripping faggot-ass niggas done got Daddy's pussy all wet?"

"No, Daddy got Mommy's pussy all wet. I didn't want to fuck none of them niggas. Mommy don't stray, no matter what. She knows who this pussy belongs to."

"If you ever give my pussy away, just remember, I'm shootin' the nigga," Trae warned.

"If I find out you are fucking that Chinese bitch, I'm not going to shoot anybody. Because it takes two to tango, I'm just going to give the bitch a royal ass-whipping and then I'm leaving your ass," she warned him right back.

They rode in silence until he pulled into their driveway. "Trina, get up," Tasha yelled as she jumped out of the front seat and slammed the door.

Trae got out and made himself comfortable on the front porch. They had a swing bench that had been custom-made when they first moved in. He pulled out a blunt and lit it. Halfway through it Trina got out of the truck and stumbled up the steps. He didn't bother to look at her or say anything. He was lost in thought. *Was it worth it? To launder a few mil and have this crazy bitch sweating him and his wife mad at him and being suspicious?*

He sucked on the blunt for another half hour before Tasha came out. She had showered and was smelling like sweet pears, and had on one of his nightshirts and booties on her feet. She sat next to him as he rocked back and forth.

"Can I have some of that?" He kept rocking back and forth. "Trae, you heard me."

"Don't you think you had enough intoxicants for one night?"

"No," she pouted.

"Well I think so." They heard a plane off in the distance.

"I still love you, Trae," she confessed.

"Why would you stop loving me? Shit, I love you more." She reached over into his sweatsuit jacket and pulled out another blunt and a lighter. He watched her as she fired it up. "Why would you stop, Tasha?"

"I'm not as happy as I used to be."

"That's because you are allowing the bullshit to take that happiness away."

After she took a few tokes he took it from her and took a few hits before putting it out. *Damn this nigga is sexy*, she thought. His long legs were stretched out, ending in his signature Timbs. He took off his jacket, revealing muscular arms, placing the jacket across her shoulders.

"Why'd you put it out?"

"That's enough for you. Listen to yourself. You talking crazy." He unbuttoned the top two buttons on her shirt and gazed at her nipples. "This is my shirt. How are you not going to speak to me and wear my shirt?" He leaned down and began to suck lightly on one of her nipples and then switched to the other one.

"I miss us," Tasha whispered.

"I don't like it when we fight," he told her and then leaned in for a kiss.

"Me neither." Tears began to stream down her cheeks. "You usually make me so happy."

"You'll stay happy if you stop being so damn suspicious and insecure. That ain't your steelo, Tasha." He was wiping her tears with his thumbs.

"It's not my steelo, Trae, but I'm not some stupid bitch." She got up and left him sitting on the porch.

CHAPTER TWENTY

Marvin's sweaty back was burning from Kyra's nails scratching it up. Her legs were wrapped around his waist and she lay limp against him.

He whispered in her ear, "We halfway there, baby girl. You gonna come for Daddy four more times, I promise."

She didn't know what had gotten into Marvin. He had come into the house and woken her up with a hard-on. Since Aisha was in the bed with her he swooped her up and put her in her own bed and come back and told Kyra she was gonna come eight times tonight. Why that number, she had no clue.

He gently unwrapped her legs, but held her ass tight. He didn't want her warm, juicy pussy to release his dick, but he wanted to lay her on her back.

Kyra, sensing this, moaned, "Umm, umm, baby. I had enough."

He ran his thumb over her nipple. "Four more times, baby. We almost there," he begged.

"I can't, baby."

"Yes, you can. I got you."

He slowly and gently managed to keep his dick inside her while laying her on her back.

"This is Daddy's pussy," he whispered as he began getting his stroke on. "Daddy's pussy is good." He grabbed one of her legs and put it in the crook of his arm. Now he was in deeper.

"Marvin," Kyra moaned. He grabbed the other leg and put it over his shoulder. Her fingers grabbed at the sheets. He was hitting her G-spot and somehow stroking her clit at the same time. He knew that drove her crazy. "Baby," she squealed as she bust an even harder nut, and Marvin wouldn't stop stroking.

"That's number five, baby. Three more to go." He kept stroking a trembling sweating Kyra. She was half unconscious. He took the leg off his shoulder but held on to the other one as he rained kisses all over her face. "Baby, you feel so good." He stroked. "When you come...oh, the way your pussy squeezes my dick. Oh, baby, I love this pussy. C'mon," he pleaded. "Stay with Daddy. Three more to go." He stroked and ground his hips into hers. He was determined to get her off three more times.

"Baby, no." She tried to push him off of her.

"C'mon, baby girl, three more times." He grabbed both of her tiny wrists in one of his hands and continued to stroke.

"Marvin, please. I'm drying up. Stop, baby."

"Baby girl, you still real wet," he grunted. "This pussy feels so good. Let's keep fucking. C'mon and fuck Daddy." He was stroking faster.

"Marvin, stop!" she screamed. "What is the matter with you?"

He kept grinding and moaning. She opened her mouth to scream but instead sank her teeth down into his shoulder as hard as she could and wouldn't let go until he pulled out and rolled off of her.

"What the fuck is the matter with you!" he barked. She

had drawn blood. Before he knew it she had knocked him in the mouth and started throwing punches.

"What the fuck is the matter with *you?*" she cried. Now she was trying to choke him. "What did you have, Marvin?"

He easily swatted her hands from around his neck. "You're crazy, girl." He jumped out of the bed.

She jumped up and pushed him. "Marvin, I am not fuckin' playing with you." She punched him in the chest. "What the fuck did you have tonight? Don't lie to me, baby."

"What are you talking about? I ain't have nothing."

"Oh, God," she cried as she held her stomach as if she were getting sick. She did not want to even entertain the thought that he was back getting high. "Marvin, you forgot how well I know you. When I look at you I see me, baby. This is me. You can't lie to me."

"Why you bite me, Kyra?"

"Damn you, Marvin. Don't change the subject. What did you have tonight?"

"I ain't have nothing. What the fuck are you talking about?"

Kyra put her face into her hand and started crying. "Get out, Marvin. Please, just get out of my face." She jumped up and pushed his naked body out of her bedroom and locked the door.

"Trae, where are you going? I told you I needed to run to the mall real quick. Take me to the mall." Tasha pouted.

"The mall? Baby, this is Sunday. The king's day. Have you forgotten? You got work to do at home."

"Of course I didn't forget. But my king wants his Valentine's present, doesn't he? Valentine's Day is only a few days away."

"This king doesn't want any Valentine's present from a mall. You slippin', baby."

She mushed him on the side of his bald head. "A part of your gift is at the mall, smartass."

"I was getting ready to say."

"Say what, Trae?"

"My baby is turning into a mall rat."

"I've always been a mall rat. I was a mall rat when you met me, and I'm gonna always be one. Let me find out you forgot where you came from."

"Naw, I'm just sayin'," Trae said.

"Sayin' what?"

"You'll see. The gift I got for you is going to make you take whatever you got for me out of shame, back to some damn mall," he teased.

"Yeah right. Nigga, you ain't never outdo me for Valentine's Day. What makes you think you going to start now?" she challenged.

"Aiight. I'ma remember those words. The same words that I'ma make you eat."

"I don't think so." When they pulled up in front of their house Tasha jumped out, leaving Trae to take the groceries inside. She headed to the mall, excited about getting everything ready for Valentine's Day.

As soon as Tasha pulled off, his cell phone rang. Trae looked at the caller ID and it was Bo. "What's up in New York, my nigga?"

"Yo, man, it sounds like everthing happenin' out there in Cali to me. Y'all crazy out there. But check it, I've been thinking about yo ass. I know you, nigga. You up to something," Bo told Trae.

"This world is too fuckin' small," Trae spat.

"So...what you wanna do?"

"I don't know yet. Shit, I'm going to see her today. She working on something for me."

Bo started laughing. "See her? I knew my gut was right. I know you crazy for real. Don't make no moves yet, nigga."

"Chill out, fool. I ain't crazy, just careful. I have her doing a drawing of Tasha for Valentine's."

"You better be careful, nigga, even though the tape is destroyed. I don't see where you have to take any drastic measures. Plus, she don't know who you are, do she?"

"I don't know. I'm feelin' her out, just to be sure."

"Man, you stupid. Stay away from that broad."

"Bo, don't you think it's too much of a coincidence that she's out here? I gotta check this out. I won't be able to rest until I do."

"Man, your head is hard. If you don't leave shit alone, I know you gonna be calling me in a few to clean shit up."

"So what if I do?"

"You playin' with fire, nigga. But go ahead, do you, I'm out. Peace." Bo hung up.

CHAPTER TWENTY-ONE

It was breakfast time in the Macklin household. Trae was seated at the head of the table, Pop Pop at the other end. Trae's parents were up for Valentine's Day. This was his gift to Nana. She had wanted to visit her grandchildren. The twins and Caliph were in their high chairs. Of course Shaheem was seated next to Aunt Marva, Kareem by Pop Pop, and Nana had Caliph.

Tasha was feeding Trae and Nana grinned as she watched them interact. Tasha was spoon-feeding him, giggling, and they were whispering back and forth. Every now and then they would look over at the children.

"This is all the time," Marva said to Nana. "That is how they eat. She feeds him, they share a plate, and whisper and giggle throughout the entire meal. I've never seen anything like it."

"Oh, leave them alone. Let the flame burn as long as it can. They're in love," Nana told her. "I was beginning to think that my son would never settle down."

Trae and Tasha were oblivious to their conversation. Trae was trying to get some pussy since she hadn't given him his morning fix. She told him he had to wait until tonight, after all it was Valentine's Day.

"I'm built like that, you can still give me a little bit and I'll still be ready for tonight."

"Unh-uh, it ain't going down like that. Plus your parents

are here. If we up and disappear they're going to know what's up."

"Man—"

"Shhh, why you gotta get all loud?" Tasha whispered.

"Because you poppin' bullshit right now."

Tasha giggled. "You're just a spoiled brat. You can wait until tonight. I told you I got you." She kissed his lips that tasted like pancake syrup.

"Oh, this better be good because you owe me."

"I got you, big daddy."

"Aiight then. I'ma hold you to that."

Later on that evening, Trae and Tasha finished up an intimate dinner on a yacht. They visited the California Yacht Club in Marina Del Rey where they watched the sunset. Now Trae was waiting outside on the porch for Tasha. She had to change clothes and they would be on their way to their hotel suite.

He puffed on his blunt in anticipation; so far everything was going perfectly. This was actually his favorite day of the year, their anniversary was second. He never saw himself loving a woman more than the way he loved Tasha.

"You ready?" Tasha stepped out onto the porch.

"Yeah, but hold up. Damn, baby," was all Trae could get out.

"Don't start drooling and what's this?" She went toward the big package that was wrapped with a bright red bow.

"Hold up. Hold up, slow down. Don't touch that yet." He pulled up his camera. "Let me get a shot of this. Come stand in front of me. All of this red is gettin' my dick hard. Open up the trench coat for me."

"No, I said don't start drooling, you're going to have to wait."

"Oh, so it's like that?"

"Yes it is." She smiled at him.

Her hair was piled high on top of her head, curls dangling everywhere; she had on a red spaghetti-strap Versace dress under the black Versace trench coat. The red stockings and red garter belt had her feeling very sexy. She twirled around for him, spinning on the red stilettos. She handed him a red-and-white rose and turned around and gave him a kiss. "Can I open my other gift now?" The red dust on her cheeks was shimmering.

"Who said it's your gift?"

"Trae, stop playing."

"Actually it's mine. I bought it for me. I just want you to open it. But first come stand right here." He pointed between his legs. He was seated in the swing holding the camera. She did as she was told and stood there in front of him. "Can a nigga get a shot of his pussy?" She raised her right leg and placed her foot on the bench. He moved the camera to the side, zooming in on her garter belt and neatly shaved pussy. "Looka here," he panted. "If this ain't a work of art I don't know what is."

"Can I open *your* gift now?" Tasha asked as if she were bored.

"Hold up, Ma, can I get another minute?"

"Baby."

"Go ahead, Tasha."

"Oooh, goody," she squealed as she took her leg down and went to untie the big red floppy ribbon. When she opened it up, she frowned. "A picture?" She obviously was not thrilled.

"It's not a picture, it's a drawing, baby."

Tasha snatched off all the paper and got a better look. "Baby, you didn't."

It was a drawing taken from a picture that he had taken of her one morning after he fucked her damn near into a coma. The covers were sprawled across the bed and she was knocked out. Her hair lay across the pillows and she was sleeping peacefully. It was one of Trae's favorites.

"Who did this for you? How could they draw with so much detail?" Tasha was in complete awe over the drawing.

"I paid this college student to do it. You like it?"

"Oh my God. Look at me."

"Do you like it?"

"Where are you going to put it?"

"Right over the bed."

"I didn't realize you liked this picture so much. I can't believe how real it looks. This person has skills."

"Do you like it?"

"Well, yeah. It's just strange seeing a lifelike picture of yourself." Tasha was getting all choked up.

"Baby, you are larger than life. Let me take it inside so we can get the rest of our evening under way." He practically had to pry it out of her hands before he winked at her and disappeared into the house.

When he came back onto the porch he eased up behind her, wrapping his arms around her waist, then whispered in her ear, "You got something real nice planned for Daddy?"

"Real nice. You have no idea."

"Aiight then, let's go."

"Let's!"

They headed for the drop-top Beamer and drove to their presidential suite.

Trae led the way into the plush hotel suite. There were red, white, black and yellow rose petals everywhere. There were also six-foot-tall white long-stem roses and candles throughout the room. This was one of their favorite suites so they were already familiar with the suite itself. The living room had the bucket of ice with four bottles of Patrón.

"You are not getting drunk tonight so don't even think about it," Tasha warned him.

"After we fuck, I'ma do whatever I feel like."

"The only thing you're going to want to do is fall into a comatose sleep when I finish with you."

Trae broke into a wide grin and rubbed his hands together. "That's a bet. Don't take off the coat yet. Let me make sure the camera is set up in the bedroom and let me freshen up. You get the whipped cream and strawberries. Plus, I got a surprise for you, look in the fridge and the freezer."

"You ain't got to tell me twice." Tasha grinned. They both went happily on their separate ways.

Tasha skipped to the freezer, snatched it open and pulled out a long box with a ribbon. With trembling hands she lifted the top and ran her fingers across the icy ankle bracelet that he had bought her when they first met. It had TRAE written in diamonds. Now he had had it upgraded, adding more diamonds. She started crying at the memories. They had been on their way to Kaylin's birthday party and it was also the night he had proposed to her.

Swiping the tears away, she opened the refrigerator and pulled out her favorite, chocolate-covered strawberries. She sat them on the table and pulled out the whipped cream and a bowl of fresh fruit slices. On the counter was honey and a bowl of warm chocolate syrup. When Trae came into the kitchen he caught Tasha crying as she fingered the diamonds on the ankle bracelet. "You are such a crybaby." He stood there holding the camera.

"Come here, baby." She held open her arms for Trae. He

put the camera down and held her close. "I love you so much," she sobbed.

"I love you more," he told her, loving every minute of it.

"Do you remember the day you put this bracelet on my ankle?"

"Of course I do. I even remember what you had on. I was sitting on the bed watching you get dressed."

"You remember those days? Oh God, you made the magic."

"Of course I do. Now stop crying and give me my gift."

"It's in the bedroom."

"Where at?"

"You have to find it."

"Oh, I see you got jokes."

"What, you forgot? I am one not to be outdone." She laughed through snivels.

"Oh, we'll see about that. Meet me in the living room. I'll be right back."

"Happy hunting," she teased.

She busied herself getting everything set up in the living room where the party was to get started. A phone rang but since they had the same ring tone she wasn't sure whose phone it was. She grabbed the one that was ringing since they were both sitting on the coffee table.

"Hello." There was silence. "Hello," Tasha said again.

"I'm sorry, I was interrupted. Is Mr. Macklin available?"

Tasha was stunned. *Here this bitch is calling my husband on Valentine's Day. I ought to— No, breathe. Be cool, Tasha. Breathe. Think with a level head.*

Tasha finally spoke. "Who is calling?"

"Charli. Charli Li, his attorney. Is this Mrs. Macklin?"

Tasha sat down on the plush sofa and crossed her legs. Trae must have found his present because she could hear him coming back into the living room talking smack.

"Yo baby. I hate to give you the crown, but I think you got me this year." He held up a small box that held a set of keys, the manual to a Maybach and a Maybach umbrella and cupholder. "I can't believe you did this shit. How much did it set you back?" She was trying not to laugh because he looked as if he was trying not to cry. He had wanted that car for almost a year now but had kept putting it off. "What nigga you know gets a Maybach for Valentine's?" He leaned over and gave her a kiss on the lips. "I love you, baby. But, yo, this shit here looks gay. I'm not feeling this." He held up the cell phone.

"I knew you would say that. So I'm going to keep that for myself. That's mines. Give it to me." She held out one hand to claim the cell phone and the other one to pass him his. She had bought him—well, actually her—a GoldVish diamond-studded mobile phone. She wasn't planning on telling him how much it had cost.

"Fuck that little shit. This is the real deal!" He was now thumbing through the manual and cheesing from ear to ear. "When do we go pick it up?"

"Sit down and take this call, Trae."

"Who is it, baby? Damn, it's Valentine's Day. When can I go pick up my car?"

"That's what I said. It's Valentine's Day. And at this rate I may cancel the fuckin' car."

"Are the kids okay?" He took the phone. "You ain't canceling shit. Why you trippin'?"

"The kids are fine."

"What up?" Trae spoke into the receiver. He looked over

at Tasha and frowned. She folded her arms across her chest and had her eyes glued on him. He listened attentively for a couple of minutes, then said, "Cool. Give Benny a call." He ended the call and turned his phone off.

"Your phone is on, right?"

Tasha looked at him, not bothering to respond.

"Don't look at me like that, Tasha. That was big business right there."

"I can't tell. Why the bitch keep blowing up your cell phone and buying you gifts and shit, Trae? Hell, it's Valentine's Day and the bitch calling you as if you owe her something."

"Tasha, I told you, that was business. She about her money and don't care if it was Christmas. But fuck her. Let's move on with our evening." He rubbed his hands together.

Tasha laughed and shook her head in disbelief.

"Tasha, let it go, man. Fuck her. Stop the insecure shit. I told you that ain't you."

"Insecure? Nigga, please. Having gut instincts is not inse-cure. You taught me that, remember?"

"Yes, you are acting insecure. I told you I ain't fuckin' the bitch, so what the fuck? You want me to stop getting money with the broad?" he yelled.

She could see that Trae was pissed off. But hell, so was she. They sat across from one another staring each other down and not saying a word.

"Come here, Tasha. I didn't mean to raise my voice like that. I'm sorry, baby." He made an attempt at bring-ing the peace back into the room. "Tasha, come here baby. Please? So what now? You gonna let a phone call disturb our groove? Fuck her, Tasha. Now come here. And I'm not going to ask you again." He glared at her. She sucked her teeth, rolled her eyes, and stood up. He eased up to the edge of the sofa as she slowly made her way over to him and stood in front of him. He began rubbing the outside of her thighs before sliding his hands over her ass cheeks. She didn't have any panties on under the dress.

"See." He massaged and squeezed her ass. "This is what I'm talking about. You gonna let that bitch stop you from enjoying a good fuck from your husband that worships the ground you walk on? Drop that trench coat so I can see what you been hiding all night, with your fine ass."

"Since you can't seem to take care of that bitch, I will, Trae."

"Tasha, I'm not telling you again, later for her!" he spat. "Let's enjoy our evening. Now open this coat."

"Take your hands off my ass."

"This ass belongs to Daddy."

"Well take your hands off of Daddy's ass." He let go and she stood back and untied the trench coat and let it fall to the floor. She took off the Versace dress and slowly twirled around for him.

He was speechless. She had on the sexiest set of lingerie he had ever seen. Tasha had gone to La Perla and had them alter a $750 corset that was made of lace and fishnet. They cut out the nipples and the crotch. The bloodred color accented Tasha's cocoa brown complexion perfectly. She bent over seductively and spread her legs and gave him a shot at her pussy.

Trae threw his hands up. "You outdid yourself this year, baby."

She went over to him, leaned over and kissed him nice and soft on the lips. "Oh, it ain't over yet."

"Baby, stick a fork in me. I'm done. Ain't shit else you can do. Take off the lingerie." She did as she was told and was standing there in front of him with only the heels, stockings, and garter belt on.

"You like?"

"Like?" He unzipped his pants and out sprung a long hard dick. "Ask him if he likes what he sees."

Tasha smiled as she watched him stroke his joint. Veins were popping everywhere. "C'mon baby, let's go to the bedroom. I'm ready to talk to that guy. I think he has something to tell me," she purred.

"He got something to tell you all right." Trae stood up and got behind Tasha. He slipped one hand around her waist and the other hand began playing with her nipple as he led her to the bedroom. Since the camera was rolling he led her to the chair and bent her over, spreading her legs.

"Baby, I wanted to suck your dick first," she cooed.

"In a minute. I gotta get up in this tight pussy first."

She looked back at him, pouted her lips and clapped her ass cheeks together, which made him want to do some damage. He spread those cheeks and put his dick all the way in.

"Ooooh, Daddy," Tasha moaned as the dick banged at her walls. "I'ma be a good girl for now on." She spread her legs wider and was throwing the pussy at him.

"See what you would have missed out on?" Trae was stroking long and deep, watching his dick appear and then disappear into the pussy.

"Oh, Daddy," she groaned, "that's...Oh..." She squeezed her eyes tight.

"Your spot?" Trae banged harder.

"My spot," she squealed. "Oh, yes, fuck me, baby. Oh, oh, shit. Oh, God, right there, that feels so good," she groaned before her legs began to tremble and she was skeetin' nonstop.

Trae slowly pulled out while watching her body twitch

and was proud of his handiwork. He slapped her ass real hard. "C'mon, let me eat some pussy." He stood her up.

"Wait baby," she gasped, "that was a quick one but a good one."

"Naw, ain't no waiting, come on," he teased while planting soft kisses on her neck and reaching around to play in her pussy.

"I love you, baby." She moved his hand, wanting her pussy to settle down a little bit.

"You think you slick, don't you?"

"Shut up, boy. Let me get my bearings straight first. Lay down on your back." She wiggled away from him.

Tasha snatched up the hotel robe.

"Where are you going?"

"To get the whipped cream, my strawberries, the chocolate syrup, some ice and the bowl of fruit. Is that all right?"

"Just hurry back."

"I got you, Daddy." She floated away on a cloud.

Trae lay on the bed, rested his hands behind his head and closed his eyes. When he opened them again Tasha was standing at the foot of the bed.

"Baby, let me introduce you to Mysterious."

Tasha had arranged to have her wait in the room next door. Mysterious wore a mask that covered half her face. She had Tasha's rich brown complexion and was the same weight and height. Her hair was twisted up into a ponytail and she had red and white glitter sprinkled throughout her hair. She was trembling as she undid her trench coat and allowed it to fall to the floor. She wore a red teddy, stockings, garter belt and stilettos just like Tasha. She was fine.

"Put your tongue back into your mouth, baby. You are not fucking her, so sorry to burst your bubble. The rules of this game is she is not to contact us ever again, she's only here to give you extra pleasure, and again you are not allowed to touch her or fuck her. That's what I'm here for. Comprende, big pimpin'?"

"Let me get this straight. I'm—"

"What part of *you ain't gonna fuck her or touch her* didn't you understand?" Tasha cut him off. "Now are you going to let me do me or what?"

"It's your show and from what I can tell I don't have a choice in the matter." Trae couldn't believe what was happening.

"You damned right you don't."

Tasha dropped her robe and sixty-nined Trae. He immediately began sucking on her pussy. She took his dick into her mouth and Mysterious began sucking on his balls. If her sister and brother had known she was doing this they would have killed her. But shit, five hundred for two hours of work? She wasn't complaining. Her main job was to suck balls and toes and lick ass cracks until Trae couldn't hold back anymore.

Damn, I know I'm halfway good at what I do but how this nigga can hold back a nut for this long is beyond me. I see why this bitch said I couldn't fuck him and if I ever tried to contact him she would kill me, Mysterious thought as she stood up and was preparing to leave. Her two hours were up. She didn't want to and couldn't believe that she was feeling like this.

Tasha was wrapped up in Trae's arms and was spent; she had had at least four orgasms.

"Hold up," Trae said to Mysterious. "Don't leave yet." Mysterious wanted to jump with glee.

"Trae, don't even think about it," warned Tasha.

He studied Mysterious closely before saying, "I want her

to do something for me. I ain't finished with you yet." He leaned over and began sucking on Tasha's nipples.

Mysterious was elated, on fire and dying to hop on Trae's big black dick. She was hoping that she was getting ready to get the opportunity. *Damn, could he get it up again?* she wondered. *The bitch is being so selfish, she won't even let me suck his dick. She is on him like white on rice.*

Mysterious watched as he lovingly kissed Tasha and played with her pussy. She watched in greedy anticipation as his dick sprang to life. She couldn't help but lick her lips. She sat in the chair in front of the bed and not even realizing it began playing with her pussy.

Trae got up first and sat on the edge of the bed. *Damn.* He looked like a god to her.

"Tasha baby, come here and sit in big daddy's lap," he instructed while keeping his eyes on Mysterious.

Mysterious could tell that Tasha was worn out but she still looked hungry and obviously loved pleasing her man. Mysterious wished she had a man who loved her more than she loved him, which she could see was the deal with these two. She watched in jealousy as Trae stroked his dick and Tasha seductively crawled to the edge of the bed. She went to suck his dick but he stopped her and guided her to sit in his lap with her back to his chest. Mysterious watched in anticipation as Tasha straddled him and the dick disappeared up in her pussy. She was so agitated that she couldn't bring herself to come. She wanted Trae to watch her masturbate but he was too into wifey.

Tasha's head was thrown back and her eyes rolled up toward the back of her head as she slowly rode Trae.

He pointed to Mysterious.

"Come do her."

"What?" Tasha moaned but didn't stop grinding on his dick.

Mysterious crawled over to the bed.

"I got this," he told her. He nodded to Mysterious, who began blowing on Tasha's clit. The ladies at Divine Escort Service had taught her well.

Tasha grabbed Mysterious's hair in an attempt to stop her. But Trae moved her hand.

"Relax, baby." He dug into Tasha's pussy even deeper, causing her to tremble.

Mysterious began sucking on Tasha's pussy.

"I don't...want...no...bitch...eat. Oh, shit," she groaned. "Trae ssttop...wait."

Trae was trying to hit that G-spot as he watched Mysterious eat his wife. He couldn't wait to replay this tape.

"Fuck," he gritted. Tasha was screaming as Trae felt his nut coming and Tasha was already coming. "Keep licking her," he growled to Mysterious and he gripped Tasha tighter and shot a huge load up into her.

Tasha fainted.

The next morning, as they were leaving the hotel, Trae stopped by the gift shop and bought Tasha a teddy bear.

"What's this for?" Tasha asked him through a stifled yawn. She was worn out.

"Since when have you asked me what a gift was for?" He started the car and leaned over to get a kiss. "This is for that wonderful Valentine's Day."

"This is all I get?" Tasha teased.

"You are so damned spoiled. You know yo ass celebrate Valentine's all year-round."

"Yeah, and that's the only reason I ain't trippin'."

"But I bet you won't be able to top this Valentine's."

"Nigga, you said that last year. I'm hip to your reverse psychology."

Trae gave her that dazzling grin. "You love me or what?"

"You know I do. And don't think about contacting that ho from last night!"

"Aww, man!" Trae acted as if he were hurt. "Yo, I'm ready to go pick up my Maybach." Trae pulled off and headed home.

CHAPTER TWENTY-TWO

M arvin, it is one o'clock in the morning on a Sunday night and the club is closed. Where are you and why aren't you home? Aisha has been asking me why are you gone so much."

"Baby." Marvin's voice was low and raspy. "I'll be there in a few," he told her.

"Guess what, Marvin? You said that last night and the night before!" Kyra snapped.

"For real. I'll be there in a few!" He hung up.

Little did he know that Kyra was already dressed and on her way to go get him.

"Zip up your jacket, Aisha."

"Okay, Mommy. Can I take my Bratz doll?"

"Yes. Let Mommy get her keys. And hurry up."

Kyra snatched up her keys, her purse and some mace. She turned out the lights and headed out.

"Where are we going, Mommy?" Aisha asked while being thrilled by the night lights and night sounds.

"I told you. We're going to pick up Daddy. Roll your window up."

"Aww, Mom."

"Aisha," Kyra snapped.

"Okay, Mommy." She pouted as she watched the window close.

Kyra stuck in the lecture tape from her last physics class. She had a test coming up and she was barely halfway prepared, thanks to Marvin and his recent antics. She had followed him to this house just the other night so she knew exactly where she was going. She felt she needed to put a stop to this shit right now.

They drove for another twenty minutes before hitting the 'hood. It was all the way live. Children were outside as if it were noon, folks were sitting on their porches and of course the feens and hustlers were in full effect. The only thing that slowed the night up for a good minute was the sound of gunshots in the distance.

Aisha spotted Marvin's truck before Kyra did. "There go my daddy's truck," she squealed with glee.

"I see it, baby. I'm going to pull up into the driveway."

"Whose house is this?"

"It's more of your daddy's relatives. C'mon, baby."

They both got out of the car. Kyra grabbed her hand and they climbed the cement stairs. NWA's "Gangsta Gangsta" was booming through the sound system. She heard laughter and smelled the weed. A fire truck was blaring in the distance. Aisha squeezed her mother's hand tighter as Kyra rang the bell.

"It's okay, baby." Kyra honestly hoped as she rang the bell again.

"Okay, okay, damn." A tall, slim, older woman came to the door. She looked as if she had definitely been around the block several times. She looked at the little girl and then back at Kyra before opening the door.

"I'm here for my husband, Marvin."

"You didn't have to come to my home. Me and Blue ain't fuckin'!"

"After seeing you, there's no doubt in my mind that y'all aren't. Number one, you're too old. Marvin likes them young. Number two, your feet are too big. He has this thing about a woman's feet being over a size seven. He said some shit about his daughters not having big feet. You must be his get-high buddy. So if you were a young bitch with small feet, then I'd be worried." Kyra smirked.

Just then Marvin's cousin Lo came to the door. "MiMi, who dat be?" He had his hand on his waist, ready to go for his burner. When he saw Kyra he broke into a wide grin and then it quickly turned into a frown. He knew Marvin was busted. "Cousin, come on in." He pushed the door all the way open. "What y'all doing out here this time of night?"

"What's up, Lo?" She rolled her eyes at MiMi. "I'm glad somebody got some manners around here."

"This is my house. I don't have to have any damn manners." MiMi rolled her eyes and walked away.

"Where's Marvin, Lo? I need to speak to him." She and Aisha remained on the porch. "Tell him me and his daughter are outside."

"Come on in, Cousin. Don't pay her any mind. She always had a crush on Marvin," Lo said as he went into a nod, but immediately shook it off. He was now scratching his arm.

"Tell Marvin to come outside, Lo. I know he's in here so don't even think about trying to cover for him."

Lo scratched his head and disappeared.

Kyra and Aisha went back down the stairs and stood by the car. A few minutes later Marvin came out of the house with a surprised look on his face.

"Daddy." Aisha bolted, ran off and jumped into Marvin's arms.

He rained kisses all over her face, causing her to giggle. "What's up, baby girl. It is way past your bedtime."

"I know. It's real, real, real late but Mommy said we had to come and get you."

"I see." He kissed her again and put her in the backseat.

Kyra noticed that he had a fresh haircut, he was clean-shaven and his clothes were neatly pressed. He swooped her up and plopped her on the hood of the car. He kissed her nice and slow, damn near making her forget why she was out in the streets of LA at two in the morning.

"Baby girl, I told you I was coming home. You got my baby in harm's way as well as yourself. What was so urgent that couldn't wait?"

"Wait how much longer, Marvin? You've been gone for three days. We want you to come home."

"I was on my way." He kissed his wife again. This time it was so good that she wrapped her legs around his waist.

"Yeah, right," Kyra moaned as he pulled her to the edge of the car so that she could feel his hard-on.

"Tell Daddy what's that supposed to mean." He squeezed her ass while making her grind on his dick.

She kissed him, playing and sucking on his tongue. Then went to kissing his neck, rubbing her nose up and down his neck and chest.

"You forgot we are one and the same, baby. You practically raised me, Marvin. I can taste it. I smell it. It's all in your pores, Marvin." Just then a gold kitted-out Caddy came to a screeching halt at the end of the driveway. "You ready, Blue?" That was the nickname Marvin's West Coast relatives had given him.

Kyra held on to Marvin even tighter. He checked out the

car. "Where the fuck am I supposed to ride, on the roof? Y'all niggas packed in there. And say what's up to Kyra."

"Oh, my bad. How you doin,' Mrs. Blue? What's up?" the other voices said.

Aisha's head popped up. She wanted to see all of the action. Kyra just waved at them.

"Come on, man. Let's roll out," the driver of the Caddy yelled.

Marvin looked at Kyra and Aisha. Then back at the car full of homies and relatives.

"We droppin' Skip off so it'll be room for you." Chuck nodded. "C'mon, man, you said you wanted to do this."

Kyra was massaging his back and whispering in his ear, "Don't go, baby. Come home with us. Your wife and daughter need you to come home."

Marvin kissed and hugged Kyra the way only Marvin could do. "Baby girl, I'll be home in a couple of hours. I promise." He kissed Aisha on the cheek and sprinted for the Caddy.

Kyra knew right then and there that she had lost him.

Who is this laying on my bell like this? Sabeerah reluctantly got up from her desk. She was almost finished with the new sketch she was working on. She peered out of the peephole and jumped back. The bell rang again. She peeped out again and held her breath. All she could do was stare. *Boing.* Sabeerah jumped. She then ran to the mirror and smoothed back her ponytail and fixed her shirt and shorts. She took a deep breath and cracked the door. Trae pushed it all the way open. She then watched as he stepped inside and closed the door behind him. He looked around the living room and then waltzed through the kitchen. He came out and when she saw that he was heading for her bedroom she jumped in front of him.

"What do you think you're doing?"

"Somebody back there?"

"No, but you can't just come in here going through every-thing. I don't know you like that."

"I can't tell, *Mysterious*. You end up at my hotel suite on Valentine's Day. You obviously know more than you are letting on. Tell me why I shouldn't make you disappear?"

"You knew who I was?" Sabeerah panicked.

"Not at first."

"Make me disappear? Oh my God. I swear, I was just as surprised as you were. I work part-time for an escort service and they told me the client looked through the pictures and she chose me."

"You expect me to believe that? Out of all the escort services in California, my wife chose the one you worked for and chose you? C'mon now."

Sabeerah was getting offended. "I work for the best escort service in California. You don't think your wife would choose the best? And what do you mean chose me? I am young, beautiful, smart and that is not the first time I was chosen," she snapped, forgetting that he had just threatened to take her out.

"I don't mean it like that." Trae shook his head in disbe-lief. *This shit is unreal.* "Why the fuck are you working for an escort service? Does your family know what you are doing with your spare time? How old are you? Your draw-ings are not making you enough money?"

"Who do you think you are? I am grown!" She walked to the door and opened it. "Don't come over to my house judg-ing me. For your information, I have not slept with anyone.

I just accompanied a few clients on outings and with you I was told no sex. So keep your judgments to yourself. And you can leave now." Tears welled up in her eyes. "How did you find out where I lived? Get out now before I call the police."

"You need to quit that escort service. Those dates don't always turn out as planned." He walked out the front door and she slammed it behind him.

She began ransacking her living room. "Why didn't you tell him?" Sabeerah screamed. She stopped dead in her tracks and Mysterious calmly said, "Not yet. He'll be back. Stop being a sucker. He doesn't want you. You are a geek, a nerd for crying out loud. You wouldn't know what to do with him."

"Fuck you!" Sabeerah began smacking herself. "This geek or nerd, as you call me, strategically set you up with that Valentine's date, didn't she?" Sabeerah was now foaming at the mouth.

"But you fucked that up," Mysterious challenged. "The wife was there. I couldn't even enjoy myself. The bitch wouldn't let me fuck him." Mysterious spat.

"Bitch, just leave me alone," Sabeerah said before lying down on the couch to cry.

CHAPTER TWENTY-THREE

Tasha was in the kitchen putting together a snack bag for their trip to the drive-in and wondering where Trae was when the house phone rang. "What's up, big daddy?" Tasha cooed into the phone. "Are you on your way home? Of course you aren't. Buying you a Maybach was not a smart move," she teased.

"Yes it was. I'll be there in a few. Y'all almost ready?" Trae asked.

"By the time you get here we'll be ready."

"Make me a turkey pastrami on rye. Love you," Trae told her.

"I already did and I love you more."

Tasha hung up and headed for the laundry room to put some clothes away. Concita was cooking and the kids were playing as Aunt Marva entertained two of her girlfriends. The doorbell rang and she wondered who it could be. "Auntie, are you expecting somebody else?"

"Miss Carrie said she was coming but then called and canceled, maybe she changed her mind. I hope so, we need one more spades player."

Tasha had a puzzled look on her face because she wasn't expecting anyone. She peeped out the front window and the person she saw made her blood boil. "No! I know this bitch didn't bring her ho ass over to my house!" Tasha spat in disbelief.

She snatched open the door. "Can I help you?" Tasha was having a hard time controlling the shakiness in her voice.

"Is Mr. Macklin in? I only need to drop off these files," Charli calmly stated as she pointed to a box on the ground. "Do you mind picking these up and taking them inside?"

Tasha fought like hell to remain calm. "Oh, that won't be a problem. Give me a sec, hun," Tasha said, being real fake. She then hurried to the sliding glass doors that separated the kitchen from the patio.

"Auntie, I need you to call 911 in about five minutes. Tell them that a lady just forced her way into our home and she is attacking your niece. You got that?"

Aunt Marva looked confused. "Girl, what in the hell is going on?"

"Concita," Tasha called the nanny. "Stay out here with the boys, okay?"

"Okay, Missus Macklin. Not a problem. The boys, they fine."

Tasha pushed Marva back, shut the door, locked it and dialed Trae.

"Ma, what's up?"

"Since you can't keep your bitch in check, I'm about to do it for you." She began taking off her earrings as she hurried up the stairs.

"What are you talking about?"

"Your bitch is at my front door. You thought I was playing? I warned you to handle her or I would. Ain't no way you can convince me, nigga, that you are not fucking this ho or didn't fuck her. This bitch done lost her mind over what is supposed to be mines, Trae." She ended the call and wrapped her hair up into a tight bun, greased her face up and went back downstairs.

Trae was frantically dialing Rick. "C'mon Rick, answer the phone," he gritted.

"Yeah," Rick answered.

"Rick, where are you?"

"On my way home. You ready for me to tap that ass on the pool table? Game of eight-ball, that's all I want. If you win I'll—"

"Man, fuck the game, I need you to get to my house. Tasha getting ready to whup my lawyer's ass. I can't have my wife going to jail for some bullshit. I'm on my way now. I'm about ten minutes away."

"I'm on my way too. I got you," Rick said, glad to be able to do something to help Trae.

"C'mon in." Tasha held the door open for Charli, who stepped inside, leaving the box of files on the front porch.

"Thank you." Charli smiled, feeling empowered now that she had made her way into Trae's home. "I know we got off to a bumpy start but I'm not all that bad. Maybe we can do lunch sometime."

Tasha closed the door. "I'm only going to tell you this one last time, stop calling my husband, stop buying him gifts, and don't bring yo' ass by the club, and especially on this property ever again. Do you understand what I just said?"

"Excuse me?" Charli got indignant. "Myself and Trae, we have business together. And this house? I'm the one who made it possible for you to live here." When she said that, if you could have bought Tasha for a penny, that would have been the time. Tasha couldn't even breathe or speak. But Charli wasn't done. "And the club? I arranged the financing on that. The club wouldn't even be in existence without my help," Charli said with an air of smugness. "So if you think it's any more than just business, you need to check yo husband," Charli said in a mocking round-the-way-girl voice.

Plop. Tasha's fist landed in her mouth. "Bitch, I'ma check you." She punched her again.

It was now Charli's turn to become speechless and to lose her breath. When she recovered she hauled back and slapped the shit out of Tasha. Tasha didn't blink but grabbed two handsfuls of Charli's hair and pushed her neck down, damn near snapping it, and kneed her in the face. She then hauled back and punched her in the jaw. Charli grabbed her hair this time and got a nice punch at Tasha's mouth. Just when the ladies were about to really get it on, Trae burst through the door. "Tasha, hold up." He grabbed her and swooped her clean up into the air.

Charli used this opportunity to sneak her in the face. "Bitch, now we even." She smirked.

"Ho, it's on now. We can do this. Trae, put me down so I can handle this bitch," Tasha growled. When Charli saw the look on Tasha's face she started backing up.

Rick burst through the door, almost knocking Charli over. He looked at Trae struggling to hold Tasha in the air and grabbed Charli.

"Get your hands off of me. Do you know who I am? Trae, who is this? Tell him to get his hands off of me."

"Get her out of here, man," Trae told Rick.

"No. Rick, let the bitch stay," Tasha spat as she tried desperately to squirm out of Trae's grasp.

"Rick, you got her, man?"

"Yeah. Handle your business. I got you." Trae carried Tasha upstairs into their bedroom.

"I can't believe you didn't allow me to whup that ho's ass!"

"Why the fuck would I want my wife to be fighting some bitch. Fuck her! I married you, Tasha." He finally let her go.

"Nigga, now I know that's exactly what you are doing. Fucking her. Trae, pack your shit and get the fuck out," Tasha screamed.

"What?"

"You heard me, nigga. Pack your shit and get the fuck outta my house!"

"Your house?"

She turned around and got in his face. "That's right. I *said* my fuckin' house. What? Better yet. I may leave for a couple of days to get some shit straight. While I'm gone, you better get your shit and get the fuck out of my house. Oh, no. I'm sorry. It's yo' bitch house. She ain't have no problem telling me that I wouldn't be living here if it wasn't for her. I can't believe you. We could have gotten a house anywhere. You ain't need her. Nigga, I got A-one credit. Let me refresh your memory. I'm not one of them chickenheads you used to fuck with back home. Oops. My bad. You came out here and called yourself stepping ya game up. Well, you know what? Fuck you, yo' game and that bitch. Because I don't need you."

"Tasha, what I do?"

"You know what you did! Just have your shit out of here by the time I get back." She went into their bathroom, slammed the door, and locked it. She then started breathing as if she were having an asthma attack.

CHAPTER TWENTY-FOUR

Trae was sitting in Rick's living room. They were getting blunted out. "Man, you're a detective. They don't give y'all random piss tests?" he asked Rick. They were on their third blunt as they watched Roy Jones, Jr. get his ass beat by Calzaghe.

"I'm a boss, nigga."

"So. Bosses have a boss."

"Well, I have a unique situation. I'm good. Don't worry about me. You know how lucky you are that I am who I am? That Asian chick you fuckin' with is connected. We even now, homey," Rick told him.

"Nigga, we ain't even. That's what you get paid to do, serve the public," Trae joked.

"Dude. Who you know can call 911 and request a specific officer by name and he comes running? Nobody," Rick joked. "But seriously," he said, "ole girl is *very* connected. How did you get hooked up with her?" He wanted to see how much Trae knew. But Trae didn't bite. Rick paused to take a toke. "She said Tasha *invited* her inside the house. So that means that wifey took her time and premeditated the ass-whipping. Dawg, you better not sleep on Tasha. That's the type of woman you can't sleep on, man."

"Man, I know my wife."

"I can't tell. What were you thinking fuckin' with that rich crazy and very connected bitch? I underestimated your willingness to live on the edge. Shit, I need you on my team, Rick kept prodding. "I mean, it's obvious that you love the ground your wife walks on and she worships you. Man, you know how many folks wish they had it like that? Sheeit, I hate my wife. We together for convenience. The bitch got money." Rick was watching Trae and waiting on an answer. Because they had been investigating Charli Li's law firm hoping to get something on Charles Li, which led them to Stephon, who had led them to Trae. They didn't want Charli, Stephon or Trae. They *wanted* the man himself, Charles Li.

Their attention went to the front door. Rick's wife walked in, frowned and slammed the door. "Speak of the crooked-horn devil," Rick said.

"Rick, we talked about you smoking that shit in my house." She rolled her eyes and kept going, ignoring Trae.

Rick looked at his watch. "Here this bitch comes in at almost one in the morning, no explanation, no previous phone calls, no dinner on the stove, and got the nerve to check me about smoking weed in the privacy of my own goddammed house? This bitch got me fucked up!"

"What did you call me?" his wife Rachel screamed from the stairs.

"Ohhkay." Trae stood up. "I think it's time for me to bounce."

"Naw, man. You ain't gotta leave."

"What did you call me?" Rachel screamed again as she stormed down the stairs.

"Rachel, we have company."

"I don't have shit. That's your company," she yelled as if Trae weren't standing there.

"Aiight, man. I'm out. It's time for me to get my ass home."

He gave Rick some dap. "I'll holla at you tomorrow and thanks for everything."

"Anytime, man. I got your back," Rick said as he walked him to the door.

Trae thought, *Damn, seems like everybody got issues.* He inhaled the night air before walking off the porch. Rick's house was situated in the cul-de-sac on the block and Trae's was in the middle. It was a beautiful star-filled night. The kind of night that he and Tasha liked to sit on the front porch and watch. Trae pulled the trash cans out in front of the house before going inside.

His first stop was the children's room and he was surprised to see it was empty. Anxious to find out what was going on, he headed to his bedroom. It was shut. He wasn't in there, so of course he was wondering why the door was closed.

He eased it open and breathed a sigh of relief when his eyes adjusted and he saw that the boys were in the bed with Tasha. He could barely hear her but he knew that she was crying. When he stepped all the way inside their bedroom, she raised her head up. "Get the fuck out, Trae. I told you I want you out of my house," she gritted.

"Why you got them boys in the bed with you? They have their own beds."

He saw the swift move of her arm and then a picture frame came flying at him, causing him to duck.

"Get out, Trae." She jumped out of the bed like a madwoman. "Please, just get the hell out of my house!" She tried to push him out of the bedroom. He shoved her, sending her flying onto the floor.

"Why are you trippin' like this, Tasha? We need to talk about this!"

"Talk? Trae, the only thing that has been coming out of

your mouth is lies. You know you are fuckin' that bitch, so just say it." She jumped up and tried again to get him out of the bedroom.

"I'm not fuckin' her, Tasha." He grabbed hold of both of her wrists.

"Look at you. You're busted and you're still lying. The bitch said she got you this house and that muthafuckin' club. So, you're not fuckin' her? Nigga, just get out. I can't stand the sight of you right now. Please. Just go."

"She got me this house? I didn't know the bitch when we bought this house," Trae said, obviously baffled.

"Nigga, get out!"

Days had passed by when Trae decided to return home. He had been staying at the condo that Marvin insisted that he use. Marvin said it would be stupid of him to go to a hotel.

Trae pulled up into his driveway.

"Daddy, Daddy." The boys and Aisha all ran to the truck.

"Uncle Trae, can you take us to the park?" Aisha asked him. She had on the pair of Mickey Mouse shades that he had bought for her. He stepped out of the truck with a few groceries and handed them each a Popsicle.

"What's up y'all?" He looked at Marvin sitting on the porch steps. "Aisha, you might as well move in. You're over here every day."

"Oh, can I, Daddy? Please? Please?" She looked back at Marvin as she hopped up and down.

"What about your daddy? You're just going to leave me home by myself?" Marvin asked.

"You won't be by yourself. Mommy will be there," she giggled.

"Oh, you think it's funny?" He teased her.

Aisha took off running. "C'mon, y'all." All of the boys took off running behind her as if she were the queen.

"Man, you need to have another baby. That girl of yours is too lonely."

"Her momma ain't tryna hear that. Plus you gotta get some pussy to have a baby. I ain't had no pussy in almost two weeks. I'm in the doghouse right along with you."

"Word?" Trae laughed because he was glad he wasn't the only one in the doghouse.

"Yeah. She thinks I'm gettin' high."

"What?" Trae sat the grocery bags on the ground. "Man, what makes her think that? Are you?"

"Calm down, nigga. All I had was some E."

"Nigga, c'mon now. You know as well as I do that you don't need to be fucking with that shit. What made you pop some E?"

"You don't want to know," Marvin sighed.

"That's fucked up, yo." He pointed to the limo in the driveway. "Who the fuck is in my house? The President?"

Marvin looked at him as if he were crazy. "That's Jaz and Angel in there. I forgot you and Tasha ain't speaking so I guess you didn't know that they were flying in."

"What are they here for?" He was actually surprised.

"You know what they're here for."

"What?" Trae was honestly clueless.

"To male-bash your ass! So you better watch your back, they might jump you. Your name is mud right about now and if I was you I wouldn't even go inside the house. Your ears should be burning. I told them niggas Kay and Faheem how you been living at the club."

"Damn, you got a big mouth."

Marvin started laughing.

"Yeah, those fools had the nerve to call me up and talk shit," Trae said, picking the grocery bags up. "Like they ain't ever been in the doghouse."

Both of their attention went to the black Pathfinder creeping up the block. It slowed down when it got in front of Trae's driveway. The driver-side window came down. A smiling Sabeerah motioned for Trae to come to the car.

"Ain't this some shit. Nigga, you bold as fuck. In the doghouse and got bitches showing up at the crib. Nigga, you better get rid of that ho before the clan come out here and lynch that ass."

Trae set the grocery bags back down and went over to the car. "How do you know where I live?"

"This is the era of information, baby," Sabeerah said.

"Daddy." Kareem came running over. "Who is that?"

"Aww, he is so cute." Sabeerah swooned. "Oh my God here comes another one. You have twins?" she marveled when Shaheem came running over.

"Go back over there with your uncle. What are you doing at my house?"

"I was in the neighborhood and something told me to drop by. The last time I drove by no one was out front. I see I picked a good time," she told him, oblivious to his agitation.

"Naw. You didn't pick a good time. And if you don't want nothing specific you need to get the fuck away from here and don't come back. Stupid bitch don't come to a nigga's house," he snapped and walked away from the car.

"Trae, can I talk to you?" she asked as she watched him walk away. "Excuse me, Trae. Can we talk?"

Marvin was laughing at him. "Man, look at the bitch," Marvin yelled. "I know she not getting ready to get out the car."

Trae quickly turned around and yelled, "Yo, get the fuck off my property before I call the police."

"Man, who the fuck is that?" Marvin watched as Sabeerah finally drove off.

Trae waved him off.

When Marvin saw that he was on his way into the house, he said, "I'm telling you, man, don't go in there."

"Fuck that! This is my house. I told you she only allows me to come in the mornings to be here when the boys get up and then to put them in bed at night."

"Damn, yo! So what are you doing here now? It's two in the afternoon."

"Man, fuck this shit. This is my house. All the bullshit is about to stop." He picked up the grocery bags once again and headed for the front door.

"Aiight dawg, don't say I didn't warn you," Marvin teased.

Trae was in no way prepared for what he saw. Tasha was sitting on the sofa crying and blowing her nose. Being the drama queen that she was, she was surrounded by Kyra, Angel and Jaz. The sight of the four of them together brought back a flood of memories. He couldn't help but smile.

Jaz jumped up off the sofa and gave him a hug. "You know you messed up, right?"

"And I'm glad to see you too," he told her. "What's up with my man?" He was referring to her husband and the big brother to them all, Faheem.

She snatched one of the bags out of his arm. "This is about you, not Faheem. Now c'mon, let me read you the riot act in private."

He looked over at Angel. "So you can't speak to your brother-in-law?"

"I'm very disappointed with you, Trae," she told him.

"Can I talk to my wife in private?" Trae asked.

"I'm not trying to talk to you, Trae. I already told you that. You are not even supposed to be here."

"When can I talk to you, Tasha?"

"Trae, just leave me alone and get out of my house."

Jaz yanked him into the kitchen before he could say something. She gave him a hug. "Damn, Trae. Why I gotta visit under these circumstances?"

"You need to talk to your girl, Jaz. She is blowin' this shit all out of proportion."

"Nigga, you fucked a bitch and the bitch put you on Front Street. So how is she blowing it all out of proportion?"

"Damn, if you would shut the fuck up I'll tell you."

"You fucked up, Trae. Why you creepin' out on your wife? You really disappointed all of us and you really hurt Tasha."

"Front Street?" Trae went back to that.

"That's what Tasha said. The bitch told all your business."

"Tasha is exaggerating," Trae said as he put the groceries away.

"Jaz, Tasha said come here, she wants you now," Angel burst into the kitchen and announced as she rolled her eyes at Trae. She then left back out.

"Angel," Trae called her, only to be ignored.

"I'll be right back. I gotta see what my girl wants." Jaz left Trae standing there in the kitchen.

When Jaz walked back into the living room, Tasha snapped, "We were getting ready to hear about Kyra's problems and you run off to go fraternize with the enemy."

"That's right," Angel said.

"C'mon, Tasha. That's my nigga. I haven't seen him in ages. I only wanted to say hi." She rolled her eyes at Angel.

"You saw him at the club's grand opening so fuck him. Kyra

here has been holding back. I could sense that something was the matter but she was trying to cover it up. So tell us, Kyra. What's really going on?"

Kyra admitted, "It makes me sick, just thinking about it. Now you want me to tell it, which only means that I have to face it."

"Get it off your chest," Jaz told her.

"Please," Angel snapped.

Kyra rolled her eyes at Angel. "Y'all the same ole impatient bitches from years ago. Some shit never changes."

"What?" everyone asked.

"Anyways, Marvin is getting high. He keeps denying it but I know he is. There. I said it." She looked around at the startled faces on her girls.

"Off what?" Jaz shrieked as she held her hand over her heart.

"Dope," Kyra responded. "Y'all know what he likes."

"This news is fucked up," Jaz said.

"You ain't lyin'," Angel added. "These niggas done got out here in Hollyhood and lost their minds. Maybe y'all should never have left New York."

"Kyra, why didn't you say something?" Tasha wanted to know.

"Because"—she started crying—"he keeps denying it and I haven't figured out what to do." The three of them rushed over to her and hugged her. "I swear I don't know what to do. But give me some time. I will figure it out. And y'all don't say anything to your husbands. Not yet, okay?"

Trae walked past the girls all hugged up, crying, and had no understanding. He wanted to ask Tasha for few minutes of her time but decided not to. He went back outside on the front porch with Marvin.

Marvin looked at him, saw the expression on his face and said, "I told you not to go in there."

Trae watched the kids slide down the sliding board and Caliph enjoying the ride on his motorized SUV. He decided to call Kaylin.

"Yo," Kaylin answered.

"Man, you ain't even tell me your wife was coming up here. Why you ain't come with her? Subject me to all this bullshit by myself. I wouldn't have left you hangin' like this."

"I told you Lil' E and Lupe Black is getting ready to drop. One of us needs to be here. As a matter of fact, Red needs to get her ass back here. Dawg, I heard you creepin' around on Tasha and got caught? What's going on out there? Let me find out Hollywood is a little too fast for a city boy."

"It ain't go down like that, nigga. Why none of y'all fools listening to me? You know what, I'll talk to you when I see you."

Kaylin laughed. "Damn, nigga. You creepin'? And you got caught? That's fucked up."

"Aiight, man." Trae hung up frustrated. He then turned to Marvin and said, "Nigga, I'm out of here."

An hour later he ended up at the club and was sitting in Stephon's office. Stephon practically lived there. This was now his life. "Trae, what's up?"

"I'm trying to figure it out now. What's up with Charli, man?"

"What do you mean?" Stephon stopped the money-counting machine and turned around to face Trae.

"How did you hook up with her?"

"Man, I told you, I was out here on my grind, doin' what I do best, matching buyers and sellers, and this dude Marshall introduced us. Ever since she been respecting my hustle and sending shit my way. Why? What's up? You didn't give her the dick, did you? Say it ain't so, nigga."

"What did she have to do with the house we in?"

"I found out through her that it was available. Why? What did she tell you?"

"She ain't tell me nothing, man. She told your cousin. Aiight." Trae stood and went to give Stephon some dap.

"Hold up. What she tell Tasha?"

"It ain't important, man. I gotta go." Trae walked out. He had to go somewhere and figure this shit out.

CHAPTER TWENTY-FIVE

Kyra was doing laundry and cleaning up. She had already washed four loads and had one left. The last load belonged to Marvin and it was a pile of jeans. Kyra looked at the mountain and sighed. It looked more like two loads than one. "I gotta get a maid like yesterday," she said out loud, and began going through his pants pockets pulling out money, lottery tickets, mail, more dollars, his American Express card and something she didn't want to see. Kyra opened the foil and smelled the substance before sealing it back up. She then backtracked and went through all the pockets again. Went through all of his jacket pockets, dresser drawers and so-called hiding places, finding a little over a bundle of heroin.

Next thing you know she was on the phone. She couldn't dial Marvin fast enough.

"Marvin, bring your ass home right now."

"Baby girl, I'm at the club. They got me waiting on the deliveries. What's up?"

"I need to talk to you, Marvin. Get somebody else to wait on the deliveries."

"Nobody else is here."

"Fine. I'm on my way." She slammed the phone down, snatched up her keys and purse and was out the door, not even realizing she had dope squeezed in the palm of her hand until she got in the car.

"Shit," she said as she grabbed the steering wheel and the dope fell to the floor. She picked it up and tossed it into her purse. Pulling out of the driveway she saw that the gas tank was on E. "Kyra you got to get it together. Old baggage obviously needs to be dropped. It's not good to go backwards," she said out loud. She would tell herself this over and over again until she reached a gas station. Grabbing her purse, she got out to prepay and to get something to drink. Feeling somebody staring at her she looked back.

Detective Rick was smiling at her. "Kyra, what are you doing on this side of town?"

"I live over here, remember? What's your excuse?"

"I'm on duty, remember?" He flashed her that sinister grin. Today his locks were hanging loose.

"No. I can't say that I do. I don't know your schedule." He was dressed like a thug in Air Force Ones, jeans sagging off of his ass, wife-beater, platinum chain dangling around his neck and fitted cap turned backwards. "You don't look like you're working to me, Eric." She was now standing in the checkout line. Lots of ladies said that he reminded them of Eric Benét, so he knew she was teasing him.

"It's Rick, not Eric. I look better and sing better than Eric Benét."

"Yeah right."

He was now right up on her. When she went inside her purse to get the money to pay for the gas he saw the dope.

"Next in line, please," the young Indian kid said.

"Put forty on pump ten and give me a raspberry-apple Vitaminwater."

"That'll be forty-one fifty."

"Let me get that for you," Rick offered.

"I got it," Kyra said, feeling his body heat.

"Don't let that nigga take you down, Kyra. You're too good for that. And get rid of that shit in your purse."

"Why? Are you are going to arrest me, Detective Bryant?"

"No. Because I know it's not yours. And since your eyes are red and swollen I'm guessing that you were crying mad when you came across it and stormed out of the house to confront your man. Like I said, be careful and don't let that nigga take you down. You're too good for him."

"How do you know that? You don't know me and you don't know him."

"Well, tell me otherwise. Go ahead, I'm listening." Kyra didn't say anything as he paid for both of their purchases. "I didn't think so. I'll take you and make you mine before I let that nigga take you down." He leaned over, kissed her on the cheek.

When Kyra got to her car she sat inside staring into space for about five minutes. When she looked up Rick was standing there.

"Other people want to fill their tanks up too." She looked at him as if to say, "I don't give a fuck." He started laughing. "C'mon, lil' mama, follow me. You look like you need to relieve some stress." He went and jumped into a white-on-white Chevy Tahoe.

Like a robot, she followed him. Twenty minutes later they pulled up in front of a brick house in Long Beach. Rick got out and came over to Kyra. "This is my mother's house. I've been trying to get her to move for years. But she won't. She teaches fifth grade in the school down the street." He opened Kyra's door and grabbed her hand. "C'mon, get out."

"I'm not going to meet your mother, Rick. Look at me. I been doing housework all morning."

"Girl, my mom isn't home." He practically yanked her out of the car and dragged her up the front steps.

A nosey neighbor came to her door. "Rick? Is that you?"

"Yes, Mrs. Henderson, it's me."

He hurried up and opened the front door to let Kyra in. "That woman will talk you damn near to death." He breathed a sigh of relief.

Kyra's eyes looked around the living room. Yes, this was definitely the home of a senior citizen. Knickknacks such as saltshakers, banners from Rick's football games, baseball game paraphenalia and his drawings were everywhere. When she moved to go look at the pictures on the wall he pulled her toward the kitchen.

"Awwwww, you were so cute."

"Don't worry about that. Let me show you around." He showed her the entire house, holding on to her hand the entire time. He saved the guest room for last. When he took her in there, he pulled the door closed behind them. "This used to be my room. I used to sneak a lot of girls up here."

Kyra smiled. "Is this what you're calling yourself doing? Sneaking me in your room?"

"Yeah." He looked at his watch. "My moms will be home in an hour. Can I have a kiss?" The attraction had been there since the first day they met. And with all the bullshit Marvin had been on lately Kyra needed a good fuck. Hell, she wanted one. Matter of fact, she thought she deserved one. He picked her up, stood her on the footstool and kissed her before she could answer.

"What do you think you are going to do with me in an hour?" Kyra kissed him back.

"Whatever you allow me to. We have forty-five minutes to be exact," he said as he began unbuttoning her shirt and kissing her neck.

"Put me down." When he lifted her off the footstool, she stepped back and began to undress herself, letting him know that she was all for this. He began doing the same thing, but not before placing the two burners he had on the dresser. She glanced at the guns and realized that his bad boy demeanor turned her on. "You are tall, dangerously and forbiddenly sexy."

He licked his lips as his eyes admired her dark, huge nipples that were now poking out. He smiled. "And you are very short, extremely and make-a-nigga-wanna-kill-somebody sexy. Wait until I stick this dick inside of you."

"I'm looking forward to it," she whispered.

"Is there anything else you like about me?"

"I like your body and all of those muscles. I want to grab on to your dreads. But more than anything I want to find out if underneath all of that tough-cop shit if you are nothing but a sweetheart." She now stood there naked.

"A sweetheart?"

"Yeah, a sweetheart."

"I'll be a sweetheart only to you." He was now standing there butt naked and placing a condom on his hard dick. He then pulled the covers back off the bed and Kyra came over and lay down. He immediately got on top of her and began sucking her sweet dark nipples.

"We don't have much time, Rick," Kyra told him.

He spread her legs, put one of them in the crook of his arm and entered her. Kyra moaned, sending shivers up and down his spine. *Damn.* He really wanted to take his time and enjoy this, he thought to himself as he went in deeper. She was so hot, tight and wet. His knees buckled as he got his grind on nice and slow. It was obvious to him that Kyra had found her spot, because her eyes were shut tight and she was trying to get all the dick she could. Unlike his wife, Kyra was enjoying herself. After a few minutes, to his surprise, she was coming. She waited until her breathing slowed down before she opened her eyes and smiled at him.

"That was a nice appetizer."

"Turn over," he ordered. She did, raising that ass and pussy up in the air as if it was a challenge. He grabbed on to her hips and slid his dick in as deep as it would go, trying to knock the bottom out. She grabbed a pillow and bit down into it. "You want to get fucked like this?" Rick whispered in her ear.

"Ohhhhh, yess. Just like this," Kyra cooed back. "Harder, baby. Hurry and *make* me come again."

"I'ma *make* you mine, Kyra," was the last thing he said before he nutted inside of her and she came again as well.

"Damn I needed that," Kyra said as she closed her eyes and went to sleep.

CHAPTER TWENTY-SIX

Kyra took her time driving to the club. It was later than she had thought. After getting busy with Rick she had dozed off and it felt as if she had been asleep for hours when it was only minutes. They exchanged cell numbers and joked about leaving a public gas station and going straight to the bedroom. She left right as his mother was pulling up. Rick actually had her shook. She thought about how earlier today she had been steaming mad at Marvin, but now she felt sorry for him. She used her code to get into the club entrance marked PERSONNEL. She knew Marvin was watching her every move on the security monitors. The staff was busy getting ready for the night. They were sweeping, mopping, buffing and restocking. But what caught her attention was the young lady painting a mural of people dancing. The painting sucked you in. Kyra stopped and watched the girl whiz with the brush in her hand.

The girl reminded her of Tasha as she rattled away on her Bluetooth not missing a stroke. The girl definitely had skill and Kyra was mesmerized by how fast she worked. Kyra walked over to where she was and stood next to her. The girl smiled and kept talking.

When she ended her call Kyra asked, "Where are you from?" Kyra had noticed that she had an accent.

Sabeerah held out her hand with the paintbrush for Kyra

to shake. Realizing what she was doing she giggled. "Oops, sorry about that. My name is Sabeerah. My parents are from Haiti, and I've been over here since I was six. I just came from New Jersey. I got accepted at UCLA."

"Really. That's great. What part of New Jersey?"

"Newark."

"Newark! Get out of here. That's our old stomping grounds! Small world."

"Aiight, let us allow you to get back to what you do." Marvin walked up on them and interrupted as he led Kyra away.

"Nice meeting you, Sabeerah," Kyra told her.

"Same here." Sabeerah turned around and went back to painting.

"Where did y'all find her?" Kyra asked Marvin.

"Trae found her the day we took you out to the college. She was out there selling her art. She kept calling the club until Stephon finally got tired of her and he gave her some work."

"Ummph." Kyra smirked, full of skepticism.

Marvin wrapped his arms around her waist and kissed her on the neck. "You know you feelin' her work. She is known as Sabeerah, the artist. She's the one who did that big picture of Tasha. But before I forget, I gave Trae the keys to the condo."

"The condo? Trae has a house. What does he need with the condo?"

"He's family. Where else is he supposed to go? I ain't sending the nigga to no hotel. I'm tired of seeing him sleeping here at the club. Tasha kicked him out, remember?" Marvin said as he held the door to his office open for her.

"Then he's supposed to be sleeping at the club. Y'all niggas got out here and done lost y'all fuckin' minds," Kyra snapped.

"What is that supposed to mean?" Marvin barked.

Kyra went into her purse and pulled out the dope. She held it out for Marvin to see.

"Where did you get that from?" He tried to snatch it out of her hands but she moved away just in time.

"You know exactly where I got it from."

"No. I don't."

"Oh my God. Marvin, baby. This is me you're talking to. I'm not against you, baby. I'm not your enemy. And you know I'm not stupid. Baby, I know you are using. At first I didn't want to believe it but I know you are."

"Kyra, c'mon now."

"C'mon nothing, Marvin. And you're slipping up leaving the shit around. What if Aisha would have found the shit, Marvin? Huh? Answer me, nigga."

"Kyra I am not using. I may dabble in a little E every now and then but that's it."

Kyra sighed as she slumped down into the chair in front of his desk. "I never would have dreamed that in this point of our lives we would be having this conversation." She looked across the desk at Marvin, who was now sitting down. They had been through thick and thin together. After they had gotten their lives together and had stopped using, he had been her strength.

"Marvin, you need to choose."

"Choose?"

"You know what the fuck I'm talking about." Kyra went into her purse, snatched out one of the packages of dope, and tossed it at him. "Me and Aisha or that shit. You can't have both." She stood up and went for the door.

"Wait, Kyra."

"Me and Aisha or the dope, Marvin. If you're not ready to admit that you slipped, then I don't want to hear shit you got to say."

"Where do you think you're going, Kyra?"

"I'm going to pick up our daughter and then I'm going home." She stormed out and left him sitting there.

Kyra had ended up at Tasha's house. She was planted on the love seat in her bedroom trying to act as if everything in her world were lovely. But Tasha knew better.

"Kyra, you look awful. You might as well get it off your chest because you know I know you," Tasha said to her best friend as she stood in front of her with her arms folded.

"Tasha, I am so scared." Kyra revealed. Tasha grabbed some tissue off of the end table next to the love seat. She then grabbed the remote and turned down the Jennifer Hudson CD.

"Get if off your chest, Kyra," Tasha told her, waiting patiently as Kyra wiped the tears that were streaming down her cheeks. "To have to live without Marvin in my life, I am scared shit-less. We've been together over ten years. We've made it a habit to depend on each other and to have each other's back. But now, I don't give a fuck. I'm ready to up and leave him, Tasha. I refuse to let him take me down that road again."

"I honestly don't know, Kyra. Try something first. Shit, both of y'all are family. Maybe put his ass in rehab and see how that goes."

"How am I supposed to do that? He won't even admit that he's using, Tasha. I threw the dope right in his face and he still wouldn't admit it." Just then Tasha's house phone rang.

"Get that. It's probably Trae. I don't want to talk to him right now," Tasha told her.

"Hello."

"Hi, is Trae home?"

"Who's calling?" Kyra asked with her face all twisted up.

"Who is it?" Tasha snapped.

Kyra put her hand up, motioning for Tasha to be quiet. "Who is this?" Kyra prodded.

"Sabeerah. I'm looking for Trae, is he available?"

"No, he isn't. What can I—"

"Thank you." Sabeerah hung up.

As soon as Kyra placed the phone on the receiver it rang again. Kyra snatched it up on the first ring.

This time she looked at the caller ID and it was Rick.

"Hello, Mrs. Tasha, is your husband available?"

"This is Ms. Kyra. Who is this?" Kyra stood up and walked out of Tasha's bedroom.

"Kyra? Damn, this is my lucky day. You all right? Can you talk?" Rick asked.

"For a minute. What's up?"

"I wanted to thank you for this afternoon. I regret that everything happened kind of quick, but I still wanted to thank you. I'm still sailing off that shit."

"You're welcome." Her frown was now turned into a smile.

"But check it, I'ma take you from him, watch."

"I don't think you can do that."

"Why not?"

Kyra sighed before answering. "Rick, I just got done fucking you and now I'm over here crying about Marvin and our shaky-ass marriage. I don't know. Do you remember that O'Jays song 'You Got Your Hooks In Me'?"

Rick smiled. "Yeah, I remember it."

"Well, he got his hooks in me. I'm having a hard time walking away from him. Even worse, I feel like I can't and that's scaring the shit out of me."

"Don't sweat it. I got that," he assured her.

Kyra laughed. "Oh, it's like that?"

"Kyra, you keep forgetting that I'm the king. But listen, I'm in the middle of something and I need to speak to Trae. Is he in?"

"No he's not."

"I gotta run. Can I call you later? Better yet, can I see you later?"

"You can call me. I'll have to see about the other thing."

They both hung up.

"Who was that?" Tasha was standing right behind her.

"Tasha, not now, okay." Kyra went and sat back down on the love seat. Her eyes went to the lifelike picture above Tasha's bed.

"That's fucked up. Something is up with you and you won't even tell me," was all Tasha kept saying. "I know it was some nigga." Tasha snatched up the phone and checked the caller ID, fumbling through the numbers. "Who called my phone, Kyra?"

"Do you know the girl that did that is working at the club?" she asked, wanting to change the subject.

"That did what?"

"That picture over your bed."

"What?"

"Yeah, I met her earlier. She's a college student and, get this, she's from Newark. She is the one who just called. We need to check that whole situation out because the shit is suspect to me."

"What? She called here? What did she want, Kyra? Why

didn't you let me talk to her? Don't answer my damn phone anymore. I can't believe you didn't let me talk to her," Tasha spat. "What are you thinking?"

"Chill, Tasha. It could be nothing other than her checking in. Because she is working at the club. But then again there's no such thing as a coincidence."

"What does she look like?"

"She reminds me of you." Tasha shook her head in disbelief. "And," Kyra continued, "did you know Trae is living in that last condo we bought?"

"He's living in it?"

"Yeah, Marvin's ass said he got tired of seeing him sleeping at the club so he gave him the keys. His ass probably didn't want Trae to see him getting high." Kyra looked at her watch. "I gotta get out of here. I got some homework I haven't even looked at." She stood up. "Thanks for letting Aisha stay over all of the time. You don't know how much I appreciate it."

"Her little grown behind might as well move in. She tried to talk me into letting her spend another night." Tasha ratted her out.

"Oh yeah? She didn't even ask me. She can forget about it." Kyra forced out a smiled. "Oh, and guess what else?"

"What?"

"I was at the gas station and Rick was there. He said he'll take me away from Marvin before he allows him to take me down," Kyra said, purposely leaving out the part about her sleeping with him.

"What? How did the conversation move to Marvin?" Tasha wanted to know.

"He saw the dope in my purse and knew it wasn't mine."

"How did he see the dope, Kyra? Why are you carrying

that shit around? That's stupid, Kyra." Tasha was clearly agitated with Kyra.

"I needed it to confront Marvin." Kyra felt like a child being chastised.

Tasha sucked her teeth in disgust. "Go dump that shit in the toilet right now." Tasha stood there with her arms folded across her chest while Kyra immediatley got up and did as she was told. When Kyra came back into the bedroom, Tasha said, "Now regarding Rick, don't get any ideas, the nigga is married. Now the same way you said you feel weird about the chick that drew this painting, I feel the same way about Rick. So we both need to be on point and on guard. Do we have a deal?" Kyra didn't respond. "Kyra, do we have a deal or what? Don't fuck with him. I saw his number on my caller ID."

"I heard you, damn," Kyra mumbled.

"Now why was that chick at the club?" Tasha had to backtrack.

"She's painting a mural."

Just then Trae eased the bedroom door open to both Tasha's and Kyra's surprise.

"What are you doing here?" Tasha snapped.

"I live here, remember? What the fuck you think?"

"What's up, Trae? Tasha, I'ma grab your little babysitter, Aisha, and be on my way." Kyra could sense that things were about to get ugly, got Aisha and left.

"This is my house, you are my wife and *we* do have a family."

"You obviously never told that to the Asian bitch you creepin' with." Before Tasha could turn around good he had snatched her up around the neck.

"Daddy, Daddy." He was interrupted by their three sons,

who were running through the bedroom. He let Tasha go and ran both hands over his face.

"Get your shit and leave." Tasha was relieved that she had probably just escaped an ass-whupping.

"How long do you think I'ma put up with this shit?" Trae gritted.

"How long do you think I'ma put up with your bitches coming by and calling my house? Who is Sabeerah, Trae?"

"Sabeerah?"

"Yes, Sabeerah."

"She's the girl I hired to do the painting."

"Nigga, the ice you are skating on is getting thinner and thinner," Tasha said before she stormed out of the bedroom.

Marvin looked at his watch. It was almost noon. He hadn't been home all night. It was a homey's birthday party and he had been invited. After it was over they had just hung out. He took another hit of his demon and swore it would be the last time. "Fuck cocaine," he mused. "Heroin is a helluva drug."

Lo nudged him, interrupting his nod. "Man, cut that phone off or answer it. You got the shit turned up too damn loud."

Marvin felt around, finally finding his phone. "Yeah," he answered.

It was Kyra. "Daddy, when are you coming home? I have a surprise for you." She sounded very jubilant.

Marvin thought that he was hearing things. "Baby girl, Daddy loves you no matter what."

"I love you more. Come on home to your baby girl," she cooed. "How soon can you get here?"

Marvin stood up. "I'm leaving right now."

"Promise?"

"Right now." He ended the call.

"Gotta get that ass home, huh?" Lo was preparing to take a hit.

Marvin looked around at his shoddy surroundings and shook his head in disbelief, trying to figure out what had caused him to backslide. "Yeah, it's time for me to head on out."

"You comin' back later, right? Smoke and 'em gonna be here." Rok was sitting in the corner smoking crack.

"I'll be here," Marvin said.

"That nigga ain't coming back. You hear how weak he sounded?" Lo teased.

"I'll check y'all out later." Marvin gave them both dap and headed out the door.

"You leaving?" MiMi asked as she blocked his way.

"Yeah, my baby girl wants me to come home. I'll catch y'all later." He gave MiMi a hug and went out the front door.

When he pulled up into his driveway he fought the urge to take another hit. He fingered the packet in the ashtray and decided to leave it there. He got out of the car and went around back.

He entered the house through the back door. Kyra's back was to him as she sat in the kitchen chair. Her head was back as if she was asleep.

"What up baby girl? Daddy's home." He stepped in front of her and his heart felt as if it had dropped to his feet.

Her eyes popped open and she smiled at him. "This is what you wanted, right?" Her eyes closed and her head rolled to the side.

"What the fuck are you doing, Kyra?" he screamed as he yanked the syringe out of her vein and untied the cloth she had tied around her arm. But her whole body started convulsing and she went limp.

"Kyra," he screamed out, tears running down his cheeks. He picked her up and ran up the stairs into the bathroom and turned on the cold shower.

Trae was in his temporary condo. Marvin had it set up like a bachelor's pad. It had only the bare necessities. Ever since he had been staying at the condo he hadn't been able to sleep. He was now sitting on the couch in the dark trying to figure out what was happening with his life.

He froze when he heard a car pull up into the driveway. He glanced at his Bulgari and saw that it was ten minutes to one. His burner was on the coffee table next to him. He grabbed it and then put it down. His heart filled with glee when he heard heels click up the walkway.

"Tasha," he mumbled. "My baby misses me." He jumped up and went to the front door. As soon as the bell rang he opened it with a huge smile that instantly turned into a frown.

Charli pulled open the screen door and waltzed right past him. "Hello to you too."

Trae stood there in shock. *This bitch. How in the fuck do she know where I rest my head?*

Her flowery perfume filled the room, which only made him angry. He wanted to smell Tasha's perfume. "Charli, what are you doing here? It's one in the morning."

She gave him a smug look as she slid the shawl she had draped around her shoulders off onto the couch, revealing a skimpy blue silk strapless dress. The matching bag she set on the coffee table. "Why else would I be here at one in the morning? It was all good when I was swallowing your kids. It's always business with you. I make you millions and you can't even show me a little bit of appreciation."

"What?"

"You heard me. I want to be shown a little bit of appreciation."

"Oh, I'm supposed to fuck you, just because." Trae came across the room in one fluid motion. "You don't know who you fuckin' with do you?" He had one hand planted firmly around her neck. The other one was pulling up her dress. He tossed her around and pushed her over. "This is what you want, right?" He spread her legs roughly as she tried to stand up. He pushed her back down and pulled out his dick. "Naw, this is what you wanted, right? You want to be appreciated, right? What daddy's little girl wants to feel appreciated?"

"Ouch...wait. Not so fast," she moaned. He was already inside of her banging against her tight walls. She was tight as hell, but Trae didn't care, he wasn't trying to enjoy the fuck. *Maybe now she will leave me alone.* He knew that was wishful thinking. *This bitch got the nerve to be throwing it back at me.* This was only making him madder and his dick harder. When she started coming he pulled out of her and pushed her onto the couch. He watched as her body trembled and legs shook before putting his dick back inside his sweats. *Bitch.*

When she had first walked in not a hair was out of place. Now it was covering her face as she slowly got up off the couch. "Why are you so angry?" she asked, out of breath.

"You got some dick. What else do you want?" He went to the front door and opened it, letting her know that it was time to go.

"I can't believe you. Your club is going to be raided and"—she paused and got her clutch bag and pulled out a check. Trae looked it over. It was for 270,000 dollars. "Before you say anything, I know it's short. But give me some time."

"Short is an understatement. Bitch we talking eight million!" Trae was beginning to foam at the mouth. "Charli, don't fuck around with my money."

"Calm down. You aren't the only one who came up short with this last deal. We all did."

"Charli, eight million? You got me fucked up. I suggest you get on the phone and talk to your father or see whoever it is you gotta see and get me my fuckin' money."

"I am. Give me a few days." She waltzed by him and left.

CHAPTER TWENTY-SEVEN

"Trae, I have a meeting at four-thirty. Concita had an emergency and Marva went on her bus ride. It's almost three, can you get here in half an hour?" Tasha pleaded as she swallowed her pride.

Trae was at Marvin's condo that Marvin allowed him to use. It was only fifteen minutes from his house. He was on his way out to meet up with Rick to see if he could stop this raid bullshit.

"Trae, are you going to answer me?" Tasha rolled her eyes. She hated the fact that she had to call on him. But an emergency had come up only minutes ago. "Trae!" she snapped. "Are you there?"

"I'm here. It's just that you kicked me out my house, won't speak to me, won't even talk to me about our situation, but now that you're in a jam, who do you call?" He was trying to sound pissed but he was actually enjoying himself.

"C'mon Trae, these are your kids as much as they are mine."

"Then how come I can only come by in the mornings to get them up and at night to put them to bed? Don't be talking that yours-just-as-much-as-mine bullshit."

"Because I will never deny you the privilege to see your kids just because we are beefing but I am angry with you and I honestly can't stand the sight of you. Now are you coming to pick them up or what?" she snapped. "I need a babysitter."

Trae put a smirk on his face. "What's in it for me?"

"What do you mean what's in it for you?" Tasha asked in disbelief. "What do you want? You want me to pay you to watch your own kids?"

"Of course not, I want forty minutes with you. That's it."

After several seconds, Tasha said, "Fine, Trae," and hung up.

Trae laughed out loud, grabbed his keys and headed over to pick up his kids. They would just have to ride with him while he talked to Rick.

"Don't do this to me, baby. No, not now," Marvin cried as he placed Kyra's limp body in the bathtub and turned on the cold water. "C'mon, baby girl, snap out of it," he pleaded. He felt for her pulse and got nothing. "God, no. Please!" he screamed out. "No. No. No." He began pumping down on her chest and giving her mouth-to-mouth. "God, why? Take me instead." He gave up and began praying. Shortly afterwards, she started coughing and choking, and then she vomited.

"That's it baby. Get it out. Get it all out." He held her trembling body upward, watching her hurl. Once she finished he said, "C'mon baby. Let me get you out of this cold water." He was filled with glee as he snatched a towel off the rack and then lifted her up. He wrapped her in the dry towel and held her tight. "Why, baby girl? Why would you do this?"

"This is what you wanted, right?" She looked up at him sounding like that innocent girl he had snatched up when she was fourteen. "I thought it was what you wanted," she cried.

"Nooo, baby." He squeezed her. "Hell no. You should have known better than that."

"Then stop it, baby. Stop it," she sobbed.

"Okay, baby."

"You promise?"

"I promise."

The following day Trae was having a staff meeting of his own. Since Charli and Rick had both put a bug in his ear that a nice amount of E and heroin was moving out of Club New York, what he really wanted to do was bust some heads. But since Rick had said he would handle it, he would settle on talking some shit.

Everyone was seated on the dance floor with confused looks on their faces. Trae was the only one standing up and it was obvious that he was livid. Stephon had never seen this side of Trae, but Marvin had. He was the only one out of the bunch who wasn't nervous.

"I know y'all must be wondering why we are sitting here on a Tuesday morning. Well let me get straight to the point. How long have we been open, Steph? Ten or eleven months?"

"Twelve months, fourteen days," Stephon answered.

"Twelve fuckin' months and already we've been put on the radar for the place to cop some E and dope," he spat, allowing his words to sink in as he looked around the room. Every one of these niggas was suspect to him, including Marvin and Stephon. There was a little grumbling and mumbling but Trae didn't give a fuck. "Now check it out. I don't have a problem with the next nigga trying to eat. Shit, I hustled just about all of my life but I'm done. I barely escaped with my life and a life sentence so I'll be damned if I'ma let any of y'all muthafuckas pull me back in. And on top of that I ain't gettin' a cut? Y'all got this nigga here fucked up. So, this

is what I'm gonna do. I'ma keep it gully with y'all muthafuckas. Especially since we are supposed to be on the same
team. I'ma give y'all a heads-up. Don't fuckin' deal out of my
club. Now, if we get raided and they find some shit in here,
I'm looking forward to makin' an example out of every one
of you muthafuckas. Meeting dismissed."

Trae was so mad he only wanted to get to the condo and
chill out by himself. Here he was facing a possible raid at
the club when he was really trying to be legit, he had just
lost eight million dollars fucking around with Charli and his
wife had put him out.

The first thing he did when he walked in the door was
pour him a shot of Hennessy and turn on CNN. He listened
as they hyped up the presidential inauguration. He watched
as Barack Obama got off an airplane. He had a hell of a
swagger as he came down the steps. *A brother gettin' ready
to move in the White House. I would have never thought it.
Didn't they know that everything was already decided? This
was America, land of the Illuminati. They controlled everything and the masses didn't have a clue.* His dad's words
rang in his ear.

Trae turned off the TV and lay in bed looking at the ceil-
ing. All he could do was laugh at his current situation. Since
he was a little guilty, he was allowing Tasha to get away
with this bullshit. Yesterday her stubborn ass had called
him again. This time it was to drop the kids off at the day
camp. He told her it was gonna cost her another twenty
minutes of her time. But her slick ass was dodging him. He
hadn't been able to get a minute with her, let alone forty. He
knew she was ducking him on purpose. She was a master
at that shit.

Finally, he ended up dozing off with Tasha heavily on his

mind. He even had a wet dream about her and right before he busted a nut he woke up with a massive hard-on. Somewhat disappointed, he looked around realizing he wasn't in his bedroom, and Tasha wasn't in his bed. It only pissed him off. Here he was sleeping in another house, waking up with a hard-on, and her ass was fucking dildos. When he was at the house the other day he had seen the box sitting on her bed. When he opened it and saw what it was he threw it in the garbage and dared her to say something about it. He knew she did that shit on purpose. Just to fuck with him. But he had something for her. He was paying her a visit first thing this morning.

He got up, showered, dressed, and headed on over.

When he walked in the front door she yelled, "Twins and Caliph, your daddy is here to take you guys to your swim class."

Damn. Trae had forgotten all about that.

"Daddy." Caliph came running towards him, his sneakers untied. Tasha was not far behind him. She looked as if she had just gotten out of the shower. She was wrapped in a short robe and a towel was wrapped around her head. She was carrying a saucer of sliced cucumbers and a glass of white wine. She was barefoot. Trae bent down to tie Caliph's sneaker and when Tasha came by he grabbed her wrist. Caliph ran back out of the room.

She looked down at him and then at his hand on her wrist and frowned. "What do you think you're doing?"

He stood up and wrapped his arms around her waist. "You owe me forty minutes, remember?"

She felt his dick immediately stand at attention. But she couldn't do anything with a saucer of cucumbers in one hand and the glass of wine in the other. "I remember, but you can't get them now. I'm getting ready to give myself a facial and sit in some steam," she said haughtily.

"Too bad. You always got an excuse. I don't give you excuses for when you need me to pick up the boys, now do I?"

"They're your boys."

"You owe me forty minutes, Tasha. And I want them now."

"C'mon, Trae. What about later? I got the house all to myself, I would like to relax."

"You can relax after I get my time." He led her over to the sofa. "We're going to sit right over here and I'ma get my forty minutes. *Then* you can do whatever it is you gotta do."

"The boys, Trae. Their class, remember?" She smirked.

"Nice try, Tasha. But we got time. They're out back with Auntie."

Tasha sucked her teeth. "Okay, okay, let me set this stuff down." When she bent over to set the dishes on the glass table, Trae rubbed his dick all on her ass. "You can let me go now. You have my attention." He turned her loose and she flopped down, crossed her legs and folded her arms across her chest. She made no attempt to hide her nasty attitude.

"You can pout all you want. I'm getting my forty minutes." He sat on the glass coffee table in front of her, straddling her legs.

They sat there looking at each other. Trae had on a wifebeater, shorts and a pair of tan Gucci sandals. His bald head was shining and he smelled fresh and clean.

"Okay, talk," Tasha snapped in an attempt to get her mind off of how good he looked and smelled, and how much she actually missed him.

"Talk?" He slid his hands up her thighs. When he got to her ass he pulled her up close to the edge of the sofa, catching her by surprise.

"Trae, what do you think you're doing?"

"I'm getting my forty minutes, that's what I'm doing." He leaned over and began kissing her softly on the neck.

"Trae, we are supposed to be talking." She tried to push him away.

"Talk? I never said anything about talking. I said forty minutes of your time, right?" She didn't respond. "Right?"

"You think you are so slick. You didn't have to say *talk*. But that's what I took it to mean, Trae."

"A deal is a deal, Tasha. You owe me forty minutes."

"It's thirty-five now."

"Aiight. Thirty-five then." He gently uncrossed her legs. "This morning I had a dream that I was all up in this pussy. My dick was so hard it woke me up, hard just like it is now." He took her hand and placed it on his dick, rubbing it up and down.

"Thirty minutes," Tasha snapped, mad this joint was feeling good.

"Five minutes didn't pass that quick." He untied her robe and saw that she had on only panties. He gazed at her nipples and then began to play with one and suck on the other.

"Trae, no. This is not right," Tasha's voice squeaked.

"Oh, it's right. Thirty minutes, remember?" He skillfully lifted her up, slid off her panties and eased her back down. He spread her legs a little wider and began massaging her pussy.

"Trae, no, the kids." Tasha was shaking her head and trying to move his hand.

"They're out back."

"But I said no, Trae."

"No what? Thirty minutes." He stood her up and began eating her pussy.

She half tried to push him away. "No, Trae. I'm supposed

to be mad at you. Oh, God, don't make me feel good, baby." His tongue was causing tingles to shoot from her head down to her toes.

"Why not? This is still my pussy."

She looked down at him and his face was all into her pussy. She wondered how he could talk and eat her at the same time. She grabbed onto his head as her knees began to buckle. He always made her come so quick when he went down on her and she tried to fight it, not wanting to give him the satisfaction.

"Mommy, Mommy."

They heard the kids running towards the living room. Trae sat Tasha down and closed her robe. She had tears rolling down her cheeks. He wiped them away as she wiped her juices from around his mouth.

"I told you the kids, Trae."

Aisha made it to them first. The twins and Caliph were on her tracks. "Aunt Marva said we ready," she announced.

"Do you live here now?" Trae asked her.

"No," she giggled. "I spent the night."

"Daddy, we ready," Kareem said.

"Daddy is talking to Mommy. Aisha, tell Auntie and Concita I need them to take y'all."

"Okay," Aisha said. "C'mon y'all, and don't run." Aisha led the troops back out and had the nerve to be running. They all took off behind her.

Trae looked at Tasha, leaned in and began to kiss her. She was trying to break away from him.

"A deal is a deal," he reminded her.

She didn't say anything and kept giving him her cheek to kiss. "Ten minutes," she said.

"Nah, it's more than that. You not gonna give me a kiss?"

She shook her head. "Aiight then." He slid his dick out of his shorts and pulled her up to the edge of the sofa. Then he lifted her up into his lap.

"My glass table, Trae," she protested as he put his dick into her soaking wet pussy. "Oh, God, I hate…you. My table…breaks, Trae. I'm mad…you. Oooh, this feels good."

She was skipping her words as he dicked her down. "No. Wait." Pissed that it was feeling so good, she tried to convince him to stop pounding inside her pussy and making that rod hit all of the right places. The angrier she got, the better it felt. When she started coming her legs went to shaking and she kicked the full wineglass over.

Trae planted kisses and hickeys on her neck as her body calmed down from that early-morning and much-needed orgasm. When Tasha realized how tight she was holding onto him it was too late. Trae had wrapped her legs around his waist and was already digging deeper into the pussy.

"No, Trae. Umm, um." She unwrapped her legs and managed to get off the dick.

"What?" Trae snapped. He was ready to put in some serious work and here she had climbed off the dick, leaving it standing long and stiff at attention. "C'mon, baby. My time isn't up." He went to lift her up onto his lap.

"I said no, Trae." She stopped him. "Do you love her?"

"What?" he asked in disbelief.

"Do you love her?"

"Who?"

"That bitch, Trae. You know damn well who I'm talking about."

"C'mon, Tasha. We had this conversation already. You know damn well I'm in love with you and you only. Shit, you and everybody else know it."

"Then why, Trae? Tell me why you were fuckin' her." She sat back down, crossed her legs and crossed her arms across her chest waiting on a response. She waited as he fixed his shorts and picked up the wineglass. "Trae! Stop being so damn bullheaded and tell me why or just get up and leave."

"For thirteen million, Ma," he mumbled.

"What?"

"For thirteen million."

She gave him a cold stare, then she hauled off and smacked the shit out of him. "Thirteen million fuckin' measly dollars! You mean to tell me that's all me, your kids and what we *had* was worth to you?" she screamed as she stood up. "You stupid son of a bitch! I hate you."

"What do you mean, what we *had*? We still got it."

"Get out, Trae." She pushed him and he grabbed her. She tried to break away and they struggled, falling back onto the couch, where he pinned her down.

"Get off of me and get out." She was now crying.

"I'm not going anywhere. I admit, I fucked up. If I could, I'd go back and undo it. But at the time I was sure that was the best thing to do, Tasha. We got all of this money and it needed to be cleaned up. And that's all I was concerned with. It was business only. I swear, Tasha."

"Don't swear, Trae."

"Tasha, I'm swearing on Shaheem's grave. C'mon, baby. Can't you forgive me at least one time? I fucked up and I'm sorry. Forgive me baby." He kissed her on the cheek and hugged her tight.

"Get off of me, Trae." She tried to fight him off of her.

"Forgive me." He kissed her again. "Please."

"I can't believe you did that. Sold us out for thirteen million measly dollars."

"I'm sorry, baby. I admit that I fucked up but I thought it was the best thing to do at that time."

"Fuck a bitch was the best thing to do?"

"To get the second deal through. That's what she wanted."

"Second deal?"

"Yeah, for eight mil." He wouldn't dare tell her that he had lost eight mil.

"What, next it will be one mil? Then a thousand? I swear, I should have killed that ho."

"You did enough, Tasha. I can't have my wife sitting on death row."

"It would have been the best thing to do at the time," she mocked him. He bit down on her cheek. "Owww. Shit! Trae, that hurts," she gritted.

"Don't be smart," he warned her.

"Get off me, Trae."

"You gonna forgive me?" He bit down on her cheek once again. This time harder.

"Owww. Okay. Okay. Please. I forgive you."

He released his teeth and looked down at his handiwork. Tasha breathed a sigh of relief as she rubbed her cheek.

"Why do you keep hurting me, Trae?"

"Stop talking crazy, Tasha." He kissed her on the lips.

"I'm not talking crazy and let me up."

"Yes you are. Give me a kiss first."

"No," she spat. "Let me up."

"Not until you give me a kiss. I mean that shit. We can lay here all day." She reluctantly pecked him on the lips. "Naw, a real kiss. Kiss Daddy the way he likes to be kissed."

She obeyed and did just that. "Now get off of me."

"Mmmm. That's what I'm talking about. Give me another

one." Next thing you know Trae had spread those legs and was all up in the pussy once again. After she came he turned her over and hit it from the back, causing her to get two more orgasms. By the time he turned her loose she was dizzy, and had forgotten why she was mad at him.

Almost an hour and a half later they stood up and looked around the living room. Her panties were on the floor, her robe was strewn over the sofa, the towel she had had on her head was on the floor. The wine had dried up on the coffee table and the carpet. Trae's shirt and boxer shorts were tossed to the side.

Tasha headed up the stairs, leaving Trae to clean up the mess. When he arrived upstairs he smiled because she was in the bed. *I knocked that ass out*, he said to himself.

He walked over to the bed and sat down. He leaned over and kissed her cheek. "Can I take you out tonight?"

The house phone rang. Tasha checked the caller ID: it was Kyra. She didn't answer, but instead Trae picked up the phone and handed it to her. "What time will you be here?" Tasha asked her.

"I'll call you when I'm on my way over."

Tasha passed Trae the phone to hang up.

"Where y'all going?"

"Hair appointment."

"You already washed your hair."

"No, I didn't. That was a cholesterol treatment."

"Can we go out tonight or what?"

"I'll let you know."

"What's that supposed to mean?"

Tasha smiled. "What part of *I'll let you know* don't you understand?"

"Oh, so it's like that?"

"Sounds like your kids are home, Trae. Can I take a quick nap please?"

"You got a lot of shit with you. I'm moving back in."

"No, you're not."

"Why not?"

"Because I like it the way it is. I've gotten used to it."

"I don't give a fuck. You better get unused to it. I'm moving back in." He left out of the bedroom.

Tasha was too worn out to argue. She pulled the covers over her head and dozed off.

About two hours later, Tasha was climbing into Kyra's truck. Kyra did a double take. Tasha had on dark shades, her hair was up in a ponytail, and she was glowing and looking totally relaxed as she leaned back in her seat.

"Why are you looking at me like that?" Tasha asked.

Kyra hit the speakerphone button and dialed Angel.

"What's up?" Angel answered.

"Get Jaz on the three-way."

"Hold up." Angel clicked over.

Kyra looked over at Tasha and smirked.

"I got her," Angel said. "So what's up? Everything okay?" Angel was alarmed.

"Kyra, I've been calling you. Where have you been?" Jaz asked.

"It's a long story that I don't feel like sharing right now. But I had to call and let y'all bitches know that it's time to pay up."

The car was quiet until Angel said, "Oh, shit, she let him back in?"

"I don't know if she let him back in but she got some dick."

"How do you know?" Jaz asked. They were talking about Tasha as if she weren't nowhere around.

"This ho so worn out she can't even talk. She's laid back in the seat with dark shades on, hickeys all over her neck and a bite mark on her jaw." Kyra started laughing. "Plus she got that look that says 'I just had some boss dick.'"

"Aw, Tasha. I thought you were tougher than that. I thought you would have at least held out for ninety days." Jaz was really disappointed.

"Y'all bitches bet on me?" Tasha snapped.

"Hell, yeah," Kyra said. "And I won."

"I knew I shouldn't have taken you up on this bet. You right there with her. You probably told her to fuck him just so you could win," Angel snapped. "I can't believe I got suckered."

"Oh, stop being a sore loser. I didn't have to tell her shit. Once the cat needs to be scratched a bitch gonna get it handled. Now y'all can PayPal my dough by tonight." She turned off the speakerphone and looked at Tasha. "So how was it?"

"Fuck you, Kyra." Tasha leaned back and looked out the window.

Kyra started laughing.

When they pulled up in front of the club, Tasha said, "Don't turn the car off, I'm not getting out, and hurry back. You're going to make us late."

"Okay, this will only take a minute. Marvin didn't bring his ass home last night so I'm getting ready to bust him in the mouth." She jumped out of the car.

Several minutes later, Trae came out carrying Caliph. During the daytime the kids hung out with their fathers at the club. He knocked on the window for Tasha to roll it down.

"Mommy," Caliph said. "We are going to the park."

"To the park? Sounds fun. I love you," she said to her baby.

"Give your mother a kiss," Trae told him. Caliph hugged his mother and kissed her before Trae put him down.

"Why didn't you come upstairs?" He leaned over and got him a juicy one on the lips.

"Because we have to get to our appointment."

"Yo, Trae." Stephon came out the front door. "Come get your boy Marvin. He and Kyra are up there fighting."

CHAPTER TWENTY-EIGHT

Sabeerah had dragged her girlfriend Zina to Club New York. Her intentions were to show off her new mural as well as get a chance to speak to Trae, especially since Zina didn't believe that Sabeerah worked at the same club that she had seen on BET. Three and a half hours later, Sabeerah had given up.

"Who is that?" Zina squealed. Her excitement obvious. "He is foine."

Sabeerah's heart skipped a beat as she looked to see who Zina was talking about. "Don't even think about it." She tried to appear cool but couldn't. Sabeerah hadn't expected him to show up with the wife. "That's the wife," Sabeerah gasped. "Shit, I can't let her see me here."

"Oh my God," Zina drooled. "He is divine."

"Bitch, he is also off-limits. Start packing everything up. I need to get out of here. I have to go change and meet a client later," Sabeerah lied and was crushed as she stood behind Zina and watched as everyone rushed up to the offices.

"Bitch, please, I know you. She is not paying you any attention. She probably doesn't even remember you. So chill out instead of chickening out." Zina laughed and shoved Sabeerah in his direction. "Go say something."

"You ladies need to pack it up." Big Grip, the security guard, walked up on them and startled them both.

"What's going on?" Sabeerah snapped.

"That's none of your business. Go ahead and pack it up."

"I need to talk to Trae. He has another job for me. Can you tell him to come here for a minute?" Sabeerah pleaded.

"You can't talk to him now. Talk to him the next time you come."

"But I've been trying to. He hasn't been here and it's not a sure thing he'll be here when I come the next time." Sabeerah was adamant.

"Don't know what to tell you. It's not my problem. You got three minutes to pack up your things." He stood there crossing his arms across his chest, letting them know that he wasn't going anywhere.

Zina was rushing but Sabeerah was now taking her time. Her personality had switched up that quick. She was getting that more often since she had stopped taking her medication. Now she was disappointed that she wouldn't be able to get a few minutes with Trae. Even though she didn't know what she was going to say to him, Mysterious was dying to come out and make her presence known.

"Let's go, ladies."

"All right, all right. I'm coming." Sabeerah packed up her remaining supplies and they headed for the door. Big Grip was right behind them.

Trae and Tasha had barged into the office and if any fighting was going on, Marvin was the one who looked as if he was getting his ass beat. His lip was busted and his buttons were popped off his shirt. "Yo, I need y'all to give us a minute," he said.

"No!" Kyra yelled out. "I want them to stay. Tell them how you are getting high again, Marvin." She put him on blast.

"Kyra, shut the fuck up. Trae and Tasha, can y'all excuse us please?"

"I said no. Y'all stay here. Tell them, Marvin. Tell them," she was so pissed she broke down crying. "He doesn't want me to help him, y'all. He's ruining our family. What am I supposed to do if he won't let me help him? I'm trying not to leave him because he never left me. But enough is enough."

Tasha ran over and hugged her. "C'mon. Let's go and talk, Kyra." Tasha was pulling her away.

"That's the real reason I have Aisha staying with y'all. I don't want her to see him like this," Kyra yelled out. "She's not stupid. She's very smart, Marvin. Your daughter knows her father has changed."

Tasha led her out of Marvin's office.

"Dawg, you told me you had some E a couple of times. I wanted to believe you," Trae said.

"But now you don't?"

Trae sat down, not taking his eyes off of Marvin, who was cleaning the blood off of his lip. "Am I supposed to ignore what Kyra just said? You are using again." Trae had been in the streets long enough to know the signs. But he had to admit Marvin hid his shit well. And when you didn't want to see it, you didn't see it. Plus, he couldn't help but recall the times they were supposed to go and take care of business and Marvin had been nowhere to be found.

"Yeah, man. It ain't nothing I can't handle. Kyra just blowing shit all out of proportion."

"Man, she's concerned. And you know better than anybody that ain't no such thing as *it ain't nothing you can't handle*. It is what it is."

"I told you man, I got this," Marvin barked at Trae.

"Yo, we niggas, Marv. Talk to me, man, or else I'm gonna be very insulted."

"Nigga, I do a little snortin', that's all. Damn," Marvin confessed.

"Damn, man." Trae shock his head in disbelief. "How the fuck you hide that shit so good?" Trae wanted to know.

"Niggas get high and tweak. My tweak is hidin' the shit."

"I never see you in a heroin nod." Trae couldn't believe this shit.

"That's because I nod in private. I don't do that shit in front of everybody."

"Yo, that's crazy, man. You moving anything out of the club?"

"Naw, man. Where you get that from? Your detective friend?"

Trae stood up when Kyra and Tasha came back in.

"Marvin, if you don't go to a rehab, I'm leaving you. I'm taking Aisha and we are gone."

"Where did that come from? Tasha? You left out with her for a few minutes and now you're talking about leaving." He was now blaming Tasha.

"Tasha? I didn't have to convince her of anything. You're doing this to yourself and blaming everyone else. You forgot that I know you, Marvin? I know y'all's history. I was there the first time. Shit, don't get me started," Tasha snapped. "You know damn well that Kyra is like my sister, and I consider you to be my big brother. But you are making her very unhappy and I am worried about you. You got too much positivity around you and going on in your life to fuck it up on some dope."

"You need to choose, Marvin. And I'm giving you until tonight. C'mon, Tasha, before I put my foot in this nigga's ass again."

The ladies left out, leaving the two men standing there.

* * *

"Trae, call this chick back. She has been blowin' the phone up," Stephon said.

"Who?"

"The girl doing the murals."

"What girl?"

"The girl I hired to do the murals," Stephon said, realizing that he had never told Trae about her.

"If you hired her then why is she calling me?"

"Because she said she is doing sketches for you."

Trae though about Sabeerah. "When did you hire her?"

"Several weeks ago. She kept calling and hanging around until I got tired of her ass."

After thinking it over Trae told himself, *I didn't tell her where I worked.* "Why did you hire her to do a mural without checking with me first?"

"I didn't know I had to check with you. The bitch was persistent, plus since she said she already did some work for you, I didn't give it a second thought. What's up?"

"It's just that she been calling the house, she came by the house and I didn't even tell her where I lived or worked."

"Well damn, you obviously got a stalker."

"What do she want when she called?"

"She wants to talk to you. And now I see why she hasn't been back around to finish what we hired her for. She wants you to be here." Stephon figured it out.

"What the fuck is the matter with this bitch?" Trae mumbled. His sixth sense told him Sabeerah needed to be dealt with and fast. *Man, I shouldn't have listened to Bo and did that bitch a long time ago. Fuck!* Trae thought.

"Hello. Anybody home?" Stephon called out to Trae. "Dawg,

there is something that you are not telling me about this girl. Come on now, what's up?"

"Shit, I don't know but I'm about to find out."

"Here are all of her messages." Stephon handed them over to him. "Now, let's get to today's top agenda. Game or no game?"

"Game, nigga. That's a no-brainer. The nigga is LA's next best thing since Death Row."

"Naw, it's not a no-brainer. All them young niggas and gangbangers. We gonna have to get extra insurance, extra security, and we gonna have one hell of a headache. Plus I don't want my shit fucked up. We'll most likely have to renovate the joint all over again," Stephon joked.

"We'll discuss it in detail later. Shit, we need to be worried about the fuckin' club being shut down," Trae reminded Stephon.

"They ain't going to find nothing. I've been listening to these niggas. You got them shook."

"It's too late. We already on their radar, Steph. I don't know why you don't understand that shit. Me and Marvin got a past and the Li's? They on a whole different level. Trust me, it ain't all good. You lettin' this Hollywood bullshit go to your head."

"I ain't worried about it. I'm legal. The club is legal," Stephon told him.

Trae then went back to thinking about Sabeerah. *This bitch is starting to gnaw at me.* He tossed all of her messages in the trash except for one and called her up.

"Hello," the groggy voice answered.

"This is Trae. I'm returning your calls. What's up?"

"Oh." Sabeerah perked up. "I just wanted to tell you your other painting is ready."

"What?"

"Your other painting. The one of your wife and the kids."

"Damn, I forgot that I even gave you that picture. It sure took you long enough."

"Well I told you I was in school and you wanted me to do the murals at the club, remember? Thank you for the extra work."

"Don't get it twisted, I didn't want you to do a mural at the club, that was my partner, but since you brought it up, when are you going to finish it? My people are getting concerned and thinking you on some bullshit." He wanted to get her to talking.

"I'm not."

"I'm not what? On some bullshit or going to finish the job?"

"I'm not going back there. What if your wife sees me there?"

"My wife?" Trae frowned. "What does she have to do with anything?"

"I don't want her finding out about me and you. But if you continue to act the way you have been, I will have to let her know about us." Sabeerah started laughing. "It's bad enough that Mysterious knows. I have a hard time dealing with her. But add your wife to the equation? I had to duck her out the other day. As a matter of fact, you can come by and pick up your portrait because I mean it when I said I'm not stepping foot in there again." She instantly changed up and was making no sense to Trae.

"Hold up. Hold up. You can't just leave the job half done."

"I am. Did you know that bouncer was very disrespectful and that he practically threw me out the last time I was there?"

"What bouncer?"

"Don't act like you don't know who I'm referring to. That

big one! I don't know his name. But it doesn't matter, I'm not coming back. I need my money so please come and pick this up today!" She hung up the phone.

Trae looked at the phone in complete puzzlement. "This bitch is crazy." He replayed their conversation over again in his mind. *Something ain't right and I need to know what it is.*

Trae arrived at Sabeerah's apartment around seven-thirty. He knocked on the door and was about to kick it down when she opened it.

"Sorry for taking so long. I was expecting you. When you talk about telling wifey, that usually makes y'all niggas act right," she greeted him as she held the door open for him to come in. It looked as if she was packing to move. "Don't mind the boxes. I got some more of my stuff sent from home. As you see, I still haven't unpacked. Can I get you something to drink? I just made some fresh lemonade. It's the bomb. Have a seat, let me get you a glass." She rushed off before he could answer.

He looked around at all the boxes she had. The majority of them were marked BOOKS or ART SUPPLIES.

She came back with the glass. "Have a seat." She handed it to him.

Trae looked around. "You joking, right?"

She laughed. "All you had to do was move this box right here." She went over to the futon.

"Mind if I take a look around?"

"No, make yourself comfortable. I need to jump in the shower." She stood there staring at him. "Are you going to taste my lemonade or what?"

"As soon as you tell me you're going to come and finish the job you started, yeah."

She rolled her eyes. "You need to talk to that bouncer dude."

"I'll talk to him. Even though I don't know which one you're talking about." He finished the glass of lemonade in a few gulps. "A little too sweet for me."

"I had to put a little extra sugar in it to cover up my secret ingredient." She took the glass from him. "Have a seat."

Trae moved a couple of boxes and sat down. "Did you quit that escort service?"

Sabeerah rolled her eyes at him. "I don't work for an escort service."

That was the last thing Trae remembered as he woke up in a candlelit room. He was naked with a sheet over his body. Sabeerah was lying next to him smiling as she rested on her elbow, while with the other hand she drew circles on his chest.

"I knew you loved me," she whispered. Trae tried to sit up, but flopped back down. "It will wear off. It's an old Haitian remedy. The only side effect is a light headache but other than that you'll be okay in a few."

"Fuck," he spat. He sat up successfully this time and swung his legs around so that he was sitting on the side of the bed.

"You were great. Even though the dick was only half hard. I came *all* night. I really needed that. Let's hope we made us a baby."

"A baby?" He turned around and started choking her. She gasped, fought and tried to scratch him off of her. Right before she was about to pass out, he caught a glimpse of the drawing on the nightstand next to the bed. That's when he let her go.

"What the fuck is this?" He got up off the bed and picked up the drawing. It was a sketch of him looking up at her as she stood on the balcony. "You bitch." He looked over at her. "You still got a copy of the tape?" She was still coughing but managed to shake her head.

"Why the fuck did you draw this then?"

"It's...what...I do," she gasped.

"Where are my fuckin' clothes?" *My burner?* He began looking around the room. His gun was lying on top of the television. There were several other pictures of him on the wall. He was snatching them down. When she handed him his clothes, he smacked the shit out of her, causing her to flop across the bed. She cried as she watched him get dressed. He snatched up his burner and stuck it in his waistband.

Then he dumped out a box and put every sketch of himself he could find in it.

"Don't take my favorite one," she pleaded.

"Any more pictures of me and my family around here?" She obediently got up and opened a drawer and gave him three more. "Bitch, you are sick. So you knew who the fuck I was all this time?" he asked in disbelief. "What's stopping me from snapping your neck right now?"

"You're not sure if I have another tape of you," she said as she backed up into a corner.

He stood over her, debating whether to take her out now or wait. Deciding on right now he called Rick. Rick owed him one and he needed him to wipe clean his mess.

Rick had Kyra's back against the door in his bedroom. Her legs were wrapped tight around his waist and she was riding his dick as if it were the end of the world. She had sneaked out of the house, leaving Aisha with Marvin. Some-body was blowing Rick's phone up and it was pissing Kyra off, she was seconds away from busting another nut when he stopped grinding into her pussy.

"Ungggghhh," she groaned. Holding on to him tighter.

"Duty calls, baby. Give me a minute. Yeah," Rick screamed into the phone. "Who is this?"

"I need something handled, now."

He recognized Trae's voice. "Now? I'm in the middle of something. I can't get free for another hour."

"Yo, I need something cleaned up."

Rick was silent. "Damn, man. Tonight of all nights?" Rick spat as he looked into Kyra's eyes. He was feeling the shit out of her.

"Nigga, I didn't say that to you when them niggas was getting ready to bust you a new asshole." Rick closed his eyes as Kyra nibbled on his ear and was clenching her pussy muscles around his pole.

"Okay, okay, give me the address." Rick gave in.

Trae gave him the info and hung up. He looked over at Sabeerah, who was still cowering in the corner.

He pulled out his burner and mashed it against her temple. "I'ma ask you one time. How many copies of that tape do you have?" Sabeerah started screaming and he hit her in the head. "Bitch, I asked you how many?"

"It's just one. Please. Please don't shoot me," she pleaded.

"Then where is the tape?"

She jumped up and ran to her closet. She frantically pulled out boxes until she got to the red one. She tore it open, rummaged through it and held it out for him. He punched her in the face, causing her to fall backwards onto the bed. He tossed his gun to the side, snatched up a pillow and did his damnedest to smother her to death. She fought violently as she tried to breathe. Her arms and legs flapped wildy. "Crazy bitch!" he spat as he raised up the pillow. He tossed it to the side, revealing a dead Sabeerah with a shocked expression on her motionless face.

He threw the tape into the box along with the drawings and went into the living room. He lit a blunt and waited for Rick.

By the time Rick got there and cleaned up Trae's mess and Trae got in his Maybach the clock read five-twenty a.m. "Shit." He had just gotten back tight with Tasha and now this shit had happened. "Why the fuck is all this bad karma coming my way all at once?" he asked himself out loud.

When he finally pulled up into the driveway, it was a little after six in the morning. Tasha was sitting on the porch swing. Caliph was asleep in her lap. She had a blanket over him.

When his foot touched the steps Tasha said, "That must have been a baaaad bitch to keep you out all night and make you not answer my calls."

"Shit," he gritted.

"Just so you'll know. Two can play this game."

"Tasha, it's not what you think," was all he could tell her. *Shit.* He wondered what else he could possibly say. She didn't even know about the murder he had done in broad daylight in Jersey. What could he tell her now? That he was drugged and raped, and then had committed another murder?

Tasha got up with Caliph in her arms and left him on the front porch.

CHAPTER TWENTY-NINE

Marvin was sitting on the edge of the bed pleading his case to Kyra. He didn't want to go to rehab and he definitely didn't want to lose his family.

Kyra had all of the windows open and was busily going about cleaning up and rearranging the bedroom. She was vacuuming and dusting as if Marvin weren't sitting there.

"Kyra, are you even listening to me?"

"Marvin, just because you have been sitting around the house for the past three days don't mean shit to me. My ultimatum still stands. And the deadline came and went. Either let me check you in tomorrow or I will begin packing me and Aisha's bags. Now move, Marvin, you've been in my way all morning."

He stood up reluctantly. "I'm clean, baby girl, that's all I'm saying."

"Marvin, you've been sitting around the house for three days. So what? Tomorrow or else! Now this conversation is no longer open for discussion."

"Baby."

"Marvin!" she snapped.

"Okay, okay, but at least let me be here for my daughter's birthday party Sunday. Baby, don't make me miss that. I can go check in the next day," he pleaded.

"I'll think about that. But in the meantime the grass needs to be cut and get the pool cleaned. And answer the phone, please. Damn, y'all niggas can act like kids sometimes," she mumbled to herself.

He glanced at the caller ID and handed her the phone. "It's Tasha."

"Marvin, tell Aisha I said to put some clothes on, cut that TV off, and help around the house or help you cut the grass. What's up, girl?" she spoke into the phone, not skipping a beat.

"I don't know," Tasha mumbled through tears. "I don't know what to do, Kyra. I do know that I can't allow him to walk all over me and not do anything. I ain't built like that."

"What happened? What are you talking about?" Kyra asked.

"I can't even figure out what happened to us. Now he's staying out all night," she sobbed. "And he had scratches on him."

"Aww, man, Trae. What was his excuse for staying out all night?"

"He said it was some business and shit went bad and because it did, he has to go to New York for a couple of days."

"Why does he have to go up there?"

"I don't know. And honestly I don't want to know."

"So that's all he said? What was your reaction?"

"He tried to talk me into coming and getting in the shower with him."

"Did you?"

"I told him that he knows that I know that he already showered at the bitch's house. I said, you done fucked some other bitch all night and now you think you're going to come home and fuck me?"

"So what happened next?"

Tasha sucked her teeth. "He made me get in the shower with him and afterwards he fucked me until I fainted. When I got up I fixed him breakfast."

Kyra giggled. "Stupid bitch. You *showed* him didn't you?" she teased.

"Kyra, I'm serious."

"Tasha, your ass wasn't mad last night, so why are you bitchin' now?"

"Oh, I'm mad as hell. His ass is going to feel exactly what I felt as I sat on that fucking swing all night. I would have never thought I would see the day a Chinese bitch could come steal my shine. It must be the money. Trae has become obsessed with stacking his dough."

"When is he leaving?"

"I'm taking him to the airport in a few."

"Mmm-umm, umph. I don't know what to say about you two."

"Mommy, we ready." Kareem came barging into her bedroom, followed by Shaheem, Caliph and then Trae.

"I'll talk to you later, Kyra."

"I'm sure you will." Kyra hung up.

"You packed my bag, right?" Trae asked.

"It's right there, Trae." She pointed to the bag by the closet.

He noticed that her eyes were puffy as she walked past him, headed for the bathroom.

"I'll be ready in a few minutes," she told him as she shut the bathroom door.

Trae looked at the bathroom door, back at the kids and back at the bathroom door. He turned on the TV. "I need for y'all to sit here and watch TV while I talk to Mommy. Okay?"

"I'm ready to go," Shaheem whined.

"We're going to go after I talk to Mommy. Stay here and don't get up," he warned.

"Yes, Daddy."

When he opened the bathroom door Tasha was standing at the sink dabbing her face. He closed the bathroom door behind him.

"Give me a minute, Trae."

"Why are you crying, Tasha?" She wouldn't say anything. "Tasha, I asked you why are you crying?"

"Because."

"Because what?"

"We are not the same. It's not the same with us anymore. That magic that we had is gone."

Trae stepped up behind her and wrapped his arms around her waist. "What do you mean the magic is gone? Tasha, you know I love you with every breath I take and even when I stop breathing, I'ma love you," Trae told her as he tried not to get choked up.

"You used to, Trae. Not anymore."

"You know that ain't true." He kissed her neck.

"Then why are you cheating on me? I saw them scratches. I didn't put them there. What am I not doing?"

"Baby, I swear I am not cheating on you. I had an incident. That's all I can tell you. Trust me on that." They were both looking at their reflections in the mirror.

"Come on, Trae. What am I not doing?" She melted inside his embrace. "I love you, Trae, but you got me second-guessing myself, making me feel like I ain't pretty enough. Like I ain't sexing you right. What did I do to make you treat me like this?"

"Baby, you're doing everything and I love you now more than I did before." He was easing her sundress up over her hips. "I love you and I don't want anybody else. You're all I need. Why do you think you're my wife? Please, baby, trust me. I know I fucked up. But I love you, girl. You are my world." He moved her thong to the side. "Let me hit this real quick before I hit the road."

"No, Trae. You don't love me. You love that bitch. Why do you think that you can fuck all of our problems away? Just leave me alone. I need to work this out by myself and with myself."

He was already inside of her. "I'm not fucking our problems away. I can't help it if I love to fuck my wife."

Her eyes were now closed and she was holding on to the sink.

"Open your eyes and look at me. Look at us." He stroked her nice and slow as they looked at each other in the mirror. "Just like this pussy belongs to me, this dick is all yours. Something serious came up the other night. Trust me, baby, I wasn't cheating on you." He began to thrust faster.

She reached back to pull him in deeper. "Why...oh, God, why?" Her eyes rolled back in her head as she threw the pussy back at him and he was banging up against her spot.

He yanked her hair. "Look at me." He had a smirk on his face as he stroked long and deep.

"Baby, why?" she moaned. "Why do you make me feel...oh, shit. Right there, baby."

"Where? Here?" He wouldn't let up on that G-spot. "Here?"

"Yesssss, baby," she squealed as her knees buckled and she began to come. He couldn't hold back anymore as they both embraced a gut-wrenching orgasm.

CHAPTER THIRTY

Trae was called to New York for several important meetings. He thought he was going to find out good news and enjoy himself, but the trip was far from enjoyable. All of his meetings were negative and he was now wondering could shit get any worse. For starters, he and Kaylin were paid a surprise visit by Don Carlos. Trae was blasted in a very calm and collected way about his blatant disrespect in dealing with Charli Li after the dons had requested he didn't do so. Kaylin was sure the meeting was all about Trae until the dons mentioned that Papi and his moms could have been handled a little better. Overall, that meeting was not good.

Trae then had to break the news to Kaylin, Bo and Omar that he had had to do Sabeerah because she was getting out of hand. Of course they were not feeling that and it caught them all by surprise. Bo ranted and raved the most before coming with some news of his own. Word on the street was that Magnificent's people were coming to Cali for Trae. They did see him on BET's *Black Carpet*. Bo didn't think they were smart or bold enough and since the beef was so old and it was just talk. But to be safe he suggested that Trae tell Tasha so that she could be on point or talk about the possibility of them moving.

Now back from New York, and to make matters worse, Trae was sitting in his driveway in his truck. Marva had told him that Tasha had done something with his Maybach. She didn't know what. Now he was pissed that Tasha wasn't home and contemplating hitting the streets. He had been blowing up Kyra's phone but couldn't reach her either and figured he would call one more time.

"Kyra, it's me."

"I know your voice, Trae. What's up?"

"Damn, girl, where y'all at? I'm looking for Tasha. She's not answering her phone and she was supposed to pick me up from the airport. I've been home since seven and it's damn near midnight. Was she with you?"

"No, and she hasn't called me all day. I spoke to her yesterday and that was it," Kyra told him.

"She didn't say anything to you? At all?"

"No. Where are the boys?"

"They are with her. My aunt and Concita are here and they haven't heard from her either."

"I don't know, Trae. I don't know what to tell you. But I'm sure she'll call you before she calls me."

"All right then." Trae hung up. He was trying not to worry. But hell, it was after eleven and neither he nor anybody else had heard from his wife or kids. Tasha wouldn't even answer her cell phone.

Kyra dialed Tasha's cell. "Hello," Tasha answered on the first ring.

"Girl, he is going to tap that ass."

"Girl, please. Trae is not going to hit me. That is if he wants to keep breathing. Why? What did he say?" She smirked.

"It's eleven, you're not home to greet Daddy with his slippers, blunt and sucking his dick where you belong."

"I know he didn't say that," Tasha snapped.

"Of course he didn't say it, but that's what he meant. He's just trying not to panic. You know he is Mr. Cool, Calm and Collected but I could imagine him wiping the sweat beads off his forehead."

"Oh, well. I want him to see how it feels."

"Girl, he is seeing it and the night is not even over. I love it." Kyra squealed in glee.

"I'm doing this for me. Me and the boys got us a suite, we've been swimming, watching movies, and they are having a ball."

"Aisha is going to kick your ass if she finds out about this little trip. You've betrayed your niece's trust."

"Don't tell my little helper, Kyra. If I would have brung her, my payback wouldn't have had the same effect."

"I know. I'm just teasing you. Let me go. Marvin is calling me. I am so sick of him hanging around the house."

"All right. I'll call you tomorrow."

"Peace."

By one that morning, Trae was beginning to lose his mind. By five he had lost it.

Marva was an early riser. She came out on the front porch. "You might as well go on to bed, Trae. That girl and them boys are okay. She's just giving you a taste of your own medicine."

That statement hit Trae like a ton of bricks.

Marva saw the expression on his face change. "You know I'm right. Go on and get you some sleep. And be truthful with your wife." She went back into the house.

Around three that afternoon, Trae called her cell phone and when her voice mail kicked in he said, "Tasha, you made your point so you can stop playing these silly-ass games, put my kids in the car and bring your ass home."

Kyra was laughing as she listened to the last of the voice mail. "Girl, you are going to get it. I've never heard him that mad."

Tasha clicked the voice mail off. "Please. He got me fucked up."

"Just make sure you're here for Aisha's birthday party," Kyra reminded her.

"Girl, we already got her gifts."

"What did you get her?" Kyra asked, as excited as if the gifts were for her.

"None of your business."

"Come on, Tasha. It's not my birthday."

"My point exactly. I'll see you Sunday."

"Yo, get your tail from between your legs, dry your tears, and get your ass over here. Your wife and kids just stepped through the door." Marvin was giving Trae the 411.

Aisha's party was jumpin'. Both sides of Marvin's family were there, Crips and Bloods. They had SpongeBob, Dora the Explorer and Ben 10. Kids were swimming, playing and running around. The grown-ups were dancing, getting their drink and smoke on, playing dominoes and cards, and having more of a good time than the children.

Tasha had on a pinstriped black-and-white bikini with a matching sarong. The Prada sandals adorned her manicured toes. Her hair was up in a ponytail, allowing the diamond earrings to blind onlookers.

"Yo, man, I'm telling you. You need to get over here quick, these niggas are drooling all over your wife," Marvin told him.

"I'm en route right now, what you want me to do, fly?

Let me speak to her," Trae barked. He could hardly contain himself. Here he had to talk to her about her life possibly being in danger and here she was performing fuckin' disappearing acts and playing mind games.

"Chill out, dawg. Just bring your ass over here. You know how to handle it. Your wife and kids are fine." Marvin hung up as Tasha spotted him.

"Uh-oh. Here comes my spades partner right now," Marvin yelled. "Come over here, Tasha."

"Marvin, I am not being your spades partner anymore. I told you that."

"Why not?"

"Partners don't betray one another."

"What I do?"

"You know what you did."

"I ain't do nothing." He grabbed her and hugged her. Then gave her a big ole kiss on the cheek. "Please. Pretty please."

"Tasha, be his partner. He's been talking shit to everybody about how unstoppable he and his partner is," Loose said. "I thought you was a nigga."

"I don't care. I know you called your boy and told him I was here. Didn't you?" She was daring him to lie.

"Not yet."

She mushed him in the face. "You liar. You failed my test again."

Marvin started laughing. "C'mon, sister-in-law. I've been waiting on you." He pulled her by the wrist, leading her to a chair. "Loose and MJ, I'm ready for y'all now," he bragged.

Loose was a little brown-skinned dude with a baby face

and dreads. He had been a bangin' Crip since the tender age of ten. He had more bodies than some of the O.G.'s. Then one day he had decided that enough was enough and was now responsible for a major truce on the East Coast. MJ reminded you of the game. He was an O.G. and proud of it. Even though he wasn't bangin' anymore he still hustled big-time and still had about six hoes. And now Tasha had his tongue wagging. He couldn't keep his eyes off of her.

"Well damn, shorty. Allow me to introduce myself. I'm MJ and I swear you just made my heart skip a beat. Please tell me your name."

"This is my partna, fool. And she's married. This is Trae's wife," Marvin blocked.

MJ covered his heart with his hands. "No disrespect to my man Trae but are you happy?"

"Right now, no. I'm not," she flirted.

"Then today is my lucky day and the first day of your life."

"Nigga, shut up, sit down and let us get this game poppin'. What? A buck fifty a hand?" Marvin asked, ready to gamble.

"It's whatever, man." MJ held the chair out for Tasha to sit down.

"Now sit yo' ass down, man." Marvin began shuffling the cards. "Loose, we even gonna let y'all keep score. That's how confident we are."

As the card game went on different dudes stopped by the table to watch and to check Tasha out. Her tatas were practically spilling out of the bathing suit top.

"Let me take you out tonight, beautiful," MJ told her. "Allow me to expand your world."

She looked at him, tossed the deuce of spades out on the table and said, "I don't think you can afford me."

He looked at her expression to see if she was joking but couldn't tell. "Are you serious?"

"Very much so," she said, tossing out a joker.

Loose snapped, "Man, stop trying to get your mack on. This is my money we're losing."

"You obviously don't know who I am," MJ informed her.

"It doesn't matter, you still can't afford me."

"Don't be too sure about that. Why don't you try me?"

Tasha smiled. "What's that supposed to mean?"

"Let me take you out. Expose you to my world. And I promise you won't come back."

"Come back to what?" she flirted.

"To your world."

Trae had finally stepped foot into the festive backyard. He scanned around for his wife and kids. Of course, the twins were in the pool. The guests were in awe of the twins' swimming skills. That's why he took them for swimming lessons twice a week. Venus and Serena had tennis on lock, Kareem and Shaheem were going to have swimming. Caliph was being led around by Aisha, and they were all chasing and terrorizing SpongeBob.

He saw Tasha at the card table with Marvin. He had met MJ before and detected a little bit of hatin' coming from him. MJ was the type of cat who wanted to be the only one making all the money. He saw that MJ was all in Tasha's face and he was seriously trying to get his mack on.

"Let me nip this shit in the bud," he gritted. As he headed that way, he grabbed a chair and sat it next to Tasha, who saw him out of the corner of her eye. She was now giving MJ extra attention.

"Trae. What up, son? You already know MJ over here, and Loose," Marvin greeted him.

Loose stood up and embraced Trae. "What's good, stranger?"

"What's good with you, youngin'? What the hell are you doing way out here on what's now considered my territory?" Trae asked him.

"Oh, I see you got jokes." Loose smiled. "Man, I'm up here chillin', believe it or not. You know, tryna see what's poppin' and what moves I can make."

"Yo, deal the cards, Loose," Marvin snapped. He always took his spades games as if they were life or death. That's why Trae never played with him.

Trae turned his attention to Tasha as he sat down, totally ignoring MJ as he looked his wife over.

"Daddy, Daddy." Caliph came running over. He dived into Trae's lap.

"Lil' man, slow down and stop beating up SpongeBob. Where y'all been? Daddy missed y'all."

"With Mommy."

"I see," he said as he shot Tasha a smirk.

"Uncle Trae, it's my birthday." Aisha ran over to him, wearing her Mickey Mouse shades and big hat that read I'M THE BIRTHDAY GIRL. "Did you bring me a present?"

"Of course I did. Happy birthday, Aisha."

"Thanks, Uncle Trae, and thanks for the present. C'mon, Caliph. You wanted to see Ben 10, right?" Caliph nodded and they both ran off.

Tasha continued to act as if he weren't sitting next to her as he kissed her shoulder. "You made your point," he whispered in her ear.

"Did I?" She continued to play her hand.

"Yeah. But seriously, I got something I need to talk to you about."

"It's gonna have to wait until I finish playing this game," she told him. "And I hope it's not about the Maybach."

"No, it's more important than that. But where is it?"

"I put it away."

"Why, Tasha?"

"Because I bought it and you ain't gonna be riding no bitches in it. That's why." She slammed a joker down onto the table.

"Yeah! Yeah!" Marvin jumped up all animated. "That's why you my partner. I told these punk muthafuckas they couldn't touch you!" Marvin was now gathering up all the money on the table.

Loose and MJ just sat there staring at one another.

"Don't try and figure it out. Y'all muthafuckas lost." Marvin continued to talk shit.

Trae grabbed Tasha's hand. "C'mon, let me talk to you."

She gently snatched her hand away but stood up and followed him into the house. When the two of them stepped inside the kitchen and were on their way into the living room, they noticed Rick pick Kyra up and give her a nice long kiss. He gently put her down and handed her a motorized car for Aisha and obviously the small box was for Kyra.

Kyra smiled with a warm familiarity.

"Yo, what the fuck is this?" Trae asked Tasha.

"He looks like he's dropping off some very expensive gifts," Tasha responded, just as surprised as Trae was at the attention Rick was showing Kyra.

"Bad move, Rick," Trae mumbled.

Tasha had a look of *oh shit* on her face. She was stunned.

Kyra saw Rick out the front door. When she turned

around and saw Trae and Tasha standing there she simply said, "Rick brought these gifts for Aisha. Well, actually the motor car is for Aisha and the small box is for me."

"Bitch, anybody could have been standing here, got the wrong impression, and told Marvin. Then what?" Tasha snapped. "You in your home, Kyra. What happened to discretion?"

"You know what, Tasha? I really don't give a fuck, so fuck discretion. Shit, I don't see Marvin puttin' shit around my neck. The King says I deserve this and I can have it," she joked.

"Kyra, that's a little too close to home, don't you think?" Trae asked.

"Trae, I know you are not talking! Bitches coming by and calling your house! C'mon, y'all, it is time for the birthday girl to open the gifts. Let me gather everybody up," Kyra snapped, nixing the both of them off before leaving them standing there.

"That shit is going to get ugly," Trae said.

"Just like your shit. So, what's so important? I want to go see Aisha open up all her gifts."

"Tasha, you trippin'. But listen. I did some shit after Shaheem got killed. I just found out that dude's people saw me on BET, now they talkin' 'bout coming this way for some payback. I'm thinkin' that it is just talk but to be on the safe side I think we should move."

"What?" Tasha shrieked. "You are not serious, are you? So now we gotta be running for the rest of our lives? This is ridiculous." Tasha was now pacing the floor.

"To be safe, Tasha. I'm not running from shit but it's all about you and my kids' safety."

"You were on BET a while ago. Don't you think they

would have come by now? You know what? Never mind. I'm not moving." Tasha was so mad she was putting her hands in Trae's face but no more words were coming out. She finally mushed him in the face and left him standing in the kitchen.

Kyra went to go find Marvin to assist with opening Aisha's gifts. When she found him, down in the basement, she was in for a surprise. Marvin was sitting in front of the TV in a heroin nod.

CHAPTER THIRTY-ONE

Trae was loving the beautiful California weather as he sat enjoying the warm breeze in his backyard. The twins and Caliph were playing hard in the swimming pool. It was full of toys and even had a kiddie swing set and sliding board.

Tasha then burst through the back door with her fists balled tight.

"Damn, Tasha, you've been gone all morning. Where were you?"

"Nigga, please." She stomped over to him and threw a pill bottle at Trae, striking him in the chest. She then punched on him and began pushing him.

He managed to push her off him. The kids were now getting out of the pool.

"What the fuck is the matter with you?" he barked.

"Take your medicine, you nasty-dick muthafucka." She started crying. "How could you fuck these bitches raw?"

"What the fuck are you talking about?"

"Look at the bottle, Trae. Those are Flagyl pills. Nigga, you gave me trichomoniasis, Trae. I didn't know you were stupid. That could have easily been syphilis, gonorrhea, herpes, or worst, AIDS." She held her face in her hands. "I can't do this anymore. I want a divorce. I'm taking my kids and I'm leaving." She stomped into the house, leaving Trae sitting on the back porch dumbfounded.

He looked at the pill bottle and thought about Sabeerah. "That bitch!" he gritted through clenched teeth. "That nasty little bitch."

Aunt Marva was now in the backyard. "What you done did now? She's up there tearing the house down."

"Can you keep an eye on the boys?"

"Have they taken a nap yet? Of course not." She answered her own question. "I don't even know why I asked," she said to no one in particular, because Trae had already disappeared inside the house.

When he got upstairs Tasha was crying and talking on the phone while in the boys' room packing their clothes.

"What the fuck are you doing, Tasha?"

"I'll call you when I'm on my way." She ended her call. "I told you I want a divorce and I'm leaving you."

"You aren't going anywhere."

"Oh, yes I am. Watch me. I'm leaving you here so you can roam free. No interruptions from me while you're fucking these nasty bitches out here. We are out of here."

"Tasha, I suggest that you calm the fuck down."

"Nigga, you can't be serious. Calm down?" She was now in his face. "You fuckin' all kinds of hoes. Chinese bitches, nasty-pussy bitches, and without protection. You're doing shit that I thought you would never do. You're cheating and you're bringing home diseases. So fuck you! I am not calming down. I can't if I wanted to. I just need to get me and my kids the hell away from here and especially away from you."

"Tasha, you ain't going nowhere so put the shit back." He began taking the clothes out of the suitcase and putting them back in the dresser drawers.

"Trae, stop it. Please."

"Don't start that shit again, Tasha."

"Trae, I mean it. I'm leaving and I want a divorce."

"Divorce?"

"Yes, a divorce. I'm not going to continue to be with you and not be happy. It's over. I'm filing for a divorce," she said in finality.

"Tasha. I'm not cheating on you. Why can't you just trust me while I straighten a few things out?"

"You've had plenty of time to straighten lots of things out. But all you're doing is digging a deeper hole for yourself. We are leaving, Trae."

"Aiight then fuck it. If you can't trust me then leave. But I guarantee you two things. One, you won't get a divorce, and two, you won't be taking my children."

"What!" she shrieked in disbelief.

"You heard me. You can go, but leave my children here. They are boys and they need to be with their father. You are not taking my sons."

"Watch me."

"No bitch, you watch me," Trae spat, turned around and slammed the door.

She ran and snatched it open. "Trae, here is your cell phone." She threw it down the steps at him, damn near taking off his head. They had somehow ended up with each other's phones. "Give me mines. Rick has been blowing it up. He said that it's official. They are raiding the club today." It was her turn to slam the bedroom door.

It had been hours since Trae left the house. Now here he was standing in front of the mural in the club. Sabeerah had almost finished an updated version of Marvin Gayes *I Want You* album cover. The people looked so real it sucked you in.

Stephon walked up on him. "Why are you looking so down, man?"

"Tasha said she wants a divorce and she's making arrangements to leave. Rick said they are coming today. Hopefully they change their mind. Among a list of other shit going on," Trae said solemnly.

"They're not coming to raid shit. They would have been did that." Stephon was in denial about the raid on his dream club. "But word? Do you think Tasha's serious or is she just mad?" Stephon wanted to know.

"It sure looks like it. I want this thing painted over."

"What?"

"I don't want any signs of that bitch ever setting foot in this club," Trae said. "You know what, fuck it. They're about to close the shit down anyhow. So it don't even matter."

Right after those words left his mouth, the feds busted in the club. Rick was right. The raid was now official.

Kyra was loading up her trunk. She and Aisha were going to Atlanta with Jaz. Marvin had been supposed to go check in at rehab on Monday. Here it was Wednesday and she hadn't seen him or heard from him since the night of Aisha's birthday party. She had meant it when she said she was leaving. California had turned out to be a total bust for both her and Tasha.

"Get in the car, Aisha, and put your seat belt on. Let me make sure everything is locked up and turned off."

Kyra went back into the house and did a final sweep. She hadn't decided whether to sell the house or just leave it for Marvin to worry about.

"Okay," she sighed, "it was nice while it lasted." She looked around at her bedroom before heading downstairs. She heard Aisha giggling.

"Aisha, you are supposed to be in the car, hardheaded." Kyra was flying down the steps but came to an abrupt halt when she ran smack into Marvin.

"Mommy, Daddy said we don't have to go anywhere."

"Aisha, go get in the car like I told you."

"But, Ma," Aisha whined.

"But nothing. We are leaving in a few minutes."

"So, my baby girl was just going to up and leave me." Marvin came over and hugged Kyra tight. "Aisha, come here." Aisha came running and hugged them both.

"I gave you until Monday, Marvin."

"How the fuck you gonna give me a date? I ain't give you a date to quit fucking Detective Rick, now did I?" Kyra had a stunned look on her face. "Cat got your tongue? Maybe you'll have some words to say at that nigga's funeral. Yeah, I'ma take care of that nigga once and for all. I just haven't been able to catch up with him. So I suggest that you stick around." He took the suitcase from her and snatched the car keys out of her hands.

CHAPTER THIRTY-TWO

Two days later Tasha was in New York. "Angel, I'm at baggage claim now, where are you?"

After a knock-down, drag-out fight Tasha had left her home and kids behind in Cali. Trae hadn't lied when he said that she was not taking them with her. But she already had a plan in place to go back to Cali and get them after she got situated. For now she just needed to get away from him.

"Hey, boo. So much has come up since your flight, you wouldn't believe it if I told you. But Kaylin and Kyron are already there waiting on you. I'll call Kaylin on the other line, hold on."

"Wait a minute, Kyron? I thought he was locked up?"

"*Was* is correct. My brother-in-law is a free man. Money talks and bullshit walks. My hero, Johnnie Cochran, when asked what color was justice, his answer was *green*. Green and Kaylin fuckin' with them Italians got my brother-in-law out."

"Wow. That's deep," Tasha said.

"Yeah, but how are you holding up?"

"Girl, barely."

"Well, look at it as a break or a vacation. Get your head together, let him get his head together, and then go on back."

"Go back? Go back to what? We gotta move for our safety and even though they didn't find shit, the club is closed down until further investigation, or until Trae and Stephon can get that order lifted. I knew I should have burnt that muthafucker down to the ground when I had the chance. And Angel, you didn't hear me or you weren't listening, I'm filing for a divorce."

"Tasha, come on, now."

"Angel, I am dead serious. Here come my bags. I'll talk to you later."

"Hold on, let me tell Kaylin to come inside. Wait there so y'all won't miss each other."

"I only have two bags. What car is he in?"

"His favorite. The G-Wagon."

"Tell him I'm coming out now."

"Okay. I'll tell him and I'll see you later on this evening."

Angel hung up and called Kaylin. "We're going to have a full house, baby."

"I can see that. Where is she?"

"She's coming out now."

"Aiight then. I'll talk to you later." Kaylin hung up. He passed a leather portfolio over to Kyron. "Here, this will hold you for now."

Kyron opened it up and thumbed through it. There were a couple of stacks and a black American Express card. He tucked the cash and the American Express card in his back pocket and passed the portfolio back to Kaylin.

Kyron nodded his head in approval. "So, Trae been fucking up?" Kyron finally spoke.

"Shit. What nigga don't? He got hemmed up a couple of times but Tasha done spazzed out on him. Do me a favor and get in the back," Kaylin told him.

"Damn," Kyron said.

"Yeah. Same thing I said."

Kyron jumped out of the front and got in the back. He was so glad to be out of the bing that he didn't know what to do with himself.

"Yo, Kay, open up the sunroof." Kay hit the switch and watched as Kyron closed his eyes and lifted his face to the sky.

"Man, y'all free niggas take the smallest shit for granted," Kyron told him as he inhaled the dirty New York air. He figured he might as well dirty it up some more and lit a blunt. "Yo, is that her?"

"Who?"

"Trae's wife."

"Yeah." Kaylin opened the door.

"Damn. Shorty *is* bad."

"I don't want no trouble out of you, nigga."

"All I said was shorty is fine."

"Yeah, well, you heard what I said."

"Man, I'm the oldest. Now get the fuck out and help shorty with her bags. I give the orders around here, lil' punk," Kyron told Kaylin.

"Yeah, I got your punk." Kaylin got out to place Tasha's bags in the trunk. "What's up, my nigga?" He picked her up and gave her a hug.

"Thanks for allowing me to camp out."

"Girl, don't insult me like that. You know you can stay as long as you need to."

"It's only temporary until I get my own place."

Kaylin laughed. "C'mon, Tasha, I know my boy ain't fuck up that bad."

"Yes, he did. But I don't want to talk about that right now."

"Okay, okay. Just let me know when you're ready." He closed the trunk and opened the front door for her. "Don't be alarmed, that's just my ugly brother Kyron back there."

"Yes, I'm the member of the family no one wants to talk about," Kyron joked.

"What's up, Kyron? Good to finally meet you and that's not true. I've seen a few pictures and heard a little bit of conversation."

"I hope you don't believe everything you hear."

Tasha decided not to comment on that as she buckled her seat belt.

Kaylin jumped into the driver's seat and pulled off.

Everyone was silent. Kaylin was still in shock that his brother was home. Kyron was in shock that he was free. Tasha couldn't believe that she was back in New York and under these circumstances.

"Yo, shorty, it looks like we're going to be neighbors."

"Who is it?" Kyra rushed to the front door and snatched it open, ready to get into Marvin's ass for leaving the rehab center. It was Rick. He stood there in the doorway. They were staring at one another.

"You going to let me in, come out here, or what?"

"Rick, what's up with you?" a startled Kyra asked. "You promised me that you wouldn't come by the house." Kyra was whispering.

"I'm just checking on you. You aiight? I wanted to see you."

Kyra closed the door behind her and sat on the porch. "What's up?"

He leaned over and kissed her on the cheek. "How's he doing? He's been in there for a week now or two?"

"Rick, you know you don't give a damn."

"Nah, I don't. I only give a damn about you and the baby. Can't you get a babysitter and come see me later?"

"Now is not a good time, Rick. So what's up? Why are you here?"

"Kyra, I'm telling you. Leave now. Pack up again and go. You should have left the last time. You were almost in your car, Kyra."

"You've been stalking me?"

He laughed. "No, I'm not crazy. They are watching him, Stephon, Trae and Charli. Y'all's entire circle. You should have walked away when you had the chance. You see what he's been reduced to. He's in a rehab, Kyra, and the people he runs with have been under investigation for years."

"So why are you telling me all of this? Whose side are you on?"

"My side. Shit, I learned the hard way, my side is the only side. If it wasn't for Trae I wouldn't be telling you this. He reminds me so much of my little brother. It's like Markie reincarnated. His mannerisms and gestures. His arrogance and cockiness. He loves your family, Kyra, but he can't save Marvin. You can't save Marvin. Marvin is already gone."

"This conversation is over, Detective Bryant."

"Oh, so now I'm Detective Bryant? Why the fuck do you keep switching up on me?" He grabbed her arm.

"Don't touch me," she gritted.

"Okay look. Kyra, just leave. Take that beautiful daughter of yours and leave."

"And go where?"

"With me. I have a place for the both of you."

She snatched away from him and went into her house and locked the door.

*   *   *

Trae was just walking into the house when he heard Concita say, "Here comes Mr. Macklin now." Concita handed Trae the phone. "It's your mother, Missus Macklin."

"Tell her I'll call her right back." He tried to give her the phone back.

"No, no, I can't. She very upset. You must talk to her. I take the children. Come with me, kids."

Trae sighed before speaking. "Ma, I just walked into the house. Can I call you right back?"

"No, you cannot. Tell me why your wife is up here and you are way over there."

"We had an argument, Ma, and you know how stubborn she is. She's mad at me but give her time to cool off. She'll be back in a couple of days." Trae listened as his mother relayed what he had said to his father.

"Trae." His father had jumped on the phone.

"Shit," Trae mumbled.

"Get up here and get your wife."

"Pop, what you want me to do? Tie her up and put her on the plane? I don't think they are going to allow that."

"They? You got your own damn plane."

"Let me give her a couple of days to cool off. Pop, we've been beefin' a lot. I'll be up there to get her." Trae listened again as his dad relayed what he had said to his mother, who jumped back on the phone.

"Two days, Trae. We are giving you two days. Then get up here and get your wife. The boys need their mother." And she hung up.

Trae felt in his back pocket for a blunt, went to see what he had stiff to drink but instead ended up heading for Spinners.

*   *   *

Kyra tossed and turned all night long. Altogether she may have gotten in two hours of sleep tops. It was no surprise to her that she was wide awake at six-fifteen when her phone rang.

"Hello."

"Kyra, it's me. Come sign me outta here." It was Marvin.

She sat up and swung her legs around the edge of the bed. "Is everything okay? What happened?"

"Naw, everything ain't fuckin' okay. Kyra, just come sign me the fuck outta here." She didn't have to guess that he was pissed.

"Marvin, you haven't been in there two weeks. I knew you were going to pull this bullshit." Kyra quickly decided to try and reason with him. "Marvin, the worst part is over."

"Man, dead that clinical-speech shit. I'm not yo damn patient. I don't know why the fuck I agreed to come up in here. All I did was snort a couple of lines. And you damn right it's over, now come sign me the fuck out. Be here before I catch another case up in here." He slammed down the phone.

CHAPTER THIRTY-THREE

"Okay, shorty. Looks like we can help each other out. You around here moping around and until I get my license I need somebody to drive me around." Kyron was standing in front of Tasha with his muscled arms folded, looking like Kaylin's twin. He had Kaylin's son Malik's bedroom, it was adjacent to Tasha's. Malik was at his mother's and Kaylin and Angel were at their office.

"Drive you around? It's only seven in the morning. Do I strike you as the help?" she snapped.

"Of course not. I was just offering you something to do to get your mind off of whatever it is got you stressing."

"Like you don't already know. And get out of my room."

"It's none of my business. I'm focused on doing me. It's all about me right now. I know you can understand that. Look, shorty, I need to make a few moves today. C'mon, drive me around. I'll pay you."

"Oh, so now I look like I need money? Nigga, I'm sure my nest egg is much larger than yours." She walked away from him.

He followed behind her and couldn't help but admire her ass. "Shorty, you know I wasn't implying that. Aren't you tired of sitting around here? Look, I'm offering to pay you to do what y'all ladies love to do anyway, shop."

"I thought you had moves to make? Here you are talking

about shopping. And you may think I'm moping around but I have moves to make as well. So don't comment on shit you don't know anything about."

"Okay, okay. Damn, shorty, I apologize."

Tasha went back into her bedroom and slammed the door.

He smiled and knocked.

She snatched it open. "What now?"

"Be ready in thirty minutes, shorty. I got you."

After an hour of haggling with the staff Kyra was finally able to sign Marvin out. She was pissed off and frustrated as she paced back and forth in the waiting area. Aisha was excited, jumping from foot to foot as she waited anxiously for her father to come out.

Twenty more minutes passed and Marvin came barging through the double doors carrying his bag. He walked right past his wife without saying a word. He swooped up Aisha and kissed her on the cheek. Kyra followed behind them, barely keeping up.

"Hello to you too."

"Give me the keys," he barked.

"Why are you so angry, Marvin? I should be the one pissed off. They are not giving us that money back."

"Fuck that money. Give me the damn keys." He held out his hand. She threw the keys at him and stomped in place.

He put Aisha in the backseat and as soon as he threw his bags in the trunk and slammed it shut he asked, "So you still fuckin' Rick?"

It took a minute for his comment to register. "What? So this is what this is all about?" Kyra shrieked in disbelief. "I don't believe you, Marvin. You never cease to amaze me."

"Answer me, Kyra. Are you still fuckin' the nigga or what?"

"Marvin, fuck you. I don't even want to be around you." She went and got in the car.

He got in the car and told Aisha to put on her seat belt. As soon as he started the car he asked Kyra again, "So are you?"

"Marvin, dead that bullshit."

"Come on, Kyra, I can handle it. Tell me."

"You know what, let me the fuck out. I'd rather hitchhike than be in the same space as you."

"He was over at the house, Kyra. Why was the nigga at my fuckin' house?" he gritted, remembering Aisha was in the backseat. His pride was hurt.

"What? You had niggas watchin' me?"

"You fuckin' the nigga in my house?"

"Who, Daddy?" Aisha asked, only to be ignored.

"Marvin, our family is on the brink of collapsing all because of your drug habit and you got people spying on me to see if I'm bringing a nigga in the house? You asshole!" She swung at him, causing him to swerve in the lane and horns to beep. "Let me out now!" Kyra screamed.

"So why was he at the house? You fuckin' the nigga in our bed?"

"Who, Mommy? Daddy, no nigga was in our house."

Kyra started laughing. "Marvin, you are so stupid. I'm not going to even stoop to your level of stupidity and answer you." When the car slowed for a stoplight, Kyra jumped out.

"Kyra, get back in here." He put the car in park and jumped out to chase her, ignoring the honks and beeps. He ran and caught up to her.

"Nigga, our daughter is in the car. And listen to how you are talking to me," Kyra screamed at him.

"Get your ass back in the car." He grabbed the back of her neck, squeezed tight, and forced her back to the car.

"Stop it, Marvin," she screamed as she tried to break away. Onlookers were trying to see what was going on.

"You jump out again, I'ma fuck you up." He pushed her into the front seat and slammed the door.

She started crying and now Aisha was crying. "I can't do this anymore, Marvin. Look what we've been reduced to. Let's go back to Jersey. This was a bad move." She was now talking to herself.

He jumped into the car on the last few words of her sentence. He didn't even hear her as he pulled out of the screaming traffic behind them. Something told her to drop Aisha over at Marva's. She had a feeling that this was going to be ugly.

After about an hour and a half of prodding and promising, Kyron finally won and got Tasha to agree to drive him around. Now they were standing in Kaylin's driveway.

"Okay, Kyron, let's set the rules. I'll drive you around but do not ask me about my personal life and I won't ask you about yours. Even though you don't have one since you're just getting out of prison and all."

"Oh, so shorty over here got jokes. You already accused me of being a broke-ass nigga, now you saying that I don't have a personal life. That's ugly." He threw her the keys to the S500. "Here, start earning your keep."

She started the Benz up and it purred like a kitten. As she adjusted the mirrors and her seat she asked, "So where to?"

"First stop Motor Vehicles."

Tasha mumbled, "Why did I volunteer my services? I must be bored to volunteer to sit up at some damn Motor Vehicles all day."

"You don't have anything else to do. Now drive. I got you, shorty."

Marvin and Kyra had finally stopped arguing, only because Aisha wouldn't stop crying. They rode the rest of the way home not saying a word. When he pulled up in front of the house he didn't turn the engine off.

Kyra looked over at him in disgust. "You're not even going to come in and spend time with your daughter?"

"I'll be back after my daughter goes to sleep. If I come in now, she is going to see me put my foot all up in yo ass. I don't want that. Let me go find this nigga Rick."

"Yeah right. You gotta go find something all right. Your next hit. Marvin, don't make me come and get you. This time I'm bringing your daughter inside so that she can see what her father is doing to himself. I'm not hiding your ugly habit from her anymore."

"Kyra, get out the car."

She reached over and snatched the keys out of the ignition.

"Give me the damn keys, Kyra." He went to snatch them back. As they tussled, Marvin, being the stronger of the two, ended up with the keys. "I told you I'll be back."

"Fuck you, Marvin. I see that the urgency wasn't you thinking that I was fuckin' Rick in the house. The urgency was you wanting to get high."

"Shut your fuckin' mouth, Kyra."

"Go ahead and leave. When you look up again your daughter is going to be staring in your face and asking you why are you doing this to us." Kyra jumped out of the car and slammed the door. "C'mon, Aisha." She snatched the back door open. Marvin pulled out of the driveway and sped off.

*   *   *

By the end of the day Tasha was worn out and was beginning to look at Kyron in a whole different light. After Motor
Vehicles they stopped at his business attorneys' office.
Tasha sat in on their meeting and watched them cut and
hand Kyron a check for 2.3 million dollars as payment for
a piece of property that he had sold. From there they made
their way to the bank, his Realtor's office and then to an
apartment building in Manhattan, where he was handed
the keys to his apartment.

He led the way in. It smelled musty and it was dim. The
long hallway led to the spacious living room, high ceilings,
open kitchen and two bedrooms.

"Shorty, how much will you charge me to decorate and
furnish this?"

Ooooh. Tasha squealed in delight on the inside. *This is
going to be fun,* she said to herself, not wanting to reveal to
Kyron her excitement. "I can't answer that right now. Let me
think about it. When do you want me to start?"

"He handed her a key. I need you to start now." He also
handed her the black American Express card.

"Okay, am I on a baller's budget?"

"Don't worry about a budget. Just do what you got
to do."

"That's what I'm talking about. So you are a Santos."

"C'mon Aisha, you're moving too slow."

"Are we going to get my daddy?"

"Yes. Now hurry up and get dressed."

It was a little past one in the morning and Kyra hadn't
seen or heard from Marvin since he had dropped her off in
front of the house that morning.

"Why we got to get my daddy in the dark? My teacher said we shouldn't be out after dark."

"I don't care what your teacher said. You're with me."

"Okay, Mommy."

Kyra went and found Marvin's key to the safe with the gun stash. He thought that he had hidden it from Kyra but she knew exactly where it was. After examining about four pieces, she liked the feel of the .45 so she stuffed it in her inside jacket pocket.

"Let's go, Aisha."

CHAPTER THIRTY-FOUR

Tasha had only been in New York for a week but was missing the boys something awful. But each time she called to hear their voices, the conversation would always go in the same direction.

"Trae, I called to speak to my babies, not to argue with you."

"Who's arguing? All I said was come home because if I have to come and get you and drag your ass back, I will."

"And I already told you I'm filing for divorce, Trae."

"You can file all you want but I'm not giving you a divorce."

"It's not up to you, Trae. It's up to the courts."

"That's what you think. So are you going to come home on your own or do I have to come and get you?"

"Trae, leave me alone, okay? I need this space right now. Can I please talk to my children?"

He hung up the phone on her.

Aisha squeezed her mother's hand as they stood at the door waiting for someone to open it. She had thought that her dad went back in the hospital, not spending the night over at her cousin's house. He was going to have to take her to Toys "R" Us for this one. She was now eight years old and there were a few things, including some game cartridges, that she wanted to get.

Kyra banged on the door again. She could barely hear the footsteps over Beyoncé and Justin Timberlake.

"Who is it?" the voice drawled.

"I'm looking for Marvin."

She heard mumbling and then giggles. That same voice drawled, "Marvin ain't here."

"Then why the fuck is his car out here?" Kyra snapped as she banged on the door. "Open the fuckin' door. Tell him his wife and his daughter is out here. When I tell him that you bitches wouldn't open the door he is going to put his size elevens up y'all's ass!"

She heard silence, then the locks being turned, and then the door opened. Kyra said, "Isis, you was about to get fucked up. You are playing with the wrong bitch tonight."

Isis grinned. "Hi, Aisha." Aisha waved at Isis, Marvin's cousin. "Oh, you can't talk?"

"Leave my daughter alone. Where is Marvin?"

"He's in the back. You can leave Aisha with me."

"No. I got her. But you, you need to leave that shit alone. It's messing up your skin. You're looking bad, Isis. Get it together."

Aisha looked back at her cousin and then asked Kyra, "What shit does she need to leave alone?"

"Watch your mouth, Aisha. Drugs. Do you see how ugly she's looking? She needs to leave drugs alone."

"Yes. I can tell. Her face is dark and she's so skinny just like a skeleton."

"Exactly. Do you want to look pretty and healthy or ugly and skinny?"

"Pretty and healthy."

"Well, never do drugs. And on top of that, drugs make you crazy, stupid, and it eats your brain cells. And watch your mouth."

Aisha giggled as she squeezed her mother's hand.

"It's not funny. Do you understand what Mommy said about drugs?"

"Yes, Mommy."

"Now we are going in this room with probably lots of drug users. I want you to pay close attention." Her plan was to get in and get Marvin out as quickly as possible.

"Is Daddy in there?"

"Yes he is. But we're getting him and taking him home."

"Is he using drugs or selling drugs?"

"After you check it out closely, I want you to tell me what you think he's doing." Kyra took a deep breath to prepare herself for what was behind the door. She turned the doorknob.

Aisha's eyes widened as she covered her nose. People were smoking out of pipes, smoking blunts, which she saw her mom and dad do, and sticking needles in their arms. "Mommy, she's sticking a needle in her arm."

"I know, baby."

"Daddy!" She broke away from Kyra and dived into Marvin's lap.

He slowly came out of his nod and smiled. "Baby girl." His voice was raspy.

"Chile, get that baby outta here," a feen said to Kyra.

"Mind your fuckin' business. And don't be getting all close up on me." Kyra pushed her backwards, causing her to fall into the crew at the table splitting up some coke.

"Hey, hey! Bitch watch it," the table tenants all yelled as they pushed her away.

"C'mon, Marvin." Kyra helped him up, wrapping his arm around her neck. Aisha got on his other side. "Yeah, c'mon, Daddy."

"Both my baby girls"—he nodded out, then his head popped up—"came to see me," he finished the sentence.

"You are taking him home?" Isis asked as they walked past her.

"Yes, get the door for me. I'll be back to get his truck tomorrow," Kyra told her. "Don't let nothing happen to it, Isis."

"I gotchu, Cousin."

"Where we going?" Marvin asked her.

"Home." Kyra was trying to figure out what all Marvin had had, because the Marvin she knew was fully functional and alert when he used heroin. She made a mental note to look into that.

"Daddy, can we go to Toys "R" Us tomorrow?"

He looked down at Aisha and smiled. "Of course we can."

"Yaaay! You know what I want?"

"Aisha, open the car door and let's get your father into the car."

"I can get myself into the car. As a matter of fact, let me drive."

"I don't think so." Kyra pushed him into the seat.

"I can drive."

"No you can't, Daddy. You're high."

Marvin turned around and looked at his daughter. "Baby girl, what did you say?"

"I said you can't drive because you're high off drugs and you're not supposed to drive when you're high because you could get a ticket or have a crash."

Marvin looked at his daughter and then looked at Kyra before hanging his head in shame. Kyra had a smirk on her face. She closed the door and went around to the driver's side, jumped in, and pulled off.

"Was anybody outside the house when we left?" Kyra

asked Marvin, who wouldn't answer. "Marvin, now is not the time to be feeling guilty. You did this shit to yourself. Was somebody outside, yes or no?"

"No, why?"

"Somebody is following us, that's why."

Marvin turned around and looked back. Just then a pimped-out white-on-white Caddy cut them off, causing Kyra to mash her brakes.

"Aisha, baby, get down on the floor and stay down like Mommy showed you. Don't get up until I say so. Do you hear me?" Kyra's voice was trembling.

"Yes, Mommy," Aisha answered, already in position.

"Don't say a word."

"Tell me you holdin', Kyra," Marvin barked.

"I am."

"Give it here."

Kyra eased him her piece.

"What I tell you about carrying this little shit?"

"Baby, I saw him before."

"Oh, that's Fish." Marvin relaxed a little, placing the burner in his lap.

Fish, who was also a cousin, didn't get out of the car. But the vehicle behind them had stopped and now two niggas were coming toward them.

"Marv," one of them yelled.

"Who that be?"

"Junie," he answered as he came up on the passenger's side of the vehicle. His partner Mook was now on Kyra's side.

"Whatever the fuck y'all niggas want is going to have to wait. So y'all might as well get the fuck away from my car," Marvin barked.

"I've waited long enough. I need that dough, Blue." Junie

called Marvin by his nickname. Back in the day, Junie and Marvin rolled thick as thieves and did every dirty deed imaginable together. When Marvin jetted to go to the East Coast, Junie had it in his mind that Marvin owed him two thousand in dope and cash.

Marvin went to get out of the car. He was wondering why Fish wasn't getting out. Junie stood there blocking Marvin in, leaning against the door. Marvin raised his piece and was now poking him in the stomach.

"If you want your kidneys, I suggest you tell Fish to move his fuckin' car and I suggest you get the fuck away from my ride. I'm not going to tell y'all again."

Junie laughed. "If you want your wife, I suggest you give me my muthafuckin' dough right now."

Marvin looked at Kyra. Mook had a gun pressing against her head.

"Mook, get that fuckin' burner away from my wife."

Mook had an ugly grimace on his face and didn't move.

"I'm telling you, Blue, he's going to split her wig, just give me my dough. You owe me, nigga."

"I don't owe you shit! Nigga. That was years ago. And you talkin' about fuckin' chump change. Why you keep saying that shit?"

"Stop haggling, Marvin. Just give the nigga the money," Kyra blurted out.

"Listen to your wife," Junie told him.

"These pussies ain't going to shoot nobody. Not like I will." *Pow.* He let one loose off in Junie's stomach. "See. That's how you do that. I didn't even have to get out. Put the car in reverse, baby girl, and let's get the fuck out of here."

Mook stood there in shock as Kyra did as she was told,

crashing into the car behind them. Fish jumped out of the car waving at Marvin.

"Hold up, baby girl." Marvin jumped out of the car.

Fish snatched the gun out of Mook's hand and busted one off in his head. "Pussy muthafucka."

Marvin started laughing. "Fish, nigga, where you get these pussy muthafuckas from?"

"That's what happens when you send a boy to do a man's job." Fish turned the gun on Kyra and shot her in the head. He then turned the gun on Marvin.

"You slippin', Cuz. Then you come up here thinkin' you can just take shit over. You left us, remember? I built this. Get in my car." Fish was talking but Marvin didn't hear a word he said. All he could see was Kyra's blood splattered on the windows, steering wheel and dashboard. He forgot all about Aisha on the back floor. "C'mon, nigga, let's go. You gonna take me to the loot, man. Tonight, right now. Let's move, before I shoot yo' muthafuckin' ass!" he screamed.

A car screeched to a halt behind them. When Fish turned to look, Marvin let off three shots, striking Fish in the chest and stomach. Multiple shots were fired from the car behind them, turning Fish's body into a bloody rag doll.

"Marv. You all right?" his cousin Lo asked when he got up on the car. He was flanked by his right-hand man Joe. When he saw Kyra he said, "Aww, man." His stomach twisted into knots. He was wondering why Marvin was just standing there. He then noticed Aisha on the floor. She was still on the floor waiting on her mommy to give her the signal.

"The baby, man. We gotta get the baby." Lo opened the back door and yanked Aisha out. "Joe. Move Fish's car out the way. Make those burners disappear. Five-O is on the way. We gotta get you out of here, Blue. But check this out."

He led Marvin over to his ride and opened the trunk. There was a naked, bound and gagged King Rick. "Yeah, I knew you would like this." He beamed with pride, spat on King and slammed the trunk.

"Daddy, we can't leave Mommy," Aisha said to Marvin. "C'mon, Mommy." Aisha was talking and looking back at Kyra. Lo was carrying her to the other vehicle. "We can't leave my mommy, Uncle Lo."

CHAPTER THIRTY-FIVE

Bed-Stuy, New York City

Kaylin, Trae, Bo and Omar were in Bo's basement. Trae had come to fill them in on all of the drama that was going on with him.

Trae paced back and forth as he told them about his STD, how Tasha had left him, his club had been shut down, he had lost millions, and now after he had been convinced that he was out of the game Kaylin had the nerve to be telling him the dons were not at all pleased with his continuing his business with the Li family. Trae couldn't understand why the dons were all in his business when they were supposed to be out. So, stressing was an understatement for what was going on with him.

Omar said, "We owe the fuckin' mob for the rest of our lives. I've come to that conclusion, and I've accepted it. I'll be glad when y'all do the same. There is no such thing as out with these muthafuckas. They want you to think there is but it's not."

"Are you through?" Kaylin snapped. Kaylin looked around at everybody. He focused on Trae. He was worried about him but even more worried about his brother Kyron. His gut was telling him that Kyron was trying to make major moves and of course Kaylin didn't want him to get sucked in, like himself and everyone in the room.

"Kyron, I honestly don't understand how I allowed you to talk me into this."

"Into what?"

He and Tasha were on their way to Kyron's to unload bags after another day of shopping for the apartment, food shopping, clothes shopping and errand running. "Into chauffeuring you around and decorating your apartment. I am worn out. Between you and Angel asking me to babysit, I don't have any time for myself. This time here was actually supposed to be for me to chill."

"Don't even try it, shorty. We took care of all the major stuff."

"We?"

"Yes, we."

"Oh, I see that you got jokes, Kyron. Ha, ha. I quit."

"How are you going to quit in the middle of our agreement? You're getting ready to have two days off. I'm going out of town tonight. When I get back, I'll take the test for my license and your work for me will be done."

"So?"

"So nothing, shorty. You can't quit."

"Kyron, you are working me to death. I am supposed to be on my vacation until I get my boys and a place to stay."

"C'mon, shorty. You're just going to leave me hanging like this?"

"Yeah, unless you do me a favor."

"A favor? I'm already paying you."

"I know, but another one."

Kyron started laughing. "What, you want me to start working for you?"

"No, I want you to meet my sister, Trina."

"Your sister?"

"Yeah." Since Tasha was driving she pressed the button on her Bluetooth and hit the send button on the phone for Trina. On the third ring a dude answered.

"Who dis?"

"Tasha. Can I speak to Trina?"

"Tasha who?"

"Tasha her sister. Who is this?" Tasha asked even though she already knew that he was Fatts, an overweight hustler whom her sister was with because of his money being very long.

"This is Fatts," he announced, as if he were the president or somebody.

Tasha heard mumbling and then Trina saying, "Give me my phone. Tasha?"

"Trina, why is that fat-ass nigga screening your calls?"

"Girl, why haven't you been answering your phone? Where are you?"

"I'm up here. Why is he screening your calls?"

"Fuck him. I got his fat ass in check. But why are you up here?"

"Because I left Trae. I'm filing for divorce."

Trina started laughing. "Yeah right, Tasha. So, how long are you going to be in New York? Why are you just calling me? I want to see you. We gots to hang out." Trina was excited.

"I have somebody I want you to hook up with. It's time for you to drop that fat-ass zero."

"Who, Tasha?" Trina rolled her eyes. She had heard this one before.

"His name is Kyron."

"Where do you know him from?"

"C'mon, Trina. This is me. You've been begging me to hook you up for years and now that I finally got you, you're going to insult me by questioning my judgment?"

"Bitch, who do you think you are?" Then Trina thought about it and said, "Shit. Hold on, let me go to the other room." She peeked back at Fatts and began to whisper. "You finally hooking me up with one of Trae and 'ems crew? I don't even have to ask but I know his dough is long and he is fine. But tell me anyway, what do he look like?"

"He looks like Kaylin."

"Word?"

"It's his brother. If you saw Kaylin, you see Kyron."

"Oh, my God," Trina squealed. Tasha tried not to laugh. "I'ma give him your number."

Tasha's phone beeped. When she looked at the caller ID it was Angel. "I gotta go. Trina, I'll talk to you later."

"No, wait."

"Angel is calling me. I'll call you right back." She hung up on Trina.

"Where are you?" Angel asked.

"On my way to the house. Why? I hope you don't need me to babysit again tonight? I am beat, Angel."

"Where have you been, Tasha?"

Tasha and Kyron felt it was best not to tell anyone that she was driving him around and decorating his apartment. Kyron hadn't even told Kaylin that he had an apartment.

"Trying to get myself situated. There aren't enough hours

in the day." She rolled her eyes at Kyron, who only winked at her as he talked on his phone.

"No, I don't need a sitter tonight. It doesn't look like you're going to be available nohow."

"Why is that?" Tasha wanted to know.

"Trae just came by and got the house key from Kaylin. He's going to be waiting for you. When you get there, he is going to pack your shit and drag your ass back to Cali."

"What?" Tasha asked in disbelief.

"Yeah, you heard me right."

"What is he doing up here?"

"Bitch, are you having a blond moment? What the fuck did you just hear me say? He's come to take your ass back home."

"Shit." Tasha slapped the steering wheel, causing Kyron to look at her as if she had lost her mind. "Think. Tasha. Think," she mumbled to herself.

"Just figured I'd let you know," Angel stated matter-of-factly. "Call me later, okay? Love you but I gotta go."

"Wait! How long ago did he leave?"

"He just left. I say, to be on the safe side, you got about twenty-five minutes tops to get there, get a few things, and get out. You're going to Trina's?"

"Twenty-five minutes? You sure?"

"Give or take a minute or two. He looks pissed and discussing your options with him will not be an option." She giggled.

Tasha floored the gas pedal and ended her call with Angel.

"Yo, shorty, slow down. This ain't Grand Theft Auto. I

would like to live to see the tender age of thirty-one," Kyron joked but meant it.

"I'm going out of town with you tonight."

"No you're not."

"I have to, Kyron. I don't have anywhere else to go. You owe me this little one."

"This is business, Tasha. I'm not going for pleasure."

"Bullshit, Kyron. I know that you have a bitch up there. I can stay at a hotel right by the airport," Tasha pleaded. "I won't be in the way. Just get me as far away from New York as possible."

"Spend the night at the apartment."

"Hellooo," Tasha sang. "Kyron, there has been no furniture delivery, and the paint fumes will kill me. Kyron, please. I haven't asked you for anything. This is life or death." She screeched to a halt in Kaylin's driveway. She looked at her watch. "We have about eighteen minutes to get in, pack and get out. Trae is on his way to take me back to California," she said jumping out of the car.

"Shorty!" Kyron yelled out after her.

"What should I pack, Kyron? I'm going with you." She was practically running away from him.

"Tasha, I got some business to take care of." He hurried to catch up with her.

"Is it dangerous?" She was fumbling with the front door lock.

"Could be."

"Are you selling dope?"

"That's none of your business."

"Well, Kyron, I'm going. You owe me. So, what should I pack?"

"If you're going to go, you can't ask any questions, and you have to follow my lead and do exactly as I say."

"What do I pack?" Tasha was already on her way up the stairs.

"Something sexy in case I need you to play the part."

Kyron sat down on the couch as Tasha ran around like a madwoman. His thoughts went to his brother Kaylin. He was sure Kaylin would have his ass if he knew that he was considering accepting the dons' offer. He couldn't believe that Kaylin had suggested to the dons that his cousin Kendra could take his spot, the top spot that was supposed to be his. But suggesting a woman? Kaylin picked up from the dons that that was an insult. This game of being a don is a job for a man. A woman's place was by her man's side, not in front of him. But he understood his brother Kaylin's desperation to want out for himself. But who was Kaylin to decide if Kyron wanted in?

But instead of suggesting Kendra he should have kept his mouth shut or suggested me. Kendra is gangsta but not gangsta enough. Shit, she can roll with the toughest niggas, pretty and all.

Hell, they all dreamed of getting out of the game but there was no such thing. The game was like slavery. There were only two ways out, death or prison. Nine times out of ten, if you got caught trying to escape or get out, the penalty was death.

Now here he was behind Kaylin's back going to take care of something for the dons. He knew it was a test and he planned on passing with flying colors. This was no doubt the big time.

Tasha was high off of her own adrenaline. She didn't know what she was getting herself into but her goal was to get away from Trae and that was accomplished. This was her first time back to Chi-town and she was with three members of the Santos clan, Kyron, Kendra and Kendrick. They had checked in to two suites at the Hotel W: she and Kendra in one, Kyron and Kendrick in the other. It dawned on her that everybody in Kaylin's family had a name that started with the letter *K*. Last night she'd had the suite all to herself. When they got to the hotel, they all camped out in her room and Kaylin jumped on the phone for almost an hour, showered, got suited up and was out. Right afterwards Kendra and Kendrick took off. They were gone until four the next morning. They came in, showered, changed clothes and were out again. After that, she didn't hear from Kyron for almost twenty-four hours. The twins took turns calling in and checking on her. Kendra and Kendrick Santos were twin cousins of Kaylin's. They were a couple of years younger and from what she recalled, just like Kaylin and Trae, they had come up in the game. They obviously were close to Kyron because ever since he had been home the three of them had been running thick as thieves.

However, Tasha wasn't complaining. She was enjoying her quiet time alone in the suite. The only negative was that it was so dark. The hallways, elevators, lobby, everywhere was very dim. She kept her cell phone turned off except for when she called to check on the kids.

Since the two suites were connected she did do some snooping around. There was a briefcase full of neatly stacked cash. Kyron had left her about five grand on her nightstand. Just when she was thinking about going shopping, Kyron came through the door carrying another briefcase.

"Pack it up, shorty. We outta here in the next hour."

"Hello to you too," Tasha said to him as he whizzed by her, went into his room and shut the door.

*   *   *

"You have reached Rick and Rachel Bryant. I won't be back until the twenty-ninth. As I sit on the beach drinking margaritas, feel free to leave a message after the beep."

Trae hung up. No word from Rick, Marvin or Kyra. Seemed to him that since Tasha had left, everybody had left.

He and Stephon had been back and forth with the lawyers and court trying to get the club reopened. Trae was feeling as if Charli had something to do with it. He didn't have proof but his gut instinct wouldn't let it rest, especially since she had been ducking him out. As far as he was concerned she still owed him money. Even though she had reiterated to him there were investments that lost money and some that made money. He did lose his money and she didn't owe him anything. He felt that if he went to that office or saw her on the street, he would kill her on the spot. For a minute, she had been blowing up his phone trying to get him to meet her at Marvin's condo. Then she had just seemed to give up.

Now it was almost midnight and he was sitting on the couch in his bedroom in the dark. The phone ringing startled him.

"Yeah," Trae answered.

"Nigga, what's up?" It was Marvin.

"You tell me. Y'all went AWOL and shit. Talk to me. Where y'all at?"

"I'm trying to get shit together, that's all."

"Yeah, well where y'all at? It's like a ghost town around here. I went by y'all's house and the mail is stacking up. I've been going by and picking it up. The boys and Marva are asking about Aisha. What did you do with Kyra? She been quiet as hell. I know she can't be that mad at me."

"Kyra chillin'. We'll probably be back in a week or two. Just trying to work shit out. I'll have Aisha call the boys in the morning," Marvin lied.

"Y'all will be back in a week or two? Where y'all at? Damn, nigga. I done asked you three times."

"We in Florida. You know my shit is fucked up. We going to counseling and everything. I'll get it together."

"I hope so, nigga."

"Is Tasha back yet?" Marvin asked him.

"Naw, man. She ain't back yet. Has she been talking to Kyra?" Trae was hoping she had.

"Yeah, they've been talking. That ain't never gonna change. What's up with the club?" Marvin wanted to steer the conversation away from Kyra.

"Still working on it. I'll keep you posted, man. Handle your marriage and dead that nasty habit. I'll handle the club."

"I'm working hard on everything. What's up with Rick?" Marvin smirked.

"Ain't heard from him. I think him and his wife went on vacation."

"Word?" Marvin laughed. "That's what's up. Stay up, nigga."

"Peace." Trae hung up and Marvin snorted some more dope.

CHAPTER THIRTY-SIX

Shorty, you down to go to Great Adventure? I'm free, I'm paid, shit, I'm feelin' like a kid again," Kyron beamed.

"Sorry to be the one to burst your bubble, Kyron, but Great Adventure is closed," Tasha told him.

"Is it? You sure?" He wasn't trying to hear that.

"Kyron, its November."

"Shit, what about Disney World? Someplace warm gotta have something open."

Tasha smiled. "Are you serious?" Then she frowned. "Just me and you? That's not gonna be much fun."

"Aww, man, what you tryna say? Being around me is that bad? I tell you what, I can call the twins. Call your sister."

They were standing in the middle of Kyron's living room. Tasha had slept over; Kyron had spent the night over at Kaylin's since they had business to handle. Tasha and Kyron had an agreement that Kyron's place was a secret and so were her whereabouts. It worked out for Kyron because he didn't want anyone to know where he rested, not yet.

Two and a half hours later they had picked up Trina and Kendrick, since Kendra couldn't make it, and now they were seated in one of Game Over's private jets. They were all amped because, other than Tasha, no one had been to Disney World before.

The private plane had a wet bar, conference room, living

room and full bath. The girls were giving themselves the grand tour as the fellas rolled the weed and fixed the drinks.

"Are you ready to meet Kyron or what?" Tasha grilled her sister. Both girls had on jeans, baby tees and sneakers, and were ready to bask in the warm California sunshine. "Didn't I tell you he was fine?"

"Yes and hell yes. But, Sis, let me do me. You made the introduction, now let me take it from here," Trina told her.

"Bitch, please." Tasha waved her off. "Kyron, can you come here? My sister wants to talk to you," she yelled.

"Tasha!" Trina was tempted to snatch her sister by her hair.

Kyron stood, towering over Tasha. "What's up, shorty?" He and Kendrick were also dressed in jeans, sneaks and T-shirts.

"My sister. I want y'all to get acquainted. So go and talk to her." Tasha walked away, leaving him standing there, watching her sashay away.

"Kyron, you might as well come on and get this over with. Mrs. Matchmaker is not going to let this go," Trina told him.

"I see. But check it. You fine as hell and no disrespect, but I'm diggin' shorty. And Kendrick, well, he would like to get to know you."

Trina's mouth was hanging open.

Tasha was now seated in front of Kendrick, who had a wide grin on his face. He asked her, "You want some of this?" He held out the blunt for her to take. She took it from him and took a couple of pulls before handing it back. "That's all you want?"

"Want? That's all I need. Ever since I had Caliph, I haven't been able to indulge the way I used to."

"Caliph." Kendrick mulled over the name. "Shaheem and Kareem. What that nigga Trae know about twins? I think he's been hanging around the Santos clan too long." Kendrick laughed. All of the Santos family was brown-skinned with curly hair and light eyes.

"Obviously he knows something. Because I sure had them and was scared to death with Caliph and prayed that another set of twins was not going to happen again."

At the bar, Trina finally got ahold of herself and burst out laughing. "That's good for that chick. I wish I could be a fly on a wall when you let her know that. But damn, Kyron, I don't know about that. Actually, the more I think about it, fucking with my sister is only gonna get your feelings hurt and everybody's emotions involved. It ain't gonna be good."

"My feelings hurt?"

"Yeah. *Your* feelings. Niggas go crazy over her. Then what about Trae? I'ma be straight up. She's not gonna leave him for you. And then what happens when Trae finds out? What about your brother? And Angel? Have you thought about all of them? I don't think it's worth all of that drama."

"Let me worry about all of that." Kyron cut off her soapbox speech. The speech that he was not interested in hearing. "I didn't ask her to leave him."

"Okay then. Do you."

"Thank you."

They both headed back into the lounge area. Trina plopped down next to Kendrick and Kyron sat down next to Tasha, who was trying to get Trina's attention. But Trina was purposely ignoring her and refused to look Tasha's way.

"What happened in there, Kyron?" Tasha asked him since her sister wasn't being cooperative.

He leaned over and whispered in her ear, "Kendrick likes her and I don't think she's feelin' me like that."

Disney World ended up being a blast for everybody. They spent the day acting like kids. They rode on all of the roller coasters, visited the Tower of Terror twice, watched a Muppet show in 3-D and didn't leave until the theme park shut down.

When they returned to New York Tasha continued hiding out at Kyron's. So far nobody seemed to suspect anything. But Tasha knew that wouldn't last long and she started looking for a place.

Today Kendrick and Kyron were riding through Spanish Harlem reminiscing.

"Yo, son, remember this C-Town right here? We used to go in there and steal shit, just because." Kendrick laughed at the memory.

"Remember your little four-eyed girlfriend, Rosa? She lived on this block?" Kyron teased Kendrick.

"Man, stop hatin'. Rosa wore glasses but she was smart and she was hot. You know that. And she did my homework all of the time." Kendrick tried to defend his little childhood sweetheart.

As they headed downtown and stopped at the next light, there was a ruckus involving a big black fat dude who was slapping his chick around. Both Kendrick and Kyron noticed that the girl being manhandled was Trina. Kendrick threw the car in park and shut it off, and before you knew it he and Kyron were pulling fat boy off of Trina, who had a black eye, a ripped blouse and no coat. She was obviously dizzy as she tried to get up off the ground.

"Fatts, what's up? Why are you beating on a girl?" Kendrick asked his onetime block rival. Of course Trina was surprised that Kendrick knew him.

"K, get the fuck off me and mind your business," he spat. "Trina, get your trick ass in the car. Better yet, hell to the naw! Kick rocks bitch!" He snatched away from Kendrick and Kyron and grabbed her fur jacket off the ground.

Trina jumped up and charged at Fatts, her left hand slipping into his coat pocket and coming away with his car keys. She ran over to the Cadillac Escalade.

"Don't let that bitch take my truck." He broke away from Kendrick and Kyron, only to be put in a choke hold by Kyron.

"I don't want this raggedy-ass truck. Just give me my shit out of the trunk," said Trina.

"Let him go, Kyron," Kendrick ordered. "Let her get her shit out of the trunk, Fatts." He snatched her mink jacket out of Fatts' arms. He was holding on to it for dear life.

"He can keep that cheap-ass jacket. I can buy me another one." She grabbed two suitcases out of the trunk and tossed his keys in the sewer.

"You bitch! You stinkin' bitch! Don't come crawling your dumb ass back. I'll spit on you before I let you back in this time."

"Fuck you! You fat nasty bastard!" Trina spat as she crammed her suitcases in the back of Kendrick's ride.

"Where y'all takin her, man?" Fatts asked Kendrick, who was already walking away. Kyron shoved him out of his way and followed Kendrick. They jumped into the car and it sped off.

"Just drive me to JFK," Trina snapped.

Kyron looked back at her swollen face. "You want us to drop you off at the hospital?"

"No, I'll be fine."

"You want me to call your sister?"

"No! Please. Please don't tell her about this."

"Yo, where that fat nigga keep his stash?" Kendrick glanced back at Trina through the rearview mirror.

"Here's some of it right here." She unzipped one of the suitcases, revealing stacks of loot.

"That nigga ain't gonna let you get away with that," Kendrick told her.

"He'll have to find me first. If I tell you where one of his stash spots is what's in it for me? You got me or what?"

"You already have the answer to that," Kendrick said.

"You can't go through the airport with a suitcase full of money." Kyron was back on that.

"I got this. Just get me there and promise me you won't tell my sister. I want to do something right this time. I'm going to Cali, getting me a place, and doing something right for me for a change."

Kyron kept his promise and didn't tell Tasha about their meeting with Trina and Fatts. It was a weeknight and Kyron was bored so he snatched Tasha up and they were now in a limo on their way to Atlantic City to gamble. Kyron had stuck a *DJ Juice Video Blendz* DVD in and it was playing in the background.

Tasha had rolled herself several joints and was ready to get her party on as well.

Kyron was a wine drinker and had them both sipping on some merlot. Tasha had smoked a half a joint and had to put it out. "Damn, that's strong."

"Shorty, c'mon now, a half a joint? You killin' me, Ma."

"I'm high enough, Kyron."

"What do you mean you high enough?" He lit one of the joints, took a pull and held it out for her.

"No, Kyron. I'm good, I told you."

"No you ain't. Come here." He grabbed her by her wrist, put the lit end of the joint in his mouth, leaned over, and gave her a shotgun.

Tasha inhaled deeply, holding the smoke in her lungs for as long as she could before choking and releasing the smoke. Tears were running down her cheeks. "Okay, Kyron, that's enough."

"See, now that's what I'm talking about." Kyron had a smirk on his face. "Now, give me one." He passed her the joint and she returned the favor, and he gave her the same reaction she had given him.

Tasha started laughing. "I don't know what you're laughing at, it's your turn," he told her.

"No it's not, Kyron. You can't get but so high. And I think I'm there," she giggled.

"No you're not. We just getting started." He gave her another shotgun. This time his lips touched hers and it sent jolts throughout both of their bodies.

Kyron put the joint out and lit another one. This time he blew the smoke up her nose and then had her return the favor. By this time Tasha was wasted and it felt surreal to her when he pulled her up to straddle his lap.

"Give me another one," he told her. She did even though it was clumsy. "Okay, now I think you had enough. You about to burn us up." He took the joint from her and put it out.

"I told you I was done," she said, feeling as if she were floating. "I am fucked up," she sang with a silly grin plastered on her face.

He leaned over and kissed her on the lips. She was startled

at first and then she started giggling. "Ohhh, we gonna get in trouble," she whispered.

He kissed her again, longer and harder. "Who's gonna tell?" he whispered back.

"I don't know, but we're gonna get in trouble."

"I don't care." Kyron's lips were now on her neck and his hands were rubbing up and down her thighs and massaging her ass.

His lips were tickling her neck, causing her to laugh. "Kyron, we can play but we are not fucking."

"Why not?"

"Because."

"Because what?"

"Because I said so."

He had unbuttoned the top two buttons on her blouse and was glad that she didn't have on a bra. He began working his magic tongue on her nipples. When her breathing went into a steady rhythm and her fingers began running through his hair, he knew it was on.

She ain't laughing no more.

Kyron knew that his tongue game needed a patent. It was that point. Her sexy moans confirmed that.

Tasha's pussy was tingling and twitching and she was creamin' in her jeans. A few seconds later she was coming. Kyron began unbuckling her jeans and she stopped him. Out of breath and sweaty she said, "No, Kyron." And climbed off of his lap, feeling as if she was sobering up.

Damn, an orgasm from getting my nipples sucked! What if I get my pussy and clit done!

She lay back, stretching onto the leather seat, contemplating whether to ask him or not.

Kyron followed Tasha's movement and climbed on top

of her. He wanted her to feel how hard he was, which only scared her. She tried to push him off of her.

"I thought you said we could play?" He was now kissing her neck and grinding on her pussy.

"Get off of me. You are playing a little too fast."

Kyron grinned, got up off of her and sat back. He grabbed a joint, lit it and watched her button up her blouse and jeans. He passed her the joint and poured her a glass of wine.

The limo slowed to a stop in front of the Borgata Hotel. Before getting out they finished off another joint and glass of wine.

"C'mon, shorty, it's time to get our gamble on." Kyron got out and held the door open. "Shorty, come on."

Tasha started giggling and then burst out laughing. "My legs, I can't move my legs."

"C'mon. Get out."

"I'm serious. I can't move my legs."

Kyron sighed. "Can you put your coat on?"

She started laughing. "I think so," she slurred.

Kyron got back in and helped Tasha put on her coat, then he pulled her out of the limo and carried her into the hotel.

She whispered into his ear, "My legs are drunk, Kyron."

"I got you."

"Am I too heavy?"

"Relax, shorty. I got you." He tuned Tasha out as she rambled on—about what, he had no clue. He got their room key and stepped onto the elevators.

"This elevator is nice," Tasha slurred. There were two ladies on the elevator with them. One of them was carrying her shoes in her hand. The other one couldn't stop drooling over Kyron.

"He is fine, ain't he?" Tasha giggled. "He wants to fuck but that ain't happening. I don't care how fine he is, or how hard his dick gets," she told the strangers, who only drooled much harder, causing him to blush.

Kyron was glad when the elevator doors opened and the ladies disappeared. When they made it to their door Tasha was dozing off. He opened the door to their suite and laid her across the bed.

"Shorty, c'mon, we're supposed to be here to gamble." Tasha mumbled something, balled her body up and went to sleep. "Ain't this some shit," Kyron said as he counted up some cash and headed for the craps tables.

Tasha was downstairs at Angel's in the living room, watching TV and fooling around with a Sudoku puzzle. It was almost eleven. Kaylin, Angel, their son Malik and their baby daughter Jahara were all upstairs. She had decided to come over here to get away from Kyron for a few. At least that was her intention until the front door opened and he came waltzing in. She was seated in the La-Z Boy wearing a pair of sweats and a buttoned-up pajama shirt. Her hair was up in a ponytail and she was chilling.

When her cell phone rang she checked the caller ID and it was her sister, whom she hadn't heard from in a minute. "Damn, where you been hidin' at?" Tasha asked Trina, while trying to ignore Kyron's presence.

Kyron took off his jacket and laid it across the arm of the chair. He had on a turtleneck and a pair of slacks and a pair of black-on-black Stacy Adams shoes.

"I got a surprise for you," Trina bellowed.

"What is it?"

"I live in California," Trina yelled, unable to control her excitement.

Tasha was speechless. "You what!?"

"I live in Cali. I got me a place. I'm signing the papers in the morning and then I'll be on my way up there to see you. I love it out here!" Trina squealed. "And oh, Kyron is finally letting them throw him a welcome-home party and Kendrick invited me. We *are* going, right?" Trina had been trying to get in with Tasha and Angel ever since the two of them had met Trae and Kaylin.

Tasha looked over at Kyron, who was getting up and coming over toward her. He moved her feet off of the footstool and sat down. She tried to push him away and motioned upstairs.

"Tasha, are you listening to me? We are going, right?"

"Let me call you right back, Trina." She hung up. "Kyron, your brother and my girl are right upstairs. What are you doing?"

"When are we gonna fuck?" He was staring at her and waiting on a response as if he had asked her was she on her way to work.

"I told you we aren't." Jahara was crying, causing Tasha to keep looking toward the stairs.

"Shorty, when are we gonna fuck?" he asked again before leaning over and kissing her on the lips.

"Kyron, stop playing."

"You said we can play, remember?"

"Yeah, but there is a place and a time for everything." Her voice went up an octave because his mouth was on her nipple.

Jahara's cries were getting louder and they heard little footsteps running around, which was Malik. Tasha hurried up and buttoned up her pajama shirt. Kyron grabbed her and stood up, taking her with him. She had wrapped her legs around his waist.

"Aiight, nigga, let's play." She kissed him, forcing her tongue down his throat, and began grinding on his dick.

The little person's footsteps were now coming down the steps. Kyron sat Tasha down.

"Uncle Kyron." Malik ran over to him and began boxing with him. Kyron picked him up and tossed him in the air. Malik yelled with glee and Kyron put him down, then sat down on the sofa across from Tasha.

"Why you was kissing Aunt Tasha?"

Tasha gasped.

Kyron calmly said, "Shhh, it's our secret," and gave Malik a fist bump.

Kaylin came down the steps holding a crying Jahara. He was suited down, and passed Jahara off to Tasha. "My little princess is sleepy." He looked over at Kyron. "You ready?"

"I'm ready. Where's your other half? She changed her mind?"

"She's coming."

"Oh, I can't go out and party? I'm the permanent designated babysitter," Tasha joked.

"I believe you are." Kaylin winked at her. "Love you."

"Sure you do. You love my babysitting."

"Come on, I'm ready," Angel yelled. "Bye Tasha. Malik, it's way past your bedtime," she yelled out.

Everybody left out, leaving Tasha with the kids.

Trina and Tasha had just left Fatts's apartment. He was down in DC and Trina still had a key. He hadn't bothered to change the locks, knowing that Trina would be coming back. They had been through this many times. Trina had rented a minivan to pack the rest of her things. After they packed the van, they showered, got dressed and headed to Kaylin's. Everyone was meeting there to go to the club for Kyron's party.

Kyron had bought himself and Tasha matching full-length dark fur coats with hoods. Tasha had on thigh-high winter-white Dolce & Gabanna calfskin boots and a winter-white Dolce & Gabanna dress. Trina rocked a chinchilla-trimmed cashmere wrap with a beige skirt and blouse. Compliments of the stash she and Kendrick robbed from Fatts.

When they walked into Kaylin's house there were only three other females: one was Kendra, the other two Tasha had never met. The other six or seven people were men who all started trying to talk shit and push up on Tasha and Trina. Kyron quickly put them all in their place.

Tasha and Trina were looking fierce as they sashayed through the living room and went upstairs to Tasha's temporary bedroom. As soon as they shut the door, Kendra came up. "Kyron said for y'all to come on to the basement to shoot a game of pool right quick."

When they got to the basement Kendrick and Kyron were waiting anxiously. Kendrick was glad to see that Trina's eye was no longer black and Kyron immediately began undressing Tasha with his eyes.

"Damn you look good." Kyron leaned over and kissed her on the cheek. "I thought I was going to have to kill one of them niggas upstairs."

"Me and Trina against you and Kendrick?" Tasha asked, trying not to drool at how good Kyron was looking.

"Naw, me and you against them two."

Kendrick had already racked the balls up.

Kyron sat down on the couch as Tasha chalked up the pool stick. Trina broke the balls, knocking in the nine and the eleven.

When it was Tasha's turn, as she was bending over to shoot the balls Kyron was trying to look under her dress. And when he couldn't take it anymore he got up and stood behind her to show her how to take the shot, all over her like a glove.

"Unngh, they are making me sick," Trina mumbled. To her, Kyron seemed to be totally mesmerized and fascinated with Tasha.

"I heard that, Trina. Are y'all mad that we are whipping y'all's ass?" Tasha slammed the six ball into the side pocket.

"Shorty, I think they are," Kyron teased.

They finished off that game with Tasha banking the eight ball in the corner pocket.

"We can play one more," Kendrick challenged.

"Nah, I need to holla at shorty real quick," Kyron said, never taking his eyes off Tasha.

Kendrick grabbed Trina's hand and took her upstairs. As soon as they disappeared Kyron's hands were under Tasha's dress, squeezing her ass, and his lips were on hers. He lifted her up, sitting her on the edge of the pool table. His dick was hard and her pussy was wet, hot and throbbing. While he held her on the edge of the pool table, Tasha's hand slid down his pants and was massaging his dick. That was one of the moments Kyron had fantasized about. This was her first time feeling it and by no means was she disappointed.

"Give me some head, Kyron." What she really wanted was some dick. But Kyron's was forbidden. She was serious when she said they could play. That's as far as it could go. She leaned back, spread her legs, and closed her eyes. Instead of some tongue action, Kyron had plunged his dick into her hot and aching pussy.

Tasha's eyes flew open, her heart fluttered as Kyron grabbed one of her legs, put it over his shoulder and then...

Footsteps began charging down the steps.

"Yo, man of the hour! It's time to bounce. Kaylin said for us to leave now. He is gonna meet us at the club later on," the intruder yelled out as he was making his way down into the basement.

Kyron hurriedly pulled out of her, pulled her up and off the pool table, and then put his dick in his pants.

Tasha practically ran past and knocked over the two dudes who were now in the basement. She ran all the way upstairs to her bedroom and slammed the door. When she turned around Trina was standing there grinning, holding Tasha's coat up.

"Let's go, Sis. Time to party. We are riding in Kendra's car."

All the way to the club, Tasha was in a daze. *Forbidden. Here I am fucking a nigga without a rubber. All I wanted was some head,* she repeated to herself over and over.

"What is the matter with you?" Trina asked her.

Tasha only shook her head.

While at the club, Tasha's body was there but her mind was stuck on stupid. It was awkward because she tried to avoid Kyron and was feeling that everyone knew that she was creeping around with him. Because she was paranoid and not having a good time she was ready to go. After a couple of hours Kendra came and got her.

"Grab your coat. Kyron is waiting for you upstairs."

The club had three floors. The second floor was for the

reggae heads, the third floor was for the hip-hoppers, and Kyron's party was on the first floor where the house music was booming.

Kyron was waiting by the coat check. His fur was over his arm and he motioned for Tasha to take off hers. She did and handed it to him. When she turned around Kendra was gone.

"Shouldn't you be downstairs at your party?" Tasha asked as he checked their coats.

"I want to party with you a little bit," he said as he grabbed her by the wrist and began leading her to the other side of the dance floor. The sultry reggae music had everyone up close, bumping and grinding.

Kyron made it all the way over to the corner, where he pulled Tasha up close and they began to dance. Bumping and grinding and exchanging kisses, that was only meant for couples in love.

"What if somebody sees us?" Tasha moaned as she rocked her hips to the beat and over his hard-on. His back was now up against the wall. Both hands slid up her thighs, up under her dress. He slid her thong to the side and when his fingers ran across her clit, she dug her fingers into his shoulder and with the other hand she ran her fingers through his low-cut curly hair. Her eyes were closed and her head fell back as he played with her clit and stuck his fingers in and out of her pussy. The harder she dug her fingers into his shoulder the more skillfully he worked her pussy, bringing her to the brink of coming. He then came to a sudden stop.

Her eyes popped open! She was no longer rubbing his curly head, and the hand that had been digging into his shoulder was now grabbing the front of his shirt.

"You see somebody?" He shook his head. "Then why did you stop?" She sounded desperate.

"Let's get our coats."

"What?" she snapped, her mouth hanging open and pussy soaking wet.

"C'mon." He grabbed her and they went to get their coats. Other than a quick phone call he didn't say anything as he helped her put on her fur and led her outside and around the corner to a side street. They sat on the back of Kendrick's Beamer. He pulled her hood up over her head and did the same for himself. He pulled her close and they began to kiss, his hands all over her body.

"We fuckin' later on?" he whispered into her ear.

"Umm-um," she moaned. "No, Kyron."

He lifted her up, her knees straddling both of his thighs. He wasted no time fingering her pussy, putting her at the verge of coming. He pulled his dick out and began rubbing the head over her clit. When she started coming he plunged inside her. Shocked, she began trying to get off the dick, pushing and scratching him, which did no good. He held her firmly in place on his dick.

"No, Kyron. This is rape," she groaned as he began hitting her spot. "Oh, God. My spot."

Just then Kendra pulled up beside them. Her window came down. "Sorry to interrupt y'all's little party but they need Tasha at the house to watch the baby."

They both ignored her and continued to fuck.

"Y'all heard me? Anyway, Kaylin said he's been calling you, Kyron."

"Get rid of her." Tasha began sucking on his neck.

"I thought you said this was rape." He smirked, then told Kendra, "Drive around the block. Then you can take Tasha to the house."

Kendra sped off and Tasha rode his pole, busting a nut

right before Kyron busted his. A satisfied Kyron stuck his dick back into his sweats and helped Tasha down. He smoothed his hands over her dress and up her coat.

"You know that you were only a fuck, right?" Tasha asked him.

"Oh really?" He leaned over and kissed her on the lips.

"A revenge fuck."

"We'll see about that." Kendra pulled up right on cue. Kyron opened the passenger door for Tasha. She got in and they pulled off.

CHAPTER THIRTY-SEVEN

K endra pulled up into Kaylin's driveway, dropped Tasha off and left. Before Tasha could stick her key in the lock Angel opened the door with a crazy look on her face.

"Girl, I did not know that he was here," Angel whispered, then said out loud, "Jahara is already sleeping. She should be out for the rest of the night. Come on, Kaylin." Angel put her fingers up to her ear to say *call me*.

"Thanks, baby girl," Kaylin said, then kissed Tasha on the cheek, and just that quickly they were headed out to Kyron's homecoming party at the club.

Tasha's eyes adjusted to the dim lights. Her heart fell to her feet when she saw Trae sitting on the couch with his coat still on and his legs crossed. She took a deep breath, tried to act nonchalant and as if he wasn't there and headed straight for the stairs.

"Tasha, come here," Trae barked.

She froze in place, right there on the fourth step. There was no doubt in her mind from the tone of his voice that he was not playing.

"I need to use the bathroom, Trae." She tried to use that as an excuse to get upstairs and buy some time.

Trae turned on the lamp and got up and headed toward the stairs. He made note of the fur coat she had on as she rushed up the stairs with him right at her heels. He wanted to tell her to get her ass back downstairs even if she had to piss on herself. But since he was there in peace, he didn't.

When she made it to the bedroom, she threw off her coat and flung it along with her purse across the bed before rushing into the bathroom and locking the door.

"Shit." She gritted as she noticed that her hands were shaking like leaves. She looked around the bathroom and noticed that Angel had removed all of the towels and wash-cloths. And here she was standing there with no panties on and another nigga's come on her thighs.

Trae's knocking on the door caused her to jump. "Tasha, come on out of there," he demanded.

"Damn, can I at least use the bathroom?" She began balling a wad of toilet paper together, wetting it and then wiping between her thighs and pussy.

Trae knocked on the door again. "Trae, wait a minute." She tossed the wad into the toilet and flushed it. She stood in front of the mirror, fixed her hair and her clothes. She took a deep breath before opening the bathroom door.

She looked at her husband, who was casually dressed in a black Coogi sweater, black slacks and a pair of soft croco-dile shoes that she'd bought him.

"I came in peace, Tasha. I just want us to get an under-standing before you come back home."

"Home? I'm staying here in New York. I told you, Trae, I want a divorce." She stormed past him and headed back for the stairs. She wanted to get out of the bedroom. They were too boxed in and if she needed to make a run for it, the bedroom was not the place.

"Why are you talking crazy? I'm not giving you a divorce and you are not staying in New York." He followed her back down the stairs into the living room. She sat down on the La-Z-Boy, he sat on the sofa. He watched her as she crossed her legs and folded her arms across her chest. "You are coming back home with me."

"You said you came in peace and that you want us to talk and come to an understanding. I told you I want a divorce and I'm not going back, so let's talk about that."

"Why don't you want to come back? What the fuck you doin' up here? You got a lame up here buying you a couple of furs and some bullshit-ass jewelry and forgot who the fuck you are? Did you forget about the three kids and the home you have? Your sons need you to come home and you have a husband that *wants* you to come home."

"I don't care what my husband *wants*. My husband should have thought about that before he started trickin' himself out for houses, nightclubs, paintings and money. And, nigga, you're the one who is out here trickin'! Or did you forget all about your dick leaking?" she snapped.

Tasha was furious as she remembered the embarrassment of having to be treated for trichomoniasis. She was now standing in front of him and screamed, "Oh, you don't like it when the shoe is on the other foot, do you? Of course not. You that same nigga that sold our marriage vows and trust for a few million dollars. You started this shit, Trae, so I'm damn sure going to finish it. You got me fucked up."

"So two wrongs are supposed to make it right?" Trae asked her with calmness. She hated when he did that.

"Right? I didn't make them wrong, Trae. You did."

"I know I did, that's why I'm here. Shit, Tasha, I know I fucked up and I'm sorry. What the fuck you want a nigga to do?" He grabbed her hands. "Give us another chance, Tasha," he pleaded as he looked up at her.

"It's too late, Trae. It's over." She snatched her hands away from him.

"The hell it is. You talkin' crazy. You forgot that we said for life and death? So if you leave, you must be ready to die."

"Now you are threatening me?"

"Tasha, you know it's not over between us; you're just mad at me and I'll give you that. But I miss you and love you more than anything." He began to rub her ass. "Daddy fucked up and he's sorry, and, baby, you know I am not letting you go. I miss us, Tasha."

"Trae—" Tasha got choked up because she knew deep down and without a doubt that one of them would need to be dead before she would be free of this man named Trae. "That's not fair, Trae. Let me go." His hand was now under her dress, and his face was between her thighs. She turned to push him away a few seconds too late.

"You don't have on any panties?" He smelled her pussy and smelled the sex on her. He chuckled in disbelief. Tasha began to back away from him. "You bitch!" he spat. "Straight like that you got a nigga standing here beggin' your ho ass, and you got the nerve to be talkin' all this it's-over bullshit and marriage this and marriage that and yo' fuckin' pussy smells like another nigga's nut!" Then he stood up and smacked the shit out of her. "Who is he, Tasha?"

Oh shit. "Calm down, Trae," she squeaked. She was petrified.

He smacked her again. This time so hard she flew backwards, damn near flipping over the La-Z-Boy.

"Who is he, Tasha? I will body that nigga! Is it the same nigga who bought you that coat and the necklace around your neck?" He went over to her and snatched the necklace from around her neck.

Tasha was still in shock, holding her face.

"I asked you his name, Tasha."

She took off running for the stairs.

The next thing you know, Trae's coat was off and he was right behind her.

"What the fuck is the matter with you? We are married and you are up here trickin' my pussy away?" Trae slapped her across the back of the head, damn near knocking her up the steps. "Have you lost your muthafuckin' mind? You gonna run off and leave your children so you can fuck niggas? I warned you, *Don't make me come up here and get you.*" He kept slapping her. "What the fuck is the matter with you? You ain't no muthafuckin' teenaged chickenhead. What is the matter with you? Bitch, answer me."

Tasha's fresh hairdo was all over her head, a button had popped off her blouse and she was boo-hooing. Not sure if it was from the surprise of Trae beating her ass or from the hard slaps he was putting on her.

"Answer me, dammit!" He started choking her. "What the fuck is the matter with you? I didn't marry no damn chicken."

She let out a loud wail and then screamed, "I hate you, Trae. You have been fuckin' bitches, so what the fuck! It's over between us. I want a divorce."

The word "divorce" infuriated Trae to the point of rage. He lost all focus. He continued to beat the shit out of Tasha. They ended up back down the stairs and didn't know how they had gotten there.

Tasha was sprawled out across the living room floor. Trae was standing over her. It was as if he had blacked out and was now back to reality. He was wondering how she had gotten there on the floor.

"Tasha, baby, get up." He went to grab her arm and she started screaming, swinging and kicking wildly.

"Get away from me! I hate you! Why?" she wailed. "Why did you do this to us?"

"Baby, I'm sorry. Dammit! I'm sorry." He swooped her up and laid her down on the couch. He rubbed her back while telling her how sorry he was, and telling her that he would never put his hands on her again. "We are going back home in the morning. I miss you so much, baby."

Tasha appeared to be in shock as she lay there crying, but not releasing any sound. The tears were slowly streaming down her face as she stared blankly at the man she loved. She couldn't even protest when she felt him enter her.

Trae and Tasha left New York early the next morning before anyone was even awake. Tasha didn't want anyone to see her bruised-up face and body. As much as her heart still said that it was over, it seemed that this was the remedy to put things back in perspective. She knew exactly what type of nigga she married, and when Trae said that he would kill her she knew he meant it.

CHAPTER THIRTY-EIGHT

Back in California, Tasha had tried to stay in the house with Trae but couldn't. The house itself had too many memories and it was beginning to fuck with her mentally. She had to get out. She lasted two weeks and couldn't make it another day. She packed up herself and the kids and ended up staying with Trina in her two-bedroom apartment. They had been camped out now for almost three weeks.

Kyra, Marvin, Aisha and King were still all missing. Just the thought of something happening to Kyra and Aisha was driving her crazy as well, and to date no one knew where they were.

Tasha was in the kitchen feeding the boys. She had fried chicken, baked macaroni and cheese and the boys' favorite candied carrots. Trina had left the house early that morning so Tasha and the boys had the apartment all to themselves. She had fixed their plates and had sat down to eat when someone knocked on the door and rang the buzzer.

"The door, Mommy," Caliph yelled.

"I heard it, baby. Eat your dinner." Tasha got up to open the door. When she saw it was Trae, she rolled her eyes and left him standing there. He still hadn't gotten over the fact that he beat Tasha's ass and that she had fucked a nigga behind his back. He was trying his best to deal with it and felt that until he found out who it was so he could handle him, things couldn't go back to normal. So even though he could have, he didn't stop her when she packed up and came over to Trina's. But now he wanted her back home.

Tasha went back into the kitchen to finish her dinner.

Trae closed the door and came into the kitchen carrying an edible arrangement of chocolate-covered strawberries and chocolate-covered apples in one hand and a bag in the other. He was dressed in a black suit.

"Daddy!" all the boys yelled, jumping up from the table to greet Trae.

"I miss y'all," he greeted them and set the bag on the counter and gave Tasha one of her favorite treats.

"Where you was at?" Kareem asked.

"Daddy had to go to a funeral."

"A funeral?" Shaheem asked. "Can I go?"

"Me too, Daddy," Caliph joined in.

"A funeral is not a fun place to go. Sit down and finish your dinner." They finally found Rick, or rather what was left of his body. And his name was not Rick. It was Jason. His wife had decided to cremate him. The police were looking for Marvin, so Trae figured that was why Marvin took his family and got ghost. No one knew that Kyra was gone. Trae understood all too well that a nigga had to check another nigga about his woman, which sometimes would lead to death. And he knew that Kyra fuckin' with Rick was trouble.

"Trae, what is this?" Tasha held up the plastic bag.

"Some whiting. I'm hungry; can you fry that up for me?"

"I already cooked, Trae. There is plenty enough here for you to eat."

"I want some fish, baby," Trae said as he took off his suit jacket and hung it up. He then went to the sink, washed his hands and sat down.

Tasha sighed and dumped the fish into a bowl and began to wash them off.

"Y'all want to go see Pop Pop and Nana tomorrow?"

"Yes," all three of the boys said in unison.

"I'ma pick y'all up early in the morning, so be ready, and when we come back we all are going home." He looked up at Tasha as he said that.

He knew Tasha was still mad at him but it was too bad. If he had to drag her ass back to the house he would. He did it once and he damn sure would do it again. He needed his family at home with him.

"You're not even going to thank me for bringing your favorite treat?" Trae decided to mess with Tasha. "I got you something else and I'm glad I didn't give it to you."

"Mommy, Daddy is talking to you," Caliph said.

"I hear him, baby."

"We going back home when we come from Nana's?" Shaheem asked his mother.

"We'll see, Shaheem."

Tasha fried Trae's fish up in silence as he talked with and answered questions from his inquisitive sons.

When she finished frying the fish, she fixed the boys bowls of ice cream, fixed Trae a plate and sat down to eat hers.

"Daddy can't get fed?" Trae leaned over and whispered in her ear.

"We haven't spoken to one another in, what, two weeks? You're mad at me and I'm even madder at you. But you show up out of the blue telling me I'm coming back home and wanting me to cook for you and feed you. Did I miss something?"

"I'm tired of fighting, Tasha. We need to come to a resolution. Shit has gotten way out of hand. Don't you think so?"

"Whose fault is that?"

"It's mines but we have a family, baby."

"I know that. But you weren't thinking about your family when you were fucking up. You...Never mind. Why don't you leave? I can't talk to you right now."

"Oh, you are going to talk."

"Trae, I need time to heal. Physically and emotionally. I am not up to talking to you right now. You just want me to forgive you and act like everything is normal. I can't do that."

"C'mon, y'all, time for your bath." She stood up, waved the boys over and they all marched out of the kitchen.

Trae sat there deciding whether to leave or stay. He ended up straightening up the kitchen, rolling up a blunt and parking his ass on the living room couch.

Tasha took her time bathing the boys as they played in the tub. She then dressed them for bed and sent them into the living room with their father. She then cleaned up the bathroom and ran herself a hot bubble bath. She took her time, hoping that by the time she got out the kids would be asleep and Trae would be gone.

But no such luck, well almost. By eight the boys were knocked out on the couch and Trae was sitting there watching TV.

"Damn, I was beginning to think you drowned in there."

"I was hoping you would be gone by now," she snapped. She picked up Caliph and took him into the bedroom and tucked him in. Trae came behind her carrying the twins.

She then grabbed her blankets and pillow and took them into the living room, where she began turning the couch into a bed. As soon as she finished, Trae plopped down and began flicking channels.

"Uh, excuse me. It's time for you to go."

"Tasha, sit your ass down. You look like you gained a few pounds. It looks nice."

Tasha sat down and pulled the covers back.

"Are you done trickin' my pussy away or what?"

Before she knew it she had swung at Trae, hitting him in the mouth. He went to grab her but hit her in the eye by mistake.

"My eye, Trae!" she screamed, as he now had both her arms above her head. "My eye! Get off me!" They had tumbled onto the love seat.

"That was a mistake, Tasha."

"Get off me and get out," she yelled.

"Shut up before you wake the kids."

"Get off me."

"Not until you say you're going to stop acting crazy."

"Get off me." She gritted. "You hit me."

"You hit me first. Plus I didn't mean to."

"What about the last time? Did you mean to beat my ass then?"

"Yeah and no."

The thought of those ass whippings brought Tasha to tears and took the entire struggle out of her. The Trae she had married wasn't this man here. The Trae she had married would never put his hands on her or cheat on her. Her Trae worshipped the ground she walked on and would never hurt her.

"I don't know who you are," she mumbled through tears. "You beat on me, you cheated on me."

"Baby, listen to me. You know damn well I didn't mean to do that shit. Be for real, Tasha. All bullshit aside. Admit it, you know I didn't mean that shit." He was now hugging her tight as she cried.

"So why did you do it?" she bawled.

"I snapped. Shit, I lost control, Tasha. I didn't mean for it to go down like that, but we can work through this. We made a promise to each other that we would work through anything, remember that? I'm not going to lose you, Tasha, and I'll be damned if I'm going to sit back and approve of you dancing off into the sunset with another nigga. I'm ready to work through any and everything—no more lies, no more bullshit. I'm just asking you, Tasha, to meet me halfway," Trae pleaded.

"You begged me to take a chance with you, remember that, Trae? And I did, went against my gut and I did. I didn't want you to hurt me. And you did."

"Baby, no marriage is perfect. I'm still here and I ain't going nowhere. And I damned sure ain't letting you go. I just need you to meet me halfway."

"I can't go back to that house, Trae. We gotta move. It has too many memories. It reminds me too much of who we used to be but are no longer. I can't go back there."

"Okay, we'll move. What else do you want? I just want to make you happy again."

Tasha got up and went into the bathroom to get herself together. When she came back into the living room, Trae had turned the TV off and was sitting on the couch.

"I'm sorry, baby," he told her.

"Me too. I'm not sorry for giving you a dose of your own medicine. But I am sorry that we turned out like this. If it weren't for the children, Trae, I wouldn't have come back." She wanted to tell him that she liked Kyron, but their family was more important. She knew she had to let Kyron go and take this one for the home team.

Trae wanted to say, *Oh, you were coming back. Coming back willingly or in a coffin.* But he decided to keep his thoughts to himself.

"Come here." He patted the spot next to him and she sat down. He wrapped his arms around her and kissed her on the forehead. "I miss you, girl," he whispered.

"I miss the way you used to love me. I miss us," Tasha said as she hugged him.

"Used to love you? Don't get it twisted, I never stopped."

"Did the boys miss me?" She had been dying to ask him that.

"Aww, man, did they? I think we were running neck and neck. That's when I came and got you."

"I'm sorry," Tasha said.

"Can you forgive me?" Trae asked her.

"Trae, we probably can forgive each other but can we forget? That's where our challenge will be. I don't think things will ever be the same again."

"This is us, baby. We won't know until we give it a try," he told her.

"I'm sorry, baby."

"Me too. Looks like Cali was a total bust." Trae hated to admit.

"Yeah, it was. Look at us. Marvin and Kyra. A nightmare. I can't believe she hasn't even called me."

"He's on the lam and took his family with him."

"She still could have called." Tasha got up and disappeared into the kitchen. She came back with her chocolate-covered apples and strawberries and some napkins. They began feeding each other and smearing chocolate all over each other's lips.

"You got some whip cream and chocolate syrup in the kitchen?" Trae asked her.

Tasha giggled because she knew it was now on. Whip cream meant that Trae was ready to eat some serious pussy. "Let me check."

"Hold up, let me get some of that chocolate off your lips." She leaned over and he gave her a kiss that said *I love you more than anything and I miss the hell out of you.* Tasha took his hand and led it to her pussy. She didn't have on any panties under her nightgown. When he felt how wet she was, he grabbed one of the chocolate-covered apples and began to tease her pussy, rubbing the chocolate slice lightly over her clit until she was on the verge of coming.

"Go get the whip cream," Trae commanded. Tasha had her eyes squeezed shut. Her legs and knees were getting weak as she grabbed his head, urging him to eat the chocolate right then and there and he did, bringing her to a much needed orgasm.

As she lay on her back catching her breath, he stood up and began undressing. When she saw his dick standing straight out, she spread her thighs seductively. Trae climbed between them, she grabbed his rod and guided him in. The both of them moaned and went to kiss each other.

"No more lies, baby," Trae promised her. "We can get through this, we can get through anything. You wit' me?"

"No more lies. We can get through this, together forever. Now shut up and fuck me." She wrapped her legs around his back and he began hittin' it hard. "Slow down, baby," she whispered.

"Turn over." He pulled out and flipped her over so he could hit it doggy-style.

"Baby, slow down, you're hurting me," Tasha moaned. When he pulled out, she looked back at his frowning face. "What are you doing?"

"You're pregnant, Tasha."

"What?" she asked in disbelief. "What are you talking about? What is the matter with you? Stop playing, Trae, and fuck me."

"I know how my wife feels when I'm fucking her pregnant. Tasha, you've been pregnant three times. I know my wife's pussy." He was now putting on his clothes. He had a look of disgust on his face, as if she smelled like rotten food.

"So why are you getting dressed, baby?"

"Whose baby is it? Mines or the nigga you was fuckin'?" he spat, still gritting on her.

That bomb landed on Tasha like a ton of bricks.

"Whose baby is it, Tasha? And when or were you planning on telling me?"

"Trae, you never cease to amaze me. So now you're a fuckin' ob/gyn?"

"Yeah, I'm your fuckin' ob/gyn. I don't even know why I stuck my dick in your triflin' ass. Around here letting niggas hit it raw."

"Oh, look at the pot calling the kettle black. You got some fuckin' nerve."

"I'll be back to pick up the boys at seven. You got a couple of days to figure this shit out."

Tasha had snapped. She jumped up off the couch. "Why do I have to figure it out? What happened to we can get through this? Me and you together? No more lies?" she screamed. "No more lies, right? Well yeah, I fucked him. I fucked Kyron. There, I said it. You're probably pulling this whole pregnancy shit, just so I can say I fucked him."

"Kyron? You fucked Kyron?" Trae stood there staring at her. "Aww, bitch. I can't believe you. Who the fuck are you? Bitch, go get my wife back. My wife would never pull some shit like this. I guess you had to keep it in the family, huh?"

"You the bitch. It doesn't feel nice to be betrayed, does it?" She smirked. "And if I am pregnant, which we don't even know or not, no, I don't know whose baby I'm carrying."

"No more lies?" Trae spat. Trae raised his hand but caught himself. "Nah, I'm not going to fuck you up but I got something for you. You ready for this? Okay, well, Charli is pregnant. That's why she left the country. I told her I was going to kill her if she didn't get rid of that baby. So she bounced. You said no more lies, right?"

"No you didn't, Trae," Tasha gritted. "You fucked that bitch raw and got her pregnant?" Tasha charged at him. "I'ma kill you and that Chinese bitch. What the fuck is wrong with you?"

He grabbed her, threw her down onto the couch and left. So much for forgiveness, no more lies and getting through anything.

Two days later and no word from Trae, Tasha went out and bought a pregnancy test but refused to use it and ended up throwing it away. Trina had noticed that her big sister had been moping around. But when she tried to ask her what was wrong, Tasha wouldn't say anything. She was now trying to get Tasha to go out with her.

"C'mon, Tasha. You've been sitting around this house and I'm getting tired of looking at you like this."

"Is that your subtle way of telling me to get out?" Tasha asked her.

"No. I just want you to go out with me tonight. C'mon, Tasha. I want to go out but not by myself," Trina whined.

"You've went out without me before," Tasha snapped as she got up, then went into the bathroom and slammed the door. She pulled the pregnancy test out of the trash and opened it.

"You're turning into a couch potato!" Trina yelled.

"Fuck you!" Tasha yelled back.

"Fuck you back."

When the phone rang, Trina was going to ignore it, but when she looked at the caller ID she saw that it was Angel, she hit the speakerphone button.

"Angel, it's me, Trina. What's up?" Trina was glad to hear from her.

"Where is your sister? I can't believe this shit." It sounded as if Angel was throwing stuff around, and she was not hiding the fact that she was ready to hurt somebody.

"She's in the bathroom. Is everything all right?" Trina wanted to know. It seemed as if everyone was starting to go crazy.

"No, it's not. Just tell her to come to the phone. As a matter of fact, I know you got something to do with this shit. Your trick ass probably talked her into this."

"What?" Trina asked in shock.

"Bitch, just get your sister," Angel snapped.

"Bitch!? Angel, I know you didn't just call me a bitch. Ho, you always did think you was better than the next man."

The two girls were going at it to the point that Tasha

threw away the pregnancy test once again and came running out of the bathroom.

"What's going on? And will y'all shut up!" Tasha screamed.

"Tasha, this is the ultimate fuckup," Angel spat. Her voice was coming across loud and clear over the speakerphone. "Why in the hell did you have to go and fuck Kyron? Kyron, Tasha? Of all people? Now Kaylin is accusing me of knowing all about this bullshit and not telling him. He's talking about now he can't trust me and shit and the nigga is going off. I don't know what the fuck happened, and at this point I really don't care, but you need to tell him and make him know—and believe—that I didn't have shit to do with this. I can't believe you." Angel continued to rant and rave. "Tasha, what is the matter with you? Hell, you got everybody mad. Trae is mad at Kaylin because he thinks my husband was in on the bullshit. Kaylin is mad at me. Shit, I'm pissed at you. Kyron is pissed at his sister for telling Kaylin she saw y'all outside the club fucking, Tasha. Bitch, that's not even your husband. You could have fucked anybody in the world, but you had to go and play it close like this? On top of that, you fucked the nigga outside the club. You that pressed for some dick? Fresh-out-of-jail dick at that. You know them niggas come home with all kinds of shit! Y'all bitches done went to California and lost y'all's fuckin' minds. Yeah, Tasha. You fucked up for real this time. Say something! I am dying to hear this one."

"I might be pregnant, Angel. And I don't know who the father is."

Both Angel and Trina gasped and were holding their chests.

The next evening Trina was running through the house cleaning up, trying not to appear so obvious.

"How many times are you going to paint your toenails?" Trina stood over Tasha with her hands on her hips.

"Mind your business, Trina."

"You are my business. I don't know why you keep polishing them crusty joins anyway. All the color in the world ain't gonna help them." Trina laughed at her own joke.

"Bitch, I got model's feet and toes. You better recognize."

"Whatever." Trina knew it was true.

Someone knocked on the door. Tasha looked up at Trina. Trina looked at the door.

"Are you expecting someone?" Tasha asked her.

"Hell no," Trina lied.

"Then why are you cleaning up like a madwoman?"

Trina went to the door, looked out the peephole and opened the door. To Tasha's surprise in walked Kendrick and Kyron.

"Y'all niggas ain't right, and Trina I know you had something to do with this. All of y'all are crazy and y'all gonna get me killed," Tasha snapped.

"Chill out, girl. We ain't gonna let nothing happen to you," Kendrick told her as he came and kissed her on the cheek. She pushed him away. "Aww, man. That's cold. I travel all the way across the country to check on you and this is how you do me."

"Y'all are wrong for coming here," Tasha said.

Kendrick turned his attention to Trina. "What's up? Can a nigga get some love?"

"You are what's up, big daddy." Trina was all smiles, and Kendrick picked her up and carried her toward the back.

Tasha continued to paint her toenails as Kyron sat down next to her on the couch. He grabbed the remote and put the TV on mute. He took the nail polish from her and closed the bottle. He then leaned over, punched her on the thigh and kissed her on the cheek.

"Oow, Kyron." She punched him in the chest. "Why did you hit me?"

"Shorty, you got something to tell me?"

"No."

"Yes, you do." He punched her thigh again.

"Oow. What's wrong with you niggas thinking that I'ma let y'all hit me and not retaliate?"

"You got something to tell me?" Kyron wouldn't let it go.

"I already told you. Our little game playing is over. Me and Trae, we are going to work it out."

"That's bullshit, Tasha. You know that shit is over."

"No, it's not over. The little game me and you was playing is over."

Kyron's cell vibrated. He looked at the caller ID.

"Get out, Kyron." She tried to push him off the couch.

"Why are you getting so mad?"

"Get out, Kyron." She pushed him again, but he barely budged as he flipped open his cell.

"Because you know I'm right— Hey, Ma." He looked over at Tasha. "I'm with her now."

Tasha looked over at him, obviously puzzled, wondering why Mama Santos was inquiring about her. *Damn, I only fucked Kyron once. How did she find that out?* Kyron had shoved the phone to her face. "What?" Tasha whispered, damn near shaking in her skin.

"She wants to talk to you."

"About what?"

"Take the phone, shorty." He shoved it in her hands.

Tasha took a deep breath, forced a smile on her face. "Mama Santos, how are you?"

"I don't know yet. You kids are always getting into situations, not thinking about no one but yourselves. You know that Trae is like a son to me and I've accepted you as my daughter-in-law. But I am confused as to why you would get pregnant by Kyron?"

Tasha's body became numb and she was speechless.

Mama Santos, sensing that, continued, "I told Kyron that I don't foresee anything but problems, big problems at that. You and Kyron should not have done this. I just want you to know that whatever happens, don't let anything happen to the baby. We will take the baby. The baby is our family. Now I've said all I needed to say about this matter." She hung up.

Tasha's mouth was hanging open. Kyron took the phone from her. "What did she say?"

"You know what the fuck she said. Why did you ever tell her anything?" Tasha screamed at Kyron and jumped up off the couch and began pacing the floor, tears filling her eyes. "I haven't even taken a pregnancy test yet or been to the doctor's. Now your mother is all in my business. Why did you even tell her that, Kyron? And who says I'm having it?"

"I didn't. Trae told my brother and Kay told me and my moms. But check it, if you didn't take a pregnancy test then how do Trae know?"

"Because we fucked, Kyron. We fucked and he says he knows how I feel when I'm pregnant!" she screamed at him.

"Y'all fucked?" It was Kyron's turn to scream at Tasha.

"Yes, we fucked. He is my husband. I told you, me and

you was over. You were just a fuck and I was not leaving Trae. So don't look shocked now."

"Hey, hey, keep the noise down," Kendrick said. He and Trina came out of the bedroom to see what all the commotion was.

"Can we handle this in private?" Tasha snapped.

"Private? The last time I checked this was my place," Trina stated. Kendrick pulled her back into the bedroom.

"Look, Kyron. I can't think of another way to say it. I told you that you were just a revenge fuck and this could never go anywhere and that's that. We shouldn't have never fucked. Look at us now. I feel like we are the new niggas on ABC. The niggas to watch. We on some *One Life to Live* shit. It's over. That's it, that's all."

"That's bullshit. Shorty, you know that baby is mines. And that nigga ain't going for that."

"Look. We're not even sure if I'm pregnant, so that's all speculation. And who says I'm having it?"

"Oh, you're gonna have it," Kyron threatened. "I'm going to get you a pregnancy test. Where's the closest store?"

"No," Tasha yelled.

"No? What do you mean, no?" He looked at her as if she were crazy.

Tears began streaming down Tasha's cheeks. Kyron stood up and hugged her. "I fucked up, Kyron. I really fucked up. What if this is your baby?"

"We'll work it out."

"And how do you think we are supposed to do that? Trae is not going to act like everything's all good."

"Just promise me you won't get an abortion."

Tasha didn't respond, only cried harder.

"Shorty, I know you heard me. Have the baby. It's mines. I'll take him."

Now she was laughing through tears.

"Him?"

"Yes, him." Kyron was dead serious.

"This is crazy." Tasha sighed.

"Just promise to give me my baby, all right?"

"If you promise me that you understand that it's over and you'll leave now."

They stood in the middle of the floor, hugged up as Kyron thought about it for several minutes.

"If that's my baby, then it will never be over for us. I will take the baby and let you play house with Trae and your other kids, but I will always have access to this pussy." He grabbed her crotch. Tasha just looked at him and was speechless. "Don't look shocked. A nigga won't be able to let go of this pussy that easy. But give me a kiss and it's over. For now."

"That's it? And you're out of here?"

"You owe me that, shorty."

"How do you figure that?" Kyron was the ultimate at making Tasha hot. One kiss led to another, and before you knew it they were on the floor fucking like rabbits. Despite the fact that Trina and Kendrick were in the back bedroom.

That was the last thing Tasha remembered when the sunlight hit her in the face. She was wrapped tight in Kyron's arms.

"Shit." She gritted, "Kyron." She shook him. "Wake up. Y'all need to get out of here."

"Relax, shorty. I'll be gone before the big bad wolf gets here." He started sucking on her nipples.

"Kyron, don't do that. You said a kiss and a hug, not a marathon fuck." She couldn't help but close her eyes and enjoy. She still couldn't figure out how he could make her come by just sucking on her nipples. And now she was wet all over again. He was now between her thighs as she submitted and took him in.

As he made slow strokes they talked.

"This wasn't supposed to go down like this. I wasn't supposed to catch feelings for you." She wrapped her legs around his waist.

"I know, baby. We both in the wrong, but we can't undo it." He thrust deeper. "Damn, this pussy is good. I can't do it. I can't stop fuckin' with you."

"Kyron, you promised." She moaned. "You gave me your word. Oh shit, my spot. Slow down." It was too late, she was already coming. When she got that off, Kyron turned her over and hit it from the back until she came again and he came right after her. He got up, threw on his boxers and headed for the kitchen to look in the refrigerator. When he came back, he got dressed. Tasha was still lying on her stomach with her eyes closed.

"Y'all ain't got no meat in the refrigerator. I'm a big nigga. I need some meat. He leaned down, pulled the sheet off her naked body and lightly ran kisses along her spine and her ass cheeks.

"I want you to cook me some breakfast when I get back. I'm also going to bring back a pregnancy test. I need to know."

As soon as Kyron left for the store, Tasha jumped up, threw something on and headed for Trina's bedroom. She knocked on the door until finally Trina snatched it open.

"What is it?" Trina whispered, standing there with a blanket around her.

Tasha grabbed her by her wrist and damn near snatched her out of the room before shutting the door.

"What is the matter with you?"

"Trina, we need to get them out of here. Trae can pop at any time."

"No. You need to get Kyron out of here. Trae is not my husband. And I'm not creeping around with Kyron, you are."

"Trina, if you don't wake that nigga up and get them out of here, I swear I'ma—"

"Okay, okay," she cut her off. "Damn, Tasha. You shouldn't be creepin' if you don't want to get caught," Trina offered those words of advice.

"Listen. I ain't thinking about that right now. I am only concerned for the safety of all of us."

Trina sucked her teeth, stomped in place, turned around and went back into her bedroom, slamming the door.

Tasha headed back to the living room, where she went to clean up, washing linen and blankets and the whole nine. By the time Kyron came back the living room looked as if he was never in it.

"Damn, shorty. Are you kickin' me out?" He handed her the preganancy test.

"Yes, y'all need to be going. We don't know when Trae will pop up. I already have enough to deal with."

"Shorty, I'm not leaving until you take this pregnancy test."

Tasha plopped down onto the couch. Kyron shrugged. "Do you. But I know I'm not leaving until you make it happen." He went into the kitchen and started unpacking the groceries. He turned the broiler on, opened up his T-bone, washed it, seasoned it and put it in the broiler.

When he went back into the living room, Tasha had disappeared and Trina was coming up the hallway.

"You cooking?" she asked him.

"Yeah. A nigga is hungry."

"That makes two of them. Hook me up," Trina told him.

Tasha came out of the bathroom and sat down on the sofa.

"So what's up? We pregnant or what?" Kyron asked. He and Trina stood there looking at her. Trina didn't know what was going on.

Tasha didn't say anything. "She wants y'all to leave just in case Trae shows up," Trina told him. "Go wake Kendrick up because her paranoia is rubbing off on me."

Kyron headed for the back.

"Get them out of here," Tasha griitted.

"What the fuck do you think I'm trying to do?" Trina snapped.

The doorbell rang.

"Wait." Tasha gasped. "Don't open it."

"What?" Trina ran and opened it anyway.

"Nooo," Tasha yelled. But it was too late. Trae and Kaylin were already standing there.

Kaylin waltzed in first. Trae remained standing there in the doorway. The twisted look on his face let her know that he was ready to wreak havoc.

"I swear I don't want to catch a case, Tasha," an exasperated Trae told her.

"Baby, can we talk? Please?" Tasha thought that she would piss on herself.

"What's left to talk about?"

"I'd say a lot. But remember you started this shit." She

then turned to Kay and said, "Kaylin, I swear your wife had nothing to do with me and Kyron."

"Tasha, this shit is ugly," Kaylin told her. "I came up here with him to try and clean shit up. But damn, I don't know where to start."

"Don't you think I know that?" Tasha screamed.

Kyron came out of the bathroom looking puzzled and holding up the pregnancy test. As soon as Trae saw Kyron he looked at Tasha, then at Kyron, and then at the pregnancy test.

Tasha almost pissed on herself for real. Then her cell phone rang. And out of nervousness and wanting to do something with her hands, she hit the speaker button by mistake.

"Auntie Tasha," the little voice said. It was Aisha.

The whole room grew quiet.

"Aisha, baby, where are you?"

"I don't know."

"What do you mean, you don't know? Where is your mother?"

"I don't know. My mommy was bleeding and...and...I think she's dead. Can you come and get me, Auntie Tasha?"

READING GROUP GUIDE

1. Did Trae give Tasha enough justification to leave him?

2. Did it surprise you when Kyra met with her tragedy?

3. Was Kyra justified in cheating on Marvin?

4. Was California a good move for Trae and Tasha?

5. How do you feel about King Rick's character?

6. Was it a predictable ending or did it have you guessing?

7. What part of the book stood out to you the most?

8. Would you consider Trae's actions with Charli cheating or just business? What about with Sabeerah?

9. Do you feel Marvin got away with everything scot-free?

10. Did Kyra wait too long to leave Marvin or should she have stayed as long as she did?

THE COIN TOSS

By

WAHIDA CLARK

CHAPTER ONE

GBI

"Congratulations, Bob! You did it! Are you sitting down?" Alexis Greenspan shouted in excitement. She could feel Bob's adrenaline rush through the phone.

"Oh God, Alexis. Did I really do it?" Bob could barely contain his breathing.

"You did it, Bob Tokowski! You have just won your fair share of one million dollars of American Eagle Gold Coins! One million!" Alexis screamed out. "I told you to hang in there, Bob. The road was rocky, but you did it. Your perseverance paid off. Again, congratulations to ya, Bob. You deserve it! You finally hit the big time."

Bob was now crying tears of joy. "Thank...you, Alexis. Oh, my God. Thank you."

"Now, Bob, I need you to grab your pencil and paper. You must write down this claim number. Go ahead, Bob, grab a pen and a pad."

Alexis could hear Bob piddling around in the background. Then she heard a moan and then a thud.

"Bob!? Bob!?"

The excitement must've gotten the best of him.

Click.

Agent Houser turned off the recorder. Houser had been the lead investigator for the past two years, heading up the Georgia Bureau of Investigation. Two more years and Houser, who reminded you of the undercover detective played by Robert Blake in the 1970s hit *Baretta*, could retire. However, he was ready to retire now. His impetigo was spreading, and pus was oozing out of the skin infection on his legs. But he told himself it would all be over soon.

Retirement, here I come!

The bright side of his gloomy lining was that he lucked up and got an interview with Erica McCoy, aka Alexis Greenspan. She was one of the top salespeople at WMM advertising, aka We Make Millionaires. All of law enforcement knew that this was one of the biggest and hardest-to-penetrate fraudulent telemarketing firms in the state of Georgia; they knew how to operate in that gray area.

Houser had screamed at his team of four, "Screw the FBI! We can do just as good a job as they can."

He had pulled one of the not-so-oldest tricks in the book, but old nonetheless. He sent Erica an official-looking certified letter explaining that she had inherited some money, to the lovely tune of $250,000. The letter stated that she would have to come and get processed to see if she was eligible to claim it. When she pulled up to the Bureau's fictitious office, which they had set up just a few blocks away from WMM, Houser flashed his badge, introduced himself and told her to follow him.

She did. To the Bureau's main office.

"Why are we at the GBI?" Alexis's curiosity was piqued.

"We have to make sure that you are claiming what's rightfully yours," Houser simply stated.

As they walked past the front desk and down the long,

bright white corridor, Erica got really curious. "Are you sure I'm here to claim some kind of inheritance?"

Houser smiled. "Depends on how you look at it."

"How I look at it? What does that mean? Don't have me down here on no bullshit! I got better things to do with my time," she spat.

Houser pulled out his keys and unlocked his office door. He moved to the side and motioned for Alexis to step inside. He then flicked the light switch.

"Please have a seat, Ms. McCoy. Would you like a cup of coffee? Tea? Bottled water?"

"No. I just want you to tell me what this is really all about." Erica was growing agitated.

Houser sat his six-one, two-hundred-pound frame behind his desk. He lifted his spectacles off his nose and rubbed its bridge. He then leaned back into the chair, resting his hands behind his head. Erica cringed at the patches of impetigo on his chin and elbows. He obviously picked up on her discomfort because he hastily sat up, resting his arms on the chair's armrest.

He hit the intercom button on his phone. "Doris, tell Parker and Radcliff to bring the WMM file."

"WMM? What is this about? You fucker! You tricked me to come to your office under false pretenses. I should sue your ass!" She stood and grabbed her purse. "My name is Erica McCoy, not WMM." She turned to leave the office.

That's when Houser hit the play button on his recorder. Booming through its speakers was the conversation between her and Bob Tokowski. Erica abruptly turned around at the sound of her sales voice and stood frozen in place.

Agents Parker and Radcliff entered the office. They both slid several folders in front of Houser and took their seats.

Agent Parker looked as if he had a blond toupee sitting on top of his head. His wrinkled plaid suit drooped over his scrawny frame. He reminded Erica of an anorexic Bart Simpson. Radcliff was grossly overweight and sloppy looking. His oily black hair was slicked back into a ponytail. He looked like a goldfish.

After they listened to Alexis yell "Bob!? Bob!?" Houser turned off the tape recorder.

The room grew silent, except for Radcliff's heavy breathing.

"Please have a seat, Ms. McCoy."

Erica clutched her Gucci bag tighter.

"Fuck you! I am going to sue your ass for deceit and for wasting my time. Kiss my ass!" With that said, she stormed out of the office.

Houser jumped from his chair and headed for his office door. He stood in the hallway in front of his office and said, "Murder, Ms. McCoy! If you don't get your ass back in here, you're going down for murder."

Erica spun around and practically ran to get in Houser's face.

"Murder!? You wannabe FBI agent! I ain't got nothing to do with no murder. You people have really lost your minds. Find someone else to hassle," she said through clenched teeth.

"Ms. McCoy, your client Bob Tokowski, he died. Dropped dead of a heart attack, right while you were trying to scam him with your 'millions' in gold coins."

Houser motioned with two fingers from each hand to emphasize quote unquote "millions."

"That's right, we know all about the scamming and scheming of WMM. We know your boss, Rinaldo Haywood, aka Brian Stout, aka Tommy Green, aka John Bennett. We know about his office in the Florida Keys run by his cohorts

Brandon Ingram and Charlie Adams. We know your phone name Alexis Greenspan. Very catchy. We—"

"Hold up, you asshole. I don't give a fuck what you know. I'm a sales associate. A damned good one at that. I sell to business owners. If the client decides to patronize our firm and at the same time gamble at a chance of getting a bunch of gold coins, so the fuck what? That's not illegal!" Alexis ranted as she turned to walk out.

"Alexis or Erica, whichever character you're in right now," fat boy chuckled as Houser began his negotiations, "this is your only chance to help yourself. You know what's going on over there is against the law. All I have to do is say the word and the feds'll be all over that place. And not only will you go down for money laundering, conspiracy and fraud, you also have a murder hanging over your head."

Parker finally decided to put his two cents in.

"Look, Alexis. The company is going down whether you help yourself or not. If I was—"

"Look," Alexis sighed as she stepped back into the office and shut the door. "If y'all had something then you wouldn't need me."

Alexis snatched open the door and then slammed it shut behind her.

ABOUT THE AUTHOR

After serving a nine-and-a-half-year prison sentence, WAHIDA CLARK was released to a halfway house on June 13, 2007, from the federal prison camp in Alderson, West Virginia.

She was crowned The Queen of Thug Love Fiction by Nikki Turner, the Queen of Hip-Hop Fiction. Wahida's style of writing is the "template" for urban literature. When you read her novels, they are so real you are convinced of one of three things: you know the characters; you want to know the characters; or you *are* one of the characters. Her *Essence* and *Black Issues Book Reviews* bestselling novels include *Thugs and the Women Who Love Them, Every Thug Needs a Lady, Payback Is a Mutha, Payback with Ya Life*, and her latest anthology with Kiki Swinson titled *Sleeping with the Enemy*. She has just completed part 4 of her Thug Series, the highly anticipated *Thug Lovin'*.

She is vice president of the nonprofit organization Prodigal Sons and Daughters Redirection Services, a reentry program for convicts and ex-convicts, based out of East Orange, New Jersey. She has given motivational speeches and shared her story at high schools in New York and halfway houses such as Bo Robinson and Tully House in New Jersey.

She is also vice president of Phoenix Academy Inc., an organization that also provides support groups and mentors for at-risk youth. The ultimate goal is to establish a charter and vocational training schools.

She also has had several appearances on BET's *My Two Cents.*

Today, Wahida operates her publishing company, Wahida Clark Presents Publishing, out of East Orange, New Jersey. Her first releases include *Trust No Man* by Cash, *Thirsty* by Mike Sanders and *Cheetah* by Missy Jackson.

Visit her at:

www.myspace.com/wahidaclark, or www.wclarkpublishing .com.